# ASSIGNMENT CYPRUS

# ASSIGNMENT CYPRUS

Middle East Mission

*A NYLES HAWKSPURR ADVENTURE*

## *TROOPER*

Writers Club Press
New York  Lincoln  Shanghai

## Assignment Cyprus
### Middle East Mission

Writers Club Press
an imprint of iUniverse, Inc.

For information address:
iUniverse, Inc.
2021 Pine Lake Road, Suite 100
Lincoln, NE 68512
www.iuniverse.com

ISBN: 0-595-27341-6

Printed in the United States of America

Dedicated to the memory of my son Mike.
He fought his own battle with dignity and courage and yet died to young.

# CHAPTER 1

The heavyset man with a ruddy complexion and receding red hair rapped a meaty fist on the table. "Gentlemen your attention please."

The chatter of conversation ceased immediately, and the only sound in the room was the monotonous whirr and clunk of an overhead fan in need of lubrication. A dozen perspiring men swiveled in the ridiculously small desk benches at which they were seated. Before the emergency had necessitated its closure, this had been a village school for Cypriot children.

Inspector Jack O'Connor showed his large teeth, in what he fondly imagined was an appreciative smile.

No one responded.

The Special Branch policeman was dressed in a white shirt, knee length white socks with brown leather boots, and the ludicrous baggy shorts known universally as 'Bombay Bloomers'. This was the uninspired, unofficial off-duty uniform worn by those in the colonial service wherever the sun still shone on the British Empire. At his waist sagged a scruffy webbing holster, encasing a Webley service revolver.

"Thank you." O'Connor paused to wipe perspiration from his face with a green bandana.

Under the fan, thick cigarette smoke spiraled and swirled before dispersing to every corner of the stuffy warm room. For security reasons, someone had nailed chicken wire over the windows to prevent bombs being thrown in for-getting that now they could not be opened.

O'Connor continued with his customary growl, in an unmistakable Liver-pool Irish brogue. "I'll keep this as brief as possible gentlemen as we have a guest whom I want you to meet. Hopefully you will recognize him again should you encounter each other in unusual circumstances."

He beckoned with his hand, and Hawkspurr moved from the back of the room where he had been leaning close to the door in an effort to inhale a little fresh air.

"Lieutenant Nyles Hawkspurr, Special Air Service."

The other men examined Hawkspurr with critical with eyes, and just a touch of antagonism. They were a mixture of Army, Air Force, and police officers dressed in either khaki uniforms or mufti.

Hawkspurr was neat in a tan civilian safari suit, and suede desert boots. Out of sight was a .45 caliber Colt semi automatic—a souvenir from the Korean War. The pistol was tucked in the waist-belt of his trousers at the small of his back, and was retained in a linen bag to prevent the weapon falling into his underpants should he have to run.

A disgruntled infantry major spoke. "I thought we were doing very well containing the situation, without any interference from the glamour boys!"

His cronies laughed with him, but one by one fell silent, as Hawkspurr looked each man in the face with a disarming smile. A smile belied by the piercing cold of his dark brown eyes. Eyes that reflected his every mood from the warmth of passion, to flat chips of black onyx when he killed.

O'Connor allowed himself a wry lift at the corners of his own hard mouth as he observed the other men's reaction. "A little background. Mister Hawkspurr is here with the approval of a certain section in Whitehall, and on the recommendation of a trusted colleague of mine—Inspector Alex Compton currently serving in Malaya. Don't let these youthful good looks fool you gentlemen." O'Connor grinned like a tiger.

"Hawkspurr is a professional soldier commanding a troop of specialists. Talon Troop has proved its worth on several operations in Malaya, and their last assignment involved parachuting at night into a Mau Mau stronghold in the Aberdare Mountains of Kenya, and before joining SAS, Hawkspurr served with distinction during covert guerrilla operations behind enemy lines in Korea."

A murmur of renewed interest rose from the assemblage, and the Inspector continued. "We are all appreciative of the difficulties facing regular infantry battalions, locating and destroying the hard core cells of EOKA in the mountains. All approaches are watched and sympathizers report every troop movement. EOKA intelligence encompasses an approximate 80% of the Greek population: women and children, the priests, fishermen, farmers, shepherds and no doubt some policemen. Talon Troop will operate wherever guerilla groups think they are safe, and Hawkspurr's men will live in the mountains and forests with them. If necessary the Troop will parachute onto difficult targets, and coordinate with infantry and armored patrols to close the net around any evaders. Comments thus far?"

"Yes Jack."

The major replied again. "Does Mister Hawkspurr realize that there are no nice fields, on which to parachute in the mountain forests?" He looked around for approbation, with a contemptuous smirk on his face.

Hawkspurr answered for himself. "Thank you sir, my men do not require a nice field to land on. We intend to destroy EOKA groups—not challenge them to a game of cricket."

The major's cheeks flushed with anger. "Young pup." He muttered to himself. He glared at the 6'2" tall, dark haired Lieutenant.

He did not care for the aristocratic features and aquiline nose—a legacy of Hawkspurr's Anglo/Norman heritage. 'Looks like a bloody wog!' He thought

Inspector O'Connor intervened. "That'll be all for now gentlemen I just want you to be able to recognize Hawkspurr should you encounter him during operations. Wouldn't want to shoot him as a terrorist would we?" He smiled at the major.

The officers dispersed in varied forms of transport, and O'Connor ushered Hawkspurr to a waiting black Humber saloon car. The driver and his escort were Turkish Cypriot policemen in plain clothes, and both were carrying the familiar Sten sub machine gun.

Although a newer 9mm Patchett SMG was now in service, the old faithful of WW2, Korea and Malaya was still the predominant automatic light weapon in use by the security forces.

As the car left the village, they passed through a roadblock manned by soldiers checking all vehicles and the occupants for arms and explosives. Nervous young National Servicemen fresh from England appeared slightly embarrassed as they examined the shopping bags of ladies old enough to be their mother.

O'Connor laughed grimly. "They'll harden up when they've seen a few torn, bloody bodies."

"Yes, I'm afraid so." Hawkspurr agreed. "Now please tell me what's behind the whole emergency, my brief was a bit vague."

"Right. Basically the Greek population of the island has always wanted enosis, which means union with Greece. But since Archbishop Makarios was elected in 1950 his preaching has renewed the demands, and naturally upset the Turkish citizens.

To gain their ends, the Greeks planned a campaign of insurrection to make it impossible for Britain to retain sovereignty over the island. They created a military wing called EOKA (Ethniki Organosis Kyprion Agoniston) the National Organization of Cypriot Fighters, which is led by George Grivas, a retired Greek Army officer. Grivas uses the nom de guerre Dighenis—a legendary Greek hero and started to plan his terror campaign in 1952. Make no mistake about the quality of our opponents, Grivas has experience of guerilla warfare going back to 1940, he is ruthless and knows all the tricks." The policeman paused, and took a pull of water from a bottle in the car.

"Grivas returned to Cyprus in 1954, and demonstrations were quickly followed by the first bombings in April 1955. Now we have open violence, which Makarios refuses to condemn. Police are often the targets, and murders take place in broad daylight. Mr. Anthony Eden the Prime Minister has since appointed Field Marshal Sir John Harding, KCB. DSO. MC. as Governor. A State of Emergency was declared on the 26th November 1955 and this has enabled us to take a harder line, and now the solution lies with men like you and I and the security forces."

Hawkspurr digested the information. "That's clear enough Inspector, now since you've brought me to this particular district to meet local commanders, I presume it's to be my center of operations?"

"Exactly. You'll be based close to Limassol, which is my own area of responsibility. You'll have full support from RAF Akrotiri, and good roads up into the Troodos Mountains. By the time you return from leave, I'll have your logistic details worked out with my joint security committee."

"That sounds fine." Hawkspurr agreed. "Depending on available transport, I should be back within two or three days. Talon Troop are undergoing basic ski training in Norway at the moment, and we'll polish up our climbing skills in Wales before leaving U.K."

The policeman smiled at Hawkspurr apologetically. "Sorry to delay your leave like this Lieutenant, but when Colonel Hazlett informed me that you were in Nairobi I thought it best to divert you en route. You may have to make special arrangements for deployment with Whitehall."

Hawkspurr smiled. "I don't expect any difficulty with the War Office. The Colonel has a way of cutting through any red tape."

As Hawkspurr finished speaking, the car slowed to enter the town of Limassol, and he noticed a stiffening in the posture of the Turkish driver.

Inspector O'Connor glanced at Hawkspurr as if sensing his reaction. "The Turks in this town are outnumbered six to one." He explained.

"Right." Hawkspurr felt a sudden foreboding, his instincts finely tuned to danger from the experience of three years of warfare.

The big car maneuvered awkwardly into a narrow street of open fronted shops, but even above the noise of the high revving engine, traditional Greek music blared in an irritating cacophony of sound—echoing within the confines of whitewashed walls. From the corner of his eye, Hawkspurr noticed the sudden descent of a roller shutter over the front of a store. He looked quickly over his shoulder through the rear window, and a silent alarm triggered in his brain—the few pedestrians had now disappeared.

Even as he reached for his pistol and cocked it with a single smooth action, the driver braked his vehicle to an abrupt halt with a curse and a warning shouted in his own language. An empty handcart had careered from an alleyway, effectively blocking the car's progress before the startled policeman could effect any evasive action.

Hawkspurr was still off balance, as an intense looking young man wearing a white shirt and brown slacks stepped from a sheltering doorway and aimed a revolver through the driver's open window.

With taut face turned towards his colleague beside him, the hapless Turk was unaware of the two shots that smashed into his skull and neck, robbing him of life in an instant of detonation and muzzle flash.

His compatriot stared in horror as the dead man fell across his lap, pinning his hands and the weapon they held. His plaintive cry to Allah was cut off abruptly, as the gunman leaned forward and emptied the remaining four shells of the cylinder into his chest.

The speed of the attack had caught Inspector O'Connor completely by surprise, but dropping to the floor of the car he reached for the handle and slammed the car door open, hitting the gunman and knocking him to his knees.

Hawkspurr had rolled out of his side of the vehicle as the first shots were fired, but he tripped in the gutter and fell sprawling on the road. With leveled weapon he assessed that no further attack was threatening from their rear, and he scrambled to a crouch peering cautiously around the car boot.

The youthful terrorist, who was quite obviously working alone, had disappeared into an adjacent doorway with O'Connor pounding after him yelling in Greek for the man to halt and surrender. Very properly he wanted to capture and interrogate him about his associates and affiliations.

Hawkspurr the soldier had other ideas, nurtured by his own horrendous experiences in dealings with terrorists. Race or creed did not color his judgment—all killers must be terminated instantly, not pampered whilst their comrades plotted and incarcerated innocent hostages to negotiate for their release.

Hawkspurr stepped swiftly into the dark opening after O'Connor, pausing only to adjust his eyes to the gloom, and pushing forward the safety catch on his pistol. The street had lapsed into a stunned, apprehensive silence and the building which the protagonists had entered was as still as the tomb, and redolent with the stale essence of spices, herbs, and flour.

Hawkspurr became aware of the stertorous breathing of the big Inspector, but strained his hearing beyond—listening for a telltale creak from ancient timbers or a careless step. He could now discern the bulk of the policeman poised hesitantly between a set of stairs and two yawning door openings, and moved silently to his side. "Which way?" He whispered.

"I don't know!" The inspector shook his head nervously. He was more at home in the back streets of a noisy city.

Hawkspurr moved decisively. "I'm going up." Placing his feet carefully on the inside tread of the steps to diminish any squeals of protest from the old wood, he started to climb.

Reaching the bare boards of a landing he flattened his body protectively against the back wall—a single window was shuttered, but enough light filtered through the warped boards to reveal an open door.

In the narrow fingers of sun, dust motes swirled and danced as they sank inexorably to the floor. Someone had passed this way.

Hawkspurr was almost sure that the gunman had fired the six shot capacity of his revolver, but had he reloaded? Warily he reached into his left trouser pocket and extracted a coin. He was barely breathing, and with a sudden gasp of inhalation for his starved lungs he threw the object to the far corner of the dark room.

A practiced roll and he flung himself through the opening to lie prone upon the dusty floor.

Cautiously he searched for an alien movement as his gun barrel traversed from left to right, and back to the center. Then from the corner of his eyes he saw the faint silhouette of an extended arm against the lighter fabric of a flour sack.

The hand encompassed the unmistakable outline of a gun, and without hesitation he squeezed off two shots at the torso of the terrorist. The body crashed back with the certainty of instant death, but Hawkspurr rolled once more to the side and lay again with bated breath, gun still leveled in the Stygian blackness.

A cry echoed from below. "Hawkspurr! You Ok?"

Hawkspurr remained silent, but crawled backward to the entrance until he was able to scramble through and regain his feet, alert to the remote possibility that the gunman might still be alive and dangerous—he covered the doorway with his weapon.

"Inspector! I'm fine, get some bloody light up here please!"

Below in the street Hawkspurr could hear the sound of a police siren, and the clamor of multi-lingual voices screaming in protest and abuse.

A broad beam of light suddenly illuminated the stairs and landing, and O'Connor called out. "I'm coming up Hawkspurr."

The panting inspector reached Hawkspurr. "What's the situation?"

"Just shine your torch in there, carefully now." Hawkspurr flattened his body against the doorjamb and searched the room in the light of the wavering beam.

Amidst a jumble of sacks, crates and cardboard boxes lay the inert body of the terrorist.

The gaping mouth, wide eyes, and look of utter dread frozen on the features confirmed Hawkspurr's conviction. That man would kill no more.

O'Connor moved towards the dead gunman, followed closely by Hawkspurr. As the policeman stooped to empty the man's pockets for identification, Hawkspurr examined the room—no windows, no other exit.

"Poor blighter didn't plan this too well!" He remarked, as he removed the magazine from his weapon and topped it up with two cartridges from a jacket pocket. Hawkspurr looked around the floor until he located the spent shells from the shots that had dispatched the terrorist; he bent to retrieve them and slipped them into a pocket. Nice and tidy—no evidence.

The Inspector turned the corpse over, and straightened up with a curse. "Just what sort of artillery are you carrying Mister Hawkspurr? This poor bastard has no back left!"

Hawkspurr grunted. "Forty-five soft lead nose. Doesn't matter where you hit them—they're dead!"

O'Connor looked angry. "Lucky you're not a police officer, I'd have you before a board of enquiry!"

Hawkspurr stepped up to the inspector and looked him straight in the eyes from a distance of four inches.

His face was grim, his lips an aggressive thin line. "And you sir, have a lot to learn about this kind of warfare!"

O'Connor looked repentant. "You're probably right. Where I come from they use razors and boots."

Hawkspurr relaxed and grinned. "Ok. Let me get on with my well-deserved leave, and before you know it I'll be back with my lads and sort this lot out for you!"

The inspector laughed in spite of himself. "Right bighead let's go! The uniforms can take care of this mess."

The pair started down the stairs.

"By the way Inspector, if we're going to be working together please stop addressing me as Mr. Hawkspurr. My friends call me Hawk."

"Ok Hawk" the policeman replied, "anything else?"

"Yes. Lend me that bloody great neckerchief you're wearing please."

O'Connor looked puzzled, but released the green bandana from his throat and handed it to Hawkspurr.

"Thank you." Hawkspurr tied the large square high up on his face with only the top of his eyes showing. "First rule in my job is no photographs, and no interviews."

In the street uniformed policemen backed by British soldiers were lining up noisy, protesting civilians and checking their identity.

The Humber was about to be towed away by an army Scammel Truck, and British attendants of an ambulance were loading the bodies of the two Turkish policemen into their vehicle.

A camera flash intruded upon Hawkspurr's anonymity as he and O'Connor moved from the shadows into the sun-washed street. "Blast!" His hands moved instinctively to shield his eyes. "Get me out of here Jack."

O'Connor shouted an order, and another black car moved forward. As it halted the driver reached back and opened the rear door without leaving his seat. The inspector bundled Hawkspurr in and flopped onto the seat beside him. "Move it Mike."

The driver accelerated away swearing softly in Greek as he steered the car through the other traffic and gesticulating policemen, in the restricted confines of the street.

O'Connor sighed with relief and relaxed in the leather seat. "Hawk, meet Detective Sergeant Mike Landris."

Hawkspurr leaned forward and pulled the bandana from his face. He tapped the Greek policeman on the shoulder. "Thanks."

The darkly handsome man grinned at Hawkspurr's reflection in the rear view mirror. "You're welcome." He responded. "Where to Guv'?"

"Straight through to Nicosia Mike, the Palace Hotel. Lieutenant Hawkspurr is booked in for the night and flying on to London tomorrow." O'Connor turned to Hawkspurr. "I'll try and get you an appointment with the Governor General first thing in the morning."

"Whatever you say Jack." Hawkspurr pondered for a moment. "Who was that bloody woman who tried to take my picture back there?" He gestured over his shoulder.

"I really don't know, have you any ideas Mike?"

"Yes, Amanda Carson. Hotshot Canadian freelance war correspondent with impeccable credentials, but too pushy for a nice old-fashioned Greek boy like me."

"Is she a bleeding heart in favor of EOKA?"

"I doubt it," the Greek answered, "just after a scoop story with her byline on it."

"Ok, but keep an eye on her whilst she is on my patch." O'Connor sat back again.

Hawkspurr too relaxed and lay back wearily closing his eyes. Then suddenly he came upright. "My bags! They're in the other car."

Mike Landris spoke reassuringly. "Don't worry sir, they're with us in the boot."

"Thanks again Sergeant." The tension left Hawkspurr and lowering his lids he attempted to recall all he had read about this wild, beautiful island.

Cyprus is smaller than Sicily with a population of around half a million. Eighty percent of these are Greek Orthodox Christians, and the other twenty percent Turkish-speaking Moslems. The enmity between them dates back to the Middle Ages as the Turks began a gradual conquest of the Greek speaking Byzantine Empire.

Britain gained control of Cyprus in 1878 by a convention made with Sultan Abdul Hamid of Turkey, and Disraeli, the British Prime Minister of the time described the island as 'a place of arms' that Britain must control in order to defend the empire of her ally, against the ambitions of Russia.

The legendary birthplace of Venus, also lays claim to the champagne vines brought home to France by a noble Crusader. Certainly the island was visited in turn by Egyptians, Babylonians and Minoans, Greek and Phoenician traders. A tribute paid to the Egyptian Thothmes 111 provides a written record of history around 1500 BC, and from 300 BC the island's rulers have been in turn the Ptolemies, Romans, Byzantines, Lusignans, Venetians, Turks, and the British.

The island's area of 3,572 square miles is divided between mountain and plain. Two mountain chains, the long narrow Kyrenia range, and the heavily forested Troodos massif in the southwest are divided by the great plain of Mesaoria.

The climate on the plain is very hot and dry in summer, with snow on the mountains in winter. The landscape is magnificent, with boldly eroded mountains, deep valleys and pine forests. The lower slopes are terraced with vineyards and olive groves, and on the plain, grain-fields, vegetable gardens and orchards thrive. Spectacular medieval castles, monasteries, Gothic churches, Venetian fortresses, and other historical monuments adorn the island.

# CHAPTER 2

Hawkspurr removed the pistol from behind his back, and placed it more comfortably in his waistband. Despite the convolutions of the road, he did what every good soldier does given the chance—he went to sleep.

A tap on his shoulder brought Hawkspurr instantly awake.

"Nicosia Hawk."

The evening dusk was gathering now as the car entered the almost English tidiness of the suburbs, and approached the Venetian built fortress walls of the old city. To Hawkspurr's mind, the dying sun bestowed a mysterious golden cloak over ancient sandstone walls and shadows cast by green cypresses. A mixture of the Orient, and medieval Western architecture that reached into his romantic spirit and gave him a thrill of danger, yet an anticipation of pleasure and romance.

"When did you book me into the hotel Jack?"

"Yesterday."

"Any problems with accommodation?"

The inspector laughed dryly. "Hardly! Cyprus is not number one on the tourist itinerary at this time."

"Fine. Take me to a different hotel please."

The two policemen simultaneously raised eyebrows at each other in the rear-view mirror.

It was Hawkspurr's turn to laugh. "You coppers had better start learning a little basic security."

Mike Landris smiled. "He's right Guv'. Hôtel des Gourmets Ok?"

"Sure, let's humor the gentleman Mike."

The Cypriot handed Hawkspurr his bags from the boot of the car, and held out his hand. "Have a safe journey home sir. I shall look forward to working with you, and showing you our beautiful island."

"Thank you Sergeant. Is there anything I can bring you back from London?"

The Greek thought for a moment, and then leaned forward to whisper in Hawkspurr's ear.

Hawkspurr chuckled. "My pleasure."

O'Connor moved to the rear of the vehicle. "What are you two cooking up?" he growled.

"Personal matter Inspector."

"I see. Ok Mike you get off home, I'll have dinner with Lieutenant Hawkspurr and telephone for a car later."

The sergeant raised fingers to forehead in a half salute. "Goodnight sir. See you later Guv." He climbed into the car and drove away.

Inside the hotel lobby, O'Connor checked Hawkspurr with a hand on his elbow. "And what name will you be using to register with, mister security?" His voice was heavy with sarcasm.

Hawkspurr smiled at him unabashed. "How about Carruthers of Nairobi? It has a quaint colonial ring about it. What!"

O'Connor grunted and shook his head. "I think you're going to be more trouble than you're worth!"

In the dining room Hawkspurr tucked heartily into a plate of succulent roast lamb with capers, and a traditional Greek salad of lettuce, cucumbers, tomatoes, scallions, black olives, chunks of white feta cheese, and anchovies, all mixed together with a vinaigrette sauce and sprinkled with fresh mint.

O'Connor had ordered a bottle of a wine rarely found outside the Greek mainland; Monte Nero, an outstanding smooth red as rich as the fables of its native land.

Hawkspurr glanced down the comprehensive wine and spirit list. "Good heavens look at these prices, my boys are going to love it here. Is everything as cheap?"

O'Connor nodded. "Yes, the breweries, wineries and distilleries are well established. They were making wine here long before the Crusaders discovered the delights of this island."

Hawkspurr leaned back from the table appreciatively. "I haven't tasted lamb and fresh salad like that for years. One gets a little jaded with eternal curry." He savored the wine. "And what about you Jack, is your family here with you?"

"No I'm afraid not. Even a thick old copper like me realizes that the situation here could get much worse."

He paused reflectively. "I have to admit though, I miss the old lady and my cheeky kids. I share a bungalow with another expatriate Brit next to the police station."

He looked at his wristwatch. "Time I was off. I have arrangements to make for tomorrow and reports to write. Which reminds me—will you make out a statement tonight regarding the incident, and let me have it in the morning?"

"Certainly Jack, I'll take care of it as soon as I've bathed. Look at the state of me! Unfortunately I was too ravenous to wait any longer for a meal."

"Don't worry about it, the place is practically deserted anyway. I'll see you early tomorrow, and just sign for anything you need, you're a guest of the government."

Hawkspurr smiled engagingly. "Would that include a bottle of the local brandy for my room? Purely research you understand."

"Ok!" O'Connor waved a hand in despair as he walked away. "More bloody trouble than you're worth." He muttered to himself.

Hawkspurr was shown to a comfortable room, with a double bed and en suite bathroom. From the smiling Turkish porter who carried his bags he ordered a bottle of brandy, and asked him to have a suit pressed, then hanging his uniform bag from a hook on the door he unpacked a dark gray lightweight woolen suit, and black leather shoes.

"I'm going to soak in a bath for a while Achmed." He read the young man's name from a plate on his white coat. "Just leave the bottle and a soda siphon on the table, and lock the door behind you."

When the porter had departed, Hawkspurr ran the bath water and then rolled up his soiled safari suit, and stuffed it into the bottom of his bag along with underwear and socks.

In the bathroom, Hawkspurr locked the door and as an added precaution jammed a chair under the handle. He placed his pistol on a handy stool and slipped sensuously into the soothing water.

"Aaaah!" He bent his knees and ducked his head, but the length of his legs precluded his body from stretching completely, still he laid his head back and wallowed in the sheer luxury of hot clean water.

Hawkspurr heard the outer door open, and close with a turn of the key. He would have loved a drink in the bath, but was too lazy to move.

As the water cooled, Hawkspurr reluctantly rinsed off the dying soapsuds and stepped from the tub. He wrapped himself in one of the huge fluffy Turkish towels hanging on a rail, and glanced down at his body. "Don't want to get too wrinkled, do we old son?"

'Now for that brandy' he thought. With pistol in hand, he unlocked the door and stepped into the adjoining room.

A startled movement on the bed, and he flattened himself against the wall aiming his weapon towards the sound. Swiftly his eyes traversed the rest of the dimly lit room, but the intruder was alone. In the soft light of a bedside lamp a pair of very wide, very bright, almost black eyes stared back at him in alarm. Moist red lips were parted to reveal small even teeth, and the impudent face was crowned with pale blonde hair cut in a boyish bob.

"Ye gods woman, do you have a death wish?" The pistol did not waver from a point below the slender neck.

The feminine mouth closed with a nervous swallow.

"Before you answer, would you kindly show me both of your hands?"

The woman complied, and the pouting lips turned up in an impertinent grin as the upraised arms allowed the bed covers to slip from her shoulders.

The pistol wavered.

Hawkspurr moistened his lips and drank in the beauty of pale golden breasts. Smallish, but pert and firm with honey colored aureoles tipped by light brown nipples.

"I should warn you madam, it's been rather a long time since I had my mouth upon breasts that fair." Hawkspurr took a step closer to the bed, and did not attempt to retain the damp towel as it fell to the floor.

"Amanda Carson." The woman examined Hawkspurr's slim body, and smiled at the erection taking positive form atop the long muscular legs.

"And you sir are Nyles St.John Hawkspurr. The Princess Fazima sends her very warmest regards!" As she spoke, Amanda Carson slowly drew back the sheets to reveal her naked body. "See? I'm not armed—of course I still might be dangerous!" She spoke with a slightly aggressive Canadian accent.

Hawkspurr ignored the taunt, crossed to the large wardrobe and cautiously checked inside.

"Just let me make sure." He slipped a chair back under the outer door handle, and examined the curtained windows.

Amanda's eyes never left the now fully erect penis. The provocative bobbing motion of the member was making her feel quite heady.

Hawkspurr halted with his thighs pressing against the high bed, and the woman looked into his face from behind half closed eyelids. She glanced from his penis to the gun.

"Well," she whispered, "which one are you going to use on me?"

Hawkspurr bent and placed the semi-automatic under the mattress. He leaned his weight on the bed, and with his free hand gently pulled the enticing mouth to his loins.

"Try not to speak with your mouth full Amanda."

Sharp teeth bit lightly, and Hawkspurr moaned with delight. He sank onto the bed and moved his hands to the seductive white thighs then, gently parting them he lowered his lips to the mound of tight curls and probed with his tongue.

The response from the woman was electric, and her body stretched and arched in ecstasy as she sucked with renewed intensity upon the swollen head of Hawkspurr's manhood. Hawkspurr too was intoxicated with the sexual scent of the female, and bit down harder, his fingers caressing the writhing buttocks. Together they rolled and undulated in abandon stimulating each other voraciously—until Hawkspurr felt the overpowering need to possess the woman.

He extricated himself from the position, and knelt between the raised suppliant thighs. With rigid arms he looked down upon Amanda and slowly inserted the rampant penis into her moist being.

The woman's eyes rolled back into her head and the parted lips begged to be kissed. "Yes Hawk. Yes!"

Hawkspurr thrust deeper with his hips, and lowered his body to cover the woman. His lips sought hers and they mingled with a deep hunger both needed to assuage. Their bodies moved in unison, giving and receiving with a fierce desire, until in a momentous spasm of fulfillment they spent the lust within them.

Hawkspurr rolled over onto his back, panting with exertion and perspiring in the pleasant warmth of the room. He turned his head to look at Amanda, and grinned as he extended an arm across his body.

"Since we haven't been presented formally, allow me to introduce myself. Nyles St.John Hawkspurr, Lieutenant."

Amanda took the hand, and wriggled her body to nestle into Hawkspurr's shoulder. Her piercing raven eyes mocked the man. "Amanda C. Carson, free spirit! And I've been following your career for some time Hawk."

"Indeed madam."

"Indeed yourself. I was covering the story of our Canadian boys in Korea, when I heard about a mad young Englishman creating mayhem behind the enemy lines with a Korean guerilla group."

Hawkspurr made no comment.

Amanda continued. "I picked up your trail again in Japan, while I was visiting the military hospitals and it seemed like you were busy creating another reputation with the ladies of various nationalities!"

Hawkspurr smiled modestly. "One does one's best in time of war."

"As you say—indeed. By then, you were providing the copy that my readers back home lap up over their breakfast tables. And those Chinese twins in Hong Kong! When did you ever find time to catch up with Gunter Von Harzburg?"

At the mention of his archenemy's name, Hawkspurr sat up and grasped Amanda's shoulders none to gently. His eyes narrowed, and his mouth was a ruthless slash in the handsome face. "Just what do you know about Von Harzburg?"

Amanda was unperturbed. "Ha! Got your undivided attention now have I?"

Hawkspurr did not reply. Instead he swung his legs off the bed, and padded to the table where a bottle of brandy and two glasses stood.

He spoke over his shoulder. "Two glasses. Pretty sure I wouldn't throw you out eh?"

"Listen buster, I interviewed that pretty little blonde in Germany, and the Princess Fazima in Malaya. You were even screwing that Chinese lady detective in Singapore before you found it necessary to kill her!"

Hawkspurr poured a glass of the Metaxas brandy, and swallowed the contents savagely before turning to face Amanda with blazing eyes. "And I thought you might be just another bleeding heart."

"Bah! I live only for the story Hawk—just as you live for soldiering." Amanda added with a wry smile, "And screwing."

Hawkspurr shrugged, his anger quickly spent. "Fair enough. Drink?"

"Bring the bottle over, and get back into bed."

Hawkspurr filled two glasses and crossed to the bed. He sat on the edge with one leg on the floor.

"I have a report to write, and I'm bloody tired. Have a drink and go to your own room." He sipped at the brandy appreciatively. "By the way, how did you find me?"

Amanda raised a hand and rubbed thumb across fingers. "American dollars buster. I've got informants everywhere. You were too quickly in and out of Kenya, but sooner or later I knew that I would catch up with you."

"How long are you going to be in Cyprus?"

"As long as the job takes."

Obviously the journalist didn't yet know that he was leaving for London in the morning.

Amanda examined the tall soldier shrewdly. "You're not telling me all Hawkspurr. Where are your men—Talon Troop?"

Hawkspurr took another sip of brandy. "Cheers."

Amanda ignored the rebuff and continued coyly, "I might have a snippet of information that would interest you. I've already interviewed Archbishop Makarios and an aide of George Grivas in Athens?"

Hawkspurr turned to refill his glass, and hide the sudden flicker of interest in his eyes. "Try me." He invited.

"Did you think that your old pal Gunter died, after he saved you from drowning in Malaya?"

Hawkspurr went pale, and spun around to face woman again. "Repeat that!"

Amanda smiled like a tiger. "EOKA have hired the German to train and coordinate their intelligence network in Cyprus. Apparently Grivas himself tried to organize the locals, and they made a total balls of it."

Hawkspurr suddenly felt chill, and retrieving the towel from the floor draped it over his shoulders. He sat in a chair. "It's a well known fact that Grivas hates communists, he would never hire Von Harzburg."

"Not so. Von Harzburg has deserted his red masters, and built an organization of his own—rent-a-terrorist if you like. He now works independently for anyone willing to pay his price. He thought you might approve!"

"You've seen him?" Hawkspurr frowned.

"Sure have."

"Is he undercover?"

The journalist laughed. "Good god no! The British have nothing on him. He's even using his own name, as a wine and spirits merchant from Geneva."

Hawkspurr sat deep in thought, and Amanda wisely remained silent.

Gunter Von Harzburg: Born 1926 of a noble Russian mother and aristocratic German father. He was raised on the family estate in the Harz Mountains of Germany, and educated in a military academy. As a nineteen-year-old S.S. Officer in Hitler's Nazi army, the Red Army captured him at the fall of Berlin. Both parents had perished during the war, and the Stalinist regime had decided to reeducate the young man as an Insurrection Leader.

Von Harzburg is a natural linguist—speaking French, Russian, English, Arabic, and some Mandarin in addition to his native German. During the Korean War of 1952 Hawkspurr captured Von Harzburg during a raid behind enemy lines. Von Harzburg escaped from U.S. Intelligence custody in Japan, and was pursued by Hawkspurr through Hong Kong to his home in the Easter Zone of Germany. On that occasion, Hawkspurr had been certain he had killed the German in retribution for the murder of a Chinese constable. (See: Korean Raider)

Subsequently, Von Harzburg and Hawkspurr found themselves as adversaries during the Malayan Emergency, when the communist agent was engaged to advise the terrorists of the Malayan Races National Liberation Army.

Hawkspurr and the German have a mutual respect for each other, stemming from their similar backgrounds. Certainly Von Harzburg had spared Hawkspurr's life during an incident in Malaya, and another officer who knows both men well, described them in a poetic moment as the two heads of the hammer of Thor, bonded until death.

Hawkspurr scoffs at the simile, but like Von Harzburg has always been reluctant to kill his nemesis.

Amanda emerged from the bathroom, and completed her toilet with an application of lipstick. She was simply dressed in light green slacks and a cream silk blouse, but Hawkspurr was staring at her with unseeing eyes.

"Perhaps I'll see you at breakfast Nyles?" Amanda reached into the capacious brown leather bag that hung from her shoulder, and produced a camera.

Hawkspurr returned to the present with a threat on his lips. "Touch a button on that contraption, and you'll be eating celluloid for breakfast."

Amanda laughed mockingly. "Poor baby, so vulnerable!" She stepped closer and pulled the towel from Hawkspurr's body. "And so naked. Fazima would really appreciate a personal portrait."

"Good night Miss Carson. Thanks for the ride, I needed it."

"The pleasure was all mine Lieutenant, perhaps we can do it again sometime?"

Hawkspurr pushed the woman gently to the entrance, and kissed her lightly on the lips.

He closed the door firmly behind her.

# CHAPTER 3

✿

Hawkspurr awoke later than was his habit. Somewhat chagrined he attributed this lapse to travel fatigue—or perhaps his energetic encounter with Amanda Carson?—No certainly not!

After his ablutions he dressed carefully in the neatly pressed suit, with pale blue shirt and blue and red Guards' tie.

Speculatively he weighed the pistol in his hand. Normally he carried the weapon across international borders concealed in the false bottom of his hold-all, but British Customs Officers were more diligent than most. He removed the shells from the magazine, and meticulously cleaned and oiled the semi-automatic. He would leave it with Inspector O'Connor until his return to Cyprus.

Since he habitually unpacked only the bare essentials wherever he slept for the night, Hawkspurr wasted no time checking drawers and wardrobe. Carrying his own luggage, he made his way downstairs to the reception lobby where he confirmed that he was checking out that morning.

He headed for the dining room still retaining his bags.

All of the tables were unoccupied with the exception of one. Amanda Carson was patently waiting for Hawkspurr's arrival, and turned her head expectantly as he pushed through the doors. Hawkspurr halted abruptly, and his gut tightened as he saw the journalist's companion rise to his feet and face him. So the woman had been telling the truth—Gunter Von Harzburg was here in Cyprus.

Each man appraised the other with set faces; only the eyes glittered with emotion. Hawkspurr's cold brown, Von Harzburg's steely gray. Without looking away from the German, Hawkspurr thrust his bags towards the steward standing deferentially beside the entrance.

"Put these where I can see them please."

"Yes sir."

Hawkspurr advanced to the breakfast table.

"Good morning Miss Carson." He halted with both hands on the back of her chair and examined Von Harzburg.

Amanda did not move or speak as she stared down at the coffee cup in front of her; only a sudden uplift of her bosom betrayed some tension.

"Guten morgen Gunter. You look better than the last time I saw you."

The German was a couple of inches shorter than Hawkspurr with fair, cropped hair and a square handsome face. The three-inch long scar on his left temple was a permanent reminder of Hawkspurr's attempt to kill him in the forests of the Harz Mountains.

"And you a little drier Nyles!" He was referring to the incident in Malaya, when as Hawkspurr's captive their dugout canoe was wrecked in a jungle river. Hawkspurr had been trapped under water, and Von Harzburg had freed him before making good his own escape.

Hawkspurr allowed the corners of his mouth to lift a fraction in a grim smile. "I had an idea you would surface again somewhere in my life Gunter. Pardon the unintentional pun." He moved to a vacant chair. "Mind if I join you?"

Both men sat liked coiled springs in a gun magazine.

Amanda Carson laughed a trifle too loudly. "How lovely—a touching reunion of old comrades." She waved a hand over her shoulder to summon a waiter. "More coffee please, and I'm sure that Mr Hawkspurr requires a hearty English breakfast."

Hawkspurr nodded to the elderly Greek waiter. "Ham and eggs, toast, marmalade, and a pot of tea please."

He turned his attention back to Von Harzburg. "Now tell me Gunter, what brings you to this beautiful island?"

"Wine and spirits old boy. We Swiss are a self indulgent race, and the cellars of Europe are somewhat depleted since the end of the war."

"Really! Swiss you say, and no doubt you have the appropriate passport and papers to prove it?"

"Naturally." The German replied with a disarming smile. "And I see that you are in civilian clothes. Have you too retired from the military?"

Hawkspurr ignored the query, and looked at Amanda. "I imagine you'll be returning home to Canada, now that you have your story?"

"Oh I think I'll stay around a tad longer. I need a vacation." Then a new thought struck her, and she turned sharply towards the door. "Your bags, you're leaving!"

"I'm afraid so. I need a holiday too, and I fly to London later today."

Amanda was furious, and her facial expression showed it. "You're a tight lipped bastard Hawkspurr."

Von Harzburg laughed in wry amusement. "Miss Carson, you are one of a very long line of ladies to arrive at that conclusion."

Before the journalist could form a suitable repartee, a not too distant explosion followed by a burst of small-arms fire rattled the hotel windows.

Hawkspurr rose quickly from the table, and shouted an order to the startled waiter.

"Close the curtains!" He moved to assist the man, and looked out into the street. A noise like muffled surf was coming closer, and peering further along the road Hawkspurr saw a solid phalanx of children in school uniform advancing.

Boys and girls who appeared to be of secondary school age were chanting, "Liberate the fatherland, death to the tyrant!" Their ludicrously small, yet threatening arms waved aloft, holding rocks and sticks.

Behind the children and urging them on, Hawkspurr spotted bearded Orthodox priests in the distinctive black cap and flowing robes.

More akin to demoniac figures from the dark pages of Greek mythology, than men of a Christian god. Other adults—probably teachers—encouraging them to greater violence accompanied them.

And all this was in a country where a benevolent government permitted teaching the same curriculum as that in Greek mainland schools.

Even to the point of criticizing the policies of a British Crown Colony without any fear of censorship or retribution.

The front ranks were comprised of all girls—angelic faces contorted with hatred and Hawkspurr could well understand the devastating effect that this would have on impressionable young English soldiers. Evil, clever minds were orchestrating this demonstration.

He drew back from the windows as the column passed by, and stones rained upon the glass. Amanda was wisely sheltering under a table, and fumbling to get her camera out of a bag.

Von Harzburg had not bothered to move from his seat, and was calmly sipping his coffee.

Hawkspurr looked down on the German. "You don't seem surprised by the riot Gunter. Maybe you had a hand in it?"

Von Harzburg returned the Englishman's level gaze. "Not my style Nyles. You should know better than that."

The German reached into a pocket and produced a sheet of folded paper.

"See for yourself. This is the oath administered to children by their priests."

Hawkspurr read the malediction uneasily.

'I swear in the name of the Holy Trinity that: (1) I shall work with all my power for the liberation of Cyprus from the British yoke, sacrificing for this even my life.

(2) I shall perform without objection all the instructions of the organization, which may be entrusted to me, and I shall not bring any objection however difficult and dangerous these may be.

(3) I shall not abandon the struggle unless I receive instructions from the leader of the organization, and after our aim has been accomplished.

(4) I shall never reveal to anyone any secret of our organization, neither the names of my chiefs nor those of the other members of the organization even if I am caught and tortured.

(5) I shall not reveal any of the instructions, which may be given me, even to my fellow combatants.

If I disobey my oath, I shall be worthy of every punishment as a traitor and may eternal contempt cover me.

E.O.K.A.

Hawkspurr shook his head in sadness. "How can you condone this Gunter, you were a soldier once?"

Von Harzburg shrugged. "It is easy for you to condemn Nyles, you have your country and your military traditions. My army was destroyed, and my country divided, now I make a living in the only way I have been trained for."

Hawkspurr had no reply to the German's logic.

Amanda Carson snorted with impatience. "If you two old warriors have finished philosophizing, I'm off to shoot some hot pictures."

"Goodbye Miss Carson. Sorry I can't provide you with a story." Hawkspurr mocked. "Watch out for those young priests—I'm told that they don't wear pants under their robes!"

Von Harzburg stood. "I too must get to work. Auf wiedersehen Nyles."

"Wiedersehen Gunter. Don't let me find you with a gun in your possession." Hawkspurr was not smiling, and the two did not shake hands.

Carson and Von Harzburg departed, and Hawkspurr sat again, as Porters appeared to clean up the broken glass.

"Bring me a fresh pot of tea and two cups please. I'm expecting a guest." Hawkspurr glanced at his watch—no doubt O'Connor had been delayed by the riots.

Some five minutes later a harried looking O'Connor arrived. "Good morning Hawk," the inspector watched the staff clearing away splintered shards of glass, "I see you've already had a visit from the educational community."

"Hello Jack. Yes, what's the situation like now?"

"One shopkeeper dead in Ledra Street for not boycotting British goods. One English police officer wounded, and broken windows everywhere. Right now the security forces have the mob contained outside the Government Secretariat."

"What happens now?" Hawkspurr walked over to the windows and surveyed the road. "Will this affect my travel plans?"

"Not at all." The policeman assured Hawkspurr. "I've a car outside waiting to take us to Government House. Grab your luggage, you'll be going straight on to the airport after you've seen the Governor."

"Roger, let's move then." Hawkspurr stooped and removed his pistol and a box of shells from the carryall. "Hang onto these until I return please."

Outside the hotel, a police vehicle and Ferret armored car of the Royal Horse Guards were standing ready.

"Your old mob, aren't they?" The inspector indicated the sand colored armored car with its single Browning machine gun.

"Still my parent regiment Jack—always will be."

O'Connor laughed. "Can't quite see you trotting up the Mall again Hawk."

Hawkspurr smiled to himself. Knightsbridge Barracks and Whitehall were part of another military world. Yet the same men who rode proud black horses, uniformed in blue and scarlet with silver cuirass' and gleaming brass, now controlled powerful Rolls Royce engines. They had swapped silver helmets and red plumes for a black beret, and their sabers for revolver and Sten gun—but still they remained the Queen's Guardsmen.

Hawkspurr noted that the Corporal Commander standing alertly by the Ferret wore footwear as highly polished as the thigh-length, spurred boots he had left behind in Knightsbridge.

The NCO snapped to attention and saluted. "Good morning Mr. Hawkspurr, Major Dickinson sends his compliments."

"Thank's Corporal. Where is the Major?"

"Limassol sir, commanding 'B' Squadron."

"Get mounted please Corporal." Inspector O'Connor was impatient to be moving. "Go back past the museum, and then through Metaxas Square. I want to swing round away from the Secretariat, before heading for Government House."

"Roger sir." The tall Horse Guard clambered up into the turret of the armored car, and donned a wireless headset to instruct his driver.

The little convoy moved off, and Hawkspurr relaxed in the police car. In spite of the disapproving look from O'Connor, he wound down the window on his side. It was a typically perfect morning; still cool and clear before the sun reached its zenith, and the air had a peculiarly heady scent all of its own.

O'Connor's ploy to avoid the trouble spots was of no avail. As the cars entered Metaxas Square, a small gang of youths erupted from an alley and pelted the vehicles with stones and bottles. Hawkspurr ducked instinctively and put his window back up as he caught a fleeting glimpse of the distorted, hate filled faces of the youthful Greeks.

O'Connor pointed out the burnt-out ruin of The British Institute, destroyed by students in a frenzy of hate, burning films, technical equipment, and every book of the finest British library in the Middle East.

The armored car commander had strict orders, and roared away in the lead without retaliation. At the entrance to Government House the Ferret halted, and traversed its turret to cover the back road with the Browning machine gun, as the police car swept through open gates guarded by sentries on foot.

Extra fences and barbed wire could not diminish the impact of the imposing building as it came into sight. With the tall symmetrical cypresses, and lawns in the forefront of the residence dramatizing white arches and deep shady verandahs surmounted by a single domed tower.

Antique cannon guarded the steps, and above the great door the royal coat of arms was displayed in carved stone.

The interior was magnificent with paneling of rare woods from many parts of the Empire, vast fireplaces, and wrought-iron balustrades.

Field-Marshal Sir John Harding was not a large man in stature but the power of his presence and personality dominated the room.

As the visitors were ushered into the Governor's office Hawkspurr was sorry that he was not in uniform—he felt a need to pay Sir John the military compliment of a salute. However he drew himself to an attitude of attention as he halted in front of the desk, and focused his eyes over the Governor's head.

The Field Marshal appraised the tall young soldier in front of him, "Good morning Hawkspurr, I've heard a great deal about you." He glanced down at a folio on the desk, and his eyes twinkled in the warm friendly face. "Not all of it good, I have to admit!"

Hawkspurr remained staring woodenly ahead. "Sir."

The Governor shifted his gaze to O'Connor. "Inspector. Thank you for taking time to see me, it's not a good day out there I fear?"

"No Sir John." The policeman shuffled his feet uncomfortably.

The door opened again as another officer was shown into the room, and the Governor inclined his head. "You gentlemen will know each other of course. Please be seated, and let us proceed with the business in hand."

Hawkspurr looked at the fair-haired man and smiled in recognition. It was his former commanding officer, and a distinguished soldier in his own right.

"You've come a long way since you were a Trooper in the Blues Hawkspurr." The Colonel looked at Sir John.

"A damn fine soldier, but not always conventional or disciplined!"

"Sir." Hawkspurr acknowledged.

Superfluous conversation was not encouraged in the Guards.

"That may well be why he's suited to this particular operation Colonel." The Governor turned his attention back to Hawkspurr.

"First congratulations Hawkspurr, I've approved your promotion to Captain. You will be operating independently but with full support from Army, Air Force, and Special Branch—direct liaison with Inspector O'Connor. Your brief is to play EOKA at its own game in the mountains, track them down where they feel safe and destroy them. Your area of operations will be cordoned off by regular infantry units, and armored patrols of the Blues. Any terrorists your group flushes out will run into their net. Re-supply will be your tactical choice—airdrop, or collect from a road head. Work out the details with Limassol area commanders, but strictly on a need to know basis. We have our work cut out for us in the towns and villages, and I shall expect maximum effort from you in the interior. Right, off you go now and enjoy your leave. Report to Brigadier Hazlett in Whitehall as soon as you arrive in London. Good luck."

O'Connor drove Hawkspurr straight to the airport, and escorted him through the throng of service wives and children returning to England. "We're getting as many civilians out as we can Hawk. They're all potential targets from now on, and will only distract their menfolk from the task at hand."

Hawkspurr agreed with the sentiment. He would only accept single men for Talon Troop; soldiers under extreme stress needed clear minds, uncluttered by domestic concerns. His special unit formed in Malaya was the family, and every man a brother in it.

"Good luck Hawk and get back as soon as you can, I want to get this job finished and go home too."

"I'll be back before you miss me Jack. I'll send on an advance party of my lads in a couple of days, just make sure you meet them and get a base camp organized near Limassol. For heavens sake keep them out of the hands of the regular army or neither side will be happy!"

The two shook hands warmly. "You can depend on me Hawk."

Hawkspurr waited patiently on the tarmac, as tearful women and crying children were ushered aboard the Vickers Viscount by solicitous Air Hostesses. There was a sprinkling of soldiers going home on compassionate grounds, and they cheerfully assisted with the more recalcitrant offspring.

Hawkspurr move to join an older woman in airline uniform at the bottom of the mobile steps, she appeared to be the senior flight attendant and was overseeing the embarkation with brusque efficiency.

"Good morning ma'am. Lieutenant, err…Captain Hawkspurr. I trust you still have room for me?"

The tall woman examined Hawkspurr from polished shoes to neat haircut in a single swift glance, and then returned to her immediate responsibilities. "Millie! Lift that bloody child up in your arms and get boarded."

Hawkspurr grinned at the cultured voice with the drill sergeant's tone—a no-nonsense lady.

Without turning her head the woman acknowledged Hawkspurr. "Emily Bart-Hoskin. You're a handsome rogue—are you as wicked as your reputation?"

"Mess gossip ma'am. All fabrication." Hawkspurr eyed the medal ribbons of World War Two on the woman's left breast. "I see you were partly responsible for the demise of poor old Corporal Hitler."

"Bomber Command, radar and communications. Never had a chance to fly until the war finished. Now I'm a bloody nursemaid to a bunch of snotty nosed kids including the girls I'm trying to train." She paused. "Move it Rosemary, I want dinner in London tonight not breakfast tomorrow! Right Captain, up you go."

Hawkspurr stepped back. "After you ma'am."

Emily's brown eyes glittered mischievously. "Want to check out the old girl's undercarriage eh?" She mounted the steps with a provocative waggle of her hips and bottom.

From behind, Hawkspurr admired the compact buttocks and long slender calves in the dark nylon stockings. The seams ran straight as arrows, disappearing along firm thighs into the shadowy promise of delight.

Hawkspurr smiled hungrily. Probably seven hours flying time, with at least an hour in Malta for refueling. More than enough opportunity to join the ranks of the so-called 'Mile High Club'—those who claimed to have made love aboard an aircraft in flight.

The bedlam of noise from excited children subsided, as the airplane climbed away from Nicosia and headed west across mountain ranges and out to the blue Mediterranean.

Hawkspurr was seated in the rear with Emily for take off, but as soon as the 'plane leveled out at cruising speed the senior attendant left to distribute lunch packs and beverages.

Hawkspurr ate the corned beef sandwiches with relish and lay back to doze, as Emily and her trainees settled the passengers down for the stretch to the island of Malta.

His slumber however developed to sleep, and it was a full hour before an unexpected series of jolts accompanied by cries of alarm awoke him—the airliner was experiencing turbulence.

Emily approached up the aisle, and steadied herself against the back of a seat. "Are you one of those men that can sleep on a barbed wire fence?"

Hawkspurr yawned. "I'd rather sleep on you."

"Threat or promise?"

Hawkspurr stretched his arms high, and pushed his hips forward in the seat—he had woken up with an erection. Emily looked down, and her mouth fell open, she moistened her lips with a nervous tongue.

"Care to carry out a quick reconnaissance in a recently unexplored area soldier?"

"Who bares wins ma'am—lead the way."

Emily unlocked the door to a tiny room—little more than a storage cupboard. A rail held aircrew overcoats, and items of baggage claimed most of the available floor space.

Hawkspurr closed the door behind him and carefully snipped the latch, not that there was room for anyone else to enter.

Emily had hastily removed her tunic and skirt, and stood close to Hawk-spurr clad only in blouse and slip. She reached for Hawkspurr and embraced him passionately, her lips sought his and they kissed with a mutual desire.

Emily released Hawkspurr and half sat, half stood against the pile of suit-cases. "Regrettably there is no time for the niceties Nyles." She raised the slip to her waist, revealing smooth white thighs enhanced by taut nylon stocking tops and a garter belt.

Hawkspurr quickly discarded his trousers, and stepped between the out-stretched limbs.

Wide legged panties offered no impediment as he joined with the woman, and the rise and fall of the fuselage in the turbulent air presented a new dimen-sion to the experience. Welcome to the Mile High Club!

# CHAPTER 4

❀

In a quiet unpretentious office in Whitehall, Hawkspurr sat opposite a distinguished elderly gentleman dressed in civilian clothes; Brigadier Charles Hazlett, head of a special military intelligence section.

Hawkspurr had first met the then Colonel in Korea, at which time he had been recruited to operate with a Korean Raider Unit during the war. He had later been responsible to the Colonel, for a special assignment in Malaya and again in Kenya. Although a regular officer serving with the Special Air Service Regiment, Hawkspurr realized that once more Charles Hazlett was controlling his destiny.

"Well Captain Hawkspurr, we seem to be working together again. Congratulations on a well deserved promotion, and the success of your recent operations in Malaya and Kenya."

"Thank you sir." Hawkspurr felt a deep respect for the Brigadier, but was always cautious in his presence—the older man probably knew exactly when Hawkspurr was engaged in love making, and with whom!

As if reading Hawkspurr's thoughts, the Brigadier allowed the corners of his mouth to rise a mere fraction. "Miss Bart-Hoskin was very impressed by your err…discretion."

'Ye gods, the man has bloody agents everywhere!' Hawkspurr smiled in response. "And I thought the lady was genuinely interested in my career."

Brigadier Hazlett ignored the sarcasm. "You've already received a briefing regarding your next assignment from Sir John Harding." He hesitated and fixed Hawkspurr with a speculative look.

"I now need you to cut short your leave Nyles." Again he sat silent, expecting a protest from the younger officer.

Hawkspurr remained motionless and mute; at certain times words are pointless and inadequate.

The Brigadier continued. "I would however like you to spent a few days in Spain for me."

A tiny frown creased Hawkspurr's brow.

"In three days time a Liberian freighter will dock in the port of Cadiz. On board will be a consignment of small-arms and explosive devices from an Italian factory—these weapons are en route to Cyprus in the guise of wine making equipment for certain monasteries. That in itself is not a problem—we have on our payroll a Maltese deck officer, keeping us informed of movement and timetables and as soon as the ship enters Cypriot waters, the Royal Navy will impound the cargo."

Brigadier Hazlett rose and walked around the desk to stop close to Hawkspurr, and looked down at him. "What I'm about to ask of you is outside of your military duties Nyles. I want you to kill a man—I believe the popular term is 'to remove with extreme prejudice'. A psychological profile drawn from your reports over the last four years, has convinced War Office consultants that you are emotionally capable of taking life without undue moral stress."

Hawkspurr stiffened in indignation, and the Brigadier placed a restraining yet friendly hand upon his shoulder. "I apologize, but the doctors don't know your true identity—you are merely a case history with the codename Sparrowhawk. Rest assured that you are not considered to be a psychopath, your greatest strength lies in your sense of duty and tradition, and you definitely know right from wrong."

Hawkspurr answered through tight lips. "That's a bloody comfort!"

Hazlett smiled understandingly. "I once found myself in this chair Nyles, and in the same situation. Come, we'll finish this discussion over lunch at the Cavalry Club. You can digest the proposition along with the finest fish available in London."

The Brigadier's assessment of the epicurean delight was as accurate as his judgment of men, and Hawkspurr never allowed problems of the moment to interfere with a fine meal—sometimes a soldier simply doesn't know where the next fodder was coming from.

A piquant Gazpacho soup with Chestnut Teal sherry, then melt-in-the-mouth Sole Savoy poached and topped with asparagus and mushrooms, and on the side plump succulent English garden peas, and tiny boiled potatoes, with a crisp green salad.

Hawkspurr raised a glass of chilled Gewurtztraminer—dry and spicy, the flavor intense. "My compliments sir. Grandfather always maintains that you should have been a sommelier, if not a soldier."

"Thank you Nyles. Sir Francis keeps a magnificent wine cellar himself. How are he and your beautiful grandmother?"

"Both well thank you. I had hoped to join them for the hunt this autumn, but now it seems that I'll be busy pursuing a two-legged fox."

Brigadier Hazlett looked a little sad. "These are difficult and dangerous times Nyles. Insurgency and terrorism are on the rise all over the world, especially in what's left of the old empire. Take your pleasures where and when you can, I fear you'll not see real peace in your time."

Hawkspurr laughed. "I'll drink to that!"

In a secluded corner of the members' lounge, Brigadier Hazlett detailed his plan over coffee and cognac. "You'll travel to Cadiz by channel ferry and train. I think as if on a walking holiday, there are many such tourists traveling the continent at this time of the year. I'll provide a passport showing you as a schoolteacher, interested perhaps in Spanish history. Give me a name."

Hawkspurr didn't hesitate. "Francis Drake! Should give the Spaniards a laugh, he attacked Cadiz in 1587."

"You have a peculiar sense of humor Nyles" Hazlett remarked dryly, "I hope it doesn't backfire on you." He made a quick entry in a notebook. "Now listen carefully, your contact's name is Borg and his ship the Mount Nimba. The target is a Greek national Manos Androulakis, a very unsavory character who collaborated with the Nazis during the war, and dare not go home to Athens. He's trying to gain favor with the present Greek regime by supplying arms to Grivas in the mistaken belief that if Makarios achieves Enosis, all will be forgiven. In Italy he is protected by an organization of die-hard Fascists, and has accrued a fortune through clandestine arms deals around the world. This is the first time he's ventured out of Italy since 1946, and Borg says that he stays locked in his state-room when the freighter is in port. He's extremely nervous but has a companion, his Italian mistress Claudia."

Hawkspurr raised a hand in protest. "I won't kill an innocent woman under any circumstances sir."

Hazlett shook his head in denial. "Not necessary Nyles. The woman has Mafia family connections that probably act as Androulakis' bankers. It's safe to assume that Claudia won't give evidence, whatever she sees."

"Right sir, what about a weapon? I'll have to go through Spanish customs checks."

"Borg will supply a pistol, and get you aboard the Mount Nimba. He will then establish his own alibi—we don't want him compromised. Just how and when you expedite the matter is up to you." The Brigadier glanced at his watch. "You have thirty-six hours to get to Cadiz. There's a room for you tonight at Chelsea Barracks, and your documentation and travel tickets will be delivered there early tomorrow. Speak to Captain Giles Gresham, Grenadier Guards, he works for me from time to time and will be most sympathetic to your requirements. Following your instructions he will also organize the travel movements of Talon Troop to Cyprus."

"Well then sir, I'd better go and buy some suitable clothes. Obviously there's no time for me to go home."

"Ah yes." The Brigadier reached into a pocket and produced an envelope. "Ready cash and expenses. Not overly generous but sufficient for your immediate needs, and something extra for you and Gresham to have a drink on me tonight."

Hawkspurr stood and offered his hand to the older man. "Thank you for your hospitality sir. Shall I report to you on my return from Spain?"

"No Nyles, take a few days off, I'll find you when I need you."

Hawkspurr walked quickly away. 'I'll just bet you will!' he thought.

After a taxi ride to Chelsea, Hawkspurr walked along the Kings Road looking for a second-hand clothing shop where he purchased a civilian backpack, and items of gear that he thought the well-dressed hiker was wearing abroad this year.

At the main gates to Chelsea Barracks, Hawkspurr showed his identity card to the Sergeant Guard Commander and asked for Captain Gresham.

Later in the Grenadier officer's quarters, he worked out travel arrangements to fly an advance party of his men to Cyprus.

Talon Troop was still carrying out winter training in Norway, but Hawkspurr was eager for his men to acclimatize themselves to the Cyprus environment as soon as possible. Satisfied that his soldiers would be well looked after, Hawkspurr spent a pleasant evening in the Mess with Giles Gresham.

Hawkspurr eased the unfamiliar pack from his sweating back, and sank gratefully onto the shaded chair of the waterfront tavern. The noon heat of Cadiz was oppressive, and the predominantly white of its buildings glaringly painful. He hated wearing sunglasses, but realized that if he didn't acquire a pair soon, he would seriously impair his night vision for the job ahead.

The area was strangely quiet and devoid of life. Of course—siesta! Every Spaniard with any sense was dozing behind shuttered windows, if not working in a fan-cooled office. Even the anchored fishing boats bobbed indolently at their moorings, and taut cables extended and slackened as if they were a mother's arms, gently rocking their progeny to sleep.

Hawkspurr did not possess the energy to shout for attention, or even tap on the little round table in front of him. He opened another button of his blue cotton shirt, and leaned his head back in the shade to rest eyes for a few moments respite from the brilliance of his surroundings.

It was a shuffle of sandaled feet, and the none-too subtle scent of a female garnished within an aura of garlic that brought Hawkspurr upright in his seat.

"Senor?" The middle-aged woman didn't look too pleased at the prospect of having to fetch and carry for a gringo without the good taste to be sleeping elsewhere. The over-abundant bosom restrained in a low cut, crumpled if clean blouse, rose impatiently. "You want something?"

Hawkspurr smiled charmingly, but his eyes watched fascinated as a bead of perspiration formed in the hollow of the woman's neck. The droplet grew to a tadpole of moisture, and then slithered sensuously down to be crushed in the dark chasm of the breasts' cleavage.

"Francais?" The full lips pursed with annoyance.

Hawkspurr wrenched his gaze up to meet the angry black orbs of the woman. "Er…no. Do you speak English?"

"Si, and French, German and Italian. Now what do you want?"

"First a very long, very cold drink." Hawkspurr took a small sheet of paper from a pocket, and handed it to the woman. "Then if this is the right Taverna Alfonso, I would like to speak with Elisio Garcia."

The woman looked nervously around, and her eyes narrowed as she read the note from Giles Gresham. The paper then suffered the same fate as the tadpole of sweat as it disappeared without trace into the capacious bosom.

"You come inside quickly." Broad hips from which swirled a colorful three-quarter length skirt, swayed into the cool gloom of the cafe's interior.

The inside of the building was much larger than it appeared from the street. The front half comprised a tasca or bar with mahogany top and stools, and the usual array of wines and spirit bottles.

Continuous benches lined the opposite wall, and the bare wooden floorboards led to a short flight of steps that descended to the restaurant or tablaos below.

Predictably, a motif of fishing paraphernalia decorated ceiling and walls. Small wooden tables and chairs surrounded a polished tile dance floor, and arches on either side of an ornamental fireplace probably led to kitchen and service areas.

The atmosphere was redolent with the essence of fish, onion, tomato, garlic—and stale, pungent tobacco smoke.

At the far end of the bar, the woman pushed aside a heavy curtain and beckoned Hawkspurr to follow her through. A narrow staircase ran up to an open hall lined with doors. Here all was light and airy, with whitewashed plaster walls and white painted woodwork.

"Wait here." The woman entered a room without knocking.

Hawkspurr deposited his pack on an almost black, wooden sea chest and waited patiently.

After an interval the door opened again.

"You go in now." The woman ordered.

Again whitewashed walls and black oak furniture heavy and ornately carved, but made cheerful with bright cushions and drapes in reds, greens, yellows and blues. The garish outer sunlight was banished from the chamber by dense velvet curtains, and the subdued illumination of the room was cool and pleasant.

A rather squat, swarthy man of about fifty years rose from the sofa extending a blunt square hand, and the powerful fingers of a professional fisherman scarred by rope, crushed Hawkspurr's hand.

"I am Garcia, what do I call you?"

"Drake. Weren't you were expecting me?" Hawkspurr surreptitiously flexed aching digits.

"I was expecting someone—an Englishman." Garcia smiled like a conspirator.

"Do you have something for me?" Hawkspurr unbuttoned his shirt, and removed a slim nylon money belt from around his waist, which he handed to the Spaniard. He scratched his stomach with a self-indulgent grin. "I'm very pleased to get rid of that!"

"Good." Garcia left the room with his prize, calling over his shoulder, "Rosa, give Mister Drake a meal and a bed. I will speak with him later."

Hawkspurr looked at the woman, who merely shrugged her shoulders. "Come." She led the way to a small bedroom along the hall. "Rest here, I will bring you a tray. The bathroom is at the end of the passage."

"Thank you Mrs. Garcia." Hawkspurr assumed that the couple was married.

He examined the room that contained a wardrobe, table and two chairs, a dresser with mirror, porcelain bowl and jug. In the center was a narrow bed, and over it a heavy wooden crucifix.

Hawkspurr the atheist removed his boots and stretched out on the coverlet looking up at the cross. "I do hope it doesn't fall on me!" He fell asleep.

It was early evening when Hawkspurr awoke. On the table were a carafe of white wine, and a small empanada—a pie with fish filling mixed with onions and green peppers—now cold. He drank a glass of wine, and went in search of the toilet.

The bathroom was spacious with white tiles, and a single shower. Hawkspurr stripped, bathed and shaved, and then returned to his room to change into afresh shirt.

He hated un-ironed clothes, but realized that the crumpled effect was more in keeping with his cover character.

He wolfed down the cold meal with gusto, and enjoyed a more leisurely glass of wine. He thought it best to stay out of sight as he listened to increased activity out in the street, and below in the tavern. He did not open the curtains, and stretched out on the bed once more.

Four years of active service had taught him the value of relaxing whenever the opportunity was presented.

Soldiers termed it, 'in bed or out of barracks'.

Hawkspurr felt no concerns for the task ahead, a little fear of the as yet unknown factors was a healthy sign, and at the same time a tinge of excitement stimulated his thought process. He was not tied to a plan or timetable; once his target was identified he would take the appropriate action and think on his feet as always.

The battlefields to combat terrorism are wherever the enemy is to be found: a jungle clearing, desert, bedroom or boardroom, the purveyors of terror must be exterminated; no prisoners means no hostage demands.

Hawkspurr was glad he had declined any backup. Each of his men would cheerfully have accompanied him on the mission, but working alone gave him freedom from the natural responsibility he felt towards his soldiers.

The softly opened door brought Hawkspurr springing to his feet.

Rosa did not believe in knocking first, but alarm showed on her features as she saw the cold alertness in the Englishman's face.

"You come down now," she blustered, "Elisio will talk with you."

Hawkspurr combed his hair automatically, but as he looked at his reflection in the mirror ruffled it again and drooped his shoulders uncharacteristically.

He thought that the brown corduroy trousers and dark green creased shirt, probably looked authentic enough for a schoolteacher on a study tour.

"Scruffy bastard."

Pushing aside the weighty curtain at the foot of the stairs, Hawkspurr found the tavern transformed. The bar was crowded with local fishermen and their women, and every one of them seemed to be speaking at the same time.

Two pretty girls in Gypsy costume were dispensing drinks, and Rosa was waiting to conduct him down to the restaurant.

On a stool in front of the empty fireplace a handsome young man was plucking softly at the strings of a guitar. There was a certain air of anticipation at the crowded tables, and Hawkspurr guessed that some sort of entertainment was about to commence.

Garcia was ensconced at a central table, from where he could oversee the perambulations of his staff from kitchen to customer. He obviously had an eye for attractive young ladies, but the real manager was Mrs. Garcia.

A rapid assessment of the garrulous clientele, assured Hawkspurr that they were locals concerned only with their own hedonistic pleasures. No one paid him any attention as he sidled into a seat next to his host.

"When do I meet Borg?" Hawkspurr enquired.

Garcia waved a nonchalant hand. "Later. Relax, eat, drink, enjoy. We do not hurry life here Mister Drake."

Hawkspurr knew when not to swim upstream, and made no further protestations as a platter of fabada—succulent broad beans in a bacon and sausage stew was placed before him.

The waitress pointedly pressed her breasts on his shoulder as she served Hawkspurr, and her smoldering look clearly indicated her admiration for the handsome gringo. Hawkspurr smiled up at the girl, and moved his upper arm in response.

Garcia missed nothing, and dug a finger into Hawkspurr's ribs. "Eat your beans, they will give you stamina for later." He made a lewd gesture with his forearm.

"When your business with Borg is concluded return here, your bed will be warmed by hot Andalusian blood this night!"

"Or something just as fiery if I finish all these beans senor!" Hawkspurr tucked into the dish before him, but declined the wine.

"You are a cautious man Mister Drake," Garcia probed, "your rendezvous on the docks must be very important?"

Hawkspurr smiled. "Merely a matter of pest control Garcia—a cleansing you might say."

A hush fell upon the diners as the guitarist strummed a chord of rising crescendo, and the arrogant clatter of castanets demanded attention.

The lights were extinguished for an instant, and when they came back on a dramatic figure stood alone in the center of the dance floor.

A statuesque woman in classic pose—one arm raised gracefully above her bowed head, the other curved down and back. Her right leg, bent at the knee with poised foot pointed to the front. Her sleek hair was black gloss, pulled severely back into a tight bun on the nape of her slender neck, and she was gowned in the traditional embroidered dress of the Flamenco Dancer. She was a pure Gypsy woman, the descendant of a Hindu race who arrived in Spain in the middle ages.

A single clack of the castanets in her left hand elicited a double response from the pair in her right. Slowly her left arm rose to join the right with the rattle of ebony increasing in tempo as they met.

The dancer's right heel struck imperiously at the hardwood floor, and the figure began to stamp her feet and whirl to the cadence.

The guitar melody increased both in pace and volume, and the audience clapped and clamored with uninhibited enthusiasm.

"Ole! Ole!"

Hawkspurr admired the grace and controlled energy of the elegant woman. She did not possess the soft beauty that he sought in a woman, but he was tantalized by the glimpse of strong muscular legs displayed reluctantly by the layered swirling skirts. The dance and the ancient pulse of the music excited Hawkspurr beyond his natural reserve, and when the Flamenco finished he was on his feet applauding and shouting along with the enraptured audience of Spaniards.

The performer acknowledged the acclaim, and then threaded her way through the aficionados to join Garcia at his table.

"Mirabella, may I present Mister Francis Drake from England." The proprietor was beaming with unashamed admiration.

The Flamenco dancer sat down still panting slightly from her exertions, and loosened the colorful shawl about her shoulders. She extended a graceful hand to Hawkspurr, and he responded with a continental kiss before seating himself.

As Garcia poured Mirabella a glass of wine, she examined Hawkspurr with intense eyes under her silken lashes.

"Give me your hand Mister Drake." She demanded, speaking English with a slight lisp.

Hawkspurr complied with a teasing grin. "Don't tell me that you read fortunes as well madam!"

The woman did not return the Englishman's smile, but studied his palm for a few seconds. Then she spat on the floor, and formed a peculiar sign with the fingers of her left hand.

She muttered something in Spanish and Garcia hastily made the sign of the cross.

Hawkspurr laughed scornfully. "Tell me the worst madam—am I to die young?"

Mirabella shook her head and held Hawkspurr's fingers again in both hands. The brown eyes now glinting black in the candlelight, were boring into his very heart.

In spite of himself Hawkspurr shuddered. He joked again, with less conviction. "A goose just walked over my grave."

"No—you are destined to live long, but you cannot yet find true love. Women will give themselves to you willingly for you are touched by the ancient gods, but I also see much blood on your hands." The Gipsy woman smiled for the first time. Very gently—a mere flicker of light across her full lips, and she stood up to take her leave.

"We will meet again Mister Englishman." Mirabella was gone in a rustle of skirts and the lingering scent of wild roses.

Garcia dropped his false bonhomie. "Go now Drake. Wait outside, someone will come for you."

Hawkspurr left the table without a word and returned to his room upstairs. From his pack he removed a pair of black cotton coveralls rolled into a compact wad, and changed his footwear for blackened tennis shoes.

# CHAPTER 5

Outside the noisy tavern the air was still warm and oppressive, there was no street lighting and the sparse illumination radiated from buildings and boats.

Hawkspurr waited patiently in the shadows until a movement on the wharf alerted him, and he stiffened in expectation as a small figure approached him. The urchin boy stopped at a safe distance from the gringo and beckoned with his arm. He did not wait for a response, but turned on his heels and hurried away in the gloom.

Hawkspurr followed cautiously, as the boy led him into the quieter area of the commercial docks. No others were abroad in the night, but occasionally a lifted voice or shrill laugh caused Hawkspurr to turn his head anxiously in the direction of a dimly lit vessel.

The urchin halted and pivoted to face Hawkspurr, he pointed to the black doorway of a low warehouse, and then disappeared like a wraith into the murk.

By now Hawkspurr had regained his night vision, and examined his surroundings. The bowl of the sky was moonless but brilliant with stars, and stark against this backdrop he could discern the outline of a freighter. Stubby masts and the skeletal arms of derricks pointed accusingly upward, having been deserted by man. The only sounds were the lapping of water, and intermittent slap of rigging lines against a spar.

The atmosphere was a smorgasbord of scents—salt, tar, diesel fuel, fish, and a pot-pourri of spices. The ship was showing only dim riding lights at bow and stern, then for an instant a lamp glimmered and Hawkspurr saw the angled gangway leading down from deck to wharf.

The structure swayed and rattled slightly as a figure descended, and Hawkspurr retreated back from sight.

The man paused, and looked quickly left and right before crossing to the dark doorway.

"Drake?" He whispered hoarsely.

"Borg?"

"Yes. Listen carefully." The Maltese officer spoke English with a Cockney accent and a peaked cap obscured his face. "Apart from Androulakis and the woman there is only the night watchman on board, but don't worry about him, I have just left him in a drunken sleep." Borg pressed a cold metal object into Hawkspurr's hands. "A Beretta automatic, loaded with seven rounds. The numbers are filed off, so when you have finished drop it in the harbor."

Hawkspurr cocked the little gun and placed the safety catch on. "Ok, I'm familiar with the weapon."

"Good. Androulakis is in a stateroom below the bridge. His door is always locked from the inside, and he will not open it to anyone but the woman. You will have to go over the side. Come!" Borg whispered urgently. "I will show you where, and then leave you. I must have an alibi."

"Roger." Hawkspurr agreed. "Wait one moment please." He unrolled the coveralls and pulled them on over his clothes. From the pockets he extracted black cotton gloves and a balaclava, covering himself so that only the eyes showed. With a handkerchief he wiped all prints from the Beretta. "Let's go."

Borg guided Hawkspurr along the darkened deck, and up an internal companionway. A passage led to another short flight of steps, and they emerged on the narrow bridge deck. Crossing to the starboard rail, Borg pointed silently down to the only open porthole twelve feet below. A soft pink glow shone out like a beacon to the black sea beneath it.

Borg handed Hawkspurr a coil of knotted light rope, already tied to the rail. He gripped the Englishman's shoulder and leaned to breathe into his ear. "Give me five minutes to get clear." Then he was gone.

Hawkspurr crouched in the lee of the bridge superstructure; he could detect no movement on ship or shore but didn't want to present a silhouette against the stars.

In the silence he thought he could hear the soft murmur of voices from the cabin below. Good—he did not wish to shoot a sleeping man.

He would prefer to kick the door in, and tell the Greek exactly why he was about to die, but then he might be forced to kill the woman too. Well, this way was no different than shooting a man from ambush—except that in the field they would both be wearing uniforms.

Right, Borg should be clear by now. Hawkspurr stood upright and stretched, flexing his legs and arms. He moved to the rail and glanced down—it was lucky the night was warm or the porthole could have been closed.

Now how was he going to hold onto the rope, and fire an accurate shot at the same time? He estimated the distance from rail to porthole allowing for the length of his body, and then he formed a loop in the rope that would not slip. That should do it.

Slowly, Hawkspurr paid out the line until it hung within a foot of the open port, and almost reached the dark water. He checked the Beretta in his breast pocket, and climbed over the rail. Taking a deep breath, he wrapped his legs around the rope and lowered himself carefully over the side. His knuckles and knees scraped on the rough steel of the ship's plates, and when his shoulders reached the level of the open port he experienced some difficulty in slipping his foot into the loop.

His efforts caused him to twist away from the ship, and he held his breath, expecting a shout of alarm or the closing of the porthole.

Nothing transpired and Hawkspurr breathed easily. Reaching out with his right hand, he grasped the raised rim of the port and pulled his body over, with infinite care he peered into the cabin through one eye.

Androulakis was sitting up in the double bed of the stateroom, and facing him was the woman. She was seated cross-legged at the foot of the bed naked from the waist down, but Hawkspurr focused his attention only on the Greek terrorist.

The man was speaking softly, and gesturing with his hands as if lecturing the woman. Hawkspurr estimated his age at forty plus, with a fleshy face and balding black hair. He looked evil, or was Hawkspurr mentally trying to justify the assassination?

Hawkspurr withdrew his head and removed the gun from his pocket. He eased off the safety catch, and filled his lungs quietly through his nose. This time he pulled his body flush to the porthole, and deliberately placed the barrel of the little gun on the rim.

Calmly, he took aim at the Greek's temple and gently expelled his breath. Androulakis must have sensed the danger, yet as if mesmerized turned his head almost in slow motion to face his fate.

Their eyes met, and those of the victim widened in sudden fear.

Hawkspurr squeezed the trigger…once…twice, and the head exploded back against the bulkhead, casting an abstract crimson painting over the white wall. The woman screamed insanely and leapt from the bed, clawing at the door without once looking towards the assassin.

Satisfied that the job was done, Hawkspurr tried to kick out of the rope loop, but the twist had closed fast around his foot.

"Blast!" He eased his body down to grab the resultant knot, and accidentally dropped the Beretta in the sea. Well he had to dump it anyway. He struggled again pulling at the rope frantically, but as his foot came free his hands slipped, and he plunged headlong into the harbor.

"Ye gods!" Hawkspurr spluttered, pulling off the balaclava and spitting foul tasting water from his mouth as he bobbed to the surface. In intelligence parlance an assassination is a 'wet job'—a bloody wet job indeed!

He trod water, listening for any sound of an alarm—still all was hushed. He doubted if the shots could have been heard with the cabin facing away from the wharf, and also suspected that people hereabouts wisely kept their own council. He started to swim away with an unhurried breaststroke.

Once he was a good two hundred yards clear of the Mount Nimba, Hawkspurr swam towards a low barge tied at the wharf and scrambled aboard. He was certain that the vessel was deserted and removed his clothing, wringing out as much water as possible.

After replacing the clammy garments, he searched around for a piece of scrap metal. A short length of rusty chain served his purpose, and lashing the black coveralls, gloves and balaclava helmet securely to the links he dropped the incriminating bundle over the side.

Brigadier Hazlett had assured Hawkspurr, that the master of the ship would be unlikely to report the death of an illegal passenger to Spanish authorities.

There was therefore no real need to 'sanitize' the area, but Hawkspurr owed his survival to date by staying ahead of the opposition and leaving no detail to chance.

He had no doubt that the unmourned body of Androulakis would disappear forever in the depths of the Mediterranean, once the ship was through the Straits of Gibraltar.

Hawkspurr walked briskly back to the Taverna Alfonso along the still empty dockside. Many lights had now been extinguished, but at the front of the tavern he could hear that a few revelers were still enjoying Garcia's hospitality.

Scouting the rear of the building, Hawkspurr found an unlocked door opening into a passage that serviced the kitchen and storerooms area. Further investigation brought him to a narrow set of stairs leading to the upper story, and thence to a door adjacent to bathroom and toilets.

Hawkspurr entered his room unobserved, and after a brisk rub down and a change of clothes, was ready for a stiff drink.

Garcia and his staff, in company with half a dozen cronies had pulled together several tables and were enjoying a convivial after hour's party.

As Hawkspurr descended the steps into the restaurant, he was spotted by the exuberant if somewhat glassy eyed host and urged to join the party.

"Did our noise wake you up Mister Drake?" Garcia winked in a conspiratorial gesture, and poked a finger into the Englishman's ribs.

"Yes, I missed you Garcia!" Hawkspurr needed no prompting—his personal axiom was 'work hard, play harder.'

Room was made for the Englishman at the tables, and much to Hawkspurr's surprise Rosa Garcia greeted him like an old friend. He was pressed to the ample bosom, and in a mixture of drunken Spanish and English was told what a lovely man he was.

Hawkspurr laughingly extricated his head from the soft flesh before he smothered, and reached for a handy bottle of brandy. "I'll drink to that!"

The young waitress who had served him earlier rescued him from further risk of damage.

Carmelita's intentions were far from maternal, and with cries of approval from the assemblage, deposited her nubile body firmly in Hawkspurr's lap.

After three or four glasses of the rough brandy, the combination of heat and constant wriggling of malleable buttocks and thighs massaging his loins brought Hawkspurr to a familiar state of discomfort.

Carmelita was delighted with what she considered a personal triumph, and reached down to grasp the erection with exploratory fingers. She shouted a remark that Hawkspurr could not interpret, and the other guests responded with raucous laughter and obscene cries.

"Ay Toro—ole! ole!"

To cover his temporary embarrassment Hawkspurr gratefully accepted the wine flask being passed around the tables. The system looked easy enough; hold the soft leather bag high, and direct a stream of wine from the tiny nozzle into one's mouth.

The audience watched with bated breath and barely suppressed mirth as Hawkspurr held the bag at arms length above his head and squeezed.

Carmelita abandoned ship with unseemly haste as the jet of red wine squirted into Hawkspurr's hair, eyes and nose before finding the target area.

He choked and spluttered, and then recovering his composure joined in the general laughter aimed at the clumsy gringo.

Carmelita wiped Hawkspurr dry with a napkin, and took the wine bag from him.

"Watch Mister Drake. Start with the nozzle close to your lips, and then move the skin slowly away until you can control the wine."

Hawkspurr tried again, and succeeded to the noisy accolades of his drinking companions. By the time he had mastered the technique he was drunk enough to attempt the flamenco. Spinning and stamping in squelching wet tennis shoes, he parodied the movements of the Gypsy girls, until he collapsed in an exhausted heap and was carried off to bed.

Hawkspurr awoke in panic, and attempted to sit up in his bed. Strong hands constrained his arms before he could strike out in the dark, and a voice he associated with the perfume of wild roses calmed his thudding heart.

Mirabella whispered softly in her lisping, lilting voice. "Relax Mister Drake, I am here to serve you. Your spirit is as unfettered as the ancient shades that dwell in the mountains of my birth. Laying with you will bring me eternal good fortune."

That night Hawkspurr experienced the passionate, and savage love making of the uninhibited mountain Gypsy. With skilful fingers and tensile tongue she probed the erogenous places of the man, and initiated him in the secret of the 'Andalusian Butterfly'. As she caressed Hawkspurr, she intoned in a strange mystical language he did not recognize as Spanish.

Mirabella's sexual prowess culminated in the 'passage of the mare'—straddling Hawkspurr's loins, the muscles of her buttocks and thighs palpated and massaged, drawing him deep within her. As Hawkspurr approached a climax, Mirabella manipulated inner muscles to restrain and thwart him each time—until he could bear the pressure no longer and she permitted him a screaming release to receive his seed.

Totally spent, Hawkspurr lay debilitated and allowed the woman to sponge him and anoint his body with musky oil. He fell into a deep sleep, and dreamt he was soaring on black demonic wings above a savage landscape of mountains, canyons, and red searing rock.

Unable to dictate direction, he was carried powerless on a current of air beyond his control. His feet hanging below were talons dripping crimson with blood he knew was of other men.

Strangely, Hawkspurr awoke with a feeling of inner calm. He was aware of all that had passed, and fully realized the significance of his dream. Fate, kismet, destiny—call it what he may, the broader aspects of his life were beyond personal control—he could command only the moment.

Mirabella had disappeared as silently as she come; perhaps her sole intent was to be impregnated by the enigmatic foreigner.

Someone had dried and ironed Hawkspurr's clothing during the night, and after shaving and washing all traces of the scented oil from his body, he packed his scanty belongings and went down to the restaurant.

A young man he had not seen before served him a breakfast of omelet, bread rolls and coffee, and when Hawkspurr asked for Mr. or Mrs. Garcia in order to settle his account, the man informed him that no payment was due, and would Mister Drake leave the tavern as soon as possible.

No doubt Garcia knew more of Hawkspurr's business than he admitted, and in the sober light of day was anxious to be rid of the Englishman.

Although eager to rejoin his men and return to the job in Cyprus Hawkspurr felt he should take advantage of the day, and enjoy the sights of Cadiz.

It was one of Europe's oldest cities, founded by the Phoenicians and dating from about 1100 BC. In turn was captured by Carthaginians and Romans, and from 711 it was occupied by the Moors until recaptured by Alfonso X, King of Castille and Leon in 1262. The 551 years of Moorish influence are reflected in the picturesque architecture of the many fine buildings and promenades.

Hawkspurr found himself drawn inexorably to the docks and harbor, but the Mount Nimba had sailed and the activity around her previous berth appeared normal. The terrorist Androulakis was on his way to an unmarked grave.

In keeping with his character of the history teacher, Hawkspurr was careful to be seen taking numerous photographs with his borrowed camera. He had exhausted the single roll of film, but went through the motions of snapping the numerous scenes that delight a tourist.

Unfortunately he was so engrossed in his deception that he failed to notice the attention being paid to him by two officers of the Civil Guard, the Policia Armada who carry weapons, unlike the regular police. The dictatorship of Generalissimo Franco was at this time facing popular discontent and unrest from many workers and students, and the arrest of dissidents and malcontents was a daily occurrence.

Hawkspurr's mistake was the classic 'wrong place, wrong time'. He was quite innocently pointing his lens in the direction of warships of the Spanish Navy, when a heavy hand fell upon his shoulder.

He had to summon every ounce of self control to suppress his reaction to strike out at his captors, as the camera was snatched none to gently from his hands, ripping the neck strap from its studs.

Although offering no resistance, Hawkspurr's arms were forced behind his back and his wrists manacled. He was spun around, and for the first time was able to see the policemen properly.

Both men were squat, powerful, and ugly. Their features belonged to street brawlers rather than officers of the law, and their distinctive shiny black caps looked incongruous perched on heads of greasy unkempt hair. The uniforms were stained and scruffy and the boots unpolished.

Hawkspurr stood with bowed head, and half closed eyelids to conceal the frustrated anger blazing behind them. One man poked a grubby finger into his gut. "Name? Papers?" He demanded in guttural Spanish.

Hawkspurr shook his head. "I don't understand."

The second policeman was searching Hawkspurr's pockets, and rummaging through the pack still on his back. Triumphantly he produced a sum of money and Hawkspurr's false passport.

The cash disappeared into the policeman's own pocket with a remark Hawkspurr did not understand, and the passport was handed to his colleague.

The senior man tapped the royal crest on the black book, and spat on the ground. "English!" He thumbed to the photograph page, and viciously forced Hawkspurr's chin up to compare the likeness. He grunted with satisfaction at the match, but it was obvious that he could not read.

A brief discussion between the two policeman, and they decided to take "The English spy" to their superior officer. Hawkspurr was savagely thumped with a rifle butt to remove any doubt as to his status as a prisoner, and he was frog-marched triumphantly away.

The few witnesses averted their heads and hurried away thankful that it was not them in custody, but Hawkspurr covertly observed the spectators and for a fleeting moment thought he recognized the boy who had guided him to the docks on the previous night.

The waterfront police station was as unsavory as its tenants and after being relieved of his handcuffs and backpack, Hawkspurr was pushed quickly through the front desk area into a narrow passage housing six or eight cells. These were open fronted with bars, and no windows to the outside, the only furnishings were a foul latrine bucket and on the floor a filthy straw filled palliasse.

The once whitewashed walls were covered in graffiti and lewd sketches of naked women, whilst fingers in excrement had obviously executed some of the artwork.

The stench was overpowering with the smell of vomit and urine emanating from the other cells, along with drunken muttering and absurd threats against the police.

With a final kick Hawkspurr was propelled roughly into the narrow room, and the iron-barred door slammed behind him.

The policeman turned the key in the lock with a ribald remark to his companion, and the pair left laughing.

Hawkspurr knew better than to expend his energy on useless actions and raging against the inevitable, and skeptically avoiding the mattress he squatted in the cleanest corner and closed his eyes to plan an escape should the opportunity arise.

After an estimated hour or so—his watch had also been confiscated; an older policeman speaking English summoned him to the door. Another guard unlocked the door, and his handcuffs replaced before he was propelled along the passage to an interview room.

The English speaking Spaniard had the badges of rank denoting a commissioned or warrant officer, and in contrast to the other policemen he was relatively clean with finer features, and appeared to be about forty years of age. He held Hawkspurr's passport in his hands and sat at a plain wooden table, whilst his prisoner stood in front of him attended closely by the guard.

"Mister Drake. A teacher, yes?" The officer's face was expressionless, yet his black eyes glittered with reptilian malevolence.

"Yes sir."

'Name, rank, serial number.' Thought Hawkspurr.

"Then why are you spying upon our navy?"

"I was not spying on your navy, or anything else sir."

The officer examined Hawkspurr closely through shrewd eyes, and one corner of his lips lifted sardonically. "You do not look like a teacher in spite of your clever attempt to alter your appearance." He tapped the medal ribbons on his chest. "I too was once a soldier?"

"I did my National Service as a teenager sir, that's all."

"No Mister Drake, I do not believe you. Are you of MI6, or some other intelligence organization?"

The interrogation was interrupted by a sudden commotion in the cellblock with voices raised in anger, and then a single shot rang out deafeningly in the confined space.

Hawkspurr started and looked towards the door, but his guard and interrogator did not move or even show alarm.

Hawkspurr turned to the officer with a questioning look in his eyes.

The Spaniard stared back for several seconds without emotion. "That was probably a countryman of yours Mister Drake. A drunken English seaman who has been nothing but trouble since the time he was arrested for disturbing the peace, and saying some very nasty things about our heroic leader."

Hawkspurr remained silent.

The officer sat, staring into Hawkspurr's face and tapping the corner of his passport on the desk in an irritating manner.

Hawkspurr did not break the stare, and they searched each other's eyes watching for some sign of weakness.

The Spaniard's mouth set in a grim line as he reached a decision, then stood up abruptly and slammed the passport down hard on the table. "I am sending you to Madrid Mister Drake, the experts there will question you much more effectively than I can. Some of the senior officers were fortunate enough to have been trained by the German Gestapo in 1939. They will find the truth, I assure you." He left the room.

Hawkspurr was dragged back to his cell as the bloodstained body of a man in blue jeans and black jersey, was being carried unceremoniously through a door at the rear of the passage.

Once more he was kicked into the polluted atmosphere of detention.

# CHAPTER 6

✿

Hawkspurr now felt more optimistic, at least a move out of this repugnant rat-hole would give him some little chance to use his training and attempt an escape. At the outside chance, perhaps in Madrid he could get a message to the British Consulate. Mister Drake's passport would stand close scrutiny even there.

A pannikin of water had been placed in the cell, but obviously no food was forthcoming, so Hawkspurr wet his mouth and lips, and sponged his face with a handkerchief—he was not game to actually swallow the stuff.

Despite all of his self-control, he was forced to utilize the noisome latrine bucket. He managed this with some difficulty in an attempt to avoid contact with the filthy rim, but started to giggle—if only he had declined that plate of beans in Garcia's tavern! In the absence of any toilet accessories, he tore off a strip of his shirttail to clean himself.

Hawkspurr dozed for a while, but without natural light he was uncertain of the passage of time. The slamming of a door and the rattle of keys in his lock brought him to his feet, blinking in the light of the passage lamps now switched on.

Once more he was manacled and pushed along to the front desk, where a tall fat man in civilian clothes was signing some form of receipt for the prisoner and his passport. Hawkspurr's request for the return of his belongings was met with a sullen look from the jailer, and a wave of dismissal.

The big policeman assessed Hawkspurr with a searching look, and almost lifted him from his feet as he took a firm grip on the Englishman's arm and bundled him into a waiting car.

The driver was also in plain clothes, and drove off without a word as Hawkspurr was crushed into a corner of the rear seat by the bulk of his escort.

Hawkspurr's spirits rose when the car arrived at the railway station, any form of transport would be more comfortable than sitting in close proximity to his escort for the more than 350 mile journey.

It now became apparent that he would be traveling alone with Vincente—as the driver called the big man. Before leaving the vehicle Vincente removed the handcuffs from Hawkspurr's left wrist and attached it to his own huge arm, but once the official car drove away the escort's grim demeanor softened. He smiled at Hawkspurr, and waved a meaty fist. "You no give me any trouble. Ok?" His English was passable.

Hawkspurr managed to grin back. "Ok, no trouble!"

'I might just as well be shackled to a Clydesdale horse, as try to overpower this fellow!' He thought.

"You hungry?" Vincente enquired.

"I'm starving. Your colleagues didn't bother to feed me all day." Hawkspurr really was close to fainting from lack of sustenance and the heat of the day. In his present condition he didn't possess the energy to make a run for freedom, even should the opportunity arise.

From one of the many street vendors, Vincente purchased huge bread rolls filled with pork and tomatoes, and muffins sticky with honey and nuts. This feast was washed down with bottled, orange flavored soda. Vincente probably had a travel allowance to sustain his prisoners.

Hawkspurr was surprised at the number of people traveling that night, one possible reason was to escape the heat of the day, or maybe the fares were cheaper on the old steam train. It was certainly not the sleek, bullet-shaped Talgo of the modern Sate Railways.

Many of passengers jostling for seats in the wooden carriages were carrying baskets of goods, and Hawkspurr was informed that they and several entertainers were making for a festival fair in the city of Seville.

By sheer body weight and snarling authority, Vincente secured seats in an already crowded compartment. Fortunately it was a corridor carriage, and Hawkspurr was shoved into a corner next to the sliding door and handcuffed to a brass handrail.

The fittings were reminiscent of an English Victorian train, even down to tasseled fringes.

The other occupants looked shyly at the unfortunate prisoner, and offered food in the shape of cheese, olives and fruit, but judiciously they first presented their generous offerings to the plain-clothes policeman.

The old steamer moved off with much puffing, and the squealing of protesting wheels on steel rails as they spun seeking a purchase. In the narrow corridor a guitar started to play, and the standing passengers crammed in the available space started to sing. A wild joyful song, that had everyone within earshot clapping and joining in as best they could.

Suddenly there was a commotion at the open door of Hawkspurr's compartment, and three Gypsy women jostled their way in entreating the seated men to give up their seats. One of the girls dumped herself in the lap of the fat policeman and wrapped her arms around his neck, showering his face with kisses.

"You are such a big strong man" she taunted and cajoled, "can I sit with you for a little while?"

Hawkspurr was unable to see exactly what was transpiring as the perfumed fabric of the Gypsies gowns also covered his head, but he felt slim deft fingers manipulating a pick in the lock of his handcuffs.

The strumming guitar and boisterous singing, the crush of bodies and the rattle and roll of the train made it impossible to comprehend just what the Gypsies were up to.

The manacle separated carefully from his wrist, and Hawkspurr was promptly pulled from his seat and into the throng of humanity filling the corridor.

A man smelling strongly of fish occupied his place swiftly, but the woman dragging him through the laughing, singing peasants smelled of wild roses—Mirabella!

Following their progress to the rear of the train, the Spaniards closed ranks behind Hawkspurr in an impenetrable mass of bodies. He spared a thought of compassion for poor Vincente no doubt his next posting would be to a remote outpost in the Spanish Sahara.

"Quickly Mister Drake!" Mirabella shouted, and Hawkspurr smiled at the formal address from a woman with whom he had lain naked the previous night. "We are close to the coast, and a friend is waiting to take you to safety."

An outer door was opened, and friendly hands steadied the Gypsy dancer as she peered out into the darkness. Mirabella saw the signal she searched for, and turned to face Hawkspurr.

The lights of the train were a weak flickering orange, and the roar of air and dust from the open carriage door, combined with the raucous singing made conversation impossible. Hawkspurr smiled his thanks into Mirabella's eyes, and kissed her passionately on the alluring mouth.

The gypsy woman pushed Hawkspurr gently away, and then thrust him urgently to the entrance.

Reaching over his shoulder, she pointed to a single light towards which the train was rushing as it started to gather speed.

Hawkspurr braced his arms as if about to exit in a parachute jump from an aircraft.

"Now!" Mirabella screamed, and Hawkspurr launched himself into space.

Feet and knees together, head clasped tightly between hands and forearms, he hit the ground and rolled automatically as his training dictated. Slightly winded from the fall he recovered to crouch on hands and knees, and shielding his eyes from the flying swirling grit, watched the lights of the train fade into the night.

The light from a guarded torch suddenly shone on his face, and rough hands dragged Hawkspurr to his feet.

"Thank you." He whispered, but no answer was forthcoming. Instead the end of a short length of rope was thrust into his hands, and his rescuer turned away to lead him to safety.

Hawkspurr stumbled along behind his guide in pitch-blackness. The ground was coarse and broken with some patches shifting beneath his feet that felt like sand, and soon he could hear the comforting surge of waves upon a seashore.

His eyes had now adjusted to the starlight, and he could discern the shape of the man confidently leading the way.

Hawkspurr bumped into his guide, as the man halted abruptly on a narrow strand of sand and rocks. The cautious flash of light seaward was answered by a rapid glimmer from a small boat, and abruptly the rope was pried from his fingers the Spaniard disappeared silently. 'Probably a professional smuggler', Hawkspurr thought.

Hawkspurr cocked his head to one side, listening carefully for any sounds of pursuit in the still night. Through squinting eyes he searched the area behind his position but could see nothing, and patiently he sank to the sand on his haunches and watched the sea. He didn't have long to wait; the discernable white line of surf was broken by the bow of a small rowboat, and a figure leapt out as she beached.

"Mr Drake. Come!" It was an urgent command.

The man was already turning the bows of the boat back to the sea, as his companion steadied the oars against the swell of the current. Hawkspurr scrambled over the low stern, and moved forward to make room for the man ashore as he pushed the boat off again.

Two hundred meters out and Hawkspurr could detect the outline of a sturdy Spanish sardine-fishing smack, with her riding and navigation lights doused.

Strong hands pulled Hawkspurr up over the gunwale, as the oarsman hooked onto a davit tackle and the dinghy was hoisted aboard. An unseen man shouted instructions, and Hawkspurr was bundled below decks. He was guided to a narrow bunk that smelled strongly of tar, fish, and sweat, but was dry and more comfortable than many of the places he had slept in over his years of service.

He fell into an exhausted sleep.

It was past dawn when Hawkspurr presented himself on deck, to find a brilliantly clear day with a rolling swell that the fishing boat was smacking into almost playfully. He saw three men busy with some form of maintenance at the stern, and climbed the ladder to the wheelhouse where he greeted his benefactor cheerfully.

"Good morning, a glorious day. I'm very grateful for your help sir."

The grizzled, stocky man grunted an acknowledgment and waved an arm to port. "Gibraltar. You be Ok there, yes?"

"Yes indeed. Who do I have to thank for my rescue?"

"Friends." The laconic skipper returned his attention to navigating the vessel, and Hawkspurr examined the unmistakable bulk of the Rock of Gibraltar, which marked the southern tip of the Iberian Peninsula. One of the ancient Pillars of Hercules marking the entrance to the Mediterranean, and for over 250 years a British colony, Admiralty Harbor, and strategic naval base.

The Spanish fishermen had delivered Hawkspurr safely to the British colony as promised, and quickly departed from Gibraltar after a brief consultation and examination of their papers by the harbor authorities.

Now consular officials and a naval officer were interrogating Hawkspurr. He stuck to his cover story without mention of his incarceration by Spanish police, and played the part of the dull schoolteacher seeking a little excitement.

He claimed that he had spent the last of his money bribing the fishermen to bring him to Gibraltar after his passport and belongings were stolen from a restaurant he was dining in.

"Why didn't you report the theft to the Spanish police?"

"If I were to be detained, I could be late back for work and probably lose my job."

"Are you sure you were not involved in some illegal activity?"

"Certainly not!" Indignant schoolteacher.

"Is there anyone who can vouch for you? The Spanish authorities are not very cooperative at this time, and it may expedite a solution to your predicament."

Hawkspurr offered the official the London telephone number of Giles Gresham.

Within two hours a cable was received back from London, which left no doubt in Hawkspurr's mind that Brigadier Hazlett was once again manipulating the strings of officialdom.

The civil servants were happy to hand Mister Drake over to the naval attaché, and the deference accorded Hawkspurr reflected the contents of the cablegram.

The Lieutenant now addressed Hawkspurr as Sir, and the hospitality of the wardroom was extended to the suddenly important visitor.

Hawkspurr enjoyed the luxury of a hot bath and shave, and after changing into a clean khaki drill uniform was treated to a real English breakfast of eggs, bacon, tomatoes, toast and marmalade.

The Royal Navy certainly live well!

# CHAPTER 7

Despite all jokes to the contrary, the English summer sun shone down brightly on London and Horse Guards Parade. The clock in the tower struck eleven o'clock, and at that precise moment Her Majesty Queen Elizabeth II led her entourage of Royal Dukes, the Honorary Colonels In Chief of the Guards Regiments, onto the ancient ground. The centuries old ritual of 'Trooping The Color' was about to begin.

Horse Guards Arch in Whitehall, was originally the entrance to St.James Palace and is the oldest of royal doorways. The most exclusive thoroughfare England is guarded continuously by the Household Cavalry, and only those of royal blood are allowed to use it.

Hawkspurr and Brigadier Hazlett rose to their feet as the Royal entourage passed. For the occasion both were dressed in the off-duty uniform of officers in London, black pinstripe suit with regimental tie, black bowler hat and tightly rolled umbrella.

'Thank the gods my men cannot see me!' Hawkspurr smiled to himself.

In modern times the parade celebrates the Sovereign's official Birthday, and was a combination of two ancient drills—'Trooping The Color', and 'Mounting The Sovereign's Guard'.

The colors or standards of a regiment were once the rally point in battle, and it was essential that every soldier recognized which one he was fighting for. To this end, the flags were paraded through the ranks of men every night before combat, and suitably stirring music was played to boost morale.

Each move of marching and counter-marching is passed down by word of mouth from generation to generation of guardsmen, as some of the maneuvers are so complicated it would be impossible to write them down. The massed bands of the Guards Division, the Corps of Drums, and the Pipes and Drums of the Irish and Scots Guards provided music.

The Household Cavalry supplied two mounted bands and on parade were a total of 2,000 men and 200 horses.

The color being trooped was selected by rotation each year, and the youngest ensign in that regiment proudly carried the colors throughout the parade.

After the inspection, the soldiers marched past their Queen in slow, then quick time. The five regiments of Foot; Coldstream, Grenadiers, Scots, Irish and Welsh—uniformed identically except for the placing of buttons and facings on the scarlet tunics, and the color of the hackle in the black bearskin headgear.

Hawkspurr felt particular pride when his own regiment of Royal Horse Guards rode past on magnificent black chargers, first at the walk and then the trot, restrained by gleaming black leather reins. Tossing manes and the jingle of bright-chains against sleek groomed coats provided their own accompaniment as the mounted bands, headed by the imposing skewbald drum horses carrying the huge silver drums, played the traditional tunes of the regiment—the Grand March From Aida, and the Keel Row.

A brave sight, of bobbing fluttering red plumes cresting silver and gilt helmets, the sparkle of light on silver cuirass and lethal steel sabers. Swan necked spurs on thigh length shining black boots, with white buckskin breeches, and their tunics were the only ones of blue in a sea of scarlet.

Story has it, that the British soldier wears a red tunic so that the blood will not show in battle, and men of The Blues maintain that they wear their tunic color for the same reason!

Hawkspurr stood again in salute as the standards of his regiment, carrying the battle honors of generations, passed his position.

Luncheon with Brigadier Hazlett was by way of a debriefing, at which Hawkspurr rendered a full oral report of his assignment to Spain. The Brigadier was pleased with the success of the operation, and the fact that he had managed to extricate Hawkspurr from Gibraltar without compromising his department.

The incident would never appear on a written report; this was not a job for those wishing personal glory or official recognition.

After lunch with the Brigadier, Hawkspurr took his leave to journey to Windsor some twenty miles from London, where he was to attend a regimental ball.

The ball was a glittering affair of tall handsome men, and beautiful aristocratic ladies. As usual, the uniformed officers furnished the color and splendor of the evening. The ladies were elegantly gowned for the most part in subtle designs and muted colors, vying with each other only in the brilliance of their jeweled tiaras, and necklaces.

As well as the predominantly scarlet, blue and gold of the Guards officers, tunics belonging to other associated regiments contributed shades of blues and green; with vary hued facings and accoutrements.

Flecks of fire flashed from medals of the Second World War displayed by older men, and the newer decorations of post war soldiering worn by men of Hawkspurr's generation.

New subalterns and cornets examined Hawkspurr's tunic with envy and some awe.

His medals of the war in Korea with its bronze Oak Leaf denoting a Mention In Dispatches, the United Nations Medal, the General Service medals of Malaya and the campaign against the Mau Mau in Kenya. The Queen's Coronation Medal was followed by the American Purple Heart—worn as a special dispensation for his service under United States command. Pride of place on his upper right sleeve was the gold and silver parachute wings of the Special Air Service Regiment.

The fact that he held the rank of Captain at such a young age was also a point of speculation amongst some senior officers, but Hawkspurr was modest and confident in his bearing, showing proper deference to the soldiers of senior rank and age.

Hawkspurr was escorting a childhood friend and confidante, who had her own agenda planned for the evening. Lady Patricia Wyndyatt has set her cap at a school friend of Hawkspurr's, and he had arranged for an invitation to the Ball for Captain The Honorable John Sutton, Royal Military Police.

Hawkspurr and Lady Patricia knew each other too well to be ever involved romantically. Despite the best efforts of their respective families who had them marked for breeding, they had ridden their ponies together, been blooded at the same time in the hunting field, and comforted each other through the years of war and losses amongst their relatives.

Now they accompanied each other to formal dinners, garden parties, and endless social events confident and comfortable in the security of their friendship.

Lady Patricia was tall and slim, striking in appearance with dark bobbed hair, and bright violet eyes. Her deportment turned all heads male and female, yet her demeanor was such that even the most catty socialite did not feel threatened by her presence.

Hawkspurr grinned as Lady Patricia surveyed the room, and spotting her quarry made a beeline for the group of officers chatting at the bar. She hesitated only long enough to allow Hawkspurr to step forward and interrupt the conversation, as she waited to be formally introduced. Her direct gaze never left the face of the man she was interested in.

Captain the Honorable John Sutton, heir to a large farming estate in Devon was enjoying the relative freedom of military life, before settling down to the responsibilities of plough and cow. 6'3" tall with broad shoulders that almost made him appear squat he had blonde hair, and intense blue eyes that crinkled tightly at the corners as he greeted Hawkspurr with warmth.

"Hawk you old ba…!" He hesitated with embarrassment as he caught sight of Patricia at his friend's elbow.

Hawkspurr smiled at the big man's discomfort. "John!" he chided, "I do hope you haven't developed a penchant for nasty language since you became a copper."

Lady Patricia stepped forward and offered her hand to the big man. "Please ignore him Captain Sutton, he's a terrible tease at times."

Hawkspurr composed himself and endeavored to look suitably grave. "Captain Sutton, may I present Lady Patricia Wyndyatt."

John Sutton was enchanted. He mumbled something unintelligible, but Patricia seized the initiative and led him away from the group with a gleeful laugh.

"Let's dance John, Nyles has been longing to dump me and pursue that pretty little girl accompanying the Air Force officer."

Indeed Hawkspurr wasted no time—watching for an opportunity to appropriate at least a little of the attractive woman's attention. His chance came when the older man escorting her left the ballroom.

He moved with agility and speed, to cut off another young soldier with the same objective as himself, and with a quick grin over his shoulder at the frustrated officer, he bowed low before the seated woman.

"Captain Nyles Hawkspurr ma'am. May I have the honor of this dance?"

"Gisela Hoffinger Captain." She spoke with an attractive accent. "How could you possibly tear yourself away from that beautiful lady, is she your wife?" Gisela rose to her feet, and stood looking up at Hawkspurr with a quizzical, if amused look.

"Just a close friend Miss Hoffinger." Hawkspurr examined the Austrian woman. A little younger than himself, medium height but full breasted with shoulder length dark brown hair and warm hazel eyes. The deep red of her gown set off the slightly tanned complexion to perfection, a tan Hawkspurr noted reached well down into the plunging neckline.

She wore no jewels, and Hawkspurr appreciated that her classical features needed no artificial embellishment.

"Shall we dance now that you've completed your inspection Captain?"

Hawkspurr laughed lightly as he led Gisela onto the floor. "A good soldier always carries out a careful reconnaissance before an assault ma'am."

Gisela laughed in reply. "Does that mean I am in danger Captain?"

"Well first I have to establish who the enemy is! May I call you Gisela?"

"Of course Nyles, and there is no foe to concern you. Wing Commander Scranton is my employer, and his dear wife is sadly indisposed this evening. He is a kind man and offered to take me to the ball—like Cinderella yes?"

"Indeed. But I trust you won't disappear at midnight?" Hawkspurr twirled his partner in a sudden spin that she followed effortlessly.

"Tonight I must leave with the Wing Commander, and care for Mrs. Scranton. But I will be free tomorrow afternoon Nyles, if you still wish to see me?" Gisela answered coyly. "I confess I have been watching, and admiring you since you arrived."

Hawkspurr liked straightforwardness in a woman—so many of the socialites he was acquainted with seemed to take pleasure in deception and conniving, as if it were an amusing pastime. Sign of an empty life he suspected.

"Very well Giscla, I shall postpone my campaign for twenty-four hours. I have to lunch at Windsor Castle tomorrow, but perhaps if you'd care to meet me in St.George's Chapel at three pm, we can find something to do for the remainder of the day and night?"

After handing his partner back to the Wing Commander, Hawkspurr joined Lady Patricia and John Sutton for a cold buffet in the supper room. He excused himself soon after, assured that Patricia would be escorted safely home.

Hawkspurr retired to a room previously booked in the old Star and Garter hotel, close to the castle. Although never without invitations for hospitality, Hawkspurr at times preferred his own company and the solitude of impersonal accommodation, without obligation to a host.

Although luncheon was served in the impressive Waterloo Chamber of the castle, the occasion was informal with guests in civilian lounge suits.

The host of the all male assembly was His Royal Highness The Duke Of Edinburgh, and looking along the sixty-seat table from his position close to the bottom—as befitted his lowly rank—Hawkspurr observed that the list comprised senior officers, both military and civil of the intelligence and security services. He also noted that Brigadier Hazlett was two places removed from the Duke, which indicated to Hawkspurr that his chief was held in some esteem.

The chamber had been built in the reign of George IV, by the simple expedient of roofing over an inner courtyard to give the impression of being aboard a ship in Admiral Lord Nelson's Fleet.

Intricately adorned with woodcarvings, the room was dominated by a portrait of the first Duke of Wellington in his Field Marshals uniform. The floor covering is the largest seamless carpet in the world, and was made for Queen Victoria in Agra, India.

Following protocol after the coffee cups had been cleared away Hawkspurr paid his respects to the Duke, and after a few words with the Brigadier excused himself. He made his way to the Grand Vestibule in which are displayed numerous military relics, including the bullet which killed Nelson.

Down a staircase Hawkspurr walked to the lower ward, which houses the residences of the Military Knights of Windsor. Here, opposite the King Henry VIII Gate entrance built when the castle was already 400 years old, was Saint George's Chapel.

Hawkspurr had a special affinity for the chapel that had nothing to do with religion. The ancient regimental banners on its walls, once described by a cynic as 'moth-eaten rags on worm-eaten poles', gave the young soldier a chill of drama and glorious martial history.

Next to the Palace at Hampton Court, Windsor Castle was Hawkspurr's spiritual home. These special places where he could actually feel the presence of the nobles and warriors of old, imparted to him a sense of belonging, and he could almost believe in reincarnation of the human spirit.

William The Conqueror had built Windsor Castle, and Hawkspurr's ancestors had landed and fought with the Norman King of England in 1066. The structure is the oldest continually inhabited castle in the world, and the home of monarchs for over 900 years. The original round tower was built of timber, and replaced in the 12th century by stone on the orders of Henry II, to contain the royal archives.

Deep in thought, Hawkspurr was unaware of the approach of Gisela Hoffinger until she touched him lightly on an arm.

"Good afternoon Nyles, you appear at ease in this cold place. Do you mind if we leave? I like the bright sun and warmth."

"Hallo Gisela. Yes I'm finished here, but I don't know when I shall see it again. Let's find a secluded spot in the sun, and I shall make love to you!"

The couple walked along the old lawns known as the Brockers next to the timeless River Thames, and spoke of inconsequential matters. Gisela was affectionate and amorous, and Hawkspurr experienced that rare immediate rapport with a female.

They drove in Gisela's little Morris car to a pine scented wood, and amidst silver birch, oak, and elm trees scattered on a carpet of bluebells and daffodils, they joined in love.

Hidden from prying eyes in the tiny woodland dell, they removed all of their clothing and stood naked and unabashed, admiring each other. The human form is truly the most beautiful of all animals on earth, and it was apparent from Gisela's total tan that she worshipped the temple of her body and cared for it with a hedonistic pleasure.

Hawkspurr drew the woman towards him and kissed her gently, first upon the warm mouth and then caressed her eyes, ears, neck and shoulders with his lips.

His ardor increased as he bent to bestow his kiss on the firm breasts, and the nipples hardened with desire to the instant responsive swelling of his penis against her belly.

Gisela slipped to her knees, and took Hawkspurr greedily between her teeth, as her fingers gripped his buttocks with a ferocity that arched his back in not unpleasant pain. Her hunger for the man could not be assuaged until she had palpated and sucked the very essence from his body; instinctively timing her own climax to couple simultaneously with Hawkspurr's ejaculation.

As Hawkspurr waited for his vigor to return he laid Gisela amongst the wild flowers, and massaged her taut figure with skilful hands. Carefully spreading her legs, he worked his tactile tongue between her thighs and administered the Andalusian Butterfly enlightened for him by the Spanish Gypsy woman.

The uninhibited Viennese woman screamed with delight, shattering the silence of the isolated wood to send even the somnolent birds and indolent insects buzzing and twittering in sudden panic.

His ministering to the female had now roused his own senses, and Hawkspurr knelt between the suppliant thighs, to lift the loins with both hands and insert his penis through soft moist hairs. Gisela reached up to him with half closed eyes, urging him to thrust deep and strong, and all the time murmuring endearments in her native German.

Hawkspurr's lovemaking was passionate yet controlled; every movement of his hips and hands sensuous and solicitous, remembering all that he had been fortunate enough to learn from older, more experienced women who had taught him the expressions of love.

Ultimately as the summer air chilled with descending dusk, he brought Gisela and himself to the final consummation of their desires.

Gisela's English home was close to the town of Maidenhead, and the couple stopped to dine at a centuries old inn reaching down to the Thames before going on. Hawkspurr wanted to book a room for the night in the romantic hostelry, but Gisela was conscious of the fact that she should be home in case Mrs. Scranton needed her.

Arriving at the Scranton's residence Hawkspurr was invited in, but declined the offer. Before departing however he asked Gisela to show him her bedroom, and then borrowed the Morris car that he promised to return at lunch time the following day.

He drove back to the Inn and sat pensively sipping cognac until closing time. He couldn't afford to spend much more time in England, and he must gather his soldiers and join the advance party in Cyprus.

The main body of Talon Troop would now be enjoying embarkation leave; a situation that caused Hawkspurr some paternal concern—he knew that these very special men played as hard as they fought, and held civilian authorities in some contempt. The last thing he wanted was any confrontation with local or military police that could delay the start of operations in Cyprus.

Hawkspurr grinned. He was feeling the symptoms of withdrawal of excitement and danger himself. Well he could do something about that right now! He drove back to Wing Commander Scranton's house, and parked the little saloon car two hundred yards away in a side street, where he removed his suit jacket and tie.

Walking silently on the grass verge to avoid the gravel of the ornate driveway, Hawkspurr approached the darkened house. Fortunately the Scrantons were cat lovers and had no dogs, the only sounds in this quiet retreat were the rustlings of some nocturnal animals, probably badgers or field mice, and the lonely hoot of a barn owl as he hunted for his supper. Far off a fox barked, and Hawkspurr felt the affinity of hunters in the night although his quarry was a little different!

Hawkspurr squinted his eyes in the pale light of a mere sliver of moon. Yes there was the second story window at the rear of the house, and the sturdy drainpipe giving access to a ledge wide enough to offer passage.

The house was a solid mock Georgian building, probably built in the early thirties when British craftsmanship was in its heyday.

Hawkspurr removed his shoes, and gave the drainpipe a tentative yank—good, it stayed comfortingly anchored to the building. He grasped the cold iron with both hands, planted his feet firmly on the wall and in the manner of a native shinning up a palm tree, climbed carefully upwards.

Reaching the concrete ledge, Hawkspurr stretched out an arm to grip the upper edge of the casement window. As he had observed when visiting Gisela's bedroom earlier, one side of the window was open, not that he had expected the athletic girl to sleep without the benefit of fresh air.

Hawkspurr adroitly swung his feet to the sill, and clambered into the bedroom.

He stepped to one side so that he would not be silhouetted against the pale light from outside and stood still, listening for any sound of alarm. After a second he could just detect Gisela's even breathing—the unsuspecting woman was sleeping soundly.

He had previously memorized the layout of the room, but as his eyes adjusted to the dimness he could see the shape of the single bed, and Gisela's head upon the pillow. Tiptoeing stealthily, he knelt down beside the bed and gently placed a hand on Gisela's mouth.

The woman woke with a start, but Hawkspurr's whisper of assurance in her ear prompted her to reach out and pull his head to hers. She kissed him passionately, and then giggled quietly as she sat up.

"What kept you so long Nyles? I didn't mean to fall asleep."

"Do you mean to say that you were expecting me?" Hawkspurr was a little indignant.

"Why else would you want to see my room? And I noticed the sly look you gave the window!"

"I must be slipping." Muttered Hawkspurr. "Please move over, I'm getting goose bumps."

Gisela extended a hand and grabbed Hawkspurr penis. "Some goose bump! No not in the bed, it creaks. Make love to me on the rug and then you can come to bed."

Being a considerate lover, Hawkspurr lay on his back on the hard floor and allowed Gisela to mount him. This proved to be her favorite position, and she gyrated her pelvis with obvious delight upon Hawkspurr's rigid member.

As they once more climaxed together the effort of keeping silent nearly choked them, and they both collapsed in a fit of barely contained hysterical laughter.

Hawkspurr didn't dare sleep, but waited patiently until Gisela subsided into peaceful slumber. The luminous dial on his wristwatch told him it was three o'clock, and reluctantly he quit the snug bed and dressed quickly before creeping back over the windowsill and descending to the garden.

He then slept soundly in the cramped space of the little car for what remained of the night, until the dawn woke him at his natural time.

Back at the Star and Garter Hotel, his early—or late arrival in disheveled clothes prompted a raised eyebrow from the porter, but being a former guards NCO the elderly man greeted the Captain cheerfully and with indulgence.

Hawkspurr showered and changed into casual wear before eating a substantial breakfast. He then telephoned Brigadier Hazlett, to confirm that he could return to normal regimental duties and join his troop.

A second conversation with the S.A.S. movements officer, advised Hawkspurr that his men had departed for Cyprus the previous day, and a seat would be available for him within forty-eight hours on a Royal Air Force transport flying to Akrotiri.

Hawkspurr was elated. Without question he was enjoying his holiday and had found a woman with whom he had a complete rapport, but first and foremost he was a soldier.

The anticipation of the hunt for Grivas and his Greek terrorists was a powerful aphrodisiac in itself.

Still—he leered at his reflection in a mirror you have today and tonight.

Hawkspurr and Gisela indeed made his last day of leave memorable. They made love in the little Morris, they joined on a punt in the river, and they spent the night experiencing the pure sensual joy of each other in Hawkspurr's hotel room.

Auf Wiedersehen Gisela—I never forgot you or the summer of '56. Hawkspurr raised a cup of coffee and intoned his own special toast "a l'amour et la guerre"—to love and to war.

# CHAPTER 8

❀

Hawkspurr stepped out from the relative cool of the aircraft into the Mediterranean heat, and put on a pair of sun shields. He disliked wearing glasses, but the sharp contrast of light in Cyprus from the more filtered atmosphere of England could impair a man's vital vision.

The hoot of a monkey—jungle recognition call for an SAS patrol, brought a grin to his face. A group of men who had been waiting in the shade of a building moved towards him, and stood in a semi-circle offering their hands in welcome; Talon Troop, 22 SAS Regiment.

Hawkspurr examined each laughing face.

"Well done Billy, I'm pleased to see that you've kept these pirates out of jail." He addressed his Troop Sergeant, William Kirk McDonald—better known as Evil Billy for his less than sympathetic attitude towards anyone not of Talon Troop.

McDonald was a 6 feet tall powerfully built Australian. To compensate for a premature loss of hair he sported a huge handlebar moustache, which was trimmed barely enough to conform to army regulations. These edicts he ignored whilst on operations, and allowed the appendage to grow wild! He had fought in the Korean War with the Royal Australian Artillery, and joined the SAS Malayan Scouts to serve with Hawkspurr.

At McDonald's side and contrasting only in stature, was Corporal Jimmy McKenzie. At 5'6" he was the smallest member of the troop, but he had proved his courage and tenacity in battle on many an occasion. None more so then when Hawkspurr had first met him in a foxhole in Korea.

The Scot had been serving with the famous Black Watch Regiment when Hawkspurr had found himself inadvertently fighting in an infantry position.

(See: Korean Raider) That night they had battled side-by-side using boots and bayonets against a numerically superior Chinese force. McKenzie had later joined the SAS in Malaya, and was never far from Hawkspurr's side when danger threatened.

Hawkspurr greeted the other men individually.

Corporal Ray Watson, former Rhodesian farmer and big-game hunter. He was 6'3" tall, lean and hard with extraordinary stamina and a natural marksman. A bushy black moustache adorned his square dark face.

Corporal Ken Hall from Gloucester. WW2 commando and survivor of a Korean War prison camp. His quiet confidence and strength was a steadying influence on younger soldiers.

Lance Corporal Nobby Clarke signals specialist and Radio Operator from Newcastle.

Trooper Pat Green, cheerful Cockney Street kid, he was the troop joker and a qualified rock climber.

Trooper Kevin Richards, the dour Yorkshireman. A solid, reliable, totally unflappable soldier and a trained Frogman.

Trooper Craig Peters, former yacht builder from Southampton, and small boats expert.

Trooper Peter Nelson, explosives expert from Surrey. His trade had left him scarred, but still he kept his head shaven instead of hiding the disfigurement.

Trooper John (Sandy} Powell, Fusilier from Lancashire. Sandy hair and freckles gave him a boyish appearance; he is the youngest member of the troop, eager to tackle any difficult job to prove himself.

Trooper Grant Mason, the modest aristocrat and cavalryman of the Hussars. Fair haired with a drooping blonde moustache reminiscent of the Crimean War. A onetime Skiing professional.

Trooper Tubby Wilson, the sturdy Highlander deerstalker with an endless repertoire of recipes for cooking wild flesh.

Lance Corporal Hone Brown, a warrior from the New Zealand Army in Malaya who had volunteered to stay with Talon Troop. He had a Scottish grandfather, but the broad features and laughing black eyes of the Maori. Hawkspurr claimed he could track a shark through water.

And last but not least, the other officer in the troop: Doctor Harry 'Fab' Faulconer. His nickname came from the fact that he always referred to himself as "The Fabulous Faulconer!" He too was a New Zealander from the capital city of Wellington.

A graduate of the University of Otago, he had joined the Royal New Zealand Army Medical Corps, and later volunteered for NZSAS. He too wished to stay with Talon Troop after service in Malaya.

Tall and strong with a broken nose and cauliflower ears, his passion was rugby and his only regret was the fact that he had never played for the famous All Blacks rugby union team of his native country.

Any one of the soldiers of Talon Troop could have been an officer, or at least a Warrant Officer in a different regiment of the British Army. Hawkspurr was not really sure what made them such a cohesive unit; they were all so individually different and yet each capable of operating alone.

Although the subject was never discussed, Hawkspurr knew that they took a great pride in the achievements of the Troop as a whole, and regarded the other members as family. Whilst traditional military etiquette and discipline was observed, Hawkspurr also knew that should he ever make an error in judgment, he would be advised of it in no uncertain terms!

Standing politely to one side whilst Hawkspurr greeted his men was Inspector Jack O'Connor, and his Greek Cypriot Sergeant Mike Landris. The senior policeman gave the soldiers a few moments together, and then stepped forward to push a small bundle into Hawkspurr's hand. He grinned in welcome.

"Better put this on, if you haven't forgotten how to use it. What kept you so long?"

"Nice to see you too Inspector. Do you mean to say you haven't caught Grivas yet? Oh dear! Perhaps you do need me."

Hawkspurr unwrapped the package and buckled the belt around his waist. Removing the heavy .45 caliber colt automatic from the oiled leather holster, he checked magazine and contents. "Good." The familiar weapon felt comfortable and reassuring.

Hawkspurr peered round the bulk of the large, ruddy complexioned inspector and waved to the handsome police sergeant. "Hallo Mike. I have something special for you too."

From his carryall he produced a very light bag labeled Harrods of London, which he handed to the smiling Greek. "Enjoy!" "Thank you Hawk. I will repay you when you come to my home."

"Right. The price is one traditional Greek dinner! In the mean time let's get back to business and inspect my lads properly."

"Hold up a minute Hawk." Jack 0'Connor took Hawkspurr's elbow and the two moved out of earshot of the other men. "When will you be ready to take the field? We've some very hot intelligence regarding a EOKA group not too far distant from Limassol."

Hawkspurr glanced to where his men were standing and pursed his lips thoughtfully. "They look fit and ready Jack, but I would like a day on the firing range. Can you give me thirty-six hours?"

"Sure. I'll come out to your camp tomorrow evening, Ok?"

"Roger." Hawkspurr turned to move away, but was restrained again by the grinning inspector. "Tell me old friend" he wheedled, "just what is in that mysterious parcel you gave to Mike?"

Hawkspurr laughed softly and rolled his eyes up. "Well, if you must know it's very intimate, very exotic black lacey lingerie and hose for his wife. I believe Mike is planning a special anniversary celebration. Now, mum' s the word!"

Hawkspurr called to Sergeant McDonald. "Line up the men Sergeant, let's see what sort of fire power we've been allotted."

The relaxed men responded immediately to a barked order from their sergeant, and formed a disciplined single rank. Captain Faulconer and the sergeant took station at Hawkspurr's shoulder as he moved slowly along the line of soldiers.

Each man was uniformed in khaki drill with long pants and sleeves, tunics open at the neck. No badges of rank or regimental insignia were displayed. For footwear they had elected to retain the rubber-soled boots of jungle warfare, but had blackened the green canvas high tops.

In place of the red beret and proud winged dagger badge of the SAS Regiment, they wore a khaki soft brimmed hat. There would be no formal parades, or even acknowledgment of the existence of Talon Troop during this campaign.

Hawkspurr halted on a thought and spoke to McDonald.

"Billy grab my pack from the 'plane, also there are two gun cases, and a dozen bottles rum to offload. Thank you." The sergeant doubled away, and Hawkspurr continued his inspection. Every soldier carried on his belt a 9mm Browning semi-automatic pistol, and a fighting knife of some description—his personal choice—most still clung to an old friend, the Malay parang or machete. The addition of a brass knuckle-duster, incorporated in the handle of the machete made the versatile weapon a 'smachette'.

The new Sterling sub-machine gun was available to all men, but both Evil Billy McDonald and Ray Watson the big Rhodesian still favored the reliable Bren LMG carried on a sling with the addition of a forward pistol grip.

Brown, Hall, Powell, and the deerstalker Wilson preferred a .303 Lee Enfield rifle, and their skill was such that an enemy could be excused for thinking that they were using semi-automatic weapons.

Billy McDonald arrived with the Captain's gear, and Hawkspurr stopped to unlock the gun cases. With a grunt of satisfaction he handled his personal choice, the Ml.300 carbine he had 'liberated' from the United States Army in Korea. From the second case he removed a .308 Lee Enfield rifle with some wood removed, and fitted with a sniper's scope. "Tubby!" he called.

Trooper Wilson stepped smartly forward. "Yes boss."

"I'm lending you a special rifle of my own—don't get too fond of it, I expect it back in good order after this job is over. You have my permission to wrap it in hessian, and don't worry about losing the shine. Roger?"

"Roger boss." The Highlander's joy as he fondled the varnished eyes gleamed with stock and rubber cushioned butt plate.

"Fall the men out Billy. What sort of transport have they given us?"

"Two Austin Champs with radios, and I had the local army workshop weld up fittings for a Browning machine-gun on both. In addition we have a Bedford three ton lorry, and the Horse Guards will provide us with an armored car escort whenever requested."

"Hmm…Two rovers is a bit mean, what if one breaks down?" Hawkspurr looked speculatively at his senior NCO. If you will observe that large shed to our west, you will notice the RAF unloading several long-wheelbase Land Rovers from a Hercules. They're still painted air force blue, but if you return tonight with three lads and a pot of khaki paint…?"

"Right boss. No need to wait 'til after dark, these young National Service lads aren't quite sure who we are or what we do. I'll just drive one out in our convoy."

"By all means do it your way Billy. Load the men up and let's depart for our new home."

The tented camp was located on an old airfield, lying inland on the plain between the seaport of Limassol and the Troodos Mountains. The current occupants were an armored squadron of the Royal Horse Guards (The Blues), and Infantry with support units. Sandbag emplacements and sentries on foot guarded the perimeter and entrances.

Talon Troop's allotted area was adjacent to the The Blues for external security, but with sufficient distance to give the SAS unit some seclusion.

The camp consisted of six canvas structures—three, five-men tents, the Officer Commanding's tent, a mess tent that also served as First Aid Post, and the toilet/ablutions enclosure with a portable water tank.

"What do you think boss?" Sergeant McDonald crossed to Hawkspurr's Champ.

"Bit naked Billy. Go and visit the Infantry, give the CO my compliments and invite him over for a sundowner at 1800 hours. Then scrounge enough sandbags to built a Sanger for at least the two rovers with machine guns, and sufficient barbed wire coils to give a secure perimeter. Take the three tonner, and I'll organize some khaki paint for your borrowed Land Rover."

The big Australian called three men to assist him, and drove off cheerfully in the direction of the infantry lines.

Corporals Jimmy McKenzie, and Ray Watson joined Hawkspurr.

"Ray please take Mason over to the Blues camp, he can talk nicely to his cavalry pals and score some paint and brushes to disguise the RAF Rover—take my Champ. Jimmy, you stay by me."

Hawkspurr strode across to the mess tent. "First things first Jimmy, look after the inner man. Who's taking care of the rations?"

The Scot laughed. "Tubby Wilson sir."

Hawkspurr ducked under the eaves of the tent with the rolled up walls. Wilson was busy at a wooden table carving a small carcass.

Hawkspurr wrinkled his nose at the rather strong odor of the dead beast. "What the hell is that Tubby?"

"Goat sir. I killed it last night. A few onions and curry spices and you'll think you're eating prime lamb."

"I see, don't the army supply enough fresh meat?" Hawkspurr eyed the stacks of composite ration boxes piled in one corner.

"Not the way our lads eat sir. We all throw in a bit of extra cash, and I have an understanding with the old Greek lady that owns the tavern near the camp entrance."

"I see. Can you trust her?"

"She never tries for information sir. Just wants to get on with life and stay out of the troubles. She does me a cheap line in local wine, olives, cheese and fresh fruit."

Hawkspurr nodded his assent. "Fair enough Tubby, let me know when you want cash from me. Do the other lads take a turn cooking?"

The Highlander looked indignant. "They offer but I prefer to take care of the grub alone, as long as we're in base."

Hawkspurr turned his attention to the far end of the tent, where Harry Faulconer was inspecting the contents of two steel chests marked with a red cross.

"Do you have enough gear to support us in the field Fab?"

The New Zealand doctor continued to rummage through the chests without looking up. "I'll let you know after I've made up a kit for each man to carry Hawk. We could be short on morphine ampoules."

"Ok. What do you say we have lunch as soon as Billy and Ray get back? Then we can organize our defenses this afternoon. The lads can go to the NAAFI canteen in the Blues camp this evening while we entertain the local officers."

"Fine Hawk. What's happening tomorrow?"

"We'll be firing personal weapons, then Inspector O'Connor will brief us later in the day. We could be in the field in thirty-six hours."

"In that case I'll skip the range and visit the base hospital and see what sort of backup we have, including casualty evacuation procedures."

By five pm, the SAS camp had a rather more martial air about it. The Champs fitted with Browning machine guns were hull down behind sandbag barricades at opposite ends of the little encampment. The remaining vehicles were placed at other points of the compass to provide a ring of light outwards from their headlamps, in the unlikely event of a ground attack.

Hawkspurr sat within a circle of his men, passing an open bottle of rum between them.

"Well done lads, as soon as you're cleaned up you can head for the canteen. Take your weapons and deposit them with the guard commander, but leave your hardware in the tents. The Horse Guards don't like anything smaller than a saber hanging from a man's belt—and please don't pick any fights with my old regiment!"

"Any chance of a trip into Limassol sir?" The aristocratic Grant Mason drawled.

"Sorry Grant, the ladies will have to survive without you for the next few days."

Hone Brown the Maori soldier, put the next question. "Are we getting some action soon boss?" His laughing black eyes belied the seriousness of his query.

Hawkspurr grinned at the New Zealander. "I think I can promise you some Pakehas (Europeans) to top soon enough Hone. We'll know more tomorrow night after the Inspector has briefed us." He glanced around the group. "Any more questions?"

"Sir." Peter Nelson raised a hand. "I haven't been issued with any explosives. Surely we'll need at least some Plastic in the mountains?"

Hawkspurr's eyes probed Evil Billy McDonald. "What's the story Sergeant, I thought you would have organized that?"

"Sorry boss, I need your signature on a requisition order. We also need hand grenades and extra ammo'"

"Ye gods! And I suppose that has to come up from Nicosia?" Hawkspurr was annoyed. "Clarke! Get on the radio right away and expedite delivery within twenty-four hours. I propose to bang off most of what we have on hand in the morning. Billy, give Nobby a complete list, including operational requirements for at least one month in the field. I'll sign their bloody papers when the stuff arrives. If there's any delay I will personally contact the Governor General!"

"Sir?" Ken Hall queried. "Are we parachuting in?"

"Again I have no idea until Special Branch give me a target. It'll depend very much on the terrain, but I don't favor noisy helicopters in the open ranges. We won't be able to sneak up on the bastards as we did in Malaya."

Immediately after a light breakfast Talon Troop with Hawkspurr in the lead, and the sun still low upon the horizon doubled smartly away from base camp.

Well not exactly smartly, the excesses of the previous evening had taken their toll but Hawkspurr knew from experience that the best cure was sweat and more sweat.

The Blues had kindly supplied camp sentries for the day, so that no SAS soldier escaped the beneficial run to the firing range.

By midday Hawkspurr was satisfied with the men's, and his own performance. Individual weapons had been fired from every possible angle, position, and pace, and the rifles zeroed in to a perfect tight grouping. In the absence of live grenades, suitably sized rocks were thrown into a target circle.

The march back to camp was carried out at a more leisurely pace, and the remainder of the afternoon was given over to weapons cleaning and kit maintenance.

On the arrival of Inspector Jack O'Connor at 1700 hours, Hawkspurr summoned the men to the mess tent.

In a tight-knit group like Talon Troop every man attended briefings, and Hawkspurr knew that should he and the NCOs be lost in the early stages of an operation, each man was capable of completing the assigned task.

O'Connor was accompanied by Sergeant Mike Landris, and a man Hawkspurr had not seen before.

"Gentlemen." O'Connor called the gathering to order. "You all know Sgt Landris, and now I would like to introduce Sgt Nazim Avidar. Since the area you'll be operating in is populated by Turkish families as well as Greek Cypriots, both of my sergeants will accompany you as guides and interpreters."

The Turkish policeman bowed solemnly to the soldiers. Avidar was about 5'10" tall, stocky, with dark features, traditional black moustache, and a dignified yet sincere presence. Hawkspurr liked the look of the man immediately.

"Some political news first gentlemen." The Inspector continued. "The situation at present is rather grim, with killings and bombings almost daily. The Governor is adamant that three prisoners convicted of murder and acts of terrorism will be hanged. In my opinion, this sentence will only serve to stiffen resistance, and provide more martyrs to the cause. However…." He paused and looked around the soldiers, "our job is simply to seek out and destroy or capture the guerilla sections in the mountains."

Mike Landris was busy handing out individual copies of maps showing the operational area, as O'Connor carried on the briefing.

"If you peruse the approximate center of your maps about ten miles east of Mount Olympus, you will see the village of Kalamoulas." The Inspector waited while the soldiers examined charted terrain.

"I say village, but in fact Kalamoulas was destroyed and abandoned after a particularly bad earthquake in 1954. Yet Turkish shepherds on the neighboring hills report some movement at night in the old buildings, and ideally it makes an excellent base for a terrorist group. The route leading up to the village is open and like most mountain roads consists of a series of hairpin bends. If the group is of any substantial size they could certainly hold off a regular patrol." He paused.

"The rear of the village is sheltered by steep cliffs probably 140 to 150 feet high." O'Connor looked directly at Hawkspurr. "I have no intention of interfering with your operational plans, and I'll leave you now to work out the details. One more item of particular interest; a fair haired European has been observed visiting vineyards in the same district—Gunter Von Harzburg I suspect."

He glanced at his watch, "I have to be getting back to the Secretariat, let me know in the morning what your plans are."

Hawkspurr sat quietly for a moment digesting the information. He stood and addressed the men thoughtfully. "If Von Harzburg is advising this group, we're no longer dealing with enthusiastic amateurs. You can bet your boots he's already laid down lines of fire in the event of a frontal attack, and plotted escape routes." He stared intently at the enlarged map O'Connor had pinned to the blackboard.

"How does this sound? We climb the ridge spur at this point." With the point of a knife he indicated the contour lines approximately half a mile from the village. We march to the cliff directly behind the village," his blade traversed the map, "and drop in for breakfast!"

"Good one boss." Evil Billy liked the idea.

The two policemen looked anxiously at each other, and Mike Landris spoke for them both. "Mind if we join you after you hit the village!"

Hawkspurr grinned at the Cypriots. "Sure. You can cover the road leading out, and grab anyone doing a bunk." He turned to Trooper Green, the climber.

"Pat, do we have sufficient gear and ropes?"

"Yes boss." The Cockney soldier kept his face straight. "Although I don't think we have a harness large enough for Tubby Wilson." He ducked as the big Highlander's hat skimmed above his head.

"Ok settle down." Hawkspurr laughed. "I want as much free climbing as possible. We can hardly surprise them if we're knocking in pitons on the way down."

"Any chance of a recce' before we go in sir?" Corporal McKenzie was cautious as always.

"Not if we're to go in tomorrow night. I really don't trust the security of local intelligence."

Nazim Avidar raised a polite hand. "Captain I know the village well, and the cliffs. If I may have a piece of chalk." The Turk raised the map on the board, and sketched an outline of the cliffs behind the village. "About 50 feet from the base there is a ledge, probably 30 feet long and wide enough for a man to stand comfortably. If you can climb down to that, it's possible to rappel easily to the ground."

Hawkspurr nodded. "What do you think Pat?"

The climber considered the sketch. "Well if four men anchor each rope, we can get the first three down quietly enough, and then bang in some pitons or wedge in jam nuts to take the rest of us down. It really depends on the rock formation."

"Any comments?" Hawkspurr offered.

"Duration sir?" Tubby Wilson asked. "I might have to requisition more ration packs."

"Good point. What do you think Mike?"

The Greek sergeant considered the question. "Seems a pity to hit and run. Nazim and I can take care of any prisoners, but if you're already in place, it might pay off to stay in the area for a few days."

"My thoughts exactly. I doubt if we'll bag the lot on the first hit. I propose to follow any trails that might lead to other hideouts, and to that end we'll go in dressed as guerillas. Has brought everyone brought civilian gear as I suggested?"

There were nods of assent from the gathered men.

"Good. Now let's work out the details. Tubby, I suggest we carry two weeks rations, and cache a further two weeks supply in a suitable hiding place."

"Right sir. Can I be excused for now while I check the stores?"

"Off you go. Ray, you check the projected weather reports for the month ahead."

Tubby Wilson and Corporal Watson left the tent.

For the remainder of the evening, Talon Troop examined the maps minutely, and questioned the two policemen regarding population and local conditions.

Hawkspurr left Sergeant McDonald in command, and went to liaise with the Squadron Commander of the Royal Horse Guards regarding transport and protective escorts to the operational area.

The following morning Hawkspurr awoke with the pleasurable tight feeling in his gut that heralded the anticipation of action. In the field he always dined with his men, and as soon as breakfast was finished gave his orders in the mess tent.

"Right lads, we move tonight. All of our vehicles will remain here under guard of the Blues. They'll provide us with a three tonner, which will pick us up at 1900 hours. The truck will be completely covered, so that even the escorting troopers won't see exactly who we are. We'll be escorted by three Ferrets, and should be in the target area by 2100 hours—that will be dark enough for us to dismount without being spotted. At a certain bend in the road, the armored patrol will slow sufficiently for us to exit three at a time. Twenty seconds should give us ample time, just remember to clear the road and roll to one side before the rear Ferret runs over you! Stay quiet until the patrol has disappeared and then rendezvous in the gully on the east of the road."

# CHAPTER 9

The ride in the confines of the covered truck along torturous roads was unpleasant, and the men of Talon Troop unusually silent. It was months since they had last seen action together in the Aberdare Mountains of Kenya, and each was busy with his own thoughts. Not men given to self-psychoanalysis, they had all at some time suffered wounds or injury, and experienced fear.

Like all professional soldiers, amongst themselves they only discussed the lighter side of any action. If an outsider had dared to describe them as heroic or even dedicated—he or she, would be treated with scorn and derision. Their proud regimental motto 'Who Dares Wins' was often denigrated to 'Who Cares Who Wins'—but only by those entitled to wear the winged dagger badge!

Before leaving base camp, the mess tent had been the scene of much merriment and ridicule, as each soldier appeared in what he thought was the appropriate dress for a Greek guerilla. Evil Billy had of course gone overboard with an eye-patch, bright red bandanna on his head and a World War One ammunition bandolier across his chest.

Fortunately Mike Landris was present to correct the over enthusiastic, and after the laughter and clowning had subsided the troop were converted to a passable facsimile of mountain fighters.

Hawkspurr, who favored a modicum of the theatrical, was sporting a pair of old polo riding boots and well-worn khaki breeches from his days as a cavalry trooper. His outfit was completed with an almost threadbare battledress tunic, and a black beret scrounged from the Horse Guards. He had recently started to cultivate a military moustache, in order to give his youthful looks an air of maturity as befitted his rank, and now he was allowing the appendage to grow untrimmed and straggly.

Evil Billy referred to the moustache—in private—as a clitoris tickler!

A single prearranged toot of a horn warned Hawkspurr that the patrol was approaching the disembarkation point.

He and McDonald started to roll up the canvas at the rear of the truck, and lowered the tailgate.

Hawkspurr, with the radio operator Clarke and Maori tracker Brown, hung their legs over the back of the wagon and waited for the next signal.

A double toot and the three dropped their Bergen packs onto the road, and followed them into a shock absorbing parachute roll.

Hawkspurr grabbed for his pack, and scrambled hastily to the ditch on his left. He heard low thuds as the remainder of the troop followed suit, and then the exhaust roar of the last Ferret armored car as it passed his position.

There was a faint scrabble of loose gravel ahead, and the barely discernible breathing of someone in front of him. He lay still, listening to the armored patrol laboring in low gear up the mountain and gradually fading.

Hawkspurr rose to his feet and looked around, the starlight was sufficient for him to see the designated rendezvous, and he swung his pack onto his back after cocking his weapon and moving silently forward.

Deep in the sheltering hollow Hawkspurr whispered to Trooper Green. "Lead on Pat, and take Hone with you. I'll give you a few yards but don't get too far ahead. When you reach the ridge top look out for somewhere to cache the Bergens, I want to travel light but don't rush it."

In single file Talon Troop moved cautiously up the mountain.

Hawkspurr had the foresight to refurbish his boots with rubber commando soles, and the worn soft uppers were surprisingly comfortable.

His men were all superbly fit, and Hawkspurr listened with satisfaction to the even breathing behind him as the soldiers climbed upwards.

The night was perfect, with a cool temperature and air that tasted sweet and clean. The bluish outline of mountain tops, with clear bright stars winking down, and the aroma of bruised flora as they fell beneath crushing boots was almost romantic. Hawkspurr smiled at his own thoughts.

Topping the ridge Hawkspurr almost tripped over the crouching figure of Pat Green.

"What's the story Pat?"

"All quiet boss. Hone is scouting on to the top of the cliff overlooking the village, and I've found a spot where we can leave our packs."

"Good man. I estimate four hours before we start the descent, so we'll rest up for a spell in your shelter."

Hawkspurr and the troop followed Green cautiously to a brush covered, rocky hollow.

"Gather round lads."

Hawkspurr dropped his Bergen, and squatted on the ground. The men stooped down to his front and side. "Three and a half hours, then we move to the start point. I don't want to take a chance and brew up, so drink water only. Ok spread out, but don't fall asleep."

Hawkspurr and Faulconer moved away together, and settled to make themselves as comfortable as possible amongst the rocks.

Faulconer whispered. "You haven't said much about your trip to Spain Hawk."

"Sorry Fab, I'm really not in a position to speak about it. I think thirty years covers the Official Secrets Act, so you'll have to wait until I write my memoirs!"

"Rough was it?" The doctor was not deterred. "You've changed a little, perhaps more mature, and somewhat grimmer. You're not getting religion are you?"

"No fear of that chum. Maybe it's just the aging process. Thanks for your concern, but I really am fine, I simply had a short holiday in historic Cadiz."

Hawkspurr fell silent, and Faulconer knew him well enough to close the subject.

In fact the doctor's remarks had stirred Hawkspurr's retrospection. After some consideration, he came to the conclusion that he felt no remorse or guilt for the assassination of the Greek arms dealer, and he never again questioned the morality of removing recalcitrant terrorists by extreme means, or his role in that course.

A rattle of loose stones, and Green slid into the hollow to report to Hawkspurr. "Hone says the village is silent but earlier he caught a glimpse of flames from a fire."

"Roger Pat, you can lead us back now." Hawkspurr called softly for Sergeant McDonald.

"Time to move Billy. Hide the packs as well as possible, and check only water bottles, grenades, and spare ammo to be carried."

The sergeant nodded without words, and went to alert the men.

Hawkspurr crawled to the edge of the cliff to avoid being silhouetted against the starlit sky, and joined the Maori soldier Hone Brown.

"No movement sir."

"Ok let's do it." Hawkspurr backed away until he could regain his feet.

Each man of the troop knew exactly what his role was, as the assault had been planned and rehearsed exhaustively on the blackboard in base camp. Since there was no method to belay the ropes without making some noise, three teams of four men would fasten the ropes physically, as Hawkspurr, Watson, and McDonald abseiled to the foot of the escarpment and secured the area. The two NCOs would then man light machine guns.

Hawkspurr did not want to be encumbered by superfluous equipment such as harness and karabiners, and consequently the descent would be by the 'classical' abseil method. This was not easy for the men carrying Bren guns, but utilizing rifle slings to retain the weapons, they were confident in their ability to carry out the maneuver.

Hawkspurr stood astride his rope and ran it under his right thigh and over his left shoulder; he let the free end snake down over the cliff and signaled for his anchormen to take the strain.

Looking over his right shoulder he backed to the rim of the precipice and leaned out, then with a nervous grin at his men he stepped down on to the rock face. With gloved hands he paid out the rope until his body was at a 60-degree angle—a rapid check of McDonald and Watson—they were both in position.

"Go." He mouthed, and moved down with knees slightly bent and feet well apart. His slung carbine shifted a little, giving him an anxious moment—he didn't want the weapon to arrive at the bottom without him!

Starlight was fading as the sky lightened in the East, and he glanced again at his companions to ensure that both were keeping station six feet apart. The rope pressure on thigh and shoulder was unpleasant, but there was no need for haste; the object of the exercise was surprise.

The climbers reached a ledge, confirming Nazim Adivar's description of the feature. As arranged, McDonald and Watson paused to ease aching muscles. Hawkspurr was somewhat slower, and as he joined the NCOs he whispered, "Ok?"

Two nods of assent.

"Let's go."

Approximately forty more feet to the base, but after some thirty feet Hawkspurr's boots touched rubble, no doubt dislodged and deposited at the foot of the cliff during the earthquake of 1954. The debris shifted and rolled away under his weight with a rattle that was amplified to his apprehensive hearing. He heard a similar noise from McDonald and Watson's position and cursed under his breath, as he halted and strained to listen for any sounds of alarm from the village.

The others froze too, until Hawkspurr satisfied that they were still undetected, continued the descent. Reaching firm ground the three soldiers tugged a signal on the ropes, and moved silently away to form a defensive arc fifty yards from the outermost structures of the ruined village.

With the Bren guns fifteen yards out on either flank, Hawkspurr flattened himself behind a rock and settled to await either eventuality—an attack from the terrorists, or the arrival of the remainder of Talon Troop.

The light was still satisfactory, reassuring Hawkspurr that he was right on schedule. He turned his eyes from the village to scan the cliff top, as if by squinting up he would better hear the sound of pitons being hammered into rock crevices. He thought he captured a faint tap, tap, but nothing to warn an unsuspecting enemy. Then he saw the first figure move over the rim, followed rapidly by others.

With a satisfied smile he turned his attention back to the suspect buildings. He didn't need to confirm the arrival of his men, as one by one they circumspectly crept into a skirmish line.

The sun had not yet topped the Eastern hills, but the light was adequate. Time to move.

Hawkspurr stood and adjusted his belt-pack; taking a deep breath he held his carbine out at arms length and looked swiftly from left to right.

Fourteen men rose to their feet and moved forward.

Stepping carefully over loose rock Hawkspurr eased off the safety catch of his weapon. His tension disappeared now that the time for action was upon them, but the little knot of fear in his gut reminded him that vigilance was still his best friend.

Hawkspurr was conscious that another figure was close to his shoulder and smiled; Jimmy McKenzie felt personally responsible for his leader's safety and would cover his back whatever the danger.

The first ruin Hawkspurr reached was only a hollow shell with broken walls two feet high, and a blackened fireplace with chimney pointing accusingly to the heavens that had brought devastation. He and McKenzie skirted the rubble and moved on across a narrow street.

Other figures scurried silently across the open space, but Hawkspurr was only aware of them from the corners of his eyes.

Another abandoned home; this one with standing walls and an open doorway, empty windows glared back at him as he stepped inside and flattened his back to the wall; McKenzie did likewise to his right.

Holding his own breath whilst his eyes adjusted to the darkness, he listened for the telltale sounds of sleeping men.

There was nothing in the first room. Step by careful step he approached an open door on the far wall its lintel hanging askew, and peered inside. Yes! He was certain of two ill defined shapes stretched out close to an open window, and his nostrils informed him of the odor of cigarette smoke and unwashed bodies.

Innocent shepherds? No…two rifles were propped against the wall.

He raised a warning hand to McKenzie, not wanting the Scot to open fire. He was unsure of the situation of the other soldiers, and was reluctant to shoot first and raise the alarm. Instead he placed his carbine sling over his shoulder and unsheathed the trench knife, raising the blade to signal his intention and pointing at the figure on the left. McKenzie followed suit.

Hawkspurr nodded, and in three swift paces dropped astride the slumbering body and clamped a hand over the man's mouth. He placed the point of the knife under the exposed ear, and exerted just enough pressure for the Greek to get his message.

McKenzie was having a rougher ride, his adversary was a large man and the wee Scot was having trouble containing the heaving body. Deciding to go to McKenzie's assistance, Hawkspurr reversed his knife and smashed his fist on to his captives jaw just below the ear.

The terrorist was rendered unconscious, but Hawkspurr was no longer needed. The frustrated McKenzie had severed the man's carotid artery; well one prisoner was better than none.

Hawkspurr gagged his man with tape, and turning him onto his stomach bound wrists and ankles, and lashed them together.

"Right Jimmy, let's move on."

Even as he spoke, Hawkspurr heard a Bren gun open up, and then a return burst of fire and the detonation of a hand grenade.

Sporadic gunshots broke out on either flank of Hawkspurr's position, but he was unable to judge who was initiating the fire.

He and McKenzie moved from the gloom of the cottage, into the first rays of the morning sun.

Hugging the stone wall they sidled round the corner senses alert, fingers lightly on the triggers of their guns.

Although he had laid down strict lines of advance through the village, the original haphazard layout and subsequent damage with fallen walls and heaps of rubble, made the actual execution difficult. Clearing a defended urban area was never easy, and with Talon Troop out of uniform it was of vital importance that each target was properly identified before opening fire.

A fleeting movement to his immediate front brought Hawkspurr's weapon to his shoulder. Was that a shadow or the bulk of a man's head in the rim of a shattered window? He hesitated, not daring to breath.

McKenzie took the initiative with the SAS jungle call of the monkey. "Whoo, whoo."

No reply from the house.

The Scot shouted a warning "Grenade!" As he tossed a bomb through the window, and Hawkspurr heeding the alarm dropped to his knees.

As the explosion blasted dust and fragments from within, Hawkspurr committed himself and jumped for the aperture. With one foot on the sill, he felt McKenzie's hand on his backside. "Ups a daisy sir!"

"You'll keep Corporal!"

Hawkspurr fell into the building without a great deal of dignity, but a discharge of pellets from a shotgun storming over his head justified McKenzie's action. He squeezed off two rounds in the general direction of the blast, and rolled away from the wall.

McKenzie dropped into the building with a curse, and called out. "Are you right sir?"

Hawkspurr didn't answer; he was searching for the enemy. An anguished moan and the clunk of steel upon stone focused his aim on a shape against the far wall, and he fired again...once...twice.

The familiar sting of cordite in the confined space assailed his nostrils, a redolence that he did not find objectionable—rather in all honesty, exciting.

McKenzie moved forward to examine the body. "He's finished."

"Right" Hawkspurr scrambled to his feet, "let's move on."

Outside in what had once been the main street of Kalamoulas, the soldiers of Talon Troop were consolidating their position.

Hawkspurr called for Sergeant McDonald.

"Any casualties Billy?"

"No boss."

"Any prisoners?"

"No boss."

"I see. They all resisted did they?"

"Absolutely boss." Evil Billy almost looked contrite.

"Roger. Bring out the bodies and let's see what we have. You'll find one prisoner over there." Hawkspurr pointed to the first house he had entered, and then turned to place a finger on McDonald's chest. "Bring him alive!"

"Corporal Clarke." Hawkspurr summoned his signaler.

"Nobby, call up Inspector O'Connor please. They can move into the village." He walked to the pavement outside what had once been the local cafe and bar. Under the tattered awning his men were laying out bodies, with captured arms and equipment.

Five terrorists, rifles, shotguns, one Sten gun, ex-British army issue 44 pattern packs and pouches, and a substantial quantity of ammunition. Propaganda leaflets and personal letters would be of interest to Special Branch and military intelligence. The small amount of rations carried on the men, suggested that sympathetic occupants of the mountain villages were sustaining them.

Hawkspurr scrutinized the faces of the dead Greeks. One man appeared to be about forty years of age, the others all in their early twenties. Von Harzburg was not amongst them—hardly surprising. These men would not have been caught so easily, and without sentries if the German had been advising them.

A thorough search of the buildings was now called for. Other terrorists may have gone to ground in prepared hideouts, and possible escape routes had to be explored.

The police Land Rover ground slowly along the street, wheels tilting up over rubble and rock with the transmission whining and protesting in low gear. The uniformed driver looked around apprehensively, and spared a brief nervous glance for the dead bodies of his compatriots.

O'Connor, Landris and Adivar dismounted. The English policeman was looking very satisfied with himself.

"Good work boys." He beamed at the soldiers.

The Greek Sergeant and his Turkish colleague were more subdued—even morose.

"What's happening down the road Jack?" Hawkspurr was all business.

"Infantry and armor are still holding the cordon Hawk, but no sign of EOKA. Do you think that this is the whole cell?" The inspector waved a nonchalant hand over the dead.

"No the lads say there's evidence of a larger group than these. We're now going to carry out a detailed inspection of each building."

Jack O'Connor looked past Hawkspurr, as McDonald appeared, prodding along the now conscious prisoner.

"Good, good you've saved us one!"

Hawkspurr turned his mouth up at the corners and raised his eyebrows. "You sound surprised Jack!"

"Well there were stories from Malaya!"

"My men have only one firm instruction Jack—stay alive." Hawkspurr was not joking.

"Fair enough." The policeman accepted, as he turned away to transmit on his Rover radio and arrange for a truck to collect the bodies and captured arms.

Hawkspurr moved to confer with his NCOs. "Right, let's check out the village. Billy, Jimmy, Ray, take your sections and check every nook and cranny. Tunnel entrances, loose stones that may be letterboxes, anything out of place. Tear the bloody walls down if you have to. I'll take the coppers and start on the church and the priest's house. Pat and Nobby can climb the escarpment and retrieve the packs. Any questions.... No? Ok move out."

Inside the tiny Orthodox Church the pews and altar, together with other useful furniture and fittings, had been removed, and the roof was open to the sky.

"Not much to find in here," stated the inspector, "I think the priest's house is our best bet, I don't trust any of the bastards."

"Tut, tut, Jack. You'll never get to heaven if you speak like that!" Hawkspurr chided.

"Yeah right!"

Strangely, the roof of the rectory was still intact. Divine intervention? Hawkspurr doubted that.

Mike Landris was standing in the relatively large fireplace of the main room, staring intently at the soot-covered bricks. "Hawk." He beckoned without looking round. "What do you make of this?"

Hawkspurr squatted on his haunches and examined the hearth and back firewall. He leaned forward and placed a hand in the dead ash, brushing aside partially burnt logs he discovered that underneath the stone was still warm.

He rose and stepped into the cavity. With a finger he traced an outline approximately three feet square, then inserted the point of his knife into the exposed crack. "Bulls-eye! Give me a hand please Mike."

Hawkspurr and Landris placed their combined weight upon the stone, and with a screech of protest the segment slid back. The block traveled just far enough to admit one man, before it stopped against the back wall exposing an aperture opening off to the left, and large enough for a man on all fours to pass through.

"I'm going in Mike." Hawkspurr unhooked a torch from his belt, and shone the beam into the dark passage.

"I'll be right behind you." Answered the Greek, and drew his revolver.

Hawkspurr crawled forward, carbine at the ready.

He had only moved the length of his body, when the passage ended at a vertical shaft from which protruded the top of a ladder.

Hawkspurr held his breath, and with ears cocked strained to pick up any foreign sound.

He was sorely tempted to drop a grenade down the hole, but reasoned that the resultant blast would probably do him more harm than good. A bead of perspiration fell from the end of his nose, and he paused to rub a sleeve across his brow—he hated confined spaces.

Drawing a deep breath he sidled forward and illuminated the shaft with a ray of light. It was probably twelve feet deep, but nothing stirred and he swung his legs down to find purchase for his feet on the wooden rungs of the ladder. It was necessary to sling his weapon on one shoulder, but Landris was close to hand.

"Cover me Mike." He turned the torch off and started down. The rungs and rails of the ladder were worn smooth, evidence of frequent use.

His feet touched rock, and again he listened intently. Ok. He brought his weapon to the ready and switched on the torch again. A short tunnel high enough for a man to enter hunched over, opened off the shaft.

"Come on down Mike." Hawkspurr whispered.

As Landris reached bottom, Hawkspurr moved into the tunnel.

Now he found himself in a stone chamber approximately fifteen feet square. On a wooden table stood a stack of wax candles, and using the matches also thoughtfully provided, Hawkspurr lit one as Landris joined him.

Half a dozen stools completed the furnishings, and a cast iron stove offered warmth and comfort.

The flue pipe was cunningly constructed, to allow smoke to exit through the house chimney. Landris was busy in the cold ash box of the stove as Hawkspurr forced open a wooden door in the far wall.

Beyond, yet one more burrow led gently upwards from the terrorists' lair, and although a bend obstructed his view, Hawkspurr's keen nostrils detected fresh air.

Landris grunted with satisfaction, as he carefully placed partially burnt sheets of paper on the table.

The flickering candlelight gave his features a Machiavellian caste as he grinned at Hawkspurr. "I think I have some good stuff here Hawk." The Greek lit more candles, and taking a notebook from his pockets, started to copy script from the salvaged documents.

"Roger Mike. I'm going on." Hawkspurr acknowledged. "Obviously the game is flushed, but maybe I can pick up the scent wherever the escape tunnel comes out."

The sergeant only nodded—his policeman's mind was totally absorbed as he sifted evidence from the puzzle before him.

The shaft wound up an easy gradient, and whether the bends were tactical or simply to avoid harder outcrops of rock, Hawkspurr was not sure.

He negotiated each corner cautiously, probing with the light and searching for booby traps before moving forward. After a few minutes of slow progress, a glimmer of sunlight lanced through the gloom and Hawkspurr breathed a little easier. Steps cut into earth led up to a wooden trapdoor left carelessly open. Patently the last man through felt that the devil was behind him.

Hawkspurr found himself in one corner of a low animal shelter, stale hay and dried droppings denoted the past presence of goats, and through an open entrance he saw the broken timber rails of the holding pen. The pen was connected to yet one more ruined cottage on the outskirts of the village. Conveniently adjacent, a stream meandered out of pinewoods clothing the lower slopes of the mountain.

A close inspection of soft earth on the banks of the stream disclosed the footprints of three or four men leading up into the shelter of trees and gullies on the mountain, and fearing an ambush Hawkspurr retreated back to the shelter of the village.

Outside the cafe, uniformed police were loading the bodies of the terrorists on to a three-ton truck, and Mike Landris had returned from the underground hideout to confer animatedly with his colleagues.

Sergeant McDonald was sorting through items of equipment and papers retrieved by the soldiers, and Hawkspurr approached him first.

"How's it progressing Billy?"

"Good boss. I'm satisfied we've found everything."

"That's fine. Hand over all of this to the police." Hawkspurr indicated the pile of captured gear. "I think I know the general direction taken by at least three men who escaped, but we should eat before moving on."

Hawkspurr joined Inspector O'Connor and his men. "You chaps look very happy," he grinned, "been handing out parking tickets?"

"Even better than that." O'Connor waved Landris' note book in the air. "At last, a real lead to the whereabouts of the elusive Grivas!"

"Great. Do we have time for breakfast? I hate to fight on an empty stomach." Hawkspurr was feeling good.

"You'll be having a few meals before that eventuality Hawk."

Landris handed Hawkspurr a sheet of paper.

"I've sketched a rough map, and here we are now," the policeman pointed with a finger, "according to the notes I deciphered Grivas is at present hiding out in the Monastery of Stavadhi."

"How far is that exactly?"

Nazim Avidar answered. "As far as a Sparrow Hawk flies only five miles, but if you want to avoid the roads you'll cover fifteen or twenty miles across extremely rough terrain."

"In that case we'd better get mobile as soon as possible. We haven't expended too much ammunition here, and we have rations for two weeks plus two in reserve."

As Hawkspurr spoke, Trooper Wilson interrupted the discussion. The Scot was carrying four mugs of tea. "Here you are sir," he grinned, "if you other gents don't take sugar—don't stir!"

"Thanks Tubby. What's for breakfast?" Hawkspurr was still hungry.

"Bacon sandwich Ok sir?"

"Perfect. What about you Jack?" Hawkspurr asked the policeman.

"Don't worry about us Hawk, my driver has a meal organized. Shall we work while we eat?"

"That suits me." Hawkspurr seated himself on his pack, which had been recovered by Green.

"Mind if I join you?" Doctor Faulconer walked up.

"Pull up a bed pan and sit down Fab. Are all the boys in good order?"

"Not a scratch amongst the lot of them Hawk. How about you?"

"Bit of a rope burn under my thigh, but I'll dance again." Before Hawkspurr could continue, a warning shout from one of the uniformed policemen turned all heads.

A black Morris saloon car roared into the village, and every weapon in the vicinity of the cafe was cocked and aimed at the occupants of the vehicle as it slid to a halt.

The pale-faced driver raised his hands in alarm, but the passenger pushed open her door and swung long legs to the ground as she coolly stepped out.

"Good morning gentlemen." Amanda Carson pointed her camera and clicked the shutter, just as Hawkspurr turned his back on the journalist. "Not pleased to see me Darling!" The Canadian was unperturbed by her reception.

O'Connor was furious. "How the bloody hell did you get through the cordons Miss Carson? And who informed you of this operation?"

Amanda Carson smiled sweetly, and gestured with a document from her capacious shoulder bag. "All the correct passes and credentials Inspector, and as for my sources well…you understand, freedom of the press, confidentiality and all that rot." As she finished speaking, Amanda swung around to photograph the soldiers and the bodies in the truck.

"Blast! That's enough." Hawkspurr strode across the intervening ground and grasped Amanda's arms in a firm grip. "The film or the camera—your choice."

The woman's eyes narrowed to angry slits, and her lips compressed to a thin mean line. Hawkspurr quickly crossed a thigh to protect his groin.

Amanda smiled without warmth. "Don't worry Nyles, I'm saving your balls for a sharper fate." She looked urgently towards O'Connor for assistance, but all three Special Branch officers turned their heads away.

"The film. Now!" Hawkspurr looked savage.

"Fuck you Nyles."

"Not a second time Amanda!" Hawkspurr lifted the camera and unloaded the cartridge, before dropping the device to dangle impotently from the neck strap.

"Constable!" O'Connor roared. "Escort Miss Carson all the way back to Limassol."

"Yes sir." The policeman opened the car door and assisted the woman, none too gently into a rear seat.

The worried civilian driver wasted no time in turning his vehicle, and speeding away to relative safety.

"Blast the woman, now my tea is cold." Hawkspurr complained. "Tubby! Same again please." Hawkspurr was thoughtful as he seated himself again and passed the roll of film to O'Connor.

"Souvenir for you Jack. What do you really know about that bloody woman?"

O'Connor looked quizzically at his sergeants. "Well boys, how much do we have on the lovely lady?

Landris and Avidar exchanged glances and shrugged simultaneously.

The Greek replied for them both. "The question never came up before."

Hawkspurr shook his head in concern. "Take heed of my intuition Mike. There's something not quite kosher about that woman, she's too well informed and too well acquainted with Gunter Von Harzburg."

His mind went back to another woman he had once trusted in a distant land.

# CHAPTER 10

Hawkspurr removed a survey map from the pocket of his Bergen, and spread it for the policemen to see.

"Give me some idea of the best route to the monastery please Nazim."

"I was hoping to come with you Hawk." The Turk looked at O'Connor for confirmation.

"With all due respect Nazim, I don't believe that either you or Mike could keep up with us on a forced march. This new information has changed my original plan to seek and destroy at will in this district. We now have a specific target, and I can't see the General authorizing an air strike on a religious institution no matter who may be hiding there."

"What do you have in mind Hawk?" O'Connor broke in.

"One section under Sergeant McDonald to track the group that escaped this morning, and if they're not heading for the monastery I'll leg it straight there with the balance of the troop. Speed is of the essence so there's no time to liaise with security headquarters. However I don't want any movement of infantry or armor in the same direction until I'm in the building."

"Ok, the General did give you carte blanche in this regard." The inspector smiled wickedly. "You'll upset a lot of senior officers though."

"I'm not standing for election Jack!" Hawkspurr continued. "Now tell me all you know about Stavahdi."

"I can help you with that Hawk." Landris spoke, "I've been in the vicinity once to investigate a village murder, but it's not going to be easy to gain access."

The Greek described the ancient building as a former fortress, perched strategically on the uppermost spur of a mountain some four thousand feet above sea level.

Landris started to draw a sketch of the monastery.

"The spur is like a finger pointing out into a high valley, with the structure sitting on the nail. The foundations of the original fortress merge into almost perpendicular cliffs on three sides. The only ingress is the ridge itself leading from the main peak, and the path on this acclivity is wide enough for two men or a donkey; perhaps a motorbike could negotiate it, but no other vehicle. Grapes are carried up from the vineyards in the valley—which incidentally are owned by the monastery, and the wine they make is the source of their wealth."

Hawkspurr raised a hand to interrupt. "Could two of us infiltrate in the guise of workers?"

Landris shook his head. "No way. The single entrance is a tunnel and shaft cut through the solid rock, and closed at the end by a reinforced oaken door. The peasants deposit the grapes in bins, and the door isn't opened until they leave. The locals maintain that there are secret passages within the foundations below the monastery, which makes sense when you recall the history of this island. Probably only the Abbot knows where they are, or where they exit."

"Interesting," said Hawkspurr, "I've always been fascinated by castles and abbeys. Tell me, are the outer walls battlements or part of the building?"

Landris drafted another plan. "From what can be seen from a neighboring summit, there's an open area surrounding the main structure and tower. There are a number of small outbuildings within this area, probably storage sheds or workshops I honestly can't say."

"That's fine Mike. I think the open area is called a bailey, and the main building with a tower would be the old keep. A rappel assault from helicopters would be ideal, but I don't believe that could be achieved without alerting the whole main population, to say nothing of the red tape required, and the time factor. Parachuting is out of the question, so we climb up!"

O'Connor looked doubtful. "Can it be done Mike?"

The Greek sergeant nodded. "From what I've seen of Hawk and his men, nothing is impossible."

The inspector stood and rubbed his hands together. "In that case, I'll get back to Limassol and contact Nicosia. When you're in position Hawk, send a single coded message and I'll arrange for the security forces to surround the area. Can you give me a rough timetable?"

Hawkspurr had already completed his mental arithmetic. "Barring any complications, such as a contact with the men who escaped earlier I intend to be in place late this afternoon."

"Will you attack at first light tomorrow?"

"No. If Grivas has been warned about our presence, that's just what he'd expect, we'll go in at dusk tonight. Excuse me a moment Jack."

Hawkspurr called for Sergeant McDonald and when the NCO arrived, Hawkspurr issued his orders.

"Saddle up Billy, we are moving off immediately. Three days light rations only. Hand over any surplus to the police, and I'll give you more details shortly."

He turned to Doctor Faulconer. "Bare medical necessities Fab. I'm sure that there'll be a field ambulance with the regular troops."

O'Connor was waiting impatiently. "Just give me a code Hawk, and I'm away." "Ok Jack, how about something clerical—'bless you my child'?"

O'Connor laughed. "You're an irreligious blighter Hawk. Right, 'bless you my child' it is."

The two were about to part, when Nazim walked over from the Land Rover looking grim.

"More problems sir. A patrol of The Blues have just found the bodies of Constable Kutchuk and Miss Carson's driver. Both shot through the head, and dumped by the roadside. There's no sign of the car or the woman."

"Bugger it!" Exploded O'Connor. "It looks as though you were right about Amanda Carson Hawk. What will you do now?"

"Move faster. Of course she doesn't know that we have information on Grivas. She might have sensed that we were about to expose her though. I don't underestimate her intelligence."

"Where would she head for—that's the point?" O'Connor was talking to himself. "Kyrenia for a boat out, or a safe house?"

Hawkspurr had his own problems, and his brain was racing with each new development. "Sergeant!" He shouted.

McDonald returned with an expression of resignation on his face. "What now boss?"

"Everyone back into uniform Billy. There's no time left for subterfuge."

"Gotcha boss, head down and ass up time, right?"

"Roger. Give me time to change and we're off." Hawkspurr opened his pack and withdrew khaki pants and shirt, and his canvas and rubber boots. He changed on the spot, and swung the Bergen onto his shoulders before crossing to the police Rover to hand his riding boots to O'Connor. "Hang on to these please Jack, I'll see you later."

"Wait please!" Nazim removed the radio earphones from his head.

"I have a message relayed from London re Amanda Carson. It's a bit sketchy, but her real name is Amadou Georghiades, born at Larisa, Greece April 1920. She married a Canadian soldier, Greg Carson at the end of the war and moved back to Toronto with him. Later she returned to Greece as a Canadian Journalist and secretly joined Colonel Grivas' X Organization, which had been formed to fight the Communist group bent on taking over the whole country. She's still apparently devoted to Grivas and EOKA, and raises money for the cause amongst Greek immigrants in Canada and America."

"Well Miss Carson is wanted for murder now Sergeant. Get a description out to all stations, and warn that she's armed and dangerous. Personally, I think she'll make an attempt to get off the island; her usefulness as an agent here is finished."

O'Connor offered his hand to Hawkspurr, "Good luck Hawk, I'll join you later for a glass of the Abbot's wine."

Hawkspurr led his men from the village, and at the goat herder's ruined hut where he had seen the tracks of terrorists he called for Lance Corporal Brown.

"Take the point Hone, I want to march with all speed but we don't need to walk into an ambush. I'll keep you on the right compass bearing."

The Maori soldier moved off in the direction Hawkspurr indicated and the remainder of the troop spread out in single file behind. There was no need for further orders; each man knew exactly what was expected of him.

Disciplined and silent, Talon Troop went to hunt the enemy.

The soldiers climbed on, into one of the many steep valleys that pierce the mountains; within it a stream meandered over its bed of gray shale giving life to fertile earth and thick vegetation. As they progressed and ridge tops were gained, the men could look down to see village homes thick with bougainvillea, and gardens glowing with a profusion of colored flowers. Peasants were cultivating apple and cherry orchards, and an old woman seated on a donkey waved to girls tending their flocks of sheep and goats as she went about her business.

Up precipitous slopes the troop labored, where waterfalls cascaded down to feed this abundance of nature, and the air was heavy with the scent of predominant pine trees. Birds sang in the tangled branches unafraid—not like the Malayan jungle that fell silent at the passing of man. It was hard for Hawkspurr to equate the beauty and tranquility of these surroundings with his mission to destroy other men.

As the sun reached its zenith, Hawkspurr signaled a halt to rest and eat. Hone Brown and Jimmy McKenzie scouted on a little further, but reported back that there was no sign or tracks of the men who had escaped the village attack.

"Probably just as well under the circumstances. I don't want to split the troop at this stage—we have bigger fish to fry. Have your meal, and we'll push on."

It was with some relief that the weary, sweating soldiers with aching backs and shoulders spotted the towering bulk of the monastery of Staved through the thinning forest.

"Take five Billy, I'm going forward alone to reconnoiter." Hawkspurr thankfully removed his pack, and armed only with his pistol and a pair of binoculars crawled cautiously to the edge of the tree line.

The scene was exactly as Mike Landris had drawn it.

The colossus of the monastery, and the parent ridge leading from the mountain peak dominated the landscape. Hawkspurr couldn't see the village, but the smoke of a cooking fire betrayed its location, and the blue haze emanating from rows of grape vines clearly marked the boundaries of the vineyard.

He studied the commanding structure itself; there was no apparent sign of life as all was hidden behind solid stone battlements. Now he must find the best path up.

Meticulously, he examined the rock formation. Good, there were sufficient fissures and protrusions to afford hand and foot holds, the only difficulty might be in scaling the final exterior of the fortress walls themselves, but since it was highly unlikely that the monks posted sentries, a grappling hook through a crenellation should suffice there.

Satisfied, he returned to his troop.

With the men in a tight circle around him, Hawkspurr explained his plan for the offensive. Pat Green would lead, and he with Jimmy McKenzie and Sandy Powell the lightest and most agile of the climbers, would breach the monastery defenses and attempt to open the main entrance without disturbing the inhabitants.

Sergeant McDonald, with Doctor Faulconer and the other nine men would enter from the ridge once the gate was open. Should Hawkspurr's party come under fire, Trooper Nelson had permission to blow the gate with plastic explosive. Tubby Wilson was to find a suitable position on the peak to cover the exposed bailey with his sniper rifle.

Should any armed man present himself as a target before Hawkspurr gained the area, he was to be taken out.

Evil Billy snickered. "Just make sure he's really holding a gun Tubby, youse don't want to shoot a poor bloody monk playing with his cock in the evening breeze!"

"Thank you Sergeant!" Hawkspurr admired the Australian's use of humor to alleviate a tense situation.

"There is one problem—light. The quarter moon should be ideal, but if it clouds up your role will be redundant Tubby. So play it by ear."

Hawkspurr looked at each man in turn. "I don't need to remind you, that if we shoot an innocent monk we do ourselves no credit. Right…Billy you move off now, take your time and try not to be seen, you have at least two and a half hours to get into position. I'll start to climb when I think the light is to our advantage, so watch our progress and use your own judgment."

"No sweat boss."

Hawkspurr addressed Faulconer. "Keep your head down Fab, you could be useful later."

"Sure! Take an aspirin and call me in the morning."

Sergeant McDonald picked up his pack and checked the Bren gun. "Let's go." He shifted his weapon to a comfortable position and walked away.

When the others of the troop had left, Pat Green began to sort ropes and climbing gear. "How do you want to handle it boss?"

Hawkspurr replied. "Simple as possible Pat. Two pairs—you leading with Sandy, I'll rope to Jimmy and follow your path. Under normal circumstances we'd be safer all roped together, but this way I hope that at least two of us will reach the top. All that matters is that one of us opens the gate—Billy will take care of the rest."

He smiled at the young trooper Powell. "Here's your chance for a Mention In Dispatches, Sandy."

"Could you make it a Military Medal sir?"

"I don't think we rate that high in the War Office Sandy, besides if I fall first there'll be no-one to recommend you!"

"In that case sir, as me mum always says 'when in doubt have a cup o' tea.'"

Hawkspurr stretched out on the soft natural mattress of pine needles. "Quite right too. You brew up, and we'll rest for a while." He closed his eyes.

So much of warfare is spent in training and waiting to culminate in a brief period of excitement, sheer bloody terror, destruction, and quite possibly one's own mutilation or death!

Hawkspurr advanced from the shelter of the trees, onto the incline of shale sloping up to the fortress. His team carried only light automatic weapons and spare magazines of ammunition, one .300 carbine and three Sten sub-machine guns, a knife each, two lengths of safety line—no helmets or gloves. It was basic, but sufficient for the job in hand.

They crossed a path worn smooth by the feet of village peasants, over centuries of subservience to the priests and monks of Stavahdi. A subjugation that would no doubt be continued, long after the last British soldier had departed these idyllic shores.

Hawkspurr touched Green's shoulder. "It's up to you now Pat." He checked the rope linking himself and McKenzie, and slung the carbine across his back, to sit snugly between his shoulder blades.

Green's boots slipped a fraction on loose shale, then his fingers gripped firm rock; his feet found a crevice and he started to climb.

Hawkspurr allowed a few moments to lapse and then his hands too sought a purchase…left hand, right hand. His feet followed instinctively and he pressed his body close to the slope, but kept his head inclined up to the left as he watched Green and Powell climb steadily on.

McKenzie's foot slipped from a toehold and he swore softly under his breath.

As the rope joining them tightened, Hawkspurr clamped himself against the unyielding stone, every muscle and nerve taut, face compressed, willing his flesh to mold with the clay of Cyprus. 'Please don't fall Jimmy!' The moment of tension passed and Hawkspurr released the air from his lungs with an unconscious spasm—he did not realize that he had been holding his breath.

Still glued to the cliff he recalled a soldiers' expression—'like shit to an army blanket'.

He turned his head to McKenzie, and in the faint moonlight saw a gleam of white teeth as the Scot grinned apologetically back at him.

Ok. Hawkspurr flexed cramped digits and extended his left arm. The holds were really quite substantial—as good as any in the mountains of Wales where he had first trained. Feet followed hands, and he tried to avoid the scrape of his belt buckle against the rock by holding his gut back.

In daylight, and under different conditions this could have been a pleasurable climb, with time to enjoy the spectacular view.

Inch by cautious inch the four men progressed.

The quarter moon rose inexorably in the pure clarity of mountain air, casting oblique shadows that simplified the task of seeking handholds. A heavy door banged somewhere above, and in reply a village dog challenged the intrusive sound with a single frightened yap.

Silence fell again except for Hawkspurr's own breathing, which was a little labored now with the physical and mental strain of the ascent.

Unaware of the chronological passing of time, Hawkspurr's attention was fully focused on the mechanics of the climb. He daren't dwell on the possibility of plunging to the rocks now far below, and since he wasn't a man to pray for divine assistance he simply willed that neither he nor his companions would slip to certain death.

After a seeming eternity of probing, clawing, grasping, and heaving his body against gravity, Hawkspurr saw the shape of Green's head in a crenellation of the parapet above, followed by that of Powell's.

As he himself reached the stone masonry of the fortress walls, Hawkspurr understood why he hadn't heard the metallic sound of a grappling hook. The original mortar had decayed at the outer edge of the weatherworn blocks, leaving cavities that presented an easy climb.

At the same time, Hawkspurr was thankful to avail himself of the secure rope that Green lowered to aid him up the last thirty feet. He eased aching limbs through the capped blocks, and dropped from the ramparts to the cobblestone paving of the bailey. The inner defenses were about seven feet high, so obviously firing steps must have once been in place here for the defenders of times past.

As McKenzie dropped beside him Hawkspurr unfastened the harness tape, karabiners, and rope that had tied them together like an umbilical cord.

"Go for the gate Jimmy. Tell Clarke to send the signal to O'Connor, and remain on guard at the entrance with Wilson and Doctor Faulconer. Then you bring the others back here."

McKenzie cocked his gun and moved swiftly away.

Hawkspurr, Green, and Powell, stepped into the shadows of a stone and timber outhouse where they deposited the climbing gear, and regained their composure after the strenuous ascent. Each checked and cocked his weapon, and listened for any sounds of alarm. Nothing moved in the bailey, but a faint light shone from several windows of the keep.

Soundlessly the soldiers of Talon Troop joined their leader. Pockets were empty of anything that might rattle and betray their presence—even the identity discs suspended around their necks had been taped together.

Sergeant McDonald stood close to Hawkspurr.

"Right Billy, hoods on."

Since the incident with Amanda Carson and her camera in Limassol, Hawkspurr had asked Mike Landris to obtain the means to shield his men's features, and so guard against later reprisals. Consequently Mike's wife had sewn a number of plain black cotton ski masks.

Urban warfare was a new concept for Hawkspurr, and indeed the Special Air Service, and he was determined to protect the identity of his men in spite of any disapproval from the 'establishment'.

Hawkspurr rolled the soft material down over his head and the slits for eyes and mouth imparted a sinister aspect to his tall and now menacing figure. An added bonus he felt, in the fight against terrorism.

With a single wave of his hand, Hawkspurr initiated the next phase of the operation. The troop split into two sections and Hawkspurr made straight for the main door of the keep as McDonald led his men to check out the smaller, utility buildings located on the keep.

The huge wooden doors were locked as Hawkspurr had anticipated, and Peter Nelson placed a prepared charge of plastic explosive against the antiquated security. In nervous anticipation, the soldiers took shelter behind the protective bulk of a massive buttress.

Before the echoes of the blast had died, Hawkspurr and McKenzie were pulling on the shattered doors of the keep.

Left and right, team members charged purposely in to the monastery of Stavahdi to press home their advantage of surprise. No shouting or screaming to boost courage, just a quiet determination to get on with the job.

The foyer was smaller than Hawkspurr had pictured it—he had expected to gain immediate entry to the great hall of a medieval stronghold.

Squarely in the center of this anteroom stood a solid oak refectory table, and seated behind it a stunned and befuddled young man in civilian clothes.

His fate was sealed, as he reached belatedly for the Sten sub-machine gun lying carelessly in front of him. Two rounds from McKenzie's Sten, and one .45 caliber bullet from Hawkspurr's pistol struck the unfortunate sentry simultaneously in his chest, and he died without a murmur.

Powell and Mason dashed past the body without a glance, to open the single portal at the rear of the room. Now they were in the Great Hall, with a dozen or so closed doors set into the stone walls, and decorated with faded icons.

Working in pairs the soldiers commenced checking each door—their task was simple—assemble all the monks in the central gallery. If possible disarm any persons carrying weapons, and shoot to kill if their lives were threatened.

Sergeant McDonald ran into the keep with his section close on his heels. "All clear outside boss." He reported.

"Good. Let's see what we have up those stairs."

Hawkspurr indicated a broad staircase, which descended in two wings from a wide mezzanine floor at the far end of the chamber. "You take the left passage."

With Trooper Powell at his shoulder, Hawkspurr sprinted up the right hand flight and passed into a wider corridor. Judging from the number of windows he had plotted from the valley below, there were two stories above the lower floor plus the tower.

Corporal McKenzie and his section would search for entrance to the cellars beneath, but it would take Special Branch officers a week or more to search the monastery thoroughly.

As Hawkspurr paused and checked for a sentry before proceeding he heard yells of protest in the background, as monks were assembled for interrogation. He inclined his head to a door on the right, and Powell turned an iron ring handle to gain entry.

Hawkspurr followed the young soldier into a sparsely furnished but quite adequate bedchamber—obviously not a monk's cell.

Swiftly yet with caution, Hawkspurr and Powell examined each of the three rooms in this wing. All were empty, but one showed unmistakable signs of recent occupation.

They were now at the far extremity of the corridor, where a heavy brocade curtain covered the arched passage. Surely this must lead to the floor above or the tower.

A rustle of human presence alerted Hawkspurr, or was it simply a draught from the door he had just closed?

As he leveled his pistol the drapes swung dramatically aside and a woman stepped through the arch.

A figure clad in khaki battledress. The hair pulled back severely from a face devoid of feminine make-up or human compassion, and lips distorted below the eyelids compressed with pure hatred as she aimed a Luger pistol at Hawkspurr's head.

"No sir!" With a frantic cry of warning, Powell sprang between his officer and the woman. The soldier's momentum carried him forward onto the terrorist as her gun muzzle exploded twice, then the entwined bodies crashed to the ground with the woman screaming obscenities.

The slender form was pinned beneath the weight of the soldier, and in frustration she spat at Hawkspurr over the man's shoulder. The spittle fell short as Powell kicked himself clear, still hugging the woman's weapon to his blood stained chest as if to seal the dreadful wound.

Hawkspurr stood over the woman—looked deep into the soulless pits of her eyes—and without a word shot her between the snarling lips. Death was instantaneous, and the execution was warranted.

She was deleted from his conscious mind, and Powell was now his immediate concern. A young man who had served him, and the Special Air Service regiment unselfishly for three years, and had undoubtedly saved his life in the last few moments.

As Hawkspurr knelt beside the Trooper he removed his hood and that of Powell's, and changing his pistol to his left hand aimed it in the direction of the curtained arch.

He knew he was breaking the basic rules of security by not checking behind the drapes, but Powell's face was gray and the blood was pumping too fast for his own weakening hand pressure to contain the precious life fluid. With difficulty Hawkspurr took a field dressing from his pocket and pressed firmly on the wound.

He had to prize the Luger from cramped fingers, and he placed Powell's Sten gun beside him on the flagstones.

Powell's eyes flickered open—the pupils wide seeking light—the irises were dull, but recognition registered as he saw Hawkspurr's familiar face.

Hawkspurr as always, managed a grin. "Laying down on the job soldier?"

"Yes sir. Bit of indigestion I think."

"Something you ate no doubt." Hawkspurr's grin faded as Powell closed his eyes in a grimace of pain and the gut sucked in, seeking air.

"Don't you go to sleep on me Sandy!" Hawkspurr fumbled with one hand to find a capsule of morphine, then he unsealed the needle of the tiny tube and stuck it without ceremony into Powell's upper arm.

The eyes opened again as the lines of pain smoothed out around his mouth, and the tongue tried to moisten dry lips. "Did I do Ok sir?" Powell wheezed.

"Best of the best Sandy." Hawkspurr squeezed the man's hand in affection, his own words hoarse with emotion.

The woman's blood was oozing along the flagstone crevices to almost mingle with that of Powell's, and Hawkspurr savagely kicked out at the body to push it further away.

His eyes turned back to Powell's—they met, and silently said goodbye.

# CHAPTER 11

Hawkspurr gently straightened Powell's limbs on the cold stone, and covered the ashen face with his hood.

He picked up the soldier's gun, and as anger exploded in his brain he sprayed a burst of bullets at the inanimate curtains that had concealed the woman. Tearing the shredded drapes to one side Hawkspurr leapt through the archway and saw a spiral staircase leading aloft, spanning two steps at a time he ascended to the higher floor.

Coolness and caution returned as he reached the landing, and his hasty glance around the corner of the wall was greeted by a single rifle shot.

The bullet ricocheted and spun harmlessly into the stairwell as he tossed a grenade far back along the narrow hall, and stuffed a finger firmly in each ear. Hawkspurr waited seconds for the fireball and shrapnel to expend their energy, and stepped from shelter.

A young man wearing khaki shirt and trousers was sprawled across the top of a heavy wooden chest. A toppled chair lay close by, and beside it a discarded Lee Enfield rifle. He fired two shots from his Sten into the body, and moved on.

Hawkspurr assessed his surroundings—to the left, eight feet high double doors, on his right a series of narrow windows. The walls here had been smoothed by the application of plaster, and on them a series of frescoed saints were ranked—probably designed to frighten sinners to their knees.

Drawn with a certain linear strength in a primitive Byzantine style, their beards were parted like clumps of icicles, and the foreheads were corrugated by an intense passion as they stared down with expressions of grief. Figures in shroud-like robes they clasped their crosses before them like weapons against the devil, and offered to supplicants unscrolled parchments inscribed with the formula for eternal salvation.

The far end of the hall showed yet one more flight of ascending stairs. The rules told him to wait for backup, but instinct urged him on.

Hawkspurr let the Sten hang suspended on its sling around his neck, he was unsure of the number of rounds left in the magazine—and drew his pistol again.

He remembered to roll the black hood down over his face as he crossed to the large doors they were unlocked, and opened towards him. He entered, and found himself in a luxurious dining room hung with ornate tapestries and religious oil paintings.

The centerpiece on the dominant wall, showed the angel of the Annunciation lifting a delicate hand to announce his incarnation to the Virgin Mary. Pink and white robes flowed about his feet, and lesser angels with golden ringlets of hair attended him.

There were only two figures in the magnificent chamber, and they were both seated at one end of a polished table large enough to accommodate fifty. Fat candles dripped beeswax down antique gold ornaments placed along the length of the shining planks, and bowls of fresh fruit and bottles of wine reposed invitingly within arms reach of the diners.

The men seemed unperturbed by the appearance of an armed intruder or the explosions that heralded his arrival; rather they looked expectant, even welcoming.

Neither moved. Their hands holding a glass of wine each, betrayed not a tremor.

One—gray of hair and beard, wearing the robes of a cleric, and the other immaculate in a white dinner jacket—Gunter Von Harzburg.

Von Harzburg raised his goblet and smiled sardonically. "Very theatrical my dear Nyles. Do take off that silly hood and join the Abbot and I in a superb local wine. Most Reverend, meet Captain Nyles Hawkspurr."

Hawkspurr removed the hood with one hand, but kept his weapon trained steadily on the German's head. "I can't say that I'm surprised to find you here Gunter, but fortunately Special Branch officers will be arriving shortly to arrest you."

Before Von Harzburg could reply, the Abbot interjected. He spoke in good English, but with a smile playing around his overly plump lips that Hawkspurr found somewhat obscene.

"Herr Von Harzburg is in the monastery at my express invitation, to sample and purchase our wines for export to Switzerland. Whilst I am also pleased at your timely appearance to rescue us from the terrorists of EOKA, there is no call for you to insult my guest."

"Rescue you! From your friends?" Hawkspurr still pointed his gun.

Von Harzburg shook his head. "Dear, dear, Nyles, the Abbot and monks—and I—have been prisoners of these foul fellows for some days. They used the presence of Miss Carson to gain entry, maintaining that she was their hostage. The Superior, in his humanity had no alternative but to shelter them."

Despite his anger Hawkspurr had to smile. "Ye gods Gunter, after all these years you still take me for a bloody fool!"

Further discourse was halted by the appearance of McDonald and McKenzie, they too had discarded their hoods and both looked furious.

"Sandy's dead." The Scot stated, rather unnecessarily. "Was it this bastard boss?" Evil Billy had his weapon aimed squarely at Von Harzburg.

"No Billy. What do you have to report?"

"Apart from the monks, it's obvious that they have six visitors including two women."

"Well we've accounted for three, what about the others." Hawkspurr looked from one to the other of his NCOs.

"Short of a major search, there's nothing in the cellars sir." McKenzie spat out, "Unless you count the largest collection of pornographic photo's and books I've ever seen. Dirty bastards!" He glared at the Abbot.

"Grivas was here all right boss, and probably his personal bodyguard. Look." McDonald handed Hawkspurr some folded papers tucked into his belt.

Hawkspurr examined the pages. "I can't read Greek but the salutation to 'My Dear Dighenis' on this letter, leaves no doubt as to who the recipient was. Only a bloody megalomaniac would name himself after an ancient Greek folk-hero."

(Dighenis was said to have repelled the Saracens in mythic battles, and country people believe that this warrior whose fingerprints are still visible on the crags, hurled the off shore boulders scattered along the Cypriot coast there.)

Hawkspurr thrust the letter towards the abbot.

"Do you know George Grivas sir?"

Again the Superior shook his head in denial. "Only by name and reputation Captain. The men who forced their presence upon this holy house did not bother with introductions."

"Lying bastard." Evil Billy growled.

"I see. Just where are the other two un-named men and Miss Carson at this point in time?" Hawkspurr fixed the abbot with cold, unblinking eyes.

The 'Most Reverend' raised his hands in ignorance. "Somewhere below I imagine."

"Ok Billy start at the top of the tower and work your way down, rip the place to pieces if you need to. One man to guard the monks, and Jimmy can stay here to keep the Abbot and his guest company. I'll go to the gate and wait for Inspector O'Connor." Hawkspurr turned on his heels and marched away.

On the first landing he stopped to contemplate the bodies of Powell, and the woman who must have been Miss Carson's bodyguard. His anger vented, he straightened the woman's limbs and closed the sightless eyes still staring accusingly. He went into the adjacent room and returned with blankets from the bed to cover the corpses.

In the Great Hall the residents of the monastery sat or squatted in undignified array. What does one call a collection of monks? 'A mob'? 'A gaggle'? 'A pride' didn't fit these bearded men in underwear or night attire, they seemed to have discarded their distinction along with the robes of religious order. Perhaps a covey of clerics?

Hawkspurr was puzzled to see an obviously frightened boy of about twelve years of age amongst the men.

"Ray." He called Corporal Watson to him. "What's that lad doing here?"

"He was keeping one of the monks company boss."

"Ye gods!" Hawkspurr shook his head in disgust. "Get the boy dressed and kick him out right now, I imagine he's from the village. Have all the cells been searched?"

"Yes boss."

"Right. Does each monk have a separate cell?"

"As far as I can tell."

"Lock them all up then. One man on guard in the passage and send the rest up to Sergeant McDonald, he's organizing a thorough search of the building from top to bottom." He looked at the young Greek boy. "No pun intended!"

Hawkspurr crossed the Keep to the main entrance of the Monastery of Stavadhi. On close examination of the approaches he realized that his decision to climb to the attack had been the right one. Even two men stationed here could hold off a lightly armed company indefinitely and inflict serious casualties.

Harry Faulconer met Hawkspurr impatiently. "Is the shooting all over Hawk?"

"Yes Fab. One casualty, Sandy Powell."

As the doctor went to dash past him, Hawkspurr extended a restraining arm. "Nothing you can do, he died very quickly."

"What about Grivas?"

"I fear we've missed him, but the lads are still searching. Why don't you go inside now? It's a fascinating place, both from an historic and aesthetic point of view."

"I'll do that. How many have you accounted for?"

"Three including Amanda Carson' bodyguard. You'll find Von Harzburg and the abbot in the upper dining room."

As the doctor's mouth fell open in surprise, Hawkspurr grinned "No, they're both unharmed. In fact the bastards will probably invite you to join them in a drink!"

Faulconer moved away and Hawkspurr turned to Wilson.

"Tubby why don't you find the kitchen and cook us a nice meal, I'm told that the larders are loaded with goodies. You and Clarke eat first, and feed the lads in threes—I'll stay here and man the radio."

He addressed the signaler. "What's the present status Nobby?"

"Inspector O'Connor is on net boss. Location the village, he's waiting for a sit-rep {situation report} from you."

"Roger. Off you go with Tubby and have a meal. No wine please we'll save that for later, get back here as soon as you've finished but there's no need to rush it."

The soldiers hurried off—Wilson would be starving by now!

Hawkspurr checked and reloaded his weapons and squatted by the radio set.

"Hawk One for Bluebottle. I say again, Hawk One for Bluebottle. Do you read me? Over."

"Bluebottle for Hawk One, loud and clear. Over."

"Roger Bluebottle. The target is secure, your ETA {estimated time of arrival} Over."

"I'm leaving vehicles in village and proceeding on foot to your position now. Bluebottle out."

Hawkspurr sat patiently and considered his options.

Talon Troop's function in the monastery was complete once Special Branch and the police assumed control, and despite the search being carried out by his men, instinct told him that Grivas had already escaped.

He was bitterly disappointed, feeling that with Archbishop Makarios in exile and Grivas in custody, EOKA would wither and die like a snake without a head. He had no authority to detain Von Harzburg, and unless he received a direct order from Brigadier Hazlett to 'strategically neutralize' the German, he was loathe to execute him without provocation.

Was Von Harzburg his Achilles Heel? No—given the right circumstances he could kill the agent.

The wavering light of electric torches on the mountainside of the connecting ridge heralded the arrival of the police party. Hawkspurr watched in amusement as first one, followed by another of the beams tilted to the sky before tumbling off the narrow ledge. Judging from the screams of fright, the torchbearers had also involuntarily left the track—they were probably city cops. Well, apart from bruised pride they would come to no harm.

The column resumed the march slowly, until the leading policeman reached the monastery. A puffing and blowing Inspector O'Connor, accompanied by Sergeant Landris and Sergeant Avidar, followed him.

"Well done Hawk. What's the story here?" O'Connor was obviously pleased to have completed his enforced march.

"Sit down for a minute and catch your breath Jack." Hawkspurr grinned at the police officers.

As the rest of the police party filed past, Hawkspurr offered a detailed report of his activities to the Inspector. All three listened without comment, but their faces displayed a disheartened expression as they realized that Grivas had eluded capture once more.

"You understand that I can't hold Von Harzburg?" O'Connor stated ruefully as Hawkspurr concluded his account.

Hawkspurr simply nodded glumly.

"Ok, your job here is over Hawk. I suggest that you clear out before the press get wind of this operation." O'Connor was becoming political.

"I agree Jack. I intend to move back to Limassol cross-country, and continue the search for Grivas in any likely villages or caves en route."

"Very well. I'll inform Nicosia." 0'Connor looked at his Greek and Turkish Sergeants.

"Since you won't be in a hurry, how about taking these two dead-beats with you? They're both spoiling for a little action!"

"Fair enough. It would be expedient to send scouts into the villages who speak the language."

O'Connor rose wearily to his feet. "That's settled then. Anything more before you leave?"

"Yes, I'd like Powell's body flown straight back to England—he was an only child."

O'Connor shook his head sadly. "I'm very sorry about your man Hawk. I promise you that I'll do everything in my power to expedite your wishes. We took the precaution of bringing body bags, and there's a RAF helicopter on stand-by for casualty evacuation."

"Thanks Jack, as soon as the lads have eaten we'll disappear back into the forest."

Hawkspurr turned to Landris and Avidar, "Stay close to me gentlemen, we'll move out just before dawn."

Inside the monastery kitchen Tubby Wilson was in his element, frying slices of ham with eggs and slabs of coarse bread. The Scot had placed platters of cheese and olives, with cold mutton and boiled potatoes on a side table, but the only beverage available seemed to be earthenware jugs of red wine.

Hawkspurr poured himself a mug, grimaced and made no further comment; his men could either drink it or scour the powder residue from their weapons with it!

As he wiped the last drop of delicious ham fat from his lips, Sergeant McDonald approached him his strong jaw jutting in anger and frustration.

"What's up Sergeant?"

"Nothing boss—fuck all!"

"Ok Billy, sit down and eat. We'll take off very soon, and try to pick up the trail at first light."

As he finished speaking, Hawkspurr cocked his head to catch a familiar sound; it was the chunk-a-chunk of a helicopter settling above the monastery.

He stood upright. "Chopper. I'm going upstairs, you stay here Billy."

Atop the fortified tower, Turkish police constables were loading bodies into a hovering Sikorsky. The rotor blades had sufficient clearance, but the pilot was holding his aircraft undercarriage just above the crenellated battlements.

The SAS soldiers gathered there couldn't identify their comrade in the anonymous body bags, but as the clamor of the engine noise increased and the ungainly craft rose and tilted away, they came to attention and saluted.

Each man present is acutely conscious of his own mortality in the pursuance of warfare.

Corporal Ken Hall the sturdy quiet man from Gloucester scouted ahead with Hone Brown, the Maori warrior from New Zealand. Behind them Hawkspurr and Faulconer led the men of Talon Troop south-west to skirt the village of Stavadhi, and once again enter the forest in which they felt at ease.

Hawkspurr breathed deeply of the fragrant air, expunging the stench of decadent decay from the monastery that lingered in his nostrils. The rising sun brushed into new life the papery petals of white and pink cistus growing in the crevices of rock. Banks of crown daisies opened in greeting to the new day and curtsied to tall lupins, and the wild mint scented the soldier's boots as it was crushed in passage.

A late owl caught unawares after his nocturnal foraging, squawked and fled in alarm on strong wings—beating for altitude in the thin mountain air.

At 1000 hours Hawkspurr called a halt.

Beneath an acacia tree in a grove of eucalyptus trees, he dropped his pack and removed his boots.

"Let's call it a day, eh Doc?"

Fab Faulconer agreed. "Certainly. Doctor's orders." The New Zealander called to Sergeant McDonald.

"Anything medicinal liberated from the monks?"

Evil Billy exposed huge teeth. "Possibly! Right lads," he ordered, "tarpaulin muster." From his own pack he produced two bottles of wine and a flask of Metaxas Brandy.

Sheepishly the other men of the troop contributed to the common loot.

Red wine, brandy, chunks of cheese, grapes, oranges, and from Tubby Wilson's Bergen, a leg of cooked mutton.

Hawkspurr laughed. "Since we're not going to starve or dehydrate, we'll spend the night here. Basha down Billy, but send Jimmy and Ray out a quarter mile radius for a quick recce."

At regular intervals during the night, the sentries changed guard quietly. Hawkspurr slept comfortably and untroubled in the clean cool atmosphere, and awoke refreshed at first light. By the time he had returned from his morning toilet a little distance from the bivouac, Wilson was frying chicken pieces over a hexamine cooker.

The embers of the cheerful campfire the soldiers had burned the previous night, had been carefully dispersed to avoid telltale smoke in the still of dawn. A fire that had been lit not only to allay the cold, but as a token celebration for the successful attack, and a wake for Sandy Powell as the young soldier was remembered in a toast of brandy.

During breakfast Hawkspurr examined the area map with Landris and Avidar.

Together they plotted a route that encompassed isolated hamlets, and likely hiding places in limestone caves and abandoned mines.

With weapons loaded at the ready and safety catches on, Talon Troop sallied forth once again to seek and destroy the enemy. Moving through terrain that was pleasant and the flora open, they nevertheless patrolled in a formation perfected in the jungles of Malaya—the drills for contact and ambush being second nature to each man.

On careful feet they instinctively avoided dry branches that would betray their presence, yet their eyes never focused on one spot. The leading scout was far enough ahead to warn of possible traps, but still within Hawkspurr's sight.

'Tail End Charlie' stayed back a distance, to watch and listen for pursuit from the rear.

On the long spur of a descending ridge, Grant Mason halted and made the silent sign for a building or buildings.

Hawkspurr signaled the patrol to halt, and moved forward alone to join the scout.

Sprawled below in a wide gorge was a small community.

In the center of a group of cottages stood a tiny Byzantine church but incongruously—at least to Hawkspurr's eyes—the unmistakable dome of a shabby mosque held a prominent position at the extremity of the hamlet. Through his binoculars he observed a small group of shaven haired boys, sitting on the ground facing an elderly Muslim cleric. Was this a school or religious instruction?

"Ask the police sergeants to join me please Grant." Hawkspurr whispered to Mason.

He resumed his inspection, and noted tidy little gardens filled with the color of gladioli, rosemary, geraniums and mimosa. Beneath an ancient fig tree sat two equally benign old men, clad in vlaka—baggy breeches and high boots.

As one of the men coughed and spat into the dust, a host of multi-colored butterflies rose in alarm from the branches above them and fled for safety.

Hawkspurr handed his glasses to Avidar. "What do you make of this set-up Nazim?"

The Turk scanned the buildings below without comment, and then handed the binoculars to Landris. He waited patiently until the Greek too had assessed the village, and then voiced his opinion.

"It looks like a mixed community of Greeks and Turks who seem to be co-existing quietly together. My guess is that they are predominantly miners." He looked quizzically at his colleague.

Landris concurred with a nod of his head. "I agree. Somewhere close by there'll be a copper mine probably opened by Phoenicians or Romans."

"If you're correct," replied Hawkspurr, "all the able young men appear to be at work. Any ideas?"

"Why don't Nazim and I go down this evening and talk to the men?" Landris suggested.

"Good. In the meantime I'll split the troop into four patrols and search the immediate vicinity. You two stay put and observe—you look as though you need the rest!" Hawkspurr laughed softly, "I'll leave Clarke and the radio with you in case of trouble."

Hawkspurr issued his orders dividing the surrounding area into sections. McDonald, Watson and Hall would lead three patrols, and he would take the fourth. All were to return by dusk unless contact was made.

Bergen packs were left in the care of Clarke, and the sections moved off in light order. Hone Brown led away in the direction indicated by Hawkspurr who was followed by Faulconer with McKenzie guarding the rear.

They climbed slowly along the exposed spine of a crumbling track, and above them the crags loomed out at impossible angles.

On surrounding hillsides, poppies exploded in bursts of scarlet clumps among thyme undulating beneath the weight of marauding bees, and myriads of camouflaged insects rasped and clicked incessantly. From one of the higher crags an Imperial eagle stooped, and effortlessly lifted to circle above them. The sunlight gleamed off his back, as he banked for a closer look at the intruders.

Hone Brown halted abruptly as he spotted the primary object of the bird's attention—a five feet long snake writhing across his path with a mere rustle of roughened scales. The Maori soldier grinned nervously back over his shoulder at Hawkspurr. "You didn't tell me there are bloody snakes here boss!"

Hawkspurr laughed softly in reply. "Only your country and Ireland are free of serpents Hone."

"Right boss." The New Zealander moved forward again with a little more vigilance.

After ten minutes the track zigzagged around a shoulder of the mountain, to emerge on a wide plateau fronting a ragged cliff face pierced by a large tunnel entrance.

Angry voices greeted the patrol, and a small gathering of men stood in postures of confrontation, shaking various tools and implements in their expressions of rage. As the man at the center of the quarrel saw the patrol moving towards them, he screamed for quiet and pointed at the soldiers.

The miners lapsed into sullen silence and split into two obvious ethnic groups—Greeks and Turks.

"Spread out chaps." Hawkspurr advanced calmly and addressed the stocky man standing detached from the group.

"What's wrong here?" Although he could see no weapons, Hawkspurr's index finger rested lightly on the safety catch of his carbine.

The man replied in good English. "I am the foreman sir—Skoulas. These men," he indicated the Turks, "say there are two bandits hiding in the mine. The others deny it." He waved a hand in the direction of the Greeks.

"And what do you say Skoulas?"

The foreman shrugged. "I do not know. I am a loyal Cypriot, and we want no trouble here. For years we have worked together in peace. Now…." He lifted his shoulders again in despair.

"I see." Hawkspurr felt some sympathy for the man.

"Well Skoulas, I am now declaring a public holiday. I want you to take your men back to their homes, and I will come and talk with you later. No-one is to leave the village—do you understand?"

"Yes sir." The foreman looked relieved as the burden of responsibility was lifted from him. He went back to his laborers, and after a brief discussion the two groups walked away down a narrow road that Hawkspurr had not been aware of. No doubt a direct route to the outside, and access for the collection of ore.

Hawkspurr looked speculatively at the working site in front of him, and to a plot of ancient graves on one side. His romantic eyes seeing the sandaled footprints of a Roman Centurion in the reddish brown dust as he supervised the removal of precious metal, to sheath the hulls of battle ships and the wide bottomed corbitae—as the merchantmen wallowed from Cypriot ports stuffed with spices, and the fruits of this fertile land.

Copper to mix with the rich tin of Cornwall for the manufacture of bronze weapons, tools, coins and other objects of art.

Hawkspurr's momentary lapse into history was broken by a discreet cough from Faulconer. "Penny for your thoughts Hawk."

"A penny! Yes very appropriate. Sorry, Let's take a closer look at the mine."

Hawkspurr stepped cautiously into the maw of the cliff, and took cover beside a natural buttress. McKenzie stood close behind him, and he signaled Faulconer and Brown to move to the opposite side of the tunnel.

Hawkspurr cocked his head the better to locate any strange sounds, but only the whisper of air flowing from an unseen ventilation shaft was detected.

Gun at hip with safety catch off, he advanced deeper into the gloom of the mine until he reached a junction. Here, only Stygian blackness prevailed.

"Damn!" He hadn't brought a torch.

He raised a hand to halt the others, and taking a deep breath he yelled into the cavern.

"You are surrounded by British troops. Leave your weapons and come out now. Surrender and you will not be harmed!"

The response was a sudden assault, in the form of a flurry of beating wings accompanied by squeaks of fright as a squadron of bats swept over his head.

Hawkspurr ducked in alarm, and cursed as he involuntarily fired a single round into the dark passage.

His temporary loss of control was immediately rewarded by another rejoinder.

"Don't shoot! Don't shoot please. I am coming out!"

Hawkspurr rammed a knuckle into his mouth to stifle a near hysterical laugh, as he struggled to regain his composure. He turned to look at McKenzie—his eyes bright and watering. "All part of the plan!"

"Whatever you say sir!"

The soldiers tensed in anticipation, as a figure stumbled towards them from a branch tunnel. Brown moved like a cat, leaping to take the man's arms and twist them behind his back.

"Good. Let's get him outside." Hawkspurr followed the Maori and his prisoner. "Come with me Fab, you stay put Jimmy." He ordered.

"Let's find some shade." Hawkspurr shielded his eyes from the almost painful glare of the sun.

"Right, search him Hone." Hawkspurr examined the terrorist.

He was a scared young man of about 19 years, 5'6" in height, pale and underweight with dirty black hair and soft stubble of beard. He was dressed in heavy woolen shirt and trousers, worn boots and a threadbare jumper.

Brown produced a filthy handkerchief, komboloyia beads, and a small pocketknife from the man's pockets.

"That's it boss."

"Ok, sit him down whilst the doctor takes a look at him."

Hawkspurr removed his canteen, took a drink and then poured water into a mug that he passed to the prisoner.

With shaking hands the man drank in a single gulp, and with downcast eyes he handed the mug back.

"Right. I'll be handing you over to the police very soon. What's your name?"

"Christou Nissia sir."

"Where are you from?" No reply.

"That's Ok, I really don't care. Are you alone?"

He was answered with a negative shake of the head.

"Who else is in the mine?" Persisted Hawkspurr. He lifted the man's head to look into his eyes.

"Spiro Mavrocordatos."

"Why didn't he come out with you?"

"He would rather die."

"I see. Would you like me to talk to him?"

Again the prisoner merely shrugged his thin shoulders.

"Tell me exactly where he is."

Christou looked down once more, and then mumbled. "Where I came from. There are two side tunnels on the left, very narrow and not deep, he is in the second one."

"Is there a way out?" Hawkspurr was infinitely patient.

Christou shook his head.

Hawkspurr addressed Faulconer and Brown. "Stay here please. I'll try and talk Spiro out."

Hawkspurr paused inside the mine entrance to adjust his eyes before joining McKenzie.

"Any movement Jimmy?"

"No sir."

"There's one more in there. Let's find out if he's willing to come out."

Hawkspurr peered into the tunnel, but could neither hear nor see anything untoward.

"Spiro, this is you last chance to surrender…" Hawkspurr's entreaty was answered by a shotgun blast, which made his ears ring in the confines of the mine.

"Right Jimmy, I'm not wasting any more time on the fellow. How many grenades do you have?"

"Two sir." McKenzie pulled the Mills bombs from his belt pouch.

"I have two also, should be enough to do the job. Take out one base plate and screw them together."

Hawkspurr was busy adapting his own grenades.

"Follow me." Hawkspurr sidled around the corner, guiding himself with an outstretched arm on the surprisingly smooth cool wall of this ancient mine.

His exploring fingers found the first side tunnel, and he reached back to guide McKenzie across the opening to the far wall. Another five yards and he felt the second passage.

"Ready?" He whispered.

"Yes."

Hawkspurr extracted the safety pin from his double grenade, and heard the faint scrape of metal as McKenzie did likewise.

"Ready...now!"

Hawkspurr flung the deadly device with all of his strength into the refuge. McKenzie's grenades followed a split second later.

"Run for it!"

Hawkspurr propelled McKenzie back the way they had come. He thought he heard a cry of dismay from the tunnel behind, as he and McKenzie blundered into the main shaft.

He pressed his body against the wall, and covered his ears tightly before the blast from the detonation tore at his clothes.

An ominous roar and rumble attended the reek of high explosive, and a cloud of acrid dust billowed along the shaft.

"Outside Jimmy!" Hawkspurr tugged at McKenzie's belt, and started to sprint for the light at the entrance.

As the pair reached asylum in the open, Hawkspurr halted and looked back.

Rocks and debris were spewing from the mine, and an eerie groan of anguish emanated from the wounded mountain.

Hawkspurr grinned at McKenzie through dust-blackened lips, his teeth gleaming in stark contrast. "I've really pissed off the mountain gods today Jimmy!"

As the noise and dust subsided, Hawkspurr walked back to the ruined entrance. The main shaft was clear, but as far as he could see the branch tunnel had collapsed completely.

"Looks as though Spiro Mavrocordatos has bought himself a very classy tomb Jimmy. Let's go back and see how the other lads are faring."

# CHAPTER 12

A little before the onset of dusk, Hawkspurr's patrol together with the prisoner rejoined the others of Talon Troop. No signs of a possible terrorist group had been seen, and the Special Branch sergeants advised that it was safe to enter the village. Before moving off the high ridge, Clarke sent a radio message to Limassol requesting police to collect Christou Nissia.

On entering the village Hawkspurr took the precaution of initiating a house-to-house search. Neither Greek nor Turkish inhabitants seemed particularly upset by the intrusion, and Hawkspurr's orders were explicit: "Miss nothing, but conduct yourselves with the utmost courtesy!"

Skoulas—who was also the Mayor—and the Moslem Imam, who offered hospitality and overnight accommodation in the small Islamic community hall, met the soldiers. The Greek Orthodox representative was conspicuous by his absence, and Hawkspurr suggested to Mike Landris that he start his enquiries with the priest.

Hawkspurr set up his temporary headquarters in the poor hall stark—in contrast to any similar Greek facility, but warm and welcoming. Turkish matrons and girls had gathered to prepare an evening meal for the visitors, and a young man was playing the music of the Ottomans on a battered violin, as laughing boys brought extra wooden benches and chairs from their homes

At one end, a middle-aged man was stoking the hot coals of a tiled stove—in front of which a spit of lamb's meat was roasting—doner kebab. A younger assistant was preparing shish kebab—chunks of meat on metal skewers with green peppers, cucumber and tomato.

Hawkspurr and Clarke were served coffee by small boys fascinated with the signaler's radio, and Clarke obliged by tuning round the frequencies, and bringing disembodied voices from far away into their remote village.

Landris and Avidar joined Hawkspurr, and although the Greek was viewed with some suspicion the natural hospitality of the simple peasants overcame their reticence.

Both policemen were convinced that there was no collusion here with any guerilla group—a fact corroborated by the soldiers as they reported in from their search. Nevertheless Hawkspurr ordered the usual precaution of placing sentries at each approach to the village.

The dying sun dropped behind a sheltering hill, and darkness engulfed the mountain community like a drawn curtain. Oil lamps were lit and the hall slowly filled with the followers of Islam, bearing their simple contributions of soup, and sweet sugary deserts of halva and baklava.

Evil Billy produced a bottle of brandy, for which Hawkspurr chastised him. "Give it a rest for tonight Billy, these people don't touch alcohol at least in front of the Imam!"

The evening passed pleasantly, as food was pressed continuously upon the soldiers, and young women entertained them with the graceful dances of their ancestors.

"No belly dancers boss?" McDonald was disappointed at the display of modesty.

"Not tonight Billy. Stick your hormones in the Bergen along with that brandy!"

Soon after dawn a police section arrived, and two constables took charge of the prisoner. Christou had been locked up all night, but had been fed and allowed to wash and shave. Hawkspurr warned the Turkish escort to ensure that no harm came to the Greek, and that he must be handed over directly to Inspector O'Connor in Limassol.

Talon Troop spent the next five days patrolling slowly south.

Hawkspurr approached an isolated homestead as his men probed the surrounding forest where, to his surprise an elderly Greek Cypriot who had served with the British Army in Palestine offered him hospitality.

His plump wife brought wine she had made herself from vines around the cottage, and his daughter self-consciously produced a tray of tiny birds.

The old man beamed with indulgence. "Strouthos enjoy."

Hawkspurr's face lost its smile. The little blackened creatures reminded him of whitebait—with sightless eye pits staring at him from fragile skulls.

The hostess enjoined Hawkspurr again "Eat. Eat. See!"

She popped a bird whole into her mouth and crunched with delight. "Yumm!" The woman intoned, as if encouraging a diffident child to eat.

'For Queen and Country.' Thought Hawkspurr, and raised a bird to reluctant lips. Surreptitiously he removed the minute skull and palmed it, before biting down on the fragile bones. He reached quickly for his beaker of wine and swallowed. "Delicious thank you, now I really must join my men, they will be concerned at my absence. Goodbye." He retreated with dignity.

"Mike! Come here please." Hawkspurr sought out his Greek friend and displayed the skull he had hidden.

"Just what have I been eating?"

Landris laughed. "The local delicacy—sparrows."

"Ye gods! Do you mean to tell me they shoot sparrows?"

"Why not? Anything that moves on four legs, crawls or flies is sustenance to the mountain folk." The sergeant smiled. "Don't worry, when I take you for a real Greek meal in Limassol there will be no strouthos."

The muted thunder of machinery greeted the soldiers one morning when they awoke. An unwarranted pollution in the pristine raw beauty of the Troodos as the soldiers climbed yet another mountain slope, to find bulldozers clawing at its bowels. A crushing plant disgorged dust into the sky and the ground was covered in almost white earth.

"Asbestos quarry." Landris shouted into Hawkspurr's ear.

"Right, let's move on. There's no place here that anyone with common-sense would hide."

Once clear of the deadly dust, Landris explained that the ancient Greeks knew the secret of weaving the fibers. It formed a fireproof linen, which was used in cremation sheets—the body inside burnt to ashes, and the cloth was folded into a funeral urn, preserved forever.

On the low coastal hills, orange and olive groves gave way to shrubby evergreen vegetation, where Maquis grew from the rocks and provided habitation for pigeon, partridge, and salamanders. Here, the town of Paphos clings to the cliffs of Ktima a mixture of both Ionic and Ottoman churches, Chrysopolitissa Church, the Ayia Sophia Mosque, the Temple of Venus; shops, fishermen's homes, and old-fashioned mansions sprawling down to the western sea, but by now Hawkspurr and his men were weary and bored.

A radio call to Limassol brought the ever-obliging Royal Horse Guards to their aid with lorries and an escort of armored cars.

In the SAS base camp Inspector O'Connor was waiting for a debriefing, and to reclaim his sergeants. Mike Landris was to remain in his hometown of Limassol, and Nazim Avidar was returning to Kyrenia.

Hawkspurr discussed the operation for an hour, and promised O'Connor a written report by the following day.

The Special Branch officer was in good spirits, because despite an increase in murders, arson, and street fighting between Greek and Turkish civilians, intelligence work was producing good results resulting in the capture of several previously elusive couriers.

Talon Troop's operation had been directly responsible for flushing out one group of terrorists, into the arms of the Gordon Highlanders. These men had been ready to inform, and a considerable quantity of ammunition and other supplies were recovered from caves set deep in the mountainsides.

The man Hawkspurr had killed outside the Abbot's dining room, had been identified as one of Grivas's favorite lieutenants—a serious blow to EOKA, and the prisoner Christou Nissia had been taken back to the area in a helicopter where he was busy pointing out hideouts and supply dumps.

Regrettably Captain Nyles Hawkspurr was now listed high on the EOKA execution list, with the sobriquet 'Harding's Hoodlum'; obviously Amanda Carson or Gunter Von Harzburg had wasted no time in circulating his identity.

Hawkspurr was philosophical—"They'll just have to wait in the queue won't they!"

O'Connor shook his head. "Maybe, but keep a 'minder' with you at all times Hawk. Anyway the good news is that the troop has been granted seven days local leave, then you and I report personally to the Governor in Nicosia."

"Ok Jack. Will I see you over the next week?"

Mike Landris interrupted the conversation. "Yes, you're both invited to my family home tomorrow night, its time you sampled some real Cypriot hospitality."

"Fair enough." O'Connor agreed.

"I'll meet you at the Palace Hotel at 5 p.m. Hawk. You'll find it just past the police station."

Before going into town, Hawkspurr stopped for a chat with the motherly lady who ran a general store close to the entrance of the airfield. She and Tubby Wilson were doing a brisk business in extras for the Troop, and she made a great fuss of the British officer. Black olives, goat's cheese, and a bottle of Commanderia St John were placed before him as she proudly related the stories of Limassol.

During the Third Crusade of 1191, the self-appointed Emperor Isaac Comnenus refused an English vessel water, but unfortunately for Comnenus the ship carried Berengaria of Navarre, the fiancée of Richard Coeur-de-Lion, and King Richard's sister Joanna, the Queen Dowager of Sicily.

Seven days later the bulk of the English fleet arrived, and an angry Richard ordered a full-scale invasion. Isaac Comnenus surrendered, and was taken in silver chains to the dungeons of Margat in Palestine where he later died.

Richard married Berengaria in the chapel of St George at Limassol, crowning her Queen of England and himself King of Cyprus. He quickly realized the strategic and commercial value of the island, and subjugated the whole of Cyprus and then, always short of ready cash, the King offered the island to the knightly order of the Templars.

Limassol then enjoyed a couple of centuries of prosperity, before being sacked in turn Genoese, Egyptian Mamelukes, and Turks. It was the British late in the nineteenth century, who started the recovery of the town

Hawkspurr liked Limassol—in spite of the emergency it was lazy and a little vulgar; a sunny port with Customs Stores, ironmongeries and the twelfth century Venetian Castle.

A wide promenade, open cafes and cheerful tavernas supported by many light industries, food and tobacco products, perfumes, wine and beer.

The Landris home was a smallholding on the road to Nicosia, overlooking Akrotiri Bay. Olive and fruit trees were abundant, and goats and chickens roamed at will. A red-roofed villa sprawled amongst hazels and sycamores, and the large cobblestone courtyard was festooned with colored lights. In it, probably fifty people of all ages were gathered for the occasion decked out in their best Sunday clothes.

Amongst them a musician was softly singing rebetika—the songs of folklore and love—to the melodic embellishments of a mandolin-like instrument the bouzouki. A violinist, clarinet player, and drummer completed the quartet.

Hawkspurr and O'Connor were first introduced to Mike's wife Sophia and his cousin Eleni.

Sophia was animated and warm, and kissed Hawkspurr with an easy familiarity. "I must thank you for the beautiful lingerie you brought us from London Hawk. See!" She pulled slightly at the opening of her blouse, to reveal a fleeting glimpse of black lace, then laughing at her husband's discomfort Sophia declared. "It drives my Mikael crazy!"

O'Connor smirked and slapped Landris on the back. "So that was the mystery parcel!"

The Greek reddened, and grimaced at his wife. "Wicked woman. I shall beat you later! Take the Inspector and fill him with food and wine, I want Captain Hawkspurr to meet my beautiful cousin properly."

Mike Landris hooked his arms in those of Hawkspurr and Eleni, and led them to a circular seat beneath the branches of a gnarled fig tree. He produced a bottle of St Hilarion wine and poured three glasses.

"Yiasas Hawk, your continued good health now, as is the custom Eleni will be your partner for the evening and I will leave you two to become better acquainted."

Hawkspurr examined the girl with speculative eyes. Eleni was not exactly beautiful—perhaps pretty in an earthy, peasant mold. She had lustrous black hair, beguiling dark eyes, and a sturdy frame that would bear many strong children before declining into plump, complacent middle age.

Eleni was also bright, and certainly not shy. "My cousin admires you greatly Captain. Do you have a woman?"

Hawkspurr grinned. "Not on me!" But the humor was lost on the girl.

"I am spoken for." She stated solemnly.

"That's very nice. Where's your fiancé tonight?"

"He is working in London to save money for a home for us." Eleni smiled proudly. "I am a virgin."

"I wish I could say the same!"

Eleni smiled coyly. "Of course I can still satisfy a man…"

The glow from red wine, and the musky scent of the female were working their spell on Hawkspurr's senses, and as Eleni moved closer he could feel the heat from her body as their thighs touched. His loins stirred in response, and he quickly crossed his legs.

Eleni smiled; that enigmatic, feminine interaction of lips and eyes that always made Hawkspurr speculate that Da Vinci's Mona Lisa was being caressed during her sitting for the famous portrait. Eleni's hand moved along Hawkspurr's tense leg muscle to his groin.

"Come you two!" Sophia's sharp rebuke broke the spell. "You must eat and dance. You cannot keep the captain all for yourself Eleni."

Hawkspurr sucked in a quick sigh of relief? Or was it disappointment? He stood to his feet. "Let's dance Eleni and please, both of you call me Hawk."

Sophia took Hawkspurr's hand to lead him away, but Eleni stepped forward and raised her fingers to stroke the Englishman's nose.

"Yes you are a Hawk and the eyes!" She planted a kiss on Hawkspurr's mouth to the chagrin of her cousin's wife.

"Shameless girl!" Sophia tugged on Hawkspurr's arm. "There are others who wish to meet my husband's friend."

The tables guarded by elderly female relatives, were literally sagging beneath the weight of a traditional Greek Cypriot feast.

There was fish and octopus—baked, boiled and stewed—kakavia. Tiny meatballs in olive oil—keftedes. Meat ground with spiced rice and herbs, stuffed with vegetables and wrapped into vine leaves. Salty taramosalata, a pate made from cod roes. Salads of lettuce, radish, cucumber, tomato, with scallions, black olives, chunks of feta cheese and anchovies all mixed together in vinaigrette sauce and sprinkled with fresh mint. Spanokopita—spinach pie. Kalamari—stuffed squid. Dolmathis—stuffed cabbage leaves. Huge kidney shaped beans—gigantes. Chicken in tomato sauce and rice pilaf…The menu went on and on!

To compliment the repast, anise flavored Ouzo. Retsina—a resinated white wine, and mavrodaphni, sweet, dark and purple.

The candied fruits and sweet pastry were too much for Hawkspurr to even contemplate tasting.

Time to dance! The Tsamiko—a line dance sometimes called the handkerchief dance. Slow, dignified and warlike, and although primarily for men, women were now permitted to participate. Then the Kalamatiano—frolicsome and carefree, with the dancers moving in line each holding their neighbor's hand.

The rigors of the dance, spicy food and copious quantities of wine left Hawkspurr perspiring and wearied, and excusing himself from the company he sought respite on a bench beneath the fig trees. He still had a brimming glass in his hand—which was instantly topped up by the nearest Cypriot when the wine fell below the acceptable level.

Hawkspurr leaned back and closed his eyes, but in the background the music and laughter continued unabated. Then he heard a rustle of cotton skirts, felt a tendril of hair upon his cheek, and inhaled a musky fragrance as warm lips fastened upon his mouth.

"Would you like a swim to revive you Hawk?" Eleni sat on his lap, her buttocks conducting a tingle of electricity to his groin.

Hawkspurr's eyes flew open and he lifted the girl to her feet. "Great idea. Lead the way."

Eleni took Hawkspurr through a grove of olive trees, and down a rocky slope strewn with rosemary and wild marigolds to a warm sandy beach.

She paused only to divest herself of the simple frock, panties and bra, and kicking off her sandals ran for the water, the starlight highlighting her rotund buttocks and sturdy legs as she plunged headlong into the gentle surf.

Hawkspurr was already unbuttoning his civilian shirt and slacks as impatient feet pushed off his slip-on shoes, and he tripped to fall laughing on the fine sand.

Socks and underpants flew abandoned into the air, and in a shallow dive, he too embraced the soothing waves of the bay.

Hawkspurr surfaced to stand waist deep, and shook his head like a retriever to disperse the salt water. In front of him Eleni burst from the waves in a flurry of spray laughing gaily through enticing lips, a modern Aphrodite rising from the foam of Poseidon's dominion. The cool water cascaded down her body in a translucent veil that hardened nipples and breasts.

Hawkspurr dived again—his objective the pale thighs beneath the surface and still submerged, he turned on his back and grasped Eleni's bottom in both hands and placed his lips upon the dark mound. Taken by surprise, the woman resisted and reached down to wrestle with Hawkspurr who nearly choked.

He emerged from the depths coughing, laughing, and gasping for air as he reached out to kiss Eleni, but she dodged his advances and slapped at his erect penis.

"Please not here, come ashore."

Hawkspurr now fully aroused was in no mood for compromise, but again the woman was too quick for him as she plunged through the surf and ran for the shelter of the olive trees.

Yards ahead of Hawkspurr she flung herself on the grass and lay face down, her body heaving from the exertion. A panting Hawkspurr dropped to his knees beside Eleni, and gently rolled her over to kiss the wet face passionately. She in turn responded with a strength that took Hawkspurr by surprise as she turned him onto his back, and straddled his hips in one swift movement.

Eleni pinned his shoulders with strong hands, and smiled. "Lay still, and you shall experience your Greek!"

Standing over Hawkspurr, she reached up and picked a number of ripe olives, then with firm palms she crushed the fruit and as the rich oil flowed applied it between her buttocks.

Eleni sank down once more on Hawkspurr, and carefully inserted the hard penis into her body. She moaned in ecstasy as the man thrust forward impatiently uttering a cry of pleasurable pain and excitement.

Slowly at first then gaining momentum as her own passion reached a crescendo, Eleni manipulated her pelvis to bring Hawkspurr fulfillment in an orgasm of pent up sexual desire.

"Ye gods!" Hawkspurr released the breasts he had been kneading, and slid his hands up to the woman's neck. He pulled Eleni's face to his, and kissed her with a grateful ardor that thanked the woman for her gift of love.

As Hawkspurr lay back and relaxed tense muscles, Eleni left him to retrieve their clothes from the beach. She returned with a damp neck scarf, and tenderly washed Hawkspurr's genitals before stretching out beside him.

"Thank you Hawk—I needed to feel a man again." She stroked the handsome face now in repose.

"Tomorrow I will show you our town, and take you to secret places that the tourists do not see."

"No thank you Eleni, I am indebted to you and my need too was strong, but for you to be seen in my company would be dangerous."

Hawkspurr thought sadly of another woman in far off Malaya; an innocent girl he had loved, and who died at the hands of a terrorist because of that love.

"Although we may never meet again I will not forget you. Is that enough?"

"If you say so Hawk." Eleni kissed him gently. "Now we must return to the party and tell of our wonderful swim. Yes?"

"Indeed yes."

Breakfast in the SAS camp on the following morning, was a sorry-looking collection of hung over, bleary-eyed men. Hawkspurr fared better than most—probably because he had eaten well. The other members of Talon Troop had also patently adopted evil Billy's adage, that food spoils the taste of good liquor.

Only Doctor Faulconer was absent, as he was staying at the home of a medical colleague.

Hawkspurr surveyed his 'elite' Soldiers without pity. 'Self inflicted wounds!' indeed!

"Right lads, I suggest a day at the seaside. A run on the beach, and a hard swim will temper those flabby muscles once more. Tubby, make up sandwiches and I'll purchase a crate of beer for medicinal purposes. You can all wear civilian clothes, but carry small-arms."

After arranging for a camp guard from the Blues, Hawkspurr dressed in casual slacks and shirt and strapped on his pistol. Sergeant McDonald would drive the Champ, with Corporal McKenzie riding shotgun.

The three drove off, leaving the remainder of the troop to follow in the truck.

"Drive directly to the Keo brewery Billy. The beer will be cheaper there than the NAAFI canteen, and we'll meet the lads at the beach."

In the vicinity of the brewery, the aroma of malt and hops emanating from the chimneystacks was too much for Evil Billy. "Jeez boss I reckon if there is a place for warriors—Valhalla will smell just like this. I'd crawl through a room of 'joe blakes' (snakes) for a cold one right now."

"Ok, I'll see if we can sample a brew before we buy, I have the urge for a little fun." An idea was forming in Hawkspurr's mind.

The Champ halted in front of the administration offices, and as McDonald jumped impatiently from the vehicle Hawkspurr restrained him.

"Wait here Billy until I've spoken with manager."

An attractive, smiling woman greeted Hawkspurr at the reception counter. "Good morning sir. May I help you?"

"I hope so. I'm Captain Brownale—newly appointed inspector for central mess purchasing." Solemnly Hawkspurr flashed his SAS permanent pass, and replaced it before the woman could read his name.

"Thank you sir, I'll fetch the manager." She moved with unseemly haste through a door behind her desk.

The manager appeared promptly—rubbing his hands together in the manner peculiar to the Levant, and his smile beaming a genuine welcome.

"Captain." He bowed, "I am Mister Stavros, please accompany me and I will show you our complete range of beverages."

"I do have my driver and escort with me…?"

The manager gesticulated expansively. "By all means bring your men in. Your vehicle is quite safe here." He spoke rapidly in Greek to the receptionist, who departed to summon McDonald and McKenzie.

The party was led up a flight of stairs to the flat roof, where two young men had obviously received their orders and were opening the shutters of a display area at one end.

A blue and white awning was lowered, and wrought iron chairs and a table placed for the visitors.

"Please be seated gentlemen." Stavros clapped his hands and the subordinates brought bottles of wines and spirits, which they arranged on the table.

Hawkspurr slowly lifted each bottle in turn, inspected the label and contents intently.

McDonald coughed pointedly and raised his eyebrows in supplication.

"Perhaps a cold beer for my men to sample?" Hawkspurr smiled at Stavros.

"Of course, of course!" There was more clapping of hands and rapid instructions as Stavros smiled apologetically. "I thought it might be too early in the day."

Hawkspurr nodded sagely. "One must not shirk one's duty."

Within minutes the table was laden with chilled plates of salami, olives, nuts, and bottles of beer, and cheese.

With little urging from Captain Brownale, Mister Stavros and his assistants were soon sampling their own products, and ensuring that the soldiers' glasses never quite dried out.

After a period, Sergeant McDonald excused himself with the pretext that he had forgotten to disable the Champ's motor.

'Unlikely!' thought Hawkspurr, as the Australian disappeared on some secret mission of his own.

Even in the glow of good company and flowing alcohol, Hawkspurr kept his back to the wall and the loaded pistol in its holster. He held the manager engrossed with tales of other lands—especially London, which seemed to be the Mecca for ambitious Cypriot businessmen.

McKenzie had succumbed to the pleading of the younger men to demonstrate the working of the Sten gun, but was of course careful to remove the magazine and all ammunition.

There was no hiding the self-satisfied smirk, and flushed features that Evil Billy displayed when he eventually returned to the table, and as Hawkspurr looked into the over-bright eyes he knew; 'the bastard has just seduced the receptionist!'

Captain Brownale and his escort subsequently departed from the brewery with sufficient beer and wine to stock a small canteen.

The remainder of the day was spent pleasantly on a guarded beach, swimming, eating, drinking, and dozing in the warmth of the Mediterranean sun.

As the men tidied themselves up and changed into slacks and shirts, Evil Billy and Jimmy McKenzie sidled up to Hawkspurr.

"Boss?" McDonald wheedled.

"What's on your evil little brain Billy?"

"There's a brothel on the outskirts of town that should be searched boss."

McKenzie added his encouragement. "Regular terrorist hangout sir, I wouldn't be at all surprised to find Grivas there."

"I see. And do all the men feel the same way?" Hawkspurr tried to look serious.

"Abso-bloody-lutely sir."

"Very well, a little excitement would round off an extremely nice day."

The men gathered around Hawkspurr. "Gentlemen, since the Military Police are enormously over-worked, we are going to render them our professional assistance. You will scrupulously search each room of the target establishment, paying particular attention to all female occupants. For security reasons you must complete your task in thirty minutes, and on this occasion I will stand guard for you. Cover your collective asses—so to speak. I trust that you're all carrying prophylactics to protect your smaller weapons!"

The two vehicles drove at speed into the neglected grounds of an equally run-down villa on the outskirts of Limassol, and as they halted at the portico entrance, a dozen Cypriot men seated in line on the verandah leapt up in alarm. Like startled rabbits, they were unsure of whether to run or pretend that they were invisible to the hunter.

"Right Billy, check their identity cards and search these men first. We might as well do a proper job." Hawkspurr entered the foyer.

Gilded mirrors, several Victorian sofas and overstuffed armchairs comprised the furnishings, but the sole occupant was a large lady dressed in black satin.

Hawkspurr strode confidently across threadbare carpets, and bowed low in front of the woman as he presented her with a bottle of wine. His smile would have charmed the Eunuch of a Sultan's harem, and gained him immediate entry to the forbidden realm of females.

"I regret the inconvenience madam, but it is my sad duty to conduct a routine search of your delightful premises."

The lady in black pursed her lips coquettishly, and patted the seat beside her ample hips. "I fully understand sir. Let us enjoy a glass of wine, whilst your men err...investigate my young ladies." Her voice rose quizzically as she finished the sentence, and at the same time she lifted a small silver bell from the table at her elbow.

The tinkling chimes brought prompt response in the form of a teenage girl dressed in a diaphanous negligee—and little else—who appeared from a curtained archway.

"Open this bottle Irene, and bring two glasses."

The girl bobbed a curtsey, furtively eyeing the handsome man from under her long silken lashes before leaving the room.

As Irene departed, Sergeant McDonald and the troopers entered shuffling their feet impatiently.

Hawkspurr indicated the broad flight of stairs. "Check each room thoroughly Sergeant, but please treat the ladies with respect."

Evil Billy was already ascending the stairs two strides at a time and his men followed eagerly, playfully elbowing each other aside as they vied to be first upstairs.

Hawkspurr smiled at his hostess. "My men are very keen to perform their duty!"

The lady in black patted Hawkspurr's knee affectionately. "And what about their gallant leader? Irene is free of any engagements at the moment."

"On this occasion a glass of wine and your scintillating company will suffice, thank you madam."

As Irene poured the wine for Hawkspurr and her employer, cries of dismay and the slamming of doors echoed from the floors above. Several men in various stages of undress came scuttling down the staircase, and bolted for the front exit muttering in protest. The lady in black raised an ornate fan to cover her expression of wicked amusement, and whispered to Hawkspurr.

"Do not worry, they will be back!"

Hawkspurr lifted his glass in salute. "I have no doubt of that madam."

"You have not yet properly introduced yourself sir." The lady in black reminded Hawkspurr.

Hawkspurr didn't hesitate. "I'm sorry Madam, O'Connor. 'Jack O'Connor.'"

"And do you have any authority with the local government Mister O'Connor?"

"Very little I'm afraid."

"A pity. At this time my house is out of bounds for British servicemen. I could be most generous for the right kind of help?"

Hawkspurr grinned. "In that case madam. I will be happy to pass on your concerns to the proper authority."

Half an hour passed very quickly, as the lady in black told Hawkspurr of her early days in Athens and the many important officials and dignitaries who had been her lovers.

"In those times, my clients even brought their sons to me when they reached puberty."

She finished proudly, then reached across and held Hawkspurr's chin in her hand, looking deep into the warm brown eyes. "But you will never have to resort to whores young sir! Now go, and let my ladies get back to work." Playfully she slapped Hawkspurr's bottom as he stood up from the sofa.

"Thank you for your hospitality madam. I wish you long life and prosperity." As he kissed the proffered hand, Hawkspurr's soldiers came straggling down the stairs and quietly left the building.

It was the perfect end to a delightful day.

# CHAPTER 13

Inspector O'Connor's police car was followed into camp by a Land Rover containing four uniformed Military Policemen.

As ordered, Hawkspurr was ready and waiting, dressed in a lightweight civilian suit of tropical tan with a cream shirt. Since he had also been told to appear as inconspicuous as possible, he had substituted a rather plain dark brown tie in place of his regimental colors. His Colt pistol was snug in its customary place, in the waist-belt at the small of his back.

"Brought an old friend to see you Hawk, but don't be too long please." O'Connor did not get out of the car, as Hawkspurr handed his suitcase and carryall to the Turkish driver. Curious, Hawkspurr looked over to the Land Rover as the broad shouldered figure of an officer wearing a red-topped cap stepped out.

"John Sutton! You old ba…" Hawkspurr's smile of welcome froze as the tall officer moved away from him and entered the nearest tent.

"I'd like a word in private please Captain." Sutton looked grim.

Hawkspurr blinked blindly, as he followed Military Policeman into the dark interior of the tent and was immediately grabbed in a crushing bear hug from behind.

"Gotcha Hawk!" Sutton released Hawkspurr and stepped back laughing.

"Good to see you too John. I thought you were skiving off safely in Blighty, whilst I was defending the Empire. What's more I still haven't heard what happened to you and Patricia Wyndyatt after the Regimental Ball."

"Then you'll be pleased to learn that Lady Patricia has consented to be my wife. But! She refuses to set a date until Nyles Hawkspurr is free to be my Best Man."

"Congratulations old son, this calls for a drink."

From a hip pocket Hawkspurr removed a silver plated flask. "Have a snort of Cognac."

"I'm on duty Hawk." Protested Sutton, "And besides I have another bone to pick with you."

"Horse feathers. Take off that silly cap and sit down for a minute." Hawkspurr pushed his friend back to a camp bed and sat beside him.

"Cheers!" He swallowed a mouthful of Cognac and handed the flask to Sutton.

"Very well. Since I understand that you are off on another deed of derring-do I'll drink with you." Sutton took a drink. "Cheers! Now…during the routine inspection of certain bordellos, a lady complained that a very handsome and charming Jack O'Connor had already turned her over the day before. Since I'm well acquainted with the Inspector from Special Branch, the glowing description didn't quite fit the bill. Then I learnt that Captain Hawkspurr and his pirate crew were in the district!"

Hawkspurr reached for the flask and took another sip. He shook his head solemnly. "It sounds like a case of mistaken identity John. Sorry I can't stay and chat longer but the Governor General awaits."

Sutton laughed. "Ok you bastard, but in future keep your nose clean on my patch!" He shook Hawkspurr's hand, "Good luck on your trip."

Hawkspurr was puzzled. "I'm only going to Nicosia for a couple of days John."

Sutton tapped the side of his nose. "That's not the official word Hawk. Anyway, whenever you get back we'll fix a date for my wedding."

Hawkspurr slid onto the rear seat of the car next to O'Connor, and barely had time to wave goodbye before the driver sped off.

"I understand that you and Sutton were at school together." O'Connor looked out of the window. "He's a nice chap, and highly thought of in security circles."

Hawkspurr's brain was racing with possibilities. "What's this about a prolonged trip Jack?"

"Later Hawk. We'll be lunching with the Governor, then you'll find out."

"Right Jack, but when you asked me to pack a dinner jacket and dark suit, I assumed we were going to be partying with the brass in Government House."

O'Connor didn't reply, so Hawkspurr put his head back and went to sleep.

Lunch in Government House proved to be a rather dismal affair, and no wine was served. Hawkspurr as the junior officer present was unusually subdued and spoke only when directly addressed. The Governor was preoccupied with a middle-aged civilian simply introduced as The Minister, who was engrossed in an earnest dissertation regarding the politics of the Middle East.

Hawkspurr's curiosity and apprehension were heightened by the presence of the uncommunicative Brigadier Hazlett, whom he had not seen since his mission to Spain. Inspector O'Connor also appeared to be under some pressure and sat stolidly throughout the meal, attentive to the speaker but making no comment.

As he finished the light dessert, Sir John rose briskly to his feet and spoke to the attending steward.

"The Minister and I will take coffee in my office, please show Brigadier Hazlett and the other gentlemen to the drawing room."

As the Governor issued his instructions, Hawkspurr stood deferentially and Sir John caught his eye. "Relax Captain, you've been doing a splendid job and we'll talk later." He smiled warmly.

"Thank you sir." The Governor with his ADC and the Minister left the dining room.

"This way please gentlemen." The white-coated sergeant steward led the brigadier, Hawkspurr and O'Connor to a sunny room overlooking the gardens.

"Coffee will be served shortly gentlemen. Excuse me." The man closed the doors quietly behind him.

Brigadier Hazlett seated himself, and indicated that the others should do likewise.

"Down to business then gentlemen. I understand that you've already been briefed at your own level Inspector?"

"Yes sir."

Hawkspurr looked quizzically at O'Connor, but the policeman avoided eye contact.

The Brigadier continued. "The situation here in Cyprus is changing rapidly, and from a purely military point of view we are on top of the terrorist campaign. However the politicians in London favor a more diplomatic solution, and are pressing for the military governor to be replaced by a civilian. Be that as it may, you both know that the indiscriminate killing continues in the streets." The brigadier stopped speaking when a steward entered the room to serve coffee.

He then continued. "The minister from Whitehall, is about to embark upon a diplomatic mission to gain support from those nations with a vested interest in the Middle East, and reiterate the British position. These meetings are highly confidential, and the Minister's life will most certainly be in jeopardy should his intentions leak out."

The Brigadier opened his briefcase and handed a large envelope to Hawkspurr, and at the same time addressed O'Connor. "You have your own documentation and instructions Inspector?"

"Yes sir. I'm to accompany the Minister and his private secretary as a personal assistant."

"Correct. You on the other hand Nyles will travel incognito, remaining at all times in close proximity to the Minister, but never approaching him. Should the need arise for any discussion or change of plan, Inspector O'Connor will find a means to contact you discreetly."

Hawkspurr surreptitiously winked at O'Connor. "Yes sir."

"Right. In your folder you'll find your itinerary, travel tickets, cash and travelers checks. You have a diplomatic passport in the name of Francis Drake." The brigadier glanced at O'Connor and gave him a wry smile.

"Captain Hawkspurr has a peculiar sense of humor the name Drake is one he is particularly fond of using!"

He turned his attention back to Hawkspurr. "This time you are a Cultural Under-Secretary. The minister will cover his activities with a great deal of sightseeing, so it will not be detrimental for you to be seen in the same locations. Inspector O'Connor will organize your invitations to any official functions through the local Embassy. However your brief is to remain nondescript, and inconsequential as befits a minor diplomat. Learn to slump a little Nyles, and resist any thought of conquest regarding international secretaries!"

Hawkspurr smiled inwardly. 'Fat chance. Once the Minister is tucked up safely for the night!'

"What about carrying weapons sir?" O'Connor was all business.

"Your choice Inspector. You won't be subjected to Customs searches, and airlines still have no policy on security measures." The brigadier frowned, "That will have to change one day." He inclined his head to Hawkspurr. "Are you still sporting your cannon Nyles?"

"Yes sir, Colt .45. But I'm using a low charge and soft-nose shells. They'll stop anyone, but not exit to hit bystanders."

"Excellent. Well good luck to you both, I'm off back to London this evening." The brigadier shook hands with both men. "On the return leg of your journey Nyles you'll report to me in Whitehall, but I won't bother you with the details just now. Goodbye."

Brigadier Hazlett departed, and Hawkspurr and O'Connor drank another cup of coffee. Hawkspurr laced his drink with cognac, and offered the flask to the policeman.

"Not whilst on duty, thank you Captain Hawkspurr." He frowned with disapproval."

Hawkspurr raised his cup with a cheeky grin. "Cheers then, me old flatfoot!"

O'Connor grunted. "I'm off to my room, there'll be little rest after tonight."

Hawkspurr wandered into the garden, and down to the perimeter where the Governor's escort of Royal Horse Guards was billeted in tents. The Troop was busy washing down immaculate armored cars, each one named after Alexanda Dumas' famous musketeers, and stripping and cleaning their weapons. He knew better than to disturb the work, and walked away.

"Captain Hawkspurr." The tall, gray haired figure of the minister approached across the lawns and beckoned him.

Hawkspurr halted, and automatically assumed a position of attention. "Sir?"

The minister was wearing a shirt with the sleeves rolled up, and a pair of old khaki shorts. "Mind if I walk with you?"

"No sir." Hawkspurr was wary of all politicians. He resumed his stroll.

"Are you aware that I specifically requested you as an escort Captain?" The minister crinkled keen blue eyes.

Hawkspurr warmed to the man.

"No sir."

"Oh yes. I know a great deal about you Hawk." The lips lifted slightly at the corners. "Sorry I don't have an exotic princess for a niece!"

To his credit, Hawkspurr's face reddened with a blush. 'How on earth did the bloody man know about the Puteri Fazima in Malaya?' he thought.

The minister laughed outright. "No need to be embarrassed—all to your credit, and the Sultan awarded you a decoration to boot!"

"Well I did also top a couple of his enemies." Hawkspurr was on the defensive again.

"Quite. It's that quality of initiative, and your ability to react quickly in any given situation that I admire. I take your courage for granted."

Hawkspurr was mollified. "Thank you sir."

"We have a lot in common Hawk—do you mind me calling you Hawk?"

Hawkspurr shook his head, and the two men muttered in unison, "Just don't call me late for breakfast!" They laughed together.

"I've not always been a politician Hawk. During the last war I too was a Guardsman before joining David Stirling in the Special Air Service."

Hawkspurr halted abruptly and faced the Minister. "I had no idea sir, I feel I owe you an apology." He held out his hand to the older man. "I'm afraid I've cultured a little contempt for all politicians—always thought they were self-serving."

"Understandable—and warranted in many cases. Even now there are those who oppose our present policy here in Cyprus, and just want us to pack up and go home."

The minister looked pensive. "There are more whisperings of unrest in Suez, Aden, Jordan and Lebanon Hawk, and the communists are poised to exploit any weakness we show in this region. The whole of the Middle East is a powder keg, just waiting for someone to light the fuse."

"Then we can't afford to lose any of our military and naval bases sir."

"No indeed Hawk. That's why my mission is of the utmost importance. Did Brigadier Hazlett mention another job he has you in mind for?"

"Only that I have to report to him on the return leg of our journey sir."

"Ok we'll leave it for the time being—need to know and all that eh?"

"Sir."

"We'll speak together later when the opportunity arises Hawk. I need an impartial sounding board for some of my ideas—someone without political motives or aspirations." "Anytime sir." Hawkspurr was flattered.

The minister took a swing with an imaginary racquet. "How about a few sets of tennis before dinner? There'll be no time for exercise once we move."

"You're on sir. Just give me a moment to go and change, and I'll meet you at the courts."

Although the minister proved a more skillful player, Hawkspurr's speed and superb fitness balanced the difference. Albeit, Hawkspurr had the grace to allow his superior to win the match—just!

For Hawkspurr the following days were more intensely stressful than any active operation he had so far engaged in. He was only able to relax and sleep in the various aircraft once they were in flight. He ate the lightest of meals, and avoided alcohol in any form. Of boarding clerks he insisted they allot him an aisle seat on the opposite side of the fuselage from the minister, and at least two rows back.

Road transport was provided in each country by the relevant Embassy. A plain car that would excite no curiosity or special attention for the minister and his party, and for Hawkspurr a local taxi with an Embassy driver. This had been Hawkspurr's own idea, after considering the various scenarios he might be required to act in.

A taxi driven erratically, or taking unseemly risks by cutting in and out of traffic would not be unusual in any city in the world, and it was also imperative that the driver did not lose contact with the prime car.

The hustle and bustle of international airports entailed extra vigilance on Hawkspurr's part, with jostling crowds of people all speaking too loudly in their own language, as they tried to communicate with traveling companions served to heighten the strained atmosphere.

In these situations Hawkspurr struggled to keep close to the minister.

Ignoring the male secretary and O'Connor, his eyes roved constantly over anyone—man or woman who approached or passed Mickey, Donald and Pluto, as Hawkspurr had nicknamed his charges.

Mickey and Donald—the minister and Mr Radley moved along cool and unconcerned, but Pluto—O'Connor, displayed his nervousness with tense shoulders and jerky head movements. He was covering the minister's back so closely, that Hawkspurr had a vision of them tripping over each other—he smiled fleetingly at the thought.

The drill for formal meetings was always the same in each country; the minister met his counterpart alone whilst O'Connor guarded the door along with local security men.

Mr Radley invariably stayed in his hotel room, presumably writing up the minister's notes and reports.

Hawkspurr remained on the outside of whichever building housed the conference venue. In spite of the checks by local police he carefully scrutinized all who entered. He didn't have a great deal of confidence regarding the dedication to duty of either Greek or Turkish officials—their attitude being both casual and careless.

Hawkspurr was personally concerned with the whereabouts of Gunter Von Harzburg and Amanda Carson, neither had been seen or heard of since the incident at the Monastery of Stavadhi. A worry he had not conveyed to the Minister or O'Connor, since he was confident that whatever disguise either adopted he could detect their personal mannerisms.

As a keen student of history Hawkspurr's one regret was that he couldn't fully enjoy the sites of ancient civilizations and splendor the party visited. The Minister was considerate in the extreme, and having empathy similar to Hawkspurr, lingered wherever possible and practical in those places of special interest to them both.

Standing in the shadows cast by that masterpiece of Greek classical architecture the Parthenon, Hawkspurr could sense the palpable spirit of the ancients within the Doric Temple. In the Erechtheum he didn't see ruins—only the beauty of delicate graceful carvings, and was compelled to caress the statues of maidens eternally facing south in their task of supporting the great porch.

As they moved off the Acropolis, the Minister couldn't resist looking over his shoulder at Hawkspurr, and smiling at him in understanding.

After Athens they flew on, to where the strait of the Bosporus separates Europe from Asia. For some obscure reason, the Turkish Minister wanted to hold the conference in his country's largest city Istanbul, as opposed to the capital Ankara. The venue chosen was the magnificent 19$^{th}$ century palace Dolma Bagtcheh.

Hawkspurr was conscious of an undercurrent of excitement, and joy of living within the colorful city. It was a vibrant contrast of narrow back streets and peasants, wide boulevards, colorful bazaars, museums rich with treasures of antiquity, and dazzling buildings with slender minarets. The superb mosque of Saint Sophia once a 6$^{th}$ century church, was breathtaking in its beauty, and the Seraglio which includes the courts of the former Sultans, was imbued with an ambience of splendid decadence and opulence.

Before leaving Turkey the Minister made a pilgrimage to Scutari, and visited the hospital where Florence Nightingale served during the Crimean War.

There was no opportunity to leave Heathrow Airport during the wait for an onward flight to New York.

The minister had been assigned a private VIP room, and since British police were responsible for security he saw no reason why Hawkspurr shouldn't join him. Over a light meal the minister edited his current reports with Mr Radley, and these were dispatched by courier to Whitehall.

"Hawk, would you consider doing me a personal favor? Granted it's not in your job description but I do consider you a lot more than a 'minder'."

Now the minister sounded like a politician!

"Of course sir. I'll do anything to help—within my capabilities."

"Good man. After Washington my official business in America is finished, and I've promised myself a bit of rest and relaxation. Our host will be an old friend of mine, who served with OSS in France during the war. As you may know, the U.S. have formed a new Special Forces Group based on our own SAS—what's more they have adopted our commandos' green beret. I suppose we should be flattered! The General has requested that you have an informal chat with the officers about your experiences behind the lines in Korea, and the jungle operations in Malaya and Kenya, also as much as you want to disclose about the Cyprus campaign. Remember that these are mostly young men without first-hand knowledge of clandestine operations except from the text books, and being of a similar age I can assure you of a most appreciative audience."

"Well if it'll do some good sir—I owe my present good health to the American Forces in Korea. If it hadn't been for their nursing after I was wounded, I might still be in a wheelchair. All the same I think we should stick with my code-name 'Sparrowhawk'."

"Fair enough, and I don't have to impress upon you that old Britain needs all the friends it can muster just now."

The minister's next task was to address the Security Council of the United Nations, and the party were housed in a central New York hotel, adjacent to the Empire State building and the Rockefeller Center.

The short trip to the imposing U.N. Secretariat Building in Manhattan was a nightmare for Hawkspurr. Now the term 'concrete jungle' held some real significance for him; no other city in the world was so dominating with its noise and frantic traffic.

Everyone he met spoke too loud, and appeared to be late for an appointment elsewhere. Worst of all the minister insisted on walking along 5$^{th}$ Avenue to shop for his family, but the spectacle of a self-conscious O'Connor festooned with colorful plastic carrier bags, more than compensated Hawkspurr for his own unease.

On one occasion someone threw an Ambassadorial party at the Statue of Liberty, which entailed a ferry trip on the harbor. On the boat, there were more pretty girls from the secretariat offices buzzing around the distinguished minister from Britain than Hawkspurr could cope with.

New Yorkers seemed to eat incessantly, and the variety and quantity of food served at interminable cocktail parties and receptions was generous in the extreme.

Hawkspurr's white sharkskin dinner jacket, tailored two years earlier was getting somewhat snug around the waistline, and on the last evening before leaving the city he insisted that the party visit the hotel gymnasium and sauna.

Washington was the most beautiful—and the most sterile—city Hawkspurr had visited.

The itinerary for the minister was precise, and regulated every step of the way from the Pentagon to the White House.

His meeting with President Eisenhower was discreet and unofficial—it was only the fact that the Minister had served for a time in Europe with the former Supreme Commander that enabled him to be received as 'a friend'.

The minister's official duties ceased after a second visit to the Pentagon. Hawkspurr disliked the huge air-conditioned complex with its artificial lighting and seemingly endless corridors, but was impressed with the amount of technology available, and the enthusiasm of the military intelligence staff he met.

That night he was the recipient of the local intelligence community's generosity. After the Minister had retired for the night, a discreet knock at Hawkspurr's door announced the arrival of a 'token of alliance' in the form of a very lovely, very accommodating, very professional young lady.

Hawkspurr was very delighted.

The last day was both hectic and enjoyable, starting with a visit to Arlington Cemetery where the Minister laid a wreath on the Tomb of the Unknown Soldier. Then a tour of Washington's Colonial heritage, which was revered in carefully preserved historical buildings and by citizens wearing period costumes and performing daily tasks in the manner of their predecessors.

Flying south—this time in a military aircraft, they had a brilliant view of the Appalachian Mountains before landing at a huge military base.

Hawkspurr's 'informal chat', was delivered from a podium to a sea of eager faces.

The NCOs and enlisted men had decided that 'Sparrowhawk' was their guest as well as the officers. And in the officers' club that night, Hawkspurr instigated a favorite Mess game of the British—the steeplechase, conducted over all available furniture! Tactfully, the General and the Minister disappeared early in the evening so as not to cramp the exuberance of younger officers.

Hawkspurr woke next morning to find that he was now an honorary Sheriff of the district, and with a hangover to match. The General meantime had decided that selected men should take part in a plain-clothes exercise; therefore a military transport was authorized to convey the group to Las Vegas.

As the General hypothesized, it was not beyond the realms of possibility that subversives might some day seize the gambling Mecca!

The sojourn in a city of neon lights that never sleeps came to an end with a regular flight to Los Angeles, then on to London and a farewell luncheon with the minister in the Dorchester Hotel. Inspector O'Connor had been granted leave, and had already left for Liverpool by train.

Brigadier Hazlett telephoned during lunch to arrange a breakfast meeting, and therefore it was necessary for Hawkspurr to spend the night in the hotel.

The Minister had some advice for Hawkspurr when they parted. "You have a bright future Hawk, and I'll be watching you—metaphorically speaking. Try not to show your impatience with any fools in authority, they'll do their best to curb you. We all answer to some master, but remember that ultimately in the field only your judgment will determine the actions you take—and therefore your fate."

Brigadier Hazlett knocked on the door at precisely 0700 hours where Hawkspurr was showered, dressed, packed, and was about to pour the tea for breakfast.

"Scrambled egg and bacon suit you sir?"

"Excellent. None of that continental rolls nonsense." The brigadier peered closely at Hawkspurr's upper lip. "Good. Growing a proper military moustache I see."

"Yes sir. Someone at the base remarked on my youthful appearance, and I'm trying to look a little more imposing!"

As is the custom in most decent regimental messes, breakfast was eaten in respectful silence, and the two remained silent until a room service waiter had cleared the table and departed.

The brigadier smiled woefully at Hawkspurr. "It seems that the only time we dine together, I'm about to ask you to stick your neck out for your country."

Hawkspurr shrugged. "That's why I took the Queen's shilling sir."

"Quite. My main reason for using you this time, is because I believe that Gunter Von Harzburg and Miss Georghiades—or Amanda Carson as you know her, are involved. I do keep a man in Cairo, but he's a civilian and doesn't carry your designation, neither does he have your knowledge of the villains in question."

"My designation sir?"

"Yes. Your 'EYES ONLY' file lists you as 'Sparrowhawk OSN'—Office of Strategic Neutralization."

"Does that mean another wet job sir?"

"If required Nyles." The Brigadier frowned. "Are you still up to it?"

"I'll do my duty sir."

"Of course you will Nyles, I am sorry."

Brigadier Hazlett became brusque. "We don't concern ourselves with politics Nyles, but I'm sure that you understand the ramifications resulting from President Nasser's nationalization of the Suez Canal?"

"Yes. Egypt can now hold us to ransom, as far as our trade and troop movements to and from the Far East are concerned."

"Exactly, but it also signals the rise of Arab Unity and Nationalism, threatening not only the stability of the area but a certain rise in the price of crude oil. As we speak, the Communist bloc is pouring in modern weapons, military aircraft and Soviet officers in the guise of civilian 'technical advisers'."

The brigadier looked grim, and Hawkspurr sat quietly analyzing the implications as a soldier.

"Now for our part Nyles." The brigadier shuffled papers from his briefcase. "The MV Mount Nimba which you last saw in Cadiz, has disappeared. I've had no communication from our contact Mr Borg, so I must assume he was compromised after your disposal of Manos Androulakis. The Navy was waiting to shadow the vessel in the Mediterranean, but patently the Captain decided to remain in the Atlantic. It's possible that he has a customer for his arms in one of the emerging African states, but perhaps he is trying to deceive us by entering Suez from the Red Sea."

"So the arms shipment could still be destined for Cyprus sir?"

"Yes, my contention is that Egypt is so anxious to get us out of Cyprus, they'll assist EOKA by all means available. I further believe that Von Harzburg and Carson are acting as agents for Grivas—your job is to confirm this for me. Our best ally at the moment is a member of the Israeli Secret Service; naturally they have their own agenda, and I think they are preparing to attack the Egyptians in the Sinai Peninsular. What action Britain and France will eventually take is the major point of discussion now in both parliaments. As usual some politicians favor war, and others appeasement."

Hawkspurr snorted angrily. "So the poor old bloody soldier can expect the usual executive cocks-up!"

"Hmm…quite! This time you'll be traveling as an Irish scholar visiting the Holy Land and Egypt, I understand that you can manage a passable brogue, and Egyptians assume that all Irish hate the English!"

"Usually under the influence of Guinness in the mess sir."

"That should suffice for our Egyptian friends Nyles, just avoid any Catholic priests."

"Point taken sir. When do I leave and what's my name?"

"You'll be flying out later today under the name Michael Johnson, a genuine scholar whose background will stand up to any security checks. Once you've made contact with Yosef Buber in Jerusalem, you're free to move and act independently. However, for reasons I can't reveal you must be out of Egypt by 21October."

# CHAPTER 14

Hawkspurr, as befitted his scholarly rank booked into a modest hostelry close to the promenade in Tel Aviv. The beach looked inviting, and although it was late afternoon many bathers still disported in the sea.

Hawkspurr chose a spot near a group of pretty, suntanned girls and enjoyed himself amidst the carefree laughter for half an hour. Despite the many interested looks he received, he avoided striking up any conversation—and the resulting questions from the curious.

Later he strolled along wide, tree-lined avenues observing these energetic people. Every man and woman from the age of eighteen to fifty seemed to be in uniform, yet they had an air of anticipation and even gaiety in their posture. Without wishing to be patronizing, Hawkspurr could only wonder how they would fare when they faced the real horrors of war.

Seated in a moderately priced cafe, he savored the cosmopolitan cultures and different languages of a people united by a common religion. But to Hawkspurr's surprise the main topic of conversation was not war, but music and art—the attitude of young people who saw only a bright future, and not the possible annihilation of the State of Israel.

After breakfast Hawkspurr settled his account and walked to the bus station. His instructions were to travel to Jerusalem by road and make his way to the Old City. Since partition in 1948, the Jews held the Northern and Western suburbs as capital of the new state of Israel, and the Arabs controlled the Old City and Eastern suburbs.

At the checkpoint in no-man's-land all bags were searched perfunctorily—the Arabs still relying heavily on tourism as a major source of revenue.

He walked down Nablus Road and entered the walls through the Damascus gate, with guide book in hand and a box Brownie camera at the ready he attached himself surreptitiously to a guided party of pious tourists speaking English.

At the junction of Via Delorosa—the path of sorrow that followed the route taken by Jesus from condemnation to crucifixion—the masses of pilgrims became almost hysterical. Here at the station of the cross where the object of their worship fell for the first time, they all knelt to pray.

Many people were now carrying wooden crosses, and Hawkspurr was not at all happy in the crowd of sweating humanity; however his orders were quite clear, he was not to separate himself from the mainstream of tourists. He avoided all eye contact with his companions, and dutifully followed the pilgrims around the numerous historical and religious sites. Jerusalem was both hilly and confusing, but fortunately the heat of autumn was not oppressive.

Hawkspurr had endeavored to tone down his appearance somewhat, by combing his untrimmed hair over his forehead and rounding his shoulders. He was dressed in unpressed gray flannels, sensible walking brogues, and a short-sleeved green shirt.

Over his arm he carried a tweed hacking jacket, and his canvas backpack held only a spare shirt, underwear and toiletries. To compensate for the weight of his pistol and extra ammunition concealed in the false bottom, it also held a large bible with a prominent cross on the cover—no self respecting Muslim was going to remove that from his pack.

At five minutes to three, Hawkspurr was in position at the Moors Gate—the entrance for non-Muslims to Temple Mount and the Western Wall more commonly known as the Wailing Wall.

He had no idea what his contact looked like, but Brigadier Hazlett had assured him that Yosef Buber would find him.

As an excuse to loiter Hawkspurr had bought a snack from a street vendor—pitta bread stuffed with chick—peas and salad. He was munching happily on this and watching passing sightseers, when an Arab selling postcards approached him.

"A souvenir of the Holy Land effendi?"

Unlike most merchants, this black bearded Arab looked directly into Hawkspurr's eyes.

Hawkspurr patted his box camera with the little green shamrock painted on top. "No thank you, I take my own pictures."

The Arab's eyes moved to the emblem. "But effendi, even a poor Sparrowhawk can afford my cards." He handed a card to Hawkspurr.

Hawkspurr put a hand in his pocket and passed a coin to the Arab.

"Thank you." Slowly he sauntered away up the ramp to Temple Mount.

Although not religious, Hawkspurr's deep sense of the past kept him engrossed as he listened to a tour guide reciting the history of the rock. The site had been used for worship in turn by pagans, Jews, and Christians. Muslims identify the rock as the place where Mohammed ascended to heaven, and built the exquisite monument the Dome of the Rock in 688.

Solomon built the first temple here, and Nebuchadnezzar later destroyed it and carted the Jews off to Babylon. Herod enlarged the second temple, but again the Romans destroyed it during a Jewish revolt. Now Muslims held the sacred site, and all Jews were banned from entry.

To round off the day Hawkspurr decided to take a walk along the top of the ancient walls; from this vantage point he could look down into the fascinating one-square-kilometer area of narrow alleys thick with shops selling everything conceivable from souvenirs, fruit, vegetables, and carcasses of meat hanging on display—and everywhere people.

A close look at the postcard offered by the Arab—now identified as Yosef Buber the Israeli agent—showed a prospect of the Jaffa Gate and written on it in small print, 'Knights Palace Hotel'.

The hotel proved to be a basic but grand old building, and Hawkspurr discovered that a room had been booked for one night in the name of Doctor Michael Johnson. Tired out, he ate a simple meal of chicken and salad and then retired for the night.

Since his accommodation had been provided for one night only, Hawkspurr assumed that he would be on the move again this day. He had coffee and croissants for breakfast, and moved outside to wait for his next contact, and as the camera had served its purpose of identification—albeit with no film loaded, he had assigned it to his pack.

Within minutes Yosef Buber approached him once more. This time the agent was wearing a western business suit, with traditional Arab headdress. He shook Hawkspurr's hand and introduced himself Kahlil al-Hakim, Professor of Egyptology.

"Today I am driving my esteemed colleague Dr Johnson to Amman, where we will examine some artifacts relating to the period of King Ptolemy. Thence we will fly to Cairo and the museums of antiquity."

Buber led Hawkspurr to a black Austin motorcar, and they drove away to the first checkpoint on the road to Amman, Capitol of Jordan. The Professor was obviously well known by the Arab guards, and after a quick look at Dr Johnson's passport they were waved on with the blessings of Allah.

"What do I call you when we're alone Sparrowhawk?" Buber's accent was now pure Etonian.

"Hawk will do. I was told not to ask you any personal questions, but what do I call you?"

"I was known as Joe during my time at Sandhurst, so we'll stick to that."

Hawkspurr examined Buber more closely. He was of medium height, age early forties with a nose that could be Hebrew or Arab. His skin and full black beard were dark, which he was certain was genuine.

"What happens in Cairo Joe?"

"First we consolidate your cover by doing the expected tourist things. Museums, the Pyramids, burial sites and of course Cairo night life. We don't want them thinking you're a dull boy Doctor Johnson."

Hawkspurr grinned appreciatively. "Good. I try to balance my work with a bit of fun when the opportunity arises. If I'm going to die for Queen and country, I'd like to go out with a smile on my face." He paused and half turned to look at Buber again.

"Tell me Joe, just who are 'them'?"

"Nasser's Secret Service boys. They're usually a pretty slack mob but just now a little tense and trigger-happy. In fact all the Gippos are hyped up with nationalistic fervor. They see Nasser as the new Arab prophet, and his rhetoric has them ready to die in the streets for him."

Hawkspurr shook his head. "Messiahs and prophets scare the hell out of me, but what will you Israelis do about it?"

Buber pursed his lips and pondered the question.

He cast a hasty glance at Hawkspurr. "More to the point, what will you Brits do. Just supposing we move and capture the canal installations, would Britain attack Israel?"

"Sorry Joe, you're speaking to a foot soldier. I'm strictly expendable, and not privy to the political machinations of my superiors."

"Are you trying to tell me that you're not a 'spook'?" Buber sounded incredulous.

Again Hawkspurr shook his head. "Sorry, I'm a junior officer in a special unit, but still only a soldier."

Now Buber looked concerned. "Do you mean to say that you have no experience of this type of operation?"

Hawkspurr laughed softly. "I wasn't implying that I have no previous experience—only that I'm not an agent by trade!"

"Christ! What with you, and the prick your boss employs in the Embassy, I'll be lucky to collect my pension."

"What about our man in Cairo? The brigadier only mentioned him briefly." Now Hawkspurr was worried.

Buber snorted through his nose. "Typical bloody civil servant, he has no military service and sees himself as the ace of spies. I'll put you in touch with him, and render every assistance you require but I won't work with that man."

"That's fair enough Joe, but why are you helping us at all? I know there's still a lot of bitterness on both sides regarding Palestine."

"What I'm doing is not strictly official Hawk. I'm totally committed to the State of Israel and I'm Jewish born and bred, but my family made their fortune in Britain four generations ago. I went to the best schools and served in the British Army during the war, but in 1947 I knew where my roots lay. Not everyone in the Knesset agrees, but in regard to Egypt I believe we have a common enemy. Can you live with that?"

Hawkspurr was adamant. "Certainly and I reiterate, I'm a soldier and I follow orders, but I can think for myself. I trust we now understand each other."

Buber took a hand from the steering wheel and offered it to Hawkspurr, who accepted the gesture willingly.

After traveling in silence for a few miles—each man busy with his own thoughts, Hawkspurr remarked on the increasing flow of military traffic moving southwest.

"The Jordanian Army is very busy today."

"Yes." Replied Buber, "A border exercise is the official line. There will be more checkpoints soon but stay calm I established my cover many years ago. In fact I really am a recognized authority on ancient Egypt—thanks to my time in the Department of Antiquities of the British Museum in London."

Hawkspurr and Buber spend two days and nights in the Capitol of Jordan, and then flew to Cairo.

The airports were under heavy military guard, with armored vehicles and anti-aircraft guns ringing the perimeters. Both countries were prepared for invasion by parachute troops.

Professor Kahlil al-Hakim maintained a picturesque little bungalow in the quiet backwater of Qasr al Dubaru. It overlooked the waters of the Nile and was handy to his place of work, the Egyptian Museum.

Apart from the study—which Hawkspurr assumed was kept in a calculated academic mess to sustain his image, the house was neat and tidy.

"Are you married Joe?"

"Sure, but I don't see much of my wife and son. Sara is the administrator in a kibbutz, and a lieutenant in the army reserve."

Hawkspurr was sympathetic. "I'm sorry, this job must be a strain on you both."

Buber smiled. "Thanks. I've been promised a staff position in the New Year, besides I really am getting too old for all this dashing about. Wash up, and we'll go out for a meal."

Hawkspurr returned from his ablutions to join Buber on the veranda, where they appreciatively sipped Stella beer. The sun was dropping into the desert of Western Sahara, and feluccas and pleasure craft presented a pretty sight on the river.

Buber inspected Hawkspurr's tweed jacket. "That look is a bit out of place in Cairo old chap, we'd better get you a suit." He went to the telephone and issued some instructions in rapid Arabic.

Within thirty minutes an Egyptian tailor and his boy arrived with a selection of suits and shoes.

Hawkspurr was impressed. "That's a good deal faster than Singapore service."

"Well these chaps have been in business longer! Right Abdul, let's see what you have to offer."

Buber selected a white linen suit, shirt, tie and white shoes. "Go and try these on, doctor."

Hawkspurr returned dressed in his new apparel. "They're a tiny bit loose around the middle, but this will do nicely thanks." He had lapsed back into an Irish brogue for the benefit of the Arabs.

Buber nodded approvingly. "Thank you Abdul, send me an account please."

"Allah's blessing upon you professor."

The tailor spoke to his apprentice, who produced a black and white checked sh'magh from his bundle. Abdul handed the headscarf to Hawkspurr. "A gift to welcome the effendi doctor to Cairo."

"Many thanks Abdul." Hawkspurr took a note from his wallet and handed it to the boy.

Abdul patted the lad on his head affectionately and adroitly removed the money from his hand, to place it within his own robes. He smiled a toothy explanation.

"I look after the boy very well effendi!"

The Arabs departed, thanking Allah and all customers profusely.

Buber helped Hawkspurr to adjust the headband of his new scarf. "With that tan, and your dark eyes—not to mention the nose! You probably won't be asked for identification any more."

Hawkspurr lightly touched his fingers to mouth and forehead. "Salaam wa laykoom!"

Buber responded "Mwalaykoom a salaam."

Buber was guiding Hawkspurr through the narrow back streets of the old city. "I have to get a message to some Bedouin friends Hawk, we'll be needing them for one part of my assignment. It's not something you need be involved in." He looked impertinently at Hawkspurr. "A trip into the desert by camel might be too much for you!"

"Cheeky blighter. We Horse Guards pride ourselves on our ability to handle anything."

"Roger. We'll start you off with some typical Bedu cuisine, and entertainment fit for a warrior."

Buber led the way to a cafe decked out in the fashion of a desert tent. The establishment was crowded, noisy, and dimly lit with oil lamps.

Some of the clientele were European tourists, but the majority were genuine Arabs if not Bedouin.

Buber whispered to a man dressed in the robes of the desert, and he and Hawkspurr were shown to a table at the rear of the cafe. Buber excused himself, as merrissa was placed for the afrangi—the foreigner.

The sorghum beer was a new taste for Hawkspurr but pleasant enough, and he had emptied his glass by the time Buber came back to the table.

"All fixed. Now let's enjoy ourselves, tomorrow we go by road on a grand tour of the cemeteries of Upper Egypt."

The couple was served first with Bedouin soup lamb with pasta, eggs, tomatoes, onion, celery, and various hot spices. Harira—boiled kidney beans with rice, more spices, and Batata-be-Kamoum boiled potatoes with hot Harissa sauce, followed this course.

The entertainment served neither to cool the fierce spices in Hawkspurr's belly or his passionate desire as nubile Bedouin girls danced before them like the houris of paradise. Each dancer was festooned with her dowry of gold coins, but the costumes were not quite as revealing as the Hollywood stereo-type!

On the following day, Professor Kahlil al-Hakim and Doctor Johnson fol-lowed the Nile south to the Valley of the Kings, Thebes and Luxor, stopping occasionally during their passage to observe the people of the Nile and a way of life unchanged for centuries.

The list of Pharaohs and gods portrayed in stone, proved to be a roll call from the pages of history books that Hawkspurr had studied as a boy. The graphic fig-ures carved in relief, exhibited the everyday activities of the ordinary people of the Nile—gathering food, serving their masters, hunting and dancing.

He was overawed by the sheer scale of the statues and the magnificence of all he saw, and would gladly have spend weeks exploring and soaking up the atmosphere of grandeur and tangible history.

A further two days spent in the Museum of Egypt, and a trip to the pyra-mids of Giza spelt the end of leisure and culture. It was now time to get down to the serious task of intelligence gathering.

Buber observed that the man assigned to monitor the activities of Dr Johnson, was losing interest and had not even bothered to follow them to Giza. Hawkspurr for his part was unaware that he had a 'shadow', and on reflection he realized the inherent danger of relying on a second party for security. Work-ing alone kept a man constantly alert, and he resolved never to lapse into com-placency again.

"I think it's now time for me to put you in touch with Radcliffe Hawk, but understand that I refuse to be involved with the man. Besides I have business of my own to conduct, and I must preserve my cover at the museum. You will naturally remain as a guest in my home, but it would be more convenient for me if you use taxis to get around."

Buber fixed his intense gaze upon Hawkspurr. "Your job could now become very risky. Do not rely too much on Radcliffe and keep your meetings brief—he will most certainly be under observation every time he leaves his home. Start carrying your gun, but use it only as a last resort."

Hawkspurr experienced the familiar tingle of excitement tinged with fear, as he listened to the older man's words. Up to this point he had been completely absorbed in his role of academic tourist.

Now it was imperative that he located Von Harzburg and Amanda Carson, if indeed he was not on a fools errand. Should that part of his assignment prove redundant, he still had to find the 'Mount Nimba' in the 107-mile stretch of the canal between Suez and Port Said.

# CHAPTER 15

Hawkspurr's opportunity to speak with Radcliffe came in the form of an invitation to a diplomatic cocktail party. This was to be a multi-national affair held in the plush Palace Hotel, and hosted conjointly by all embassies and consulates represented in Egypt. Foreign nationals of any distinction visiting Cairo were expected to attend and pay their respects. Thus a brief conversation with any official was both acceptable and propitious.

Hawkspurr took a taxi alone to the Ezbekiyen Gardens. The traffic was insane, as horse-drawn gharries competing for space with stinking diesel buses and beat-up cars amidst the unregulated movement of pedestrians and vehicles.

As a cavalryman, Hawkspurr was appalled at the emaciated condition of the many horses, mules, donkeys used as beasts of burden. Tiny donkeys staggered as they strained to pull overloaded wagons, and were beaten cruelly by the men or boys responsible for their welfare. Every animal he saw bore scars or weeping, fly infested sores on deformed bones, and he would cheerfully have put them out of their misery after first thrashing their owners.

The solid stream of limousines—Rolls, Bentleys, Mercedes and Cadillacs depositing guests outside the hotel blocked both the square and its approaches, so Hawkspurr paid off his cab a block away and started to walk.

It appeared that every beggar and pickpocket from the souks had gathered in the region of the venue. Of course, they would have known about the reception long before the invitations were delivered, and barefoot boys dressed in ragged jellabiyya, clutched at every passer-by and whined. "Baksheesh effendi. Alms for the love of Allah. You want my sister? Very beautiful virgin. Very cheap!"

Beside the boys, mutilated old men stood or sat silently in their rags, holding out withered hands in the universal gesture of entreaty.

Security in the immediate vicinity of the Palace was provided by the Egyptian Police Force, and any itinerant foolish enough to approach too close was lashed at with long bamboo canes—small wonder that these people had no sympathy for animals.

It wasn't too difficult to spot the security officers of various nations on station near the entrance, and although no guest was physically searched these eagle-eyed men garbed in ill-fitting suits would have detected the smallest of weapons secreted about a man. Swordsticks, which were a popular medium of defense for gentlemen in Egypt, were however appropriated at the door.

The delicate question of a lady's armament was a different matter, but doubtless inside the building many of the waiters would have been seconded to keep a close watch on any suspect.

Hawkspurr knew it was imprudent to carry his own pistol, but nevertheless had strapped a tiny three-inch blade knife onto the inside of his thigh close to the scrotum; a small insurance policy against any unforeseen emergency.

The throng inside the huge reception hall was already overflowing onto the terrace above the brilliantly immaculate gardens. The scent of blossoms filled the air but could not quite compete with the pungency of man, albeit agitated and whirled around by overhead fans.

Once Doctor Johnson had been presented to the line of dignitaries hosting the gala, he took up an observation post outside in the fresh air. Utilizing his height, he was able to gain a view of most of the assembled guests both inside and out.

Hawkspurr was thankful that Egypt being one of the more liberal countries of Islam, allowed the sale and consumption of alcohol. The number of waiters circulating with trays of hors d'oeuvres and cool drink would have been the envy of any London hostess; there was no shortage of cheap labor in this city.

Slowly, Hawkspurr's eyes traversed the assemblage—it was a formula identical to any United Nations gathering in New York. After the polite period dictated by etiquette, officials and guests of each country represented were drawn together in associated cliques.

Hawkspurr smiled when he saw the British—stiff elderly men in dark suits and old-school ties. He identified Eton, Harrow and Winchester, but no regimental colors. Alas the women too were stereotyped, in floral frocks with summer hats, gloves and sensible shoes. Ah well, when they returned home they would not have to purchase new outfits for Ascot or the royal garden party.

Two iced brandy and sodas later, Hawkspurr espied his quarry. Gunter Von Harzburg appeared as suave as ever—in fact he looked more like a diplomat than the Greek Ambassador he was engaged in conversation with.

The dark hair of the youngest woman in the group fooled Hawkspurr for just a moment, but then a characteristic gesture of her hands betrayed Amanda Carson. Either Miss Amadou Georghiades had reverted to her natural coloring, or was wearing a wig.

The old telepathy suddenly flashed between Von Harzburg and Hawkspurr like a wireless signal. The German stopped speaking and turned his head as though stung by a bee—his surprise at seeing Hawkspurr under these circumstances was complete.

Hawkspurr raised his glass in a mocking salute, and grinned at his adversary's discomfort. He watched as Von Harzburg whispered first to Amanda Carson, and then to the two prominent bodyguards posing as under-secretaries.

Amanda Carson displayed supreme discipline, and walked leisurely away without once looking over her shoulder.

Von Harzburg leaned forward and whispered in the Ambassador's ear, before leaving the room in the company of one 'minder'.

The remaining bodyguard stepped forward a pace rather dramatically and looked Hawkspurr square in the eyes as if daring him to follow.

Hawkspurr placed his glass down upon a convenient ledge and moved to accept the challenge, but was restrained by a hand placed on his arm, and a command in English.

"Let them go Doctor Johnson, I know where to find them and we don't want a scene do we?"

Hawkspurr examined the man critically. He was tall, but too blonde and too flabby, with pale watery blue eyes, and he spoke with a pretentious English drawl that Hawkspurr found irritating.

Hawkspurr's first instinct was to ignore the advice, but the man spoke sharply again.

"You're under orders Captain!" He stressed the verb and his thin lips positioned themselves into a phony smile. "Radcliffe, British Embassy."

He thrust forward a clammy hand to take Hawkspurr's, who had to refrain from the impulse to wipe his hand on his trousers.

"Don't look so grim old boy." Radcliffe peered around the room conspiratorially like a B grade movie spy, and in spite of himself Hawkspurr was forced to grin.

Then Radcliffe muttered dramatically from the side of his mouth, and Hawkspurr nearly screamed with hysterical delight. "Meet me in room 362. Thirty minutes!" He attempted to slip a key into Hawkspurr's coat pocket, but clumsily missed and the key dropped to the floor.

Hawkspurr bent to retrieve the object. "Ye gods! Piss off Radcliffe." He walked away from the diplomat.

Hawkspurr moved around the terrace unobtrusively, avoiding eye contact with anyone until half an hour had elapsed, and then slowly made his way to the hotel foyer. Rather than use the lifts, he walked towards the main stairs but was accosted by Egyptian policeman.

Hawkspurr waved his key under the man's nose and smiled ingratiatingly. "I'm just going up to my room." He pushed confidently past the man before he could be interrogated further.

Hawkspurr climbed the marble steps with their ornate iron fretwork balustrade, until he reached the third floor where only the perpetual hum of irrepressible life from the streets reached these internal passages.

A check of door numbers indicated that Hawkspurr should turn to his left. The carpeted corridors were deserted—no doubt all available staff were engaged with the party below, and he hurried on to find room 362.

A quick look to left and right, and Hawkspurr inserted the key in the lock. It was dusk outside, but he was surprised by the darkness of the room; he had watched Radcliffe leave the reception area at least fifteen minutes earlier, and expected the man to be waiting for him.

Apprehension gripped Hawkspurr and he stepped swiftly inside to close the door softly behind him.

Closed shutters and drapes precluded even a glimmer of light, and his inherent sense of danger warned him that something was amiss. He placed his back to the wall and controlled his breathing, turning his head slowly from side to side—straining his ears for any sound that would betray the presence of some other person.

Could Radcliffe possibly be a double agent? No he doubted that.

His nostrils flared as they had in the jungle seeking the unfamiliar scent that did not belong in that particular environment. This ploy was foiled however by the domestic aroma of polish and disinfectant, submersing any lingering traces of cologne or perfume.

Hawkspurr sidled along the wall searching for a light until his exploring fingers found a switch and pushed. No result. He had no idea of the size of the room, but judging by the distance between doors in the corridor the suites were large.

Although Hawkspurr possessed the patience of the hunter, this was neither the time nor place to sit in ambush. Soon the guests would be leaving the party, and possibly some of them were staying in rooms on this floor.

Gingerly he filled his lungs. "Radcliffe!"

As he called Hawkspurr dropped to a crouch and moved to his right—fingers splayed like a runner in the blocks, legs taut on his toes.

Phutt! Plaster flew from the wall where he had been standing a moment before, but a faint muzzle flash from the silencer of the gun gave him all the information he needed.

A split second after the report, Hawkspurr launched himself to the attack. The speed and fury of his assault caught the gunman by surprise, keeping low his hard shoulders smashed into the body and their impetus carried them both through a doorway, and back into the room where the shooter had been concealed.

The instant Hawkspurr made contact and overwhelmed his assailant, he knew who he was dealing with; Amanda Carson fell winded and dropped her weapon, but still she fought back with a fury born of hatred and desperation. Kicking and clawing, she attempted to bite Hawkspurr's neck as they rolled about the floor.

Hawkspurr was merciless—the woman had murdered before, and summoning all his strength he forced Amanda Carson onto her face with her arms pinned beneath their combined weight. Holding one hand on the chin Hawkspurr took her head in both hands, twisted and snapped back, using a swift lethal technique. The slim neck broke, air whooshed from her lungs, and the Greek agent was dead.

Awkwardly, Hawkspurr regained his feet and moved to find a window in the airless room. He drew back thick drapes, and opened the louvered slats of a wooden jalousie. The windows were open, and he stood for a minute drawing in refreshing air.

When Hawkspurr turned back to the room, he saw that he was in a bedroom.

His eyes flicked over the motionless body of Amanda Carson, to rest on another corpse; Radcliffe was sprawled back on the bed, his arms and legs spread as if he had tried to lessen the impact of falling.

Two neat bullet holes over the heart displayed the mark of a professional assassin, and the expression on his face was frozen in disbelief—poor stupid bastard.

Hawkspurr found the bathroom and rinsed his face in cold water. He ran a comb through his hair, and straightened suit and tie before returning to sit on a chair facing the lifeless bodies. One a man he had taken an instant dislike to, the other a woman he had made love with.

He needed time to think, and he still had to locate Von Harzburg. What had Radcliffe known that had led to his death in this room? Hawkspurr opened the drapes over the sitting room window and started to search the suite, but all of the drawers and closets were empty—obviously Radcliffe had not intended to spend the night here.

He could find no papers or even a brief case, there was not anything hidden under seat cushions or behind the curtains; the water cistern of the lavatory held nothing more than a few spiders under the lid, and the medicine cabinet was completely clear.

Hawkspurr returned to the bodies.

Amanda Carson had placed her shoulder bag on the nightstand, but it contained only Egyptian currency, a set of keys and a spare clip of ammunition for her gun. He pocketed the keys.

Distastefully he knelt to examine her clothing, probing with reluctant fingers into the still warm bra'. She had nothing concealed about her, and her jewelry consisted simply of a bracelet watch, gold chain necklace, and stud earrings. Every label had been removed from her garments—she had indeed been a professional.

Hawkspurr turned his attention to Radcliffe, but his wallet contained only money, driving permit, diplomatic identification, and a couple of receipts for petrol. There were no letters or snapshots—maybe nobody loved the man! His pockets yielded up keys, handkerchief, comb, small change, and a gold fountain pen.

Where would a dick like Radcliffe conceal information he intended to pass on—or had he kept it all in his head?' Hawkspurr removed the shoes and looked inside for a clue, he scrutinized watch, cufflinks and tie clip, but found nothing at all.

As an afterthought he lifted Radcliffe's hands—there! Written on the left palm was a barely discernible word. The indelible ink had run slightly on the once sweaty skin, but the memory aid was just readable—Morandi, which Hawkspurr filed away in his own mind.

Now, what to do about the bodies…? Radcliffe's could stay where it was to be discovered eventually by the housemaids next morning, but he was responsible for Amanda Carson's death. Even a very thick detective would deduce that it is not possible for a man with two bullets in his heart to then break his murderer's neck-or vice versa!

Hawkspurr needed a solution to muddy the investigative waters. He entered the sitting room, and unlocked the French windows opening on to a small balcony. What if the woman had shot Radcliffe, and to avoid being seen in the hotel had then attempted to escape by climbing down via the balconies?

Darkness was gathering, but a quick look over the side of the building convinced Hawkspurr that it was possible for an active person to leave the hotel by that method. Right—he would wait until nightfall before carrying out the next step of his plan.

With a handkerchief, he wiped his fingerprints from any surface he may have touched, including the key that Radcliffe had given him. He left this on the brass coffee table before taking out his flask and sitting down to enjoy a medicinal cognac whilst pondering his options. Perhaps it would be best to discuss his predicament with Buber, before making any hasty decisions.

It was time to move, and using his handkerchief again Hawkspurr placed Amanda Carson's gun in her shoulder bag, and put the strap across her shoulders before gathering the body into his arms.

Her head fell back like a rag doll, but the expression of hatred on the face belied the simile. He closed the vacant eyes, and carried the body out to the balcony to check once more for signs of activity on this side of the building although he reasoned that most of the guests would now be out, sampling the varied nightlife of Cairo.

For a moment Hawkspurr rested the corpse upon the iron rail guard, and then let it drop. He blew a sardonic kiss after the body, and turned away—one less terrorist to bring fear and death to the innocent.

Hawkspurr opened the door of the suite and wiped both handles clean, before placing the 'Do Not Disturb' sign on the outside. Without undue haste he walked away to the far end of the passage, where he could see a fire escape door.

Moving rapidly now, he descended the concrete steps two at a time—cautiously he pushed at the locking bar on the street exit door and it opened without protest. Praise Allah indeed.

This blank wall of the hotel, faced the equally featureless side of another tall building, and Hawkspurr turned left towards the lights and noise of the square, where he inserted himself into the stream of garrulous tourists and western-ized Egyptians, and joined their promenade in the cool evening.

Hawkspurr was feeling ravenous, and after walking clear of the Ezbekiyen gardens found an Indian curry house where he satisfied his hunger with chap-attis and pork vindaloo. The night was still young when he finished his meal, but now he felt obliged to inform his host Buber of the events of the afternoon.

He called for a taxi.

# CHAPTER 16

Buber was working in his study, attempting to decipher the hieroglyphics of a parchment sealed under glass, but he looked relieved to see Hawkspurr and immediately put aside his work to invite him for a drink on the verandah.

The professor waited patiently until Hawkspurr had consumed at least half a bottle of beer, then like all good Jews he politely enquired about his guest's health before launching into more pertinent questions.

"Well what did Radcliffe have to say Hawk?"

Hawkspurr's reply was laconic and frivolous. "Not much. In fact he was dead quiet."

A frown of annoyance creased Buber's forehead.

"Sorry Joe. He literally is dead."

Hawkspurr related the precise details of his activities that day. "What do you make of the word Morandi?"

Buber screwed up his eyes with the process remembering. "Morandi…Morandi…Yes! There's a restaurant of that name in Fouad Street. Do you think it has some connection with Von Harzburg?"

"Unless Radcliffe had an assignation with some exotic popsy, I can't think of another reason. Anyway, it's my only lead."

Buber stood abruptly. "Very well, I'll get the car out and we'll carry out a reconnaissance of Fouad Street. Better wear your Arab headdress."

"Hold on a minute Joe and let me finish this beer, I'm a wee bit knackered out. How long do you think it will be before the bodies are found?"

"The woman won't be discovered in that part of town until dawn, when the street sweepers clean up. The hotel maids should find Radcliffe about eight or nine, possibly later if they take any notice of the do not disturb sign on the door."

"Ok." Hawkspurr agreed. "What then. Surely the police will want to question all foreigners who attended the party?"

Buber sat down again. "Not necessarily. My educated guess is that they'll report first to the British Embassy, and then try to identify Carson. Maybe they won't even link her with the Greeks. The other factor is that the authorities may not concern themselves about the death of any Europeans, especially under suspicious circumstances. I personally feel that all of the Diplomatic Corps associated with Britain and France, will be closing up shop and going home any day now. Word on the street, is to expect air raids by British bombers operating from Cyprus."

Hawkspurr made up his mind. "Very well, I'll make one more attempt to find Von Harzburg and if that fails, I'm clearing out to Port Said to look for the arms ship."

"In that case, your plans coincide with mine. My orders are to ascertain the state of readiness of the Egyptian Army along the canal. Do you want to join forces?"

Hawkspurr smiled. "Why not? I'm starting to get used to your rotten cooking!"

Buber and Hawkspurr drove to Fouad Street, and parked where they could observe the Morandi Restaurant. Buber commented that most of the patrons frequenting the establishment seemed to be Europeans, some of whom he knew by name and nationality—Germans, Italians, and Greeks, all members of the local business community, and all engaged in import and export.

"That makes sense." Remarked Hawkspurr. "The arms shipment on the Mount Nimba originated in Italy. Von Harzburg heads a mercenary terrorist group based in Germany, and the Greeks have the biggest stake in Cyprus."

Ninety minutes passed before Hawkspurr whispered to Buber. "There he is—Von Harzburg—the chap in the light brown suit and dark trilby hat. Radcliffe must have discovered that the arms dealers meet here."

Von Harzburg checked up and down the street but didn't seem to pay any attention to the car. Then an Arab dressed in a white jellabiyya and skullcap joined him, and the pair moved away together. Neither of them appeared to be in a hurry.

"Do you think Von Harzburg knows about Carson and Radcliffe Joe?"

Buber shook his head. "I don't see how he could, it's more likely that he thinks he is on his way to contact her now."

"Well there's only one way to find out." Hawkspurr opened his door. "We follow on foot."

"You're right, but just hold your horses." Buber went to the boot of the Austin and produced two robes. "Put on this burnoose, we'll be less conspicuous."

Hawkspurr removed his headscarf, slipped the ankle length robe over his suit, and lifted the hood to effectively hide his features."

Staying a discreet distance back in the busy streets, Hawkspurr was just able to keep Von Harzburg's hat in view. After a period, the German and his companion turned off the main thoroughfare into an unlit alley.

Their next call was to a seedy pension off al-Tahrir Square—hardly the sort of lodgings Von Harzburg was accustomed to, and the Arab remained outside the building presumably keeping watch whilst the German entered.

Hawkspurr and Buber stayed in the shadows.

Von Harzburg had only been in the pension five minutes, before he rejoined the Arab. He appeared agitated during their brief discussion, and the Arab started waving his arms about excitedly, before pointing to an alley running beside the building. Von Harzburg obviously agreed to the Arab's resolve, and they both entered the lane.

Hawkspurr and Buber allowed the couple a head start, before crossing the street to continue the pursuit. The route led through torturous streets of overhanging houses, with accumulated filth and flies in abundance.

The numbers painted on doors bore no relation to their position in the street, which must have made the delivery of mail very frustrating—if indeed such a service existed in this part of Cairo.

They passed through little more than a crack dividing two buildings which opened into another passage nine feet wide, and led eventually to a crowded bazaar. Thick dust rose from beneath their feet, and flies buzzed angrily at being disturbed during their feast upon piles of animal excrement. Dust and more flies covered the selection of fruit and vegetables displayed on rickety stalls, and Hawkspurr pulled the hood of his burnoose tightly across his mouth to deter any further exploration by the persistent insects.

In this wide-open space, the squalor was made more apparent by the romantic skyline of domes and graceful minarets outlined against a moonlit sky.

The Arab was leading Von Harzburg with more purpose now, and roughly brushed aside any trader with the temerity to approach his European colleague. Neither Buber nor Hawkspurr spoke as they focused on their quarry in the milling mass of people. For his part, Hawkspurr had no intention of opening his mouth and inhaling the foul air.

On the far side of the market place Von Harzburg plunged once more into a dark alley.

There were few pedestrians here, and Buber restrained Hawkspurr from following too closely.

Consequently, the pursuers suddenly found themselves in a small cobblestoned square containing nothing but a forlorn and broken fountain in its center.

Von Harzburg and the Arab had disappeared, but Buber pointed up with raised arm and Hawkspurr caught a fleeting glimpse of two figures moving along a high terrace. To their right a twisting flight of stone steps led upwards and Buber and Hawkspurr nodded in silent agreement before heading for the stairs.

Under their feet dozens of shiny cockroaches skittered away, and Hawkspurr automatically raised the hem of his burnoose as he climbed like a Dowager Duchess negotiating an unsavory footpath.

Reaching the terrace, Hawkspurr halted to examine their surroundings—this area too was deserted although dim lights peeped through narrow unglazed windows high up in the otherwise blank, dun colored walls.

The silence within this man-made gorge was unnatural and ominous, and Hawkspurr became conscious of his own breathing. From the corner of his eye he saw Buber draw an automatic pistol from within his burnoose, and he reached for his own Colt.

Hawkspurr pushed the hood back off his head to facilitate better hearing, and cocked the pistol under his robe to lessen the telltale slide and click of steel engaging.

Without a spoken word, Buber and Hawkspurr automatically stepped away from each other. The Israeli agent moved to the left, and Hawkspurr kept the low parapet on his right; both men knew that they were exposed in their present position, and walked on quickly but still vigilant.

Their objective was a dark opening in the wall which would afford better cover, Buber was slightly ahead of Hawkspurr and saw that the break in the parapet led to another short flight of steps, with a passageway beyond.

Hawkspurr was six feet behind Buber as the Israeli placed a foot on the step with the intention of leading the way, when the first bullet passed harmlessly through the sleeve of Buber's burnoose and imbedded itself in masonry.

As the second shot rang out in the enclosed space, Buber huddled back behind the parapet and returned fire with two rapid rounds.

After the first shot, Hawkspurr flung himself forward and lay down behind the low wall opposite Buber. "Are you hit?" He whispered.

"No."

Hawkspurr inched nearer to the steps on his belly, and peered into the gloom. He spotted a small patch of lighter material in the angle of the far passage, took steady aim and squeezed off a single shell. His marksmanship was rewarded with a yell of pain and a volley of return bullets.

In the brief silence that ensued Buber stood upright, and charged down the steps and along the passage, snapping off one more round as he ran.

Hawkspurr jumped to his feet, leapt down the steps in one bound and sped to catch up with the fleet Israeli.

He was still ten feet distant when Buber turned the corner and one more discharge echoed within the narrow walls. He heard the dull thud of a body falling and the clatter of steel on stone as a gun dropped from lifeless fingers.

Hawkspurr sprang into the passage gun leveled, ready to kill—and fell over two bodies.

He rolled over to a sitting position with a curse on his lips, and pointed his weapon at the robed figure extricating himself from the dead man beneath him.

Buber removed his hood and laughed at Hawkspurr's expression of outraged anger. "You wouldn't shoot an old Jew, would you?"

"Ye gods Joe, I really thought you'd bought it"

"Not this time old boy."

Buber bent over the Arab to check for identification. There was a wound in the man's right thigh where Hawkspurr had hit him, and Buber's fatal shot had entered beneath his left eye killing him instantly.

Buber squatted to replenish his magazine clip as Hawkspurr scrambled to his feet and moved deeper into the passageway searching for Von Harzburg.

"Take a breather Joe, I'll have a quick shufti around."

The narrow thoroughfare petered out into yet another maze of filthy back streets, where the local populace had wisely elected to stay in their hovels when they heard the exchange of gunfire.

Only a solitary pi-dog scavenging for rubbish snarled menacingly at Hawkspurr. He stooped to pick up a stone and threw it at the mangy animal, causing it to run off tail between legs.

Hawkspurr stopped to examine a single door, set in the otherwise featureless wall constituting one side of the alley. The heavy brass knob was free of dust, yet the warped timbers were as dirt encrusted as their surroundings.

He hurried back to Buber "I think I've found Von Harzburg's bolt hole."

He nudged the dead man with his foot "What are we going to do about him?"

Buber looked behind. "There's a two foot gap between the terrace wall and the adjoining building back there. Grab his legs."

Buber grasped the Arab under his shoulders and together they carried the body back the way they had come.

"On three. One, two, three."

They swung the dead man up and over the low wall, and released it. It dropped with a few bumps and a final crump like a large sack of garbage.

"He'll probably never be found." Buber rubbed his hands together in a gesture of cleansing.

Hawkspurr was already returning to the door he had discovered. "Come on Joe no time to waste. That poor devil gave Von Harzburg a good start on us."

The marauding pi-dog had by now recovered his courage and was busy lapping up the Arab's spilt blood. This time Hawkspurr encouraged it, "Good boy, bon appetit!"

Hawkspurr showed Buber the Door with the clean handle. "What do you think?"

In reply Buber raised a foot and kicked the door just below the handle. The portal flew open with a sound of desiccated, splintered wood. "Let's find out!"

The Israeli pushed the useless door aside and entered a small gallery with Hawkspurr at his heels. To their front cast iron stairs spiraled up, but this time Hawkspurr stepped in front of Buber.

"No mate, Von Harzburg is mine." He took a slim pencil torch from his pocket, and started up.

The spiral ended at one more door but this was solid, freshly varnished, and fortuitously unlocked.

Hawkspurr flattened himself against the wall and nudged the door open with his shoe.

It swung back on well-oiled hinges to reveal a whitewashed foyer, and reaching in he turned on a light switch.

The walls were decorated with traditional hanging rugs, and a hat stand and mirror with a row of brass coat hooks completed the furnishings. The apartment smelled clean with just a lingering odor of cooking.

Hawkspurr hesitated; listening for any sound of occupancy as he advanced slowly, ready to fire at the first hint of danger. He hated confined spaces, and the even tempo of his heart beat a little faster.

He was conscious of Buber at his back, and paused again before passing through the open arched entrance to a lounge. This room was also unoccupied, with more woven rugs on plain walls and a varnished wooden floor. A circular, engraved brass table stood knee high in front of an off-white sofa and matching armchairs.

Overhead an electric fan hung idle and beyond, two more arabesque arches opened off this room. Colored bead curtains covered both arches, allowing the circulation of air with some degree of privacy. Hawkspurr parted the beads of the nearest opening and saw an empty kitchen, he moved on.

The second curtain was brushed aside as he stepped through to a short corridor where a door on his right opened onto a toilet and bathroom, both vacant—that left a single door at the far end.

Taking a deep breath, Hawkspurr opened the door with a rush and jumped in to execute a forward parachute roll. He came to rest against the edge of a double bed with ornately carved posts, and swiftly traversed the chamber with eyes and leveled gun. "Blast!"

He called out to Buber. "There's no-one here Joe." He crossed to a large wardrobe and opened it half-heartedly, knowing instinctively that it was empty.

"I'm sorry Hawk, it looks as though your bird has flow the coop." Buber was busy rummaging in the drawers of the dressing table.

"He can't be far away." Hawkspurr expostulated as he opened the casement window onto a fire escape ladder. "See here." He shone his torch down onto the upper rungs. "Fresh scrapes on the paint."

Hawkspurr looked over flat rooftops and darkened streets, to the ubiquitous domes and minarets beyond, and shook his head in disappointment.

"Time to leave Cairo Joe, Von Harzburg has to be headed for the Canal now that he realizes I'm on his trail."

The next morning Hawkspurr rose early, showered, and shaved thinking that his new moustache was developing nicely. He borrowed a pair of scissors from the bathroom cabinet and trimmed a few untidy hairs, then practiced a smile in the mirror. 'Yes, I'm sure the ladies will approve!'

After dressing and packing his meager belongings, he sat to clean his gun and topped up the magazine. 'I'm slipping' he thought, 'I should have done this last night.'

Hawkspurr had fully intended to cook Buber a decent breakfast, but the Israeli was already in the kitchen preparing the inevitable scrambled eggs and toast. What he wouldn't give for a couple of slices of ham!

Over the meal Buber was strangely silent, then pushed back the chair and looked around the room at his books, photographs, and collected artifacts.

"I've a feeling I won't be returning to this home Hawk. It's funny how attached I've become to this place and my work at the museum."

Hawkspurr waxed philosophical. "Maybe you were always intended to be a serious academic Joe. Surely you can come back once the present crisis is over, and bring your wife here to settle down. You've done more than your share of time in the trenches!"

Buber smiled wryly. "That's a nice thought Hawk, in the meantime we have a 'plane to catch for the Canal Zone."

# CHAPTER 17

❀

Port Said—Mediterranean gateway to the Suez Canal, and chief port for Cairo and the rest of Egypt where an Israeli agent, using the cover name Abou Hassan, met Hawkspurr and Buber at the airport.

Hassan was the owner of a high class jewelers shop in El-Goumhouria Street and knew nothing of the real reason for the visit, as Buber conjectured that the telephone lines were probably not secure for open conversation. Professor Kahlil al-Hakim had merely called an old friend, and said that he was taking a short holiday in order to show an Irish colleague around Port Said.

In fact Hawkspurr was no stranger to this fascinating port of call, having visited on two previous occasions en route to Korea and Malaya.

The elderly Jew was dressed smartly in a business suit, as befitted his status in the community, but to Hawkspurr's surprise was wearing a fez on his head—once the hated symbol of Ottoman oppression. Buber had earlier confided to Hawkspurr, that Hassan was no more fond of the British than he was of Arabs. He had been born in Palestine, and was fanatically devoted to the new state of Israeli however, in the interests of defeating a common enemy he was prepared to offer minimum assistance to a British agent.

The jeweler had booked his friends into the Akri Palace Hotel, and accompanied them to their room. Once inside Buber placed a finger upon his lips to signify silence, and commenced a search of the most likely places to locate any electronic listening devices. Satisfied that the room was clean he asked Hawkspurr to brief Hassan.

Hawkspurr described Von Harzburg and the Mount Nimba in detail, and stressed the importance of at least finding the arms shipment, he felt sure that his path would again cross with that of the German in Cyprus.

Hassan was able to confirm immediately that the ship had not passed through Port Said into the Mediterranean. "We closely monitor every vessel and its cargo, that enters and leaves the canal. Meet me later tonight in the hotel restaurant, and today I will assign three men to locate your German. What sort of cover is he using?"

"A Swiss wine merchant, as far as I know sir." Hawkspurr showed proper respect for the older gentleman.

"Good," Hassan almost smiled at the Englishman, "that should narrow the search considerably. Such businessmen frequent only a limited number of hotels and restaurants."

"Thank you old friend." Buber shook Hassan's hand. "We will not compromise you or your network, I promise."

Hassan turned with a question for Hawkspurr. "Are you armed Doctor Johnson?"

Hawkspurr nodded.

"Show me please." Hawkspurr produced his venerable Colt .45.

Hassan shook his head. "Fine in the desert, but rather cumbersome for urban operations." He placed his briefcase down again and removed a waxed paper package, which he handed to Hawkspurr. "Allow me to make a small contribution to your continued well being. A Heckler and Koch HK4 nine millimeter, a little lighter than even the Browning you are no doubt familiar with, and less conspicuous I might add."

Hawkspurr liked the feel of the gun immediately. "I don't know how to thank you sir."

The senior Jew raised both of his hands in a fatalistic gesture. "Aaah…. The Lord will decide." He extended a hand to Hawkspurr.

"I think you are to be trusted young man—go with god, I will see you at eight o'clock tonight."

After he had shown Hassan to the door, Buber spread a map of Port Said on the table. "I don't think we'll be followed, but you saw the amount of troop deployment at the airport. We might as well check out the docks and beaches, I'm confident that Hassan's men can do a better job than us in the city."

"I agree. Besides I believe that if we discover the whereabouts of The Mount Nimba, it's of no further importance whether Von Harzburg is accompanying it or not."

As Hawkspurr and Buber checked their keys with reception prior to leaving the hotel, they were confronted by security police and ordered to deposit their camera with the desk clerk. They were further warned that any attempt to purchase a camera, would result in the shopkeeper going to prison, and their instant deportation.

"Pretty heavy stuff for the tourist industry Joe. Do you get the feeling that we're no longer welcomed by the authorities?" Hawkspurr queried once outside the building.

Buber laughed. "The official line won't carry much weight with the Arab traders Hawk!"

The Akri Palace was situated only two hundred yards from the docks, but Buber judged it more prudent to move initially in the opposite direction. They strolled along Sa ad Zaghloul Street to the junction with El-Shohada, and then turned north to the beach area.

Along the crowded promenade of New Corniche Street, curious natives were herded along and threatened with violence if they loitered. Barricades effectively isolated the beach from the general public, and heavy motor vehicles were in the process of being unloaded by men in brand new ill-fitting army uniforms.

The contents of the boxes carried so gingerly by the recruits were obvious to Hawkspurr—land mines. The language was foreign but the symbols universal and quite clear.

The engineers installing the deadly weapons were patently regular soldiers, and the origins of the mines became self-evident when Hawkspurr listened to the accent of the European supervising the arming and laying. The Russian civilian technical advisers had 'come in out of the cold'.

Towards the Eastern end of the strand, the Gezeira Casino had likewise been closed to the populace, and considering the number of ammunition boxes passing through the doors, Hawkspurr assumed that the croupiers had now been supplanted by machine gunners.

Loudspeaker vans cruising through the streets, extolled the virtues of Gamal Abdel Nasser, and berated the evil forces of English and French imperialism. Citizens were promised that every man, woman and child, would receive a rifle to defend their homes should cowardly Jews or Christians desecrate this land.

These messages were greeted with fanatical rapture, and the name Nasser was screamed aloud, over and over again. Taking his cue from Buber, Hawkspurr joined in the adulation and waved a triumphant fist in the air. Praise Allah for his well-tanned features!

Although unable to reach the dockside due to more guarded barriers, Hawkspurr and Buber could observe enough to satisfy their military curiosity.

Crates and yet more crates of war materiel were stacked in all available space, and ships flying communist flags were slinging ashore armored vehicles with indecent haste. Obviously the civilian captains wanted to unload quickly and escape into the relative safety of the open sea.

By tacit agreement Hawkspurr and Buber didn't communicate verbally in English, as Hawkspurr was learning a few words and phrases of Arabic, and this would suffice until they reached the privacy of the hotel.

Hawkspurr compared the behavior of the Arab youth to their Israeli counterparts he had watched in Tel Aviv. All displayed the same zeal, expectation, bravado and even joy at the thought of engaging a mortal enemy in combat. But would the largely indolent Egyptians fight with the same patriotic fervor when faced with the probability of death?

Hawkspurr and Buber spent the remainder of the day compiling a joint report of all they had seen of the preparations for war in the port.

Pooling their observations, they arrived at a comprehensive portrayal of the scope of opposition any invading force might expect to meet.

Buber was equipped with special paper, ink and fine pens to transcribe the intelligence gathered so far. These miniature documents could be hidden almost anywhere when it was not possible or practical to obtain microdot film, or the necessary processing.

Hawkspurr thought the Israeli was exhibiting some weird Middle Eastern humor, when he produced the light aluminum tube normally used to protect the finest cigars.

"Unless you're inflicted with hemorrhoids old boy, just roll your reports into one of these and insert it in your rectum. I've survived the most rigorous of searches and have never been compromised!"

Hawkspurr grinned. "Then you've never had bottom your exposed to British counter espionage Joe. Some of the Cambridge types they recruit might just bend you over and insert a probe!"

Hawkspurr was surprised to see so many European faces in the hotel restaurant that night; the bar was doing a roaring trade and every table full.

Fortunately Hassan had made a reservation early in the day, and as Hawkspurr surveyed the room he remarked, "This mob doesn't exactly fit the tourist profile Mr Hassan."

"No Doctor Johnson, these gentlemen represent the world press and accredited war correspondents—not to mention a few members of the intelligence community. I am also able to confirm that Von Harzburg will be attending shortly."

"In that case I'll excuse myself from your company, and wait at the bar." Hawkspurr forestalled any protest that may be forthcoming, by standing and moving away.

Weaving his way through harried waiters carrying loaded trays, he took up station in an angle of the bar from where he could guard his back and still observe any newcomers. He ordered a long brandy and soda with ice, and waited with a sense of anticipation. As an afterthought he asked a barman to fetch a scotch and water, and as if staged, Von Harzburg entered the room.

They saw each other simultaneously, and without any show of hesitation or consternation the German approached Hawkspurr with a cynical smile lifting the corners of his mouth.

"Hello Nyles, did you run out of women in Cyprus?"

"Temporarily Gunter, but I did discover an old flame in Cairo." Hawkspurr handed the scotch to Von Harzburg. "Regrettably I found it necessary to extinguish her."

A glint of anger in the steely gray eyes betrayed Von Harzburg's inwardly controlled emotion.

"You are playing a very dangerous game here Nyles. Do you know that Arab women will delight in cutting off your penis, and leaving you to die with it in your mouth? I could have you arrested right now, along with your Jewish friends."

Hawkspurr placed a hand in his jacket pocket and fingered the HK4. "And I would gladly kill you on this spot, and take my chances."

Von Harzburg shook his head disparagingly. "Don't be a fool Nyles stick to soldiering; you're not devious enough by half for this game, and no-one really admires a martyr."

Hawkspurr smiled. "Why don't you save me some time then Gunter, and tell me where the Mount Nimba is? Then I can return to soldiering, and leave you to your business."

"Ah now! That's the difference between us Nyles, I no longer have any ideals just a desire to become very rich from the fanatical stupidity of others."

Von Harzburg finished his drink and signaled a barman to replenish both glasses. He appeared to be considering his next move, scrutinized Hawkspurr's face. "I can do you one favor, Nyles just to prove my unbiased stance regarding any nationalistic considerations."

"Please go on." Hawkspurr tried to sound nonchalant.

Von Harzburg leaned closer. "In room 2B of the Canal Authority offices, there is a Libyan naval expert working on a plan of action to aid Nasser should the canal be attacked. During the day he is assisted by a senior Egyptian canal pilot and a military engineer, but the man is so dedicated that he works late into the night, and sleeps in the room."

"Why are you telling me this Gunter?"

"The outcome of any war in the Middle East is of no significance to me, only the proliferation and subsequent armament sales." Von Harzburg grinned maliciously. "You do realize that you will have to kill the Libyan to steal his blueprints?"

Hawkspurr shrugged. "The man is probably a terrorist, much like you."

Von Harzburg placed his empty glass on the counter, and from long habit clicked the heels of his shoes together. "'Til we meet again then Nyles. Remember what the Frenchman Montain said—only death quits us of all obligations." He swung away and disappeared into the crowd.

Hawkspurr rejoined Hassan and Buber at their table.

Buber had ordered him cold meat and a salad that was covered and waiting for him, and as he sat Hassan poured a glass of Riesling into his wine glass.

Hawkspurr ate pensively, and then repeated the gist of his conversation with Von Harzburg.

"Do you trust the German enough not to walk into a trap?" Hassan was incredulous.

"Perversely, yes. We've been through much conflict together albeit on opposing sides, and he did save my life on one occasion."

The Israelis looked at each other and their eyebrows rose in unison.

"Mad dogs and Englishmen!" Buber muttered.

"My next question is; can you confirm the presence of the Libyan in Room 2B, and if so is it possible for me to gain access to the Canal Authority building?" Hawkspurr smiled engagingly. "I'm sure that your Chief of Staff would love a copy of the defense plans."

Hassan touched splayed fingertips together, and tapped the indexes against his lips. "How soon?"

Hawkspurr glanced at his watch. "It's only nine thirty why not tonight?"

Hassan made his decision. "And I was under the impression that all British officers were inclined to dither and procrastinate!" He stood up. "Excuse me gentlemen, I shall join you in your room before midnight, and I suggest that you start to pack."

Buber quizzed Hawkspurr. "Why the hurry Hawk?"

"I'm anxious to get this job over and get back into uniform. Besides my men will forget who the boss is!"

They finished coffee and liqueurs leisurely, and after settling their account at reception, informed the desk clerk that they would be departing for Cairo in the morning. Buber's camera was returned to him in a sealed bag, with the proviso that it must not be removed until they had left the Canal Zone.

Back in their room Hawkspurr stretched out on his bed, whilst Buber continued transcribing his interminable notes. Neither needed Hassan's advise to pack their bags; they had never been unpacked.

Hawkspurr slept soundly for two hours, until a gentle tap on the door brought him to alert wakefulness.

Hassan looked tired and drawn, but the elderly Israeli was also excited. "It is arranged. I did not want to confide in you earlier, but I do have a night cleaner in the Canal Authority who brings me the contents of wastepaper baskets from time to time. Egyptians are so negligent." He handed Hawkspurr a suppressor to fit the HK4. "A piece of additional equipment you may find useful Dr Johnson."

"Thank you sir. A gift for the man who has everything!"

"I beg your pardon?" Hassan was dubious.

"Sorry sir—a hoary old English joke."

Hassan sat at the table. "Please sit down gentlemen and listen carefully, once I leave this room you shall have no further contact with me. At precisely two a.m. all power in the area of the Commercial Basin will be cut off for one hour. This will attract little attention, if indeed any at that time of night—but should enable you to cover the three hundred yards from this hotel to the target building in total darkness. One man will meet you at the emergency exit of the hotel and guide you to the rear service entrance of the Canal Authority offices. There you will be admitted by the cleaner, and shown exactly where room 2B is situated. My men have been ordered to take no other part in your activities."

From an inner pocket Hassan took an envelope. "Here is a sketch floor plan of the building, and two tickets for the six a.m. train leaving for Cairo. My man assures me that no person enters room 2B before eight."

"What about watchmen or a guard?"

Hassan continued. "There is only one policeman on duty and he is posted outside the main dock door." He permitted himself a smile. "When the lights go out he will be too busily engaged to concern himself."

Hawkspurr grinned. "I trust the lady is being well rewarded?"

Hassan looked slightly embarrassed. "A willing boy actually." He stood abruptly. "I leave you to work out your own details gentlemen. Good luck."

He shook hands with both men, and left the room. "Right Joe, how does this fit in with your agenda to scout the canal installations?" Hawkspurr deferred to the Israeli agent.

"Quite well actually. Instead of going back to Cairo, we'll leave the train at Ismailia and cross into Sinai where arrangements are already in place with my Bedouin friends. All this situation has done is to put the timetable forward."

"Great. What do I do between three and six a.m.?" Hawkspurr was feeling confident and excited at the prospect of positive action, tinged with enough trepidation if not fear—to keep the adrenal in pumping.

"We come back here, and leave as normal after an early breakfast. There's no need to arouse undue suspicion"

"Hold your horses Joe, what's this we—I work strictly solo."

Buber raised a hand in protest. "And since when do you read Arabic? I doubt if Nasser is thoughtful enough to provide British military intelligence with plans written in English!"

"Good point." Hawkspurr was unperturbed, and traced a finger over the floor plan of the Canal Authority offices. "2B has a window on this rear corner overlooking Ismail Basin. You wait there in the street and I'll lower the camera to you when I've photographed every scrap of paper I can find. That way if anything doesn't go according to plan inside, you can get away clean."

"I suppose that makes sense," Buber agreed reluctantly.

"Of course it does. In fact it would be better for you to make your way back independently, just remember to wedge the fire escape door open for me."

Hawkspurr started to change from his suit, into the old grey flannels, tweed jacket and scruffy tennis shoes. He checked his gun, spare magazine, pencil torch, and transferred two triangular bandages from the first aid kit to his jacket pocket. "Don't want to bleed to death if things get out of hand!"

Buber removed the seal from the hotel security bag carefully, and handed the camera to Hawkspurr.

"Here's a spare roll of film. I just hope that there are curtains over the windows in room 2B."

Hawkspurr laughed derisively. "Posh camera—and just what is a good Jewish boy like you doing with this fine example of German craftsmanship?"

Buber ignored the quip, and said thoughtfully. "I wish we could cover the break-in somehow, and avoid killing the Libyan."

"We have no alternative but to remove the man. If I tie him up the security police will realize that someone has seen the plans, and simply modify them. But I do have something in mind that could buy us time."

From his pack Hawkspurr took a lady's scented scarf.

"A keepsake of a happier moment." He explained. "I propose to leave this on the floor as a clue—the assumption being that our Libyan friend had a disagreement with a lady of the night—or a visit from a jealous husband."

"I'm not sure, but it might just do the trick." Buber was pessimistic.

# CHAPTER 18

At five minutes before two o'clock, Hawkspurr and Buber stood silently inside the hotel emergency exit.

'This procedure is becoming a bad habit.' Hawkspurr thought, as he pulled on a pair of leather gloves. An anxious moment when the hour passed and nothing had transpired, then two more minutes dragged by before a tap sounded on the door, and Hawkspurr and Buber stepped out in to the darkened alley.

A large man swathed in a burnoose took Hawkspurr's arm and tugged; no words passed between them, and Hawkspurr pulled the end of his headscarf across his face as he followed obediently.

The three men skirted the edge of Commercial Basin in complete silence, and in minutes were facing a door in a smelly service area. Hawkspurr's night vision had returned, and he watched warily as their guide scratched on the door and then walked quickly away.

As the door opened and an arm beckoned, Buber reached out and briefly touched Hawkspurr on the shoulder in a gesture of encouragement before he too left to take up his position.

Hawkspurr passed under the lintel into total blackness. He was aware of the cleaner's strong body odor and nervous breathing, and as a precaution took the gun from his trouser-band before switching on a torch. He was careful not to shine any light on the man, but could see that the figure dressed in blue overalls was thin and stooped.

"Ala tuul." The cleaner whispered, and Hawkspurr followed straight ahead.

They ascended three concrete steps to a door which opened onto a linoleum covered passage, turned right five paces on, and then climbed polished stairs to the upper floor. Hawkspurr had memorized the pertinent sections of the floor plan, but still concentrated on his exact whereabouts in case he had to beat a hasty retreat.

The rubber soles of his shoes squeaked alarmingly on the lino', and he twisted his feet to walk on the outer edges—it reminded him of clandestine, and romantic night movement along the corridors in homes of the aristocracy during country weekends!

The building encompassed him in oppressive silence—no hum of electricity, no chatter of people, not even a rodent scampered. The only human presence he was conscious of, was the garlic-laden wheeze of his companion.

Each door posed the silent threat of a concealed enemy waiting to pounce and Hawkspurr eased off the safety catch on his weapon, swiveling his eyes from left to right ceaselessly. He was so intent, that when the cleaner halted abruptly, he bumped into him. The man pointed apprehensively to brass letters that read 2B, and retreated without a single word.

Taking a deep breath Hawkspurr turned the handle, which was unlocked and lubricated as promised. 'A good omen.' He moved inside and closed the door behind him.

He was greeted by the symphony of a gentle rumbling snore, accompanied by a lip vibrato which assured him that the occupant was still asleep, and the lingering bouquet of arak spirit testified that the man had imbibed recently. At least he would die happy and in ignorance of his fate, and perhaps he was already dreaming of the houris in paradise dancing to welcome him.

Hawkspurr shone the torch again to illuminate a huge wooden desk littered with charts and papers. Two bulky cupboards, then a smaller side table with three chairs carried more papers, and against the far wall a camp bed sagged beneath the weight of a very big man.

'Ye gods, I hope I don't have to wrestle with that!'

The huge buttocks were suspended a bare two inches from the floor, and Hawkspurr moved to stand over the black-bearded man. Cautiously he reached down to lift the blanket—a bullet through the covers would not fit the scenario he was manufacturing. Good, the Libyan was naked except for a pair of green shorts.

Hawkspurr positioned the muzzle of his suppressor one inch from the torso, and squeezed the trigger so that the man died instantly with a bullet in his heart.

He applied safety catch and replaced the gun in his belt, before turning his attention to the windows. Excellent. Dark green roller blinds had already been lowered.

Holding the pencil torch between his teeth, Hawkspurr gathered the papers on the desk neatly and commenced photographing. To accomplish this comfortably he had to remove one glove, but was careful not to handle any papers with his bare hand. Buber had replaced the usual lens, and he was able to place two sheets of paper side by side and focus successfully.

On completion of this task, he rearranged the documents at random, and repeated the operation at the smaller table. Satisfied, Hawkspurr replaced his glove before tying a thin cord to the camera and moving to the window where he raised the blind. The casement was rather warped and difficult to open fully, but he managed to slide the camera out and started to lower it. A gentle tug from below, and he allowed the string to fall before pulling the blind into place once again.

One more item to take care of: he removed the ladies silk scarf from a pocket and dropped it close to the bed fervently hoping that the scene of deception was set.

The thin beam of his torch circled the room for one last check, and paused on the nightstand beside the cot. There was only one glass beside the empty bottle of Arak. Blast!

Hawkspurr crossed swiftly to one of the cupboards and opened it. The shelves displayed usual stationary supplies, and half a dozen cups—close enough.

He lifted out one of the cups, dribbled in the last few drops of spirit from the bottle, and dropped it to smash near the bedside stand.

It was time to depart.

Less worried now about noisy shoes, Hawkspurr hurried downstairs to the rear exit. On his way he neither heard nor saw the cleaner, and the darkened streets cloaked the return journey of his nocturnal excursion in perfect secrecy.

Safely back at the hotel he put the emergency door wedge into his pocket, and ran lightly up the back stairs to his room.

Buber holding a gun opened the door circumspectly, and Hawkspurr flung himself appreciatively full length upon his bed.

Hawkspurr checked the time. "Ten minutes to spare!" he chortled.

Buber smiled tentatively in an attempt to cover his anxiety. "You bloody well enjoyed that, didn't you?" He accused.

Hawkspurr sat up and faced the Israeli. "The operation yes, but I never enjoy killing I've simply come to accept it as part of my duty."

"Sorry Hawk. I believe I was more concerned for your safety than I care to admit. Throughout the war, and indeed during the ensuing years of struggle here, I've lost too many young friends."

"No sweat, please forget it Joe. I'm going bathe, then stretch out for a couple of hours."

"Good idea." Buber agreed, "I'll just finish concealing these rolls of film you took, and reseal the camera bag. Hassan decided that the safest course is to give them to his messenger before we leave. He's undertaken to process them and get copies to Israeli intelligence, and your headquarters in Cyprus as soon as possible. Does that suit you?"

"Sure, if you trust him that's good enough for me." Hawkspurr really had no alternative but to acquiesce.

On completion of an early breakfast, Professor Kahlil al-Hakim handed Hassan's messenger a jewel box with a broken hinge for repair. The transaction took place openly in front of the hotel security officer, and the vital information was passed on without arousing any suspicion.

That morning the railway station was a clamorous confusion of men in uniform, and sobbing women and children. The recruits were being transported—unwillingly judging by the outcry, to the military base of Abu Suwayr.

Hawkspurr and Buber had seats reserved in the first class section of the train and Egyptian officers, complete in highly polished riding boots, Sam Browne belts and riding crops—no doubt to keep their reluctant charges in line, already occupied their carriage.

They were charming to the professor and garrulous in the extreme, so Hawkspurr pretended he needed more sleep and lodged himself in one corner. Buber appeared cool and instigated a discussion on the value of ancient art with the interested officers.

Hawkspurr on the other hand, was experiencing a familiar cold knot of anticipation in his gut—the expectancy of a sudden disturbance heralding the arrival of security police to arrest a murderous infidel.

Although he had concealed the heavy Colt in the bottom of his pack he kept the smaller HK4 handy in his jacket pocket, and should he be apprehended before the train left Port Said he was determined not to be taken prisoner without a fight. He realized only too well that his previous internment in Spain would be a stay in the Ritz, compared to the inside of an Egyptian Jail.

The pandemonium outside the carriage grew increasingly worse as the time for departure arrived. Cursing guards tried in vain to prevent civilians climbing on to the already overcrowded train, and the situation was close to a riot. Hundreds of peasants had decided that they didn't really want to stay in Port Said and be bombed by aircraft from Cyprus, or fight the Anglo/French paratroopers they had been warned to expect.

Under the circumstances it became impossible for Hawkspurr to feign sleep any longer, but for the benefit of his traveling companions he contrived to look tired and annoyed.

One of the officers in the compartment was becoming really angry at the delay, and stood at the door screaming instructions to the nearest guard.

Hawkspurr could hear people on the roof, and others could be seen festooning the sides of the carriages like so many bundles of dirty laundry. But even he was shocked when the irate officer drew his revolver, and shot dead a more persistent civilian attempting to force his way into their compartment.

There followed one second of stunned silence as the body fell away, then the train jerked spasmodically and started to move as if the shot had come from a starters gun.

"Fuck!" Hawkspurr was not given to profanity except under extreme moments of stress—this incident however seemed to fit the bill.

The shooter made a jocular remark to his colleagues, and calmly put the gun back into its holster. The other officers laughed and congratulated the killer, slapping their thighs in glee as if he had just shot a rabid dog.

Buber sat silently until addressed by the officer next to him, and then turned to Hawkspurr. "The Major apologizes for the inconvenience, and explained that in a country of nearly 50 million citizens there will always be the odd dissident. He also explained that Egyptian discipline is fair and swift!"

Hawkspurr nodded his understanding of the situation, and smiled guilefully at the Major. "Peace be upon you."

The officer beamed appreciatively. "Mwalaykoom a salaam."

Hawkspurr assumed an air of boredom again and stared vacantly out of the window, as the laboring train rattled slowly along parallel to the canal. In fact he was mentally noting every detail of the ships moving incongruously through what appeared to be a channel of sand.

Large ships cannot pass each other in the canal except in the Great Bitter Lake and the Ballah Loop, and this convoy was moving in line astern, although spaced well apart. The flags of many nations flew above tankers, rusty freighters, large cargo ships, and a luxurious cruise ship, all forced down to a common speed.

Still ten miles out from the city of Ismailia, the train halted at the settlement of Al-Firdan, and Buber solemnly shook hands with each of the Egyptian officers.

"The doctor and I have permission to explore a recent archeological discovery in the Sinai, and we are very anxious not to waste any time, therefore we will leave the train here."

The officers nodded sagely. "Yes," one said, "it is important that the West learns more of our glorious history."

The scholars were sent on their way with best wishes.

"Ye gods, am I glad to get out of that!" Exclaimed Hawkspurr, as he and Buber pushed through the throng of peasants surrounding the train.

"I was half expecting that mad bastard to shoot us just for fun."

"Yes," agreed Buber, "that Major is one of the old Egyptian ruling class, and lower forms of life are cheaper to him than his thoroughbred horses."

"Do you mean to say that he'll get away with murder?" Hawkspurr could not compare his own punitive actions, with the unwarranted homicide he had just witnessed.

"Yes, unless the victim had relatives with him his body will be in a paupers unmarked grave before noon, and there will be no further enquiries. Come on Hawk, put it from your mind, we have to get across the swing bridge into Sinai before it is closed again."

In the Ithnayan sector Egyptian preparations for war were self-evident, where at least one armored regiment and a battalion of infantry was deployed, and judging from the tents being erected, more troops were expected.

Hawkspurr and Buber had their papers scrutinized carefully, and became the butt of the soldiers' jokes when they explained that they were going on an expedition into the desert. The average Egyptian is an urban dweller, and not fond of the desolate wastes that constitute 96% of his country.

Over the heads of the crowd, Buber spotted the tall, dignified figure of a Bedouin standing patiently aside from the Arabs.

"Follow me Hawk."

Buber wasted no time with introductions, and the Bedouin strode off to lead the travelers to the outskirts of discernible civilization where his family group was squatting down by loaded camels, and obviously ready to leave.

Their guide bowed his head deferentially to an older man and spoke a few words, then issued an order to move.

Time for the noble Bedu tribes is measured in the strides of a camel and the passing of the seasons, and without undue haste the fifteen men, women and children mounted their beasts and moved away to the east.

As the dust of their passage subsided, the Bedouin unveiled his features and extended a hand to Buber.

"Welcome Joseph, we will catch up with my father once our Ingleez friend has mastered his camel."

Buber turned to Hawkspurr. "Hawk, meet Muhammad Beg son of Sheik Omar Rashid—our host for the next few days."

Muhammad Beg was about the same age as Hawkspurr, and spoke excellent English. "Welcome to you Hawk, let me assure you that my tribe have no love for the Egyptians who have treated us with little respect over the centuries. I have sat in their university to honor the wishes of my father but was glad to return to the old ways." He smiled slyly, "Perhaps one day you may be in a position to help me?"

Hawkspurr liked the tall man with the open, handsome face. "My family too never forgets a debt of honor Muhammad Beg."

"I am sorry we have no horses here Hawk, but where we journey next only the camel can survive."

Muhammad led Hawkspurr and Buber to three beasts, each of which was couched down on their knees with a loop of rope securing one joint.

From a voluminous saddlebag, Muhammad produced two sets of dun colored robes. "Put these on over your clothes please, you will be less conspicuous."

Since Hawkspurr and Buber were already wearing the traditional head cloth, they were instantly transformed into desert nomads that met with Muhammad's approval. The Bedouin unrolled a rug attached to another camel, and handed a Lee Enfield .303 rifle to each of his guests.

"Now you are properly accoutered for a warrior—abu 'ashara—these are relics from 1914 I admit, but still accurate should the need arise. If you will place your belongings in the saddle bags, we shall make a start."

Hawkspurr walked to the head of the furthest camel and reached for the saddle, but jumped back in alarm as the beast swung his head to display huge yellow teeth and spat at him with a cough of warning.

Buber laughed at the Englishman's discomfort. "I'm sorry to tell you that you smell Hawk! At least different from his normal rider, but don't worry—after a day in the desert he won't know you from the Bedu."

Muhammad smiled politely. "Come Hawk." He bent and removed the hobble from the knee, but held the camel down by pulling on the head rope. "Stand at his left shoulder, then grasp the rear of the saddle and cock your right knee over the front horn."

Hawkspurr did exactly as he was told, but as soon as the camel felt the pressure on his back, he rose to his feet with an ungainly lurch almost unseating the rider. Hawkspurr somehow retained his balance and the dignity of the Household Cavalry, and grinned at Muhammad Beg.

"So far so good. What next?"

The Bedouin handed Hawkspurr a wooden stick. "Now cross your legs over the camel's neck, and you will find the position quite comfortable. Guide him with the head rope in your left hand and the whip in your right."

The camel grumbled as Muhammad left his side, but Hawkspurr whistled softly through his teeth as he would to calm a horse, and the beast stood still until the Bedouin and Buber mounted.

Muhammad clicked his tongue against his teeth. "Hut tut tut." And the trio padded away, along dusty tracks left by the leading party.

After a couple of hundred yards, Hawkspurr's seat had adapted to the rhythmic swaying pace of the camel. The saddle constructed of two double wedges of wood on leather supports, was well padded with a rugged cover of carpet-like fabric decorated by tassels, and was certainly as comfortable as military tack.

The sun still low in a clear blue sky shone directly into Hawkspurr's eyes, and he wondered why Muhammad Beg was leading them East away from the canal. He turned in his saddle to beckon Buber, who was riding at the rear.

Buber increased the stride of his camel and trotted up alongside Hawkspurr. Conversation was easy in the vast silence of this barren plain, and Hawkspurr queried the direction they were traveling in.

"Muhammad says that his group has been surveillance for many days." Buber explained.

"The Egyptians in the Sinai are very nervous and suspicious since Nasser grabbed the canal."

Hawkspurr searched the horizon through 360 degrees. To his left the wastes stretched back to the salt marshes of Bur Fu'ad, and far to the South West sand-pink hills broke the skyline. Due South a faint mirage shimmered on the horizon, and from the back of a camel he was suddenly conscious of how infinitely insignificant man was in this flat expanse of featureless desert.

"I don't see anyone."

"Neither do I." Answered Buber. "But Muhammad Beg knows we're being tracked through a high powered telescope, far off in the heat haze."

Hawkspurr was unconvinced. "Well it's his patch, but tell me why is a nomad helping an Israeli? I would have thought he might be happier cutting your throat!"

"Politics old boy. The Bedu don't recognize international borders—for centuries the only boundaries they knew were the Arabian Sea and the Mediterranean. Within these confines they wandered at will, living a simple life of honor and chivalry, but always ready to fight over water or grazing rights. Many successive governments have tried to settle them and restrict their movements, but we've promised them free passage in Israeli territory—and a little gold for intelligence gathered."

Hawkspurr was satisfied with the explanation. "That makes sense to me. So, what happens next?"

"We plan to lay up for the day in the oasis of Bi'r Madhkur, then after dark Muhammad and a scouting party will lead us back to the area of Ismailia and Lake Timsah. From then on we play it by ear; my intention is to recce' the length of the canal as far as Suez."

"Good. My guess is that the Mount Nimba is now somewhere in the Great Bitter Lake, and Von Harzburg with it. I can't help wondering if the German has decided to double-cross EOKA and sell the arms to the Egyptians, or maybe some other group."

The sight of date palms and the slate-colored canvas tents of the Bedouin was paradise itself to Hawkspurr's sore eyes—and other extremities! Smoke from dried camel-dung fires was rising in the still air, and heavily veiled women were cooking a meal for their menfolk. He estimated the temperature to be at least 35 degrees Celsius, and the dry atmosphere had sucked all the moisture and energy from his body.

With the assistance of a young man, Hawkspurr took his camel down on its knees and dismounted stiffly. Like a good cavalryman, he moved to 'make much of his mount' with a grateful pat on the neck, but the beast wanted no part of such niceties and being of an unforgiving nature snapped at Hawkspurr with sharp canine teeth. Only quick action by the Bedouin saved Hawkspurr's hand from being crushed.

Muhammad Beg escorted Hawkspurr and Buber to the Sheik's tent, and once inside formal introductions together with the rituals of traditional hospitality were observed, before any serious discussion could begin. Although speaking through his son as an interpreter, it was most apparent that Omar

Rashid was in complete control and command of his tribe. He approved of the help his warriors were rendering to the afrangi—especially the young Ingleez officer and he spoke with pride of his father who had fought the hated Turks with the Englishman el'awrence.

(T.E. Lawrence, British Military Intelligence Service known popularly as Lawrence of Arabia.)

During general conversation regarding the future of the Middle East the Sheik indicated that it was time to eat, and summoned the women to fetch food. Girls of the tribe brought into the tent platters of couscous, bread slightly blackened from the ashes in which it was baked, and a communal bowl of spiced lamb. From the meat dish Omar Rashid extracted an eyeball of the animal and presented it to Hawkspurr with his fingers.

Buber grinned. "This is considered a great delicacy, and an honor for a guest, it's considered a serious insult to refuse."

"In that case…" Hawkspurr placed the object in his mouth, bit it in half and swallowed—he wasn't game to chew into the delicacy. "Delicious, thank you!" He reached quickly for a glass of goat's milk, to wash the lumps down his gullet.

With the blazing sun at its zenith, the Bedouin encampment succumbed to somnolent silence, as both inhabitants and animals dozed in the shade.

Muhammad Beg allowed his guests to sleep until dusk fell, when he roused them for an evening meal. The women were busy preparing the food as usual, and children tended to the tribal herd of sheep and goats by drawing water in leather buckets from the well, and pouring it into hollowed out tree trunks that served as troughs.

Having been advised not to shave or wash too thoroughly, Hawkspurr performed perfunctory ablutions—perhaps his camel would be more co-operative if the rider smelled familiar!

The males of the tribe sat around a campfire, contained within a circle of charred rocks that Hawkspurr imagined must be centuries old.

Each warrior was meticulously cleaning all traces of dust from his rifle and magazine, as he presented his claim to be permitted to accompany Muhammad Beg and the afrangi on a scouting expedition.

Omar Rashid listened intently to each man's petition, and then wisely selected three unmarried tribesmen for what might prove to be a most dangerous mission. The unsuccessful warriors hid their disappointment circumspectly, for none would dare to challenge the authority of the tribal leader.

Later as a mark of respect and honor for the departing men the Sheik called for the warriors' to dance, and as women and children watched from a respectful distance the tribesmen formed two lines facing each other.

Moving with grace and dignity, the warriors began advancing towards each other, and then retired in a swaying rhythmic movement. Between the lines of men, Omar Rashid stood with his ancient sword above his head and began to improvise the words of a chant.

"If the enemy comes, we will drive him from our lands!"

His men repeated the monotonous verse again and again until the Sheik changed to a new verse.

"Our friend the Hawk will stand beside us!"

# CHAPTER 19

The scouting party rode quietly from the oasis and out into the darkness of the wilderness led by Muhammad Beg, and guided by stars brighter than any cut diamond set in the black velvet of the night sky.

A silence so profound Hawkspurr imagined he could hear the hum of cosmic energy emanating in stark contrast from the firmament above. This was probably the most spiritual experience of his life, and he felt the presence of his own warrior ancestors riding with him in the encapsulating darkness. At the same time he was pragmatically thankful for the comforting bulk of a modern weapon in his belt, and the ever-reliable Lee Enfield rifle slung from the saddle horn.

During the night they crossed the Jerusalem Road, and before dawn were close to the shores of Lake Timsah in sight of the military base of Ismailia.

Built by the now departed British army, Hawkspurr's own father and uncles had once served here in the thirties with a cavalry regiment. The city itself had been founded in 1863 by Ferdinand de Lesseps, as an operational base during construction of the canal.

Hawkspurr noted the frenetic activity and number of men and vehicles assembled through binoculars provided by Muhammad Beg, all the same the party prudently kept moving at the slowest possible gait of the camels.

As the sun rose high once more, the group retreated back into the furnace heat of the desert, and made temporary bivouac in a shallow depression, each man shading himself with the end of his cloak propped on a stick.

During the morning a flight of Soviet built MiGs flew high overhead, parallel to the canal. Buber chuckled, and explained that the forward Israeli air bases were only 170 miles distant—obviously the Egyptian pilots did not want to risk an aerial confrontation over the Sinai.

That night the scouts repeated their maneuver, and headed for the Great Bitter Lake, progressing slowly and calmly as if heading innocently for Suez.

Hawkspurr admired the fatalistic patience of the desert warriors—his own inclination being to gather any information with all speed and get the hell out of the Canal Zone.

Hawkspurr's restlessness was heightened when he spotted his prime quarry the Mount Nimba. The ship was lying at anchor, off shore in the lake and close to an installation still under construction and swarming with hundreds of workmen. Lorries laden with concrete were driving at regular intervals down the road from Ismailia, and a Lighter was unloading steel at a heavily guarded wharf.

"What do you make of this Joe?" Hawkspurr was excited, and a little apprehensive.

"My guess is some form of advanced communication center—radio and radar early warning—look at the towers they're building. This is important, and I suggest we abort this mission immediately and get to my radio link."

"Roger that, my job here is complete and besides I was warned to be out of Egypt by the last week in October."

Buber was fishing in his saddlebags for the camera, and as he broke the wax seal again remarked. "I suspect the time for subterfuge has passed, I'll use two film rolls on this installation so that we carry a set each. With any luck one of us will get them out of Egypt."

The next occurrence took all initiative out of the hands of the scouting party, as a burst of machine gun fire spattered the ground within yards of the camels' feet. An armored car was patrolling the lakeside road and had decided to warn them off—alternatively the gunner was a poor shot. Either way, Muhammad Beg took the hint, and headed back East at a fast trot.

Safely out of gun range the Bedouin halted to confer with Buber. "I fear we have done all we can in this sector Joseph, what are your wishes now?"

Buber looked back towards the lake. "Will that armored car follow us?"

"Not those men. They are afraid to venture further into the desert without a large escort, but that is not so of the men shadowing us. I have kept my counsel to avoid alarming you unnecessarily, but these particular soldiers of the Egyptian Camel Corps are Tuareg and our sworn enemies. They will certainly come for us now."

"How many of them?"

"I counted eleven mounted this morning, and all carrying Russian assault rifles." Muhammad Beg smiled and tapped his Lee Enfield, "But they do not have our range or such fine camels. We shall account for many before they close on us."

Buber looked at Hawkspurr. "I was hoping to escape without a fight, but we still have many miles to travel before I can signal for an evacuation flight."

"Well if we can't outrun them, I'll stay behind with Muhammad and one other man to hold them off until you reach your radio Joe. With luck we'll rendezvous with you later." Hawkspurr felt it imperative that Buber's reports were relayed to Tel Aviv as soon as possible.

As they spoke a sand-laden breeze stirred their robes, and the haze thickened on the eastern horizon.

Muhammad looked pleased. "The omens are favorable, this haboob will favor us and I suggest that we stay together a few more hours and then lay an ambush for the Tuareg. None of their aircraft will fly in this desert wind."

Hawkspurr was not displeased at the idea. "I like that, let's get cracking."

For three more hours the group rode confidently towards their destination the Wadi al Husji where, Buber assured Hawkspurr a special signal unit of Israeli paratroopers would be in place and waiting for him—their sole assignment being to ensure the agent's safe return to Israeli territory.

Riding well to the fore of the party, Muhammad slowly reigned in his camel and pointed to a feature just ahead.

It consisted of a ruined stone wall set in a large hollow surrounded by course sand.

"In Roman times this was an important well, and the site of a disastrous battle for the invaders; the water has long dried up but it is a fitting place to fight our own enemies."

Enthusiastically, the Bedouin couched their camels for shelter behind a section of the ancient wall, and unloaded water skins, dates, dried figs, and extra bandoliers of ammunition from the saddlebags.

As his men positioned themselves strategically to engage in battle, Muhammad approached Buber and Hawkspurr. "It is time for us to part company Joseph, I will send our youngest warrior Siraj with you and Hawk, to guide your journey to Wadi al Husji. Suliman and Ahmed are content to stay and fight."

Hawkspurr examined the features of these warriors from another century, hard lean bodies with predatory profiles and serious demeanor, they had evolved to live and survive in one of the most hostile environments on earth, yet retained an almost child-like quality of simplicity.

Now they were prepared to die for unbelievers, on the orders of their hereditary leader.

"No bloody way Muhammad!" Hawkspurr protested. "I for one am staying put, at least until we cut down the Egyptian numbers or they turn tail and run."

"And do you think an Israeli would leave an Englishman to protect him?" Buber smiled. "No. We all stay and fight, my men will remain in place indefinitely, or at least until the invasion starts."

Hawkspurr then confronted Buber. "So! You sneaky bastard—you do know when the attack begins?"

"Only within a week or so Hawk, much will depend on the information I have yet to submit."

"Fair enough, just as long as your lot get me back to Cyprus in time to make my report."

The discussion came to an abrupt end, as a single shot rang out above the low moan of the wind, and Muhammad, Buber and Hawkspurr threw themselves to the ground. For the first time in his life, young Siraj had laid the sights of a rifle on the enemy, and was unable to resist firing off an early round.

A fierce volley of gunfire from the Camel Corps soldiers answered the shot, which fortuitously fell short of the target.

Hawkspurr peered into the distant haze, but could barely discern the unclear figures shimmering in the oppressive heat waves. He slid his rifle forward, and levered a shell into the chamber before raising the muzzle to take aim.

"No Hawk, wait."

Muhammad placed a restraining hand on the barrel. "Soon they will advance, and you can have a clean shot. Mounted men will charge in the center while soldiers on foot attempt to attack our flanks."

Hawkspurr blinked to clear watering eyes, and turned his head to examine the Bedouin leader. Muhammad had an expectant air of elation on his face as he waited for battle, and grinned back at the Englishman.

"I know their tactics well, wait for my signal please Hawk." He crawled away to speak with his men.

Buber inched up to Hawkspurr behind the low Sanger. "You do realize that neither of us are acting responsibly Hawk?" He beamed, "You bring out the boy in me, when I should be getting this information back to my masters!"

Hawkspurr pointed to the foreground. "To late old chap, here come our guests."

Five mounted riflemen were trotting towards their position in a skirmish line, and a trick of light in the extreme heat made them appear to be floating inches above the ground.

Muhammad called out softly. "Hawk, take number one on your left. Joseph, number two."

Hawkspurr thumbed forward the safety catch and laid a bead on the thickest part of the bobbing target waiting for the command. He estimated a range of six hundred yards and adjusted his rear sight.

"Fire!"

Six weapons responded as advancing line faltered and stopped.

Hawkspurr watched with satisfaction as his bullet found its mark, and a rifleman was hurled backwards from his mount. Smoothly he reloaded, and aimed at Buber's man who was reeling in the saddle but still firing ahead.

Buber's second shot echoed his own, and the wounded man dropped to the sand dead, as Bedouin marksmen accounted for the remainder.

Five camels, riderless and confused turned and ambled away from the noise of combat.

"Hawk, Joseph, take the left flank!" Muhammad Beg was cool and in command of the situation; there was no time for self-congratulation.

Hawkspurr and Buber leopard-crawled from the shelter of the stone Sanger, and moved cautiously up to the edge of the depression. As they scrutinized the desert plain an excited Siraj joined them.

"See! There…" The sharp-eyed Bedouin indicated a barely discernible hump just 400 yards from them. "And there!" In his eagerness the young warrior stood upright, and pointed further to the right with his rifle barrel.

In the second that Hawkspurr reached desperately to pull him down, a burst of fire smashed into the Bedouin's body and he fell back to earth, his robes painted with the scarlet roses of death.

"Ye gods!" Hawkspurr pulled the body to him and placed his hands helplessly on the patterns of blood—he could neither stem the flow nor bring back the light of life to faded sight.

Enraged now and not heeding Buber's warnings, he crawled over the edge of the basin and searched the sand. There was a brief flash of reflected light as the enemy he was seeking lowered his face to conceal his location.

Hawkspurr scrambled to a kneeling position and aimed at the darker shape of a desert cloak. Once…twice…three times he fired in rapid succession…The target jerked erratically and was still.

Hawkspurr ran forward, as another exchange of gunfire split the silence of the wilderness around him.

Ignoring all else he reached the Arab soldier, and keeping his rifle aimed at the head nudged the body over with his foot.

'Good!' The bastard was even now enjoying his reward in paradise. Hawkspurr bent over the corpse, removed the ornate yet practical short-sword from the waist sash and placed it in his own belt—the ultimate humiliation for a dead Muslim warrior. Then he collected the Russian AK-47 assault rifle and a spare magazine the soldier was carrying; the Bedouin would no doubt soon adapt to new weaponry.

The firing had stopped and Hawkspurr stood upright to survey the scene of recent conflict. He cursed himself for allowing his emotions to get the better of him—he still had much to learn of control—and suddenly realized that during this assignment, his 24th birthday had passed without celebration.

Behind him Buber, Muhammad, and the other Bedouin were grouped sadly around the body of Siraj. There would be great sorrow in the tents of the tribe when they learned of the young man's fate, and Hawkspurr could not help but feel somewhat responsible.

He looked to the West, and saw camels retreating into the distance with three riders who had survived the assault. Well despite the cost, the Bedouin had achieved their objective, and gained a small victory to relate over the campfires when they were old men.

He and Buber must now consolidate that triumph, and convey their information to the right quarters.

Solemnly the Bedouin buried Siraj in the sand, and to safeguard his body from the fox and jackal, piled stones from the Roman wall upon his grave.

Muhammad Beg intoned words of praise from the Koran, and promised to return one day for a more fitting ceremony.

The remainder of the journey was uneventful, and dusk found the party at Wadi al Husji, where his fellow countrymen welcomed Buber.

The Israeli paratroopers transmitted a prearranged signal, and a coded reply verified an evacuation by air at first light.

The Bedouin stayed with them long enough to eat a hot meal provided by the soldiers, and in the cool of the night bade farewell to the afrangi. Hawkspurr shook each man by the hand and thanked him in his own tongue.

"Shukran jazeelan." He stood in front of Muhammad Beg, who placed both hands upon his shoulders and looked deep into his eyes.

"You are truly a warrior Hawk—and aptly named. One day we will fight side by side again, and until that time may Allah or your gods protect you my brother."

"Thank you Muhammad Beg, and if you ever need my help I give you this address which will always find me." Hawkspurr grinned. "Sooner or later!"

"Insh'allah Hawk. God willing."

Hawkspurr and Buber stood together silently, and watched their erstwhile comrades disappear into the desert for some minutes, before the Englishman turned to his friend the Jew and spoke.

"That was a wonderful experience Joseph, one I shall never forget."

Hawkspurr slept fitfully that night; the temperature was decreasing as autumn drew on, and he had a sense of momentous happenings to come. Was this crisis heralding the start of World War Three? Russia, America, and other Arab states all had agendas of their own, and even the British parliament was split over what action—if any—to take.

Israel was under constant attack by 'fedayun'—self-sacrificing terrorists—and as Buber had hinted, was ready and willing to push back their borders with Egypt.

Despite their present uneasy alliance, would Britain attack Israel if she in turn captured the Suez Canal? Of the western nations, it looked as if Britain and France stood alone in their determination to punish Nasser's preemptory seizure of the vital sea link.

First light saw Hawkspurr and the Israelis preparing to move out. The radio operator was sending a beacon signal and before long a helicopter became visible, skimming just feet above the desert to avoid Egyptian radar. As the big Sikorsky landed in a sand storm of its own making, a flight of Israeli Mystere fighters invaded Egyptian air space to the north, as decoys to distract any patrolling MiGs.

Arriving at the forward Israeli air base, Hawkspurr and Buber parted from the taciturn paratroopers without a word, and were shepherded onto awaiting transport bound for Tel Aviv. Once airborne, they changed from desert robes into their civilian clothes, although both were badly in need of a bath and shave—a fact confirmed by the wrinkled nose of an airman who brought them sandwiches and a flask of coffee and then hastily left them alone.

After eating Buber went forward to use the radio, and when he returned sat beside Hawkspurr and smiled a little dolefully. "I won't be getting off the 'plane with you in Tel Aviv Hawk, I've been summoned urgently elsewhere so we only have a short time together. The saddest part of soldiering is constantly saying goodbye to ones comrades—the men who become closer than any relative. To demonstrate my trust in you, I shall confide that Israel will attack Egypt across the Sinai in five days time—the 29th of October. You mustn't disclose this to a single soul, as I have no idea how your country will react."

He placed a hand on Hawkspurr's knee. "Who knows? We might be facing each other across a gun sight next month!"

Hawkspurr grinned disarmingly. "And you understand that I will have to shoot you—you old Yid!"

The aircraft taxied to a halt beside a guarded hanger, and Buber walked Hawkspurr to the door of the 'plane. The two did not speak again, but hugged each other fiercely before Hawkspurr strode away without a backward glance.

Once more Hawkspurr was greeted with reticence by dour Israeli officials—'Spooks' or army officers in plain clothes was his shrewd guess—and escorted by car to a civilian commercial airliner, where he was handed an envelope of documents.

Hawkspurr too knew how to keep his mouth shut and asked no questions, but was surprised to find in the envelope a booking for two days in a luxury Beirut hotel, all expenses paid by a certain Israeli business house with connections in London. The enclosed airline ticket included a single flight leg to Nicosia. He was on his way home.

Hawkspurr woke with a start triggered by an intrusive tapping, and instinctively reached out for his female companion of the previous night, only to find that the lady had already departed.

The unaccustomed comfort of the bed had snared him into sleeping late. "Blast!" He climbed out of the yielding mattress that was almost swallowing him, and padded across to the door. "Yes!" He was not in a good mood.

"A message m'sieur." Hawkspurr opened the door slightly and reached out a hand.

He heard the maid utter a gasp of embarrassment, and realized that he was stark naked. He smiled sweetly and slapped his thigh, "Sorry I can't offer you a tip I have no pockets, but I'll see you later.

"Merci."

He closed the door and tore open the tiny envelope. 'Mr W. Hall requests the pleasure of your company in the dining room, at your earliest convenience.' It read.

"Ye gods! Brigadier Hazlett."

So much for his first day of leave, which he had planned to spend at the beach with a supply of cold beer and a dusky damsel.

Hawkspurr bathed and dressed in his Egyptian suit—after all he was still Doctor Michael Johnson, Irish academic.

"Hallo Nyles please sit down, I've taken the liberty of ordering you a hearty breakfast. Croissants and coffee are hardly substantial fare for an Englishman, what?" The Brigadier always came straight to the point.

"Thank you sir, I did intend to stuff myself for the next two days. By the way, nice to see you too! Does this mean that my vacation is over?"

"Not at all, I just thought it expedient to debrief you quietly here. The political scene at home is rather chaotic—but I promise I won't detain you for long."

Whilst he ate, Hawkspurr summarized all details of his mission, and handed over a copy of Buber's neatly inscribed reports.

Brigadier Hazlett seemed satisfied with Hawkspurr's account, and gave him a rare smile. "Well done Nyles. Tell me, are you still interested in flying?"

"Very much sir, I've been gliding since I was sixteen with the Army Club at Lasham."

"Excellent, that's what I understood. Now I think that when this current crisis is over you should convert to light aircraft, and to that end I've enrolled you for the course at Middle Wallop. It could well prove advantageous to us both in the future. Oh by the way, you'll be pleased to learn that your friend Hassan passed on all relevant information from your foray into the Canal Authority Offices. This will most certainly have considerable bearing on any type of punitive action the government may instigate regarding Suez."

Hawkspurr's loyalty was put under pressure at that moment. Should he betray his friend Buber and disclose the date of the Israeli attack, or assume that the wily Brigadier already knew? The British politicians were still procrastinating, and a leak could cause the unnecessary deaths of many Israeli soldiers, including Buber's. He kept quiet.

# CHAPTER 20

4pm, 29 October 1956. 395 Israeli paratroopers dropped from 16 Dakota transports at Mitla Pass 30 miles east of Suez, capturing the main Egyptian border posts on the southern section.

The allied air offensive began at dusk on 31 October, when 200 Canberras, Venoms and Valiants, along with 40 French Thunderstreaks operating from aircraft carriers, swept over the delta and canal airfields. The plan was to crater the airfields at night and then destroy the airplanes on the ground at first light. Prior to the raids, radio announcements and leaflets warned Egyptians to keep away from these targets. In the Gulf of Suez HMS Newfoundland sank an Egyptian frigate.

On the night of 31 October, Nasser ordered a general withdrawal of his army in Sinai to concentrate around Cairo, which considerably relieved the pressure on the Israelis. Orders were then issued to sink 47 ships filled with concrete to effectively block the canal.

By 5 November Israel had captured all her objectives for the loss of 200 killed against 2,000 Egyptian deaths, (some at the hands of Bedouin tribesmen Muhammad Beg would now have a plentiful stock of automatic weapons and ammunition!)

One minute past midnight on the 5th of November, and a single low flying aircraft crossed into Egypt under cover of yet another bombing sortie to the west.

Hawkspurr sat next to the exit door of the transport, and glanced forward down the length of the fuselage. Next to him Jimmy McKenzie sat with his head back and eyes closed, likewise the remainder of Talon Troop looked at ease, munching on apples or otherwise pretending to sleep; all conversation ceased once the coast had been crossed.

On the starboard side of the aircraft opposite Hawkspurr, fourteen paratroopers of the Premier Battalion REP, French Foreign Legion sat with equal self-assurance. Hawkspurr had come to admire these very professional soldiers during their training period together; they were tough men with shaven heads lean hard bodies and gave total allegiance to La Legion, if not to France. Not that his own men were exactly novice nuns!

Every man in the airplane was a veteran of the wars in either Indo-China, Korea, Malaya, Kenya, Algeria or Cyprus, but due to Hawkspurr's special knowledge of their current target, he had been placed in command of this operation.

Hawkspurr had been quite prepared to carry out the attack with Talon Troop alone, but the Anglo/French accord was an uneasy alliance, with petty jealousies and national pride clouding operational decisions at high level. On the other hand, issues for the ordinary soldier were perfectly clear defeat the Egyptians, and recapture the Suez Canal.

Hawkspurr was happy with the combined effort but had insisted that the Legionnaires be English speaking, in order for the unit to be fully integrated. Thus the French unit was comprised of Australians, Americans, Canadians, Englishmen, South Africans, and a New Zealander.

During their preparations in Cyprus, Hawkspurr had built a scale model of the installation on the Great Bitter Lake reasonably accurate thanks to the photographs taken by Buber, and in recognition of the Israeli's contribution the mission had been codenamed Operation Joseph.

Hawkspurr's assignment was simple; capture the installation and hold it until relieved by a British armored unit within forty-eight hours providing the invasion went to plan.

To achieve this goal he had divided his small force into four mixed sections, each with a specific area of attack.

Hawkspurr's personal responsibility was to board the Mount Nimba and seize the illegal arms shipment, and if this was not possible he was to destroy both ship and weapons.

Of course it would have been an easy matter for the RAF to bomb the vessel and the installation, but for intelligence and propaganda purposes the High Command wanted the systems and apparatus intact—probably to embarrass the Americans whom, it was suspected had unwittingly supplied some of the technology.

"Stand up!"

"Hook up!"

"Action stations!"

The RAF dispatcher positioned Hawkspurr at the door. "Good luck sir!" he shouted as he kept an eye on the red light above the exit.

Hawkspurr steadied himself against the slight buffeting the aircraft was receiving from flying just below a thousand feet. This was to be a minimum height drop, and Hawkspurr knew from experience that he would hit the ground before his full senses caught up with his body; only instinct and hours of training would govern the descent.

Green light on—"GO!"

Hawkspurr leapt outwards, grasping his pack firmly to his chest as the slipstream hit, and swept him sideways and under the tailplane. The roar of motors diminished, and in an instance he felt a reassuring tug as the parachute was dragged away from his back and deployed with a thwack. Quickly he released his pack and weapon bag to let it dangle beneath his feet, and automatically looked around—good, in the pale starlight he could discern the paratroopers strung out behind him in a nice tight stick.

Automatically he raised his hands to grasp the rear risers and pulled down on the riggings lines, only guessing that he was drifting forward.

The maneuver became academic as he abruptly struck the ground with a thump, and instinctively his feet and knees came together as he rolled onto knee, thigh, and back. There was no surface wind to drag him, so he struck the quick release buckle and slipped out of the parachute harness. Still on his back he pulled the pack to him and recovered his carbine from the weapons bag, then discarded the obligatory steel jump helmet in favor of his regimental red beret.

He could scarcely believe their luck. The whole stick was down without a shot being fired.

Perhaps the garrison troops were expecting to find only more leaflets in the morning, assuming that they had even heard the aircraft.

As Hawkspurr squatted for a better view of the area, he was joined by McKenzie with Nobby Clarke his radio operator, Craig Peters the boat expert, Doctor Harry Faulconer, and Legionnaires Mercier and Findlay—this section designated Talon One would stay with him. Billy McDonald, and two Legion NCOs respectively commanded Talons Two, Three, and Four.

"Right Nobby, pass the signal."

Clarke whispered into his walkie-talkie radio. "Strike, strike, strike."

Hawkspurr and Talon One headed for their objective, the guard post at the jetty.

After cutting the perimeter wire and crawling through undetected, they reached the sandbag and barbed wire emplacement just as automatic gunfire sounded from the main installation.

"Grenades!" He ordered, and lobbed a bomb through the nearest gun port—crouching down until the other detonations had subsided.

McKenzie and Mercier charged into the bunker firing from the hip, and by the time Hawkspurr joined them the hapless Egyptians manning the machine guns were all dead without firing a shot.

"Right Fab, set up your aid post here. Findlay you stay and hold the fort. Don't ask any questions just shoot any Egyptians who approach. Let's move."

As Hawkspurr led his section onto the jetty, he heard bare feet pounding on the boards and nearly tripped over a pair of boots and a discarded rifle. Ahead he saw two fleeing figures, and fired a burst at them. As one man fell, the other halted with his hands in the air, and cried out in English.

"Don't shoot Johnny, don't shoot!"

Legionnaire Mercier suddenly ran ahead of Hawkspurr to shoot the man dead, and for good measure put another bullet into the Egyptian on the decking.

"Was that bloody necessary Mercier?"

The French Canadian shrugged. "We have learnt in Algeria Mon Capitaine that the only opponent you can trust, is a dead one."

"Well I've no time to moralize right now, let's get out to that ship."

As Hawkspurr spoke, gunfire and grenade explosions in the vicinity of the main installation intensified, including a heavier machine gun than his troop carried. Patently, some of the Egyptians were fighting back.

Not so the sentries stationed at the lake end of the jetty. Screams of alarm and splashes could be heard, as the soldiers threw themselves into the lake when Hawkspurr's group approached them.

'Wonder if the crocodiles from the Nile ever get over this far, or for that matter sharks from the Red Sea?' Hawkspurr idly mused.

"Here's a boat sir." Craig Peters had found what he was looking for, although Hawkspurr had included two inflatable rubber rafts in the equipment dropped with them.

"All aboard then." Hawkspurr steadied the wooden bumboat as the other four climbed in, and then positioned himself in the bow. Clarke and Mercier manned the oars, and they headed for the bulk of the Mount Nimba riding at anchor.

Due no doubt to an enforced blackout there was not a single light to be seen, all the same Hawkspurr trained his carbine up to the deck level watching for a sentry.

Level? He was puzzled for a moment and then realized that the Plimsoll line was much further out of the water than had shown in the photographs. An apprehensive thought struck him—the ship had already been unloaded.

"Blast!" Hawkspurr pointed amidships, "There." Peters steered for a ladder suspended from the hull, and attached to a floating platform. Again Hawkspurr held the boat, and tied it before swiftly climbing the ladder after his men.

"Jimmy, you and Mercier go aft. Craig check for'ad especially the foc'sle, Nobby you're with me."

Hawkspurr headed for the bridge and the Captain's cabin; once the others had cleared the upper decks they would work their way below.

Right now Hawkspurr wanted answers—he was sure that the arms had been transshipped, but he still needed to know their destination.

He felt that he had underestimated Von Harzburg, and given him too much time to formulate an alternative plan after their confrontation in Port Said.

As Hawkspurr climbed the top companionway to the bridge, a flurry of wild shots passed over his head and shattered a rail below. Firing with one hand in the general direction of his assailant, he reached the next deck to see a door close to his front.

He aimed a rapid burst at the handle, aided it with a weighty kick, and followed through by tossing a hand grenade. Charging in he saw a bloodied figure in Egyptian Naval uniform still holding an AK47 assault rifle, and finished him with a shot to the head.

Elsewhere he heard sporadic shooting as the vessel was systematically cleared of crew and guards, and he started to search cupboards and shelves for any incriminating documents.

"Nothing of importance here Nobby, we'd better find the Captain's cabin."

Hawkspurr negotiated a short ladder down to the superstructure below the bridge, and entered a narrow passageway. Four closed doors probably contained the officers' quarters, and he signaled Clarke to keep an eye on the others as he flung open the door on his right.

It was unoccupied but definitely the cabin he was seeking with a desk and extra bookshelves, and a brass sextant lying on top of the table together with charts of the Mediterranean.

One of the desk drawers was locked, and Hawkspurr forced it open with his trench knife to find the object of his search—the ship's log. Unfortunately it was written in Italian, but his schoolboy Latin was sufficient to decipher one entry regarding a rendezvous with a Greek registered yacht the 'Hermes'. Bills of lading under the log, showed a transfer of sealed crates containing 'Wine making & sundry viniculture machinery'. Right! Hawkspurr placed the documents into his pack.

"Nothing more to be gained here Nobby, but we'd better check the other cabins just to be sure."

Two cabins were empty including the stateroom which Hawkspurr remembered only too well—and where the Greek armaments dealer had received his final and just desserts in Spain.

The fourth door was locked, so Clarke shot out the lock only to be greeted with the plea that was rapidly becoming the catch-cry of the operation. "Don't shoot Johnny, don't shoot!"

Inside, another Egyptian naval rating and three Italian seamen were cowering in terror—the sailor's weapon lay discarded on the floor.

"Take charge of that Nobby," Hawkspurr indicated the gun, "and tie these fellows up."

He kept the prisoners covered, whilst Clarke secured them all with parachute cord carried for that purpose.

"Ok Nobby, let's find our lads."

Back on the main deck, McKenzie, Mercier and Peters were waiting by the gangway.

"I've checked the cargo holds boss but she's as empty as the chapel on Saturday night." Peters confirmed Hawkspurr's findings.

"Thanks Craig, I've already learnt that, but at least we know who has the arms shipment now."

Hawkspurr turned to Clarke. "Check the situation ashore Nobby."

"The firing stopped about five minutes ago sir." McKenzie reported.

"All secure at the primary target boss." The radio operator confirmed as he finished his transmission.

"Roger. Are you all done here Jimmy?"

"Aye sir—no prisoners." The Scot looked pointedly at Legionnaire Mercier, who stared back at him stony faced.

"Very good gentlemen, let's join the party at the beach!"

Hawkspurr collected Legionnaire Findlay and Fab Faulconer from the guard post, and moved on to the main installation where a jubilant Sergeant

McDonald met him. "All clear boss, and only two of ours with flesh wounds—Tubby Wilson and the South African."

"Thanks Billy. Fab, take care of Wilson and Kramer please, we can expect a counter-attack in an hour or two once the Gypos realize we're in control, and I'm going to need every man."

Hawkspurr looked around at his new command. The smell of fresh cement permeated the atmosphere, and obviously the construction work was still in progress. Well the laborers could take a rest today, with the compliments of Her Majesty's government.

"What have we got to fight with Billy, apart from our own gear?"

"Heavy machine guns, anti-tank weapons, and a small anti-aircraft battery—all Czech equipment, but one of the Legionnaires is well acquainted with it."

"Good, get him to familiarize some of our boys on it. I don't expect any heavy weapons or aircraft to be used against us, because the Egyptians will want to recover the electronics intact. As soon as Nobby Wilson has his wound dressed, have him cook a decent breakfast—we have to hold out for at least two days."

At dawn that morning the 5th of November, 600 British and 487 French paratroopers dropped outside Port Said. Operation Musketeer had begun in earnest.

The second wave landed at 1.45pm and the Egyptian commander El Moguy, decided to start talking about surrender—a course which was denied him by Nasser, who told his people that World War three had started and London and Paris were under attack by missiles.

On the following day the Anglo/French armada arrived, and destroyers commenced the naval bombardment of specific targets in Port Said. Thanks in part to Hawkspurr's intelligence report, the heavily mined beaches were 'drenched with fire' and all Egyptian fire-posts knocked out.

At 4.50am British commandos supported by tanks went ashore to capture the waterfront, and then moved swiftly through the town streets. The French landed across the canal in Port Fuad at 6.45am, while their airborne troops who had invaded the day before, held off Egyptian reinforcements. Throughout the day, sporadic fighting continued. 400 more commandos were landed by Helicopter from HMS Ocean and Theseus, and the final surrender of Port Said came in the late afternoon.

In the action, the British lost twenty killed, the French ten, and the Egyptians close to a thousand men. Ten allied aircraft were lost against 260 Egyptian aircraft destroyed.

Under economic pressure from the Americans—although there were also rumors of Russian military intervention, Britain and France then decided to accept the U.N. call for a cease-fire.

In the meantime Hawkspurr and his men fought throughout the day, and successfully held off all attempts by an Egyptian infantry battalion to retake the communications center until relieved by a British armored patrol. Hawkspurr conceded that the assault had been half-hearted, with a decided reluctance to cross the barbed wire perimeter, but still all credit went the extreme accuracy of return fire from the defenders, and the humor and competitive spirit between the British and French soldiers, as they counted their hits.

For Talon Troop, this engagement had been secondary to the task of defeating the terrorists of EOKA. It was now imperative that Hawkspurr return immediately to Cyprus with his information regarding the illegal arms shipment, especially since the Royal Navy and Marines were otherwise engaged in the Suez crisis.

# CHAPTER 21

Arriving back at Nicosia airport aboard a Royal Air Force Hastings transport, in company with other troops no longer required for duty in Egypt, Hawkspurr was driven immediately to Government House for an interview with the Governor General.

Talon Troop would be fed and remain temporarily at the Air Force base, until their next move was decided.

Hawkspurr's contingent of Foreign Legionnaires had been ordered to rejoin their regiment in Algeria, but he had no intention of letting them go before they had a farewell drink with their British comrades-in-arms, and had been treated to a night in the local brothel.

Inspector Jack O'Connor was waiting for Hawkspurr with the Governor, and after polite yet brief congratulations were offered, Sir John outlined his assessment of the current situation and ordered Talon Troop to move to Kyrenia on the northern coast of the island.

Special Branch and Naval Intelligence had specific information regarding the movements of the Greek yacht 'Hermes', and Hawkspurr was to continue operations pertaining to the capture and destruction of the armaments.

O'Connor led Hawkspurr outside to his car, where Sergeants Mike Landris and Nazim Avidar were waiting to welcome him.

"Been having some fun have you lad?" The Inspector was actually pleased to see Hawkspurr, and produced a bottle of Metaxas brandy from under his seat. "A little present from me and the boys, we understand you've not had time to celebrate your victory yet."

"Thank's, this is very kind of you all. Now tell me what the score is." Hawkspurr wanted to get on with the job.

"Right!" The inspector was a no-nonsense man himself. "You and your lads will stay under canvas, here in Government House grounds for the night, then in the morning move by road to Kyrenia. Since Nazim is a native of Kyrenia, he'll accompany you as Special Branch liaison officer."

"That's fine, but what about billets in the town? I don't want to be hampered in my movements by checking in and out of another army base camp. I intend to conduct this operation in plain clothes, and with as little restriction as possible, otherwise we'll never catch Von Harzburg red-handed."

O'Connor agreed. "Just what I had in mind, and I've requisitioned an old villa a couple of miles out of town with a perfect view of the harbor approaches and coastline. Plenty of room for the whole troop, and incidentally Von Harzburg is back in Cyprus and under surveillance in Kyrenia."

Hawkspurr nodded with satisfaction. "I knew he'd surface here again, which means that the armaments are still intended for EOKA. Do you have anything incriminating on him?"

O'Connor shook his head in negation. "No Hawk, he's as clean as a whistle—it's up to you to flush him out."

"We'll do our best Jack, now please let me have a word in private with Mike Landris, I have an enquiry you don't want to know about!"

From the Greek sergeant, Hawkspurr was able to obtain the address of the best brothel in Nicosia and an assurance that it would not be raided that night!

As he had promised, Hawkspurr laid on a farewell party for the Legionnaires in the Greek bordello that would long be remembered—especially by the Madam and her young ladies. Ample food, drink, and the spirited rendering of immortal old soldiers' ditties, together with a great deal of movement up and down the stairs contributed to an evening richly deserved—in Hawkspurr's opinion at least.

Having deposited their comrades of the Legion at the airport, Talon Troop returned to spend the night in the tents of Government House.

Most of the troop were by now exhausted and went straight to sleep, but Hawkspurr, Evil Billy McDonald and Jimmy McKenzie decided to prolong the evening with a very decent bottle of brandy.

"Jeez boss, I could eat one of your bloody horses and its saddle right now." The big Australian was always hungry after drinking.

McKenzie and Hawkspurr agreed, but there was nothing available and the mess tent was securely guarded.

"What about those chooks in the garden boss?"

Hawkspurr hesitated. "We can't possibly steal the Governor's leghorns—can we?"

The trio nodded together in inebriated conspiracy.

"Of course we can!"

Stealthily, Hawkspurr and his NCOs crept through the gardens to the wire fence of the chicken run. Fortunately it was situated close to a perimeter fence, adjacent to the dry bed of a stream that bordered the official grounds, and out of sight of the house.

McKenzie being the smallest volunteered to crawl under the fence and appropriate an unsuspecting fowl.

An anxious moment passed as the Scot disappeared into the chicken house, then a minor disturbance was heard followed by a muffled squawk and the poacher appeared triumphant.

"Well done Jimmy." Hawkspurr whispered, "let's get the hell away from here."

"Where are we going to pluck it?"

"The latrines." Suggested Hawkspurr, and the culprits made their way to the temporary toilet block.

A series of open cubicles stretched before them, and they moved to the far end of the row and lifted the wooden seat. Giggling like the delinquents they were, each man pulled, plucked and deposited his handful of feathers into the stinking maw of the toilet pit.

Finally Evil Billy cut off the head, gutted the fowl with his trench knife and closed the lid of the long box with a drunken sigh of satisfaction.

"All done!"

Then disaster struck; a sleepy soldier from the infantry guard unit wandered into the latrine, and with eyes half closed opened the lid closest to the door.

WHOOSH! An explosive updraft from the warm pit discharged a cloud of pure white feathers high into the air and engulfed him—the unfortunate young man retreated in terror, probably to complete his bodily functions in his pants.

Hawkspurr, McDonald and McKenzie all but collapsed in hysterical laughter but retained enough discretion to gather the incriminating feathers, and put them back where they belonged—this time leaving a lid open.

The resultant snack of chicken portions fried in a mess tin over a hexamine cooker was all the more delicious for it's vice regal origins.

Because of the strength of its mediaeval castle, Kyrenia had survived centuries of piratical attacks to become the favorite haunt of retired civil servants and schoolteachers. The fantastic harbor scene it presented was a painter's charm, with boats lazing at anchor in the shadow of Crusaders' walls, and the lighthouse dipping its ancient feet into crystal waters.

Along the wharf once proud Venetian mansions were now restaurants, and local fishermen loitered and drank, and cursed the military for driving away the lucrative tourist trade.

Inland, and high on a mountaintop dominating the town stood another impregnable fortress the castle of St.Hilarion. It straddles the Nicosia/Kyrenia road, and even in ruins the dramatic walls and towers of today soar from the rocky crags and ravines imparting a fairy tale quality, which still gives rise to tales of treasure, mystical rooms, and enchanted gardens.

Although dilapidated, the deserted villa had a reasonably sound roof and ample facilities to house the men of Talon Troop. Nazim had decided to lodge with the soldiers for the duration of the operation so that Hawkspurr could readily draw upon his local knowledge, and an added bonus of this, was that the Turkish sergeant had been supplied with a civilian motorcar.

Special Branch information had located the Greek yacht cruising off Cyprus but in international waters, and Great Britain's current, delicate relationship with the United Nations Organization did not allow for any leeway concerning contravention of a sovereign country's rights.

Since Greek Cypriot fishing vessels had been spotted in the vicinity of the yacht, Hawkspurr's plan was to commandeer a similar boat and keep a closer eye on any activity in the area. Craig Peters was more than competent to handle a fishing smack, and each man of Talon Troop had been trained in small boat handling.

The only other specialized equipment Hawkspurr might need was underwater breathing apparatus, and since the winter was drawing on, a few sets of frogman's' protective suits.

All members of the troop were to work in civilian clothes, and to avoid any confusion or confrontation, local British units were being temporarily withdrawn from town duties to concentrate on operations in the surrounding mountains.

When it was reported to Hawkspurr that Von Harzburg had taken up fishing as a pastime, he knew that his instincts were correct; the German was planning to bring arms into Cyprus utilizing the local Greek fishing community.

To cover this agendum as widely as possible, Hawkspurr split the troop into smaller sections, with Doctor Faulconer, Tubby Wilson the cook, and Nobby Clarke the radio operator, based at headquarters in the villa.

Three sections would covertly patrol the coast on foot to locate any possible landing sites on either side of the town, and Hawkspurr, Peters, Nelson and McKenzie would man the fishing boat.

Nazim Avidar joyfully approved of the scheme as he had been raised as a fisherman before joining the police. What was more, it would not be necessary to impound a boat, as his cousin would gladly provide the vessel.

Hawkspurr did not like to involve civilians, but at least he would ensure that Nazim's family was properly compensated in case of an accident. His only stipulation was that Nazim must skipper the boat personally, and that his cousin take no part in the operation, or even be seen with the men of Talon Troop.

The last thing Hawkspurr wanted was the blood of retaliation on his hands once he left the district.

When the unit was settled into the billet and their gear stowed away, Hawkspurr drew lots for two men to remain on guard whilst the others carried out plain-clothes reconnaissance of the town. It was intended that the men enjoy themselves in twos and threes, but ignore the other groups and mix with the natives where possible—knowing that the judicious provision of a friendly drink could provide much information.

Hawkspurr and Nazim Avidar strolled casually through the streets of Kyrenia enjoying the atmosphere, it was dusk and a faint breeze wafting down from the hills was scented with the fragrant scent of pine and herbs. They had visited Nazim's cousin and arranged for the hire of the fishing boat whilst the owner visited relatives in Famagusta, now the Turk had promised a treat in store for Hawkspurr.

Although Nazim and his Greek colleague Mike Landris were the best of friends, each scoffed at the other's idea of traditional national hospitality.

Set in a beautiful garden of blue, white, and pink hydrangea shrubs, was the white villa called the Pasha's Palace. Heavy drapes curtained the windows, but an ornate lantern at the main entrance proclaimed the palace open for business, and inside the tiled hall of the foyer a large Turk costumed in the manner of a harem eunuch stood on guard, together with an armed policeman.

"Good evening Sergeant Avidar," The Turk spoke in good English, and laughed, "you are not dining alone tonight. That is good."

"Thank you Osman. Will you kindly inform Madame Sema that I have a friend I wish to introduce to her? We shall wait in the bar." Avidar led Hawkspurr through the beaded curtain of an archway to his right, without waiting for a reply.

Within the bar elegant oil lamps gave sufficient subdued light to flatter any lady's complexion, yet highlighted the ornate fretwork panels that decorated the upper walls, their lower sections being covered in rich red and blue Turkish carpets. The furnishings consisted of gigantic cushions and small stools for the less adventurous, which were arranged around low wooden tables inlaid with brass and ivory.

Some Western women in short skirts and bare sandaled legs, together with their service husbands looked rather incongruous in their attempts to lounge at ease in this eastern opulence. All looked slightly embarrassed and laughed too loudly as they sipped exotic drinks.

Traditional Eastern music emanated from the adjoining dining room, and serving girls wearing long flounced skirts with multi-colored headdress, glided barefoot from bar to tables carrying brass trays of food dishes and beverages to the customers.

Hawkspurr followed Avidar's example and seated himself cross-legged with the ease of experience on a cushion against the wall. From this position they could observe both exits and all the guests.

Avidar ordered a bottle wine, and they did not have to wait long before a tall willowy woman entered the bar, and walked slowly and majestically in their direction. She was adorned in a gold embroidered floor length gown of deep blue velvet, with long wide sleeves modestly covering her arms and hands.

From her throat, a necklace of solid gold coins cascaded to accent the full bosom, and a cloth-of-gold Yashmak covered her head with one corner looped across, veiling her face so that only the eyes were visible. Henna colored toes peeped from gold sandals as she progressed across the room.

The statuesque figure glanced around and acknowledged her admiring patrons as she approached the table, and when she halted in front of Hawkspurr and Avidar, they both rose to their feet and bowed low.

Hawkspurr was struck by her intense eyes dramatically enhanced with kohl, and the flecks of reflected fire that flashed from the depths of black irises.

The woman raised a slim white hand to remove the veil. "I am Sema."

Hawkspurr was enchanted by this exotic female, and stammered uncharacteristically. "Nyles Hawkspurr…you are the most beautiful woman I have ever seen."

Sema's laugh was a chiming fountain of elixir in the Muslim paradise.

"And you so ancient!" She smiled gently at the embarrassed younger man. "May I sit down?"

"Of course. Forgive me." Hawkspurr poured a glass of wine for the woman.

The woman pouted ruby lips and cocked her head to one side as she looked at Avidar. "I suppose your young friend will not wish to stay in my establishment, now that he has seen how old I am?"

Avidar chuckled. "I have it on good authority that Hawk has a propensity for mature ladies."

Hawkspurr raised his glass, and turned mocking brown eyes upon the Turkish sergeant. "Perhaps my education is now complete. Allow me to toast Sema's health and happiness, as I offer my devotion and protection."

Sema laid a hand upon Hawkspurr's. "An offer you may regret! May I call you Nyles?"

"Please do."

"Come then Nyles Pasha we will dine together before, I present my finale for the evening."

Avidar spoke. "You will both have to excuse me, I am afraid that duty calls. The exploits of our young friend here have made a great deal of extra paper work for the poor old policeman, but I'll see you tomorrow Hawk." With a half salute he left the room.

Hawkspurr followed his hostess into the cabaret room, which was decorated in similar style to the bar but of loftier proportions. This area had been designed in colonial days as an intimate ballroom, with a musician's gallery high on one wall protected by a low balustrade of ornate wrought iron lace work.

Enclosed within, three instrumentalists sat wearing red Fez' on their heads and dressed in green baggy trousers with embroidered waistcoats over white shirts and red cummerbunds. One of the trio strummed the Saz—a traditional eight string guitar with a deep bowl and meter long neck—yet dominating the rhythm was the drummer as he manipulated a spoon shaped stick on one end of the Turkish drum emitting a thump. On the other skin he used a whippy twig, which produced a zinging noise and the third man played a Zouna—the trumpet like instrument which sounds like a snake charmer's pipe.

The huge dome of the ceiling contributed perfect acoustics, necessary to convey the ambience for this scene of Turkish delight.

Sema issued her instructions to a waitress garbed in striped transparent pantaloons, embroidered bodice and Arab style white head dress, and whilst they sipped more wine their table was laden with a variety of foods.

An entree of Cacik—cold yogurt and cucumber with dill and mint, followed by crayfish served with Imam Bayidi—braised aubergines, tomatoes and onions.

Bastirma—strips of mutton cured in garlic and peppers, and rice pilav, and then Beef and stuffed peppers. There were dishes of liver and kidneys, with unleavened bread to wrap around each mouthful and all eaten by hand.

Silver finger bowls of rose scented water were placed, with hot towels for convenience throughout the feast.

For sweets there were fresh apricots, honey and Pekmaz, a dessert made from mulberries good for stomach ailments and a cure for ulcers. Hawkspurr surveyed the table, and thought that the Pekmaz would probably be needed by morning.

Sema merely picked delicately at the dishes, but Hawkspurr had a healthy appetite and enjoyed the meal over a period of two hours. He blessed the wisdom of the Orient, where pleasures are to be savored and prolonged.

The combination of wine, spices, and the heady perfume of Sema were already having an aphrodisiac effect on Hawkspurr, and he began eyeing the woman lustfully.

Reading the message in his eyes, Sema leaned forward and caressed his thigh. "Patience Nyles, I must first dance for you."

At a sign from his hostess, the main lights in the room were extinguished leaving only the soft glow of table lamps, and the tempo of the music changed to a slow, anticipatory melody as Sema slipped away from Hawkspurr's side like an apparition in a mountain mist.

When he saw her next, she had changed into a Harem costume from an Arabian Nights fantasy. A transparent face veil was held in place by an elegant circlet of golden coins, and for the first time he appreciated that this woman's body was more that just willowy.

Slim yet sensuous limbs, the heavy breasts accentuated by a silken halter which scarcely contained their magnificence—down to the voluptuous curve of her abdomen with it's jeweled navel, and the splendor of her thighs, tantalizing in translucent skirt beaded with tiny silver bells.

Sema was accompanied by six other dancing girls, but Hawkspurr's eyes never left the predominate dancer and his loins ached for this exotic woman.

The performer twirled and dipped, sending the belled skirt billowing parallel to her waist, and Hawkspurr glimpsed the alluring curves of naked buttocks—skin glowing like alabaster as the waist long hair spun out like a fisherman's black net to ensnare her prey.

The artistes danced in unison, with arms outstretched and shoulders undulating rapidly as the miniature cymbals attached to their fingers clashed to the tempo of the performance. They swung and gyrated with whirling bodies, spinning forbidden creatures from an ancient paradise.

The spellbinding display rose to a thrilling crescendo, and the dancers dropped to their knees with invitingly spread thighs as the music ended in a crash of cymbal and tattoo from the drum.

Sema prostrated her body in offering before the man of her choice, her torso still heaving from the vigor of her efforts that threatened the containment of her breasts, and gallant Hawkspurr rose from his cushion, and lifted the beautiful dancer to her feet.

In front of the applauding guests, he removed her veil and kissed the still breathless woman fiercely upon her parted lips.

Sema gasped. "Please Nyles, give me a little longer."

Hawkspurr lowered Sema gently to a cushion and filled a glass of wine for her, yet his sensibilities were passionate and his hand shook spilling some of the wine.

The nearness of the swelling breasts—the feel of velvet skin glowing with the warmth of her exertions, and the brilliance of her eyes as she smiled, turned his mind to pulp, and his loins to a hardness of desire.

The traditional musicians left the gallery, no doubt exhausted by their frenzied rendering of the Houris' dance, and a western trio who smoothly performed a repertoire of more romantic, and less energetic numbers replaced them.

As the other diners led their partners to the dance floor, Sema took Hawkspurr's arm and led him through a door concealed behind a hanging tapestry, and guided him up a staircase leading to the private wing of her villa.

The heavy teak doors opened into a large room comfortably furnished with huge pillows and ornate couches, where the black tiles of the floor added contrast to a cool decor of rough-caste whitewashed walls. Color was provided in the form of exquisite Turkish rugs, and the gilded frames of oil paintings depicting village life in Sema's native land.

"Make yourself comfortable Nyles, you'll find coffee on the stove and brandy on the sideboard. There's someone you must meet." Sema vanished through a door.

Ignoring the coffee, Hawkspurr helped himself to a cognac and tried to relax in an armchair, but when the door opened again he stood up quickly in anticipation. If Sema's appearance disappointed him, he didn't show it for she was leading a little girl by the hand.

"Nyles Pasha, please meet my daughter Rahime."

Hawkspurr bowed and kissed the tiny hand offered to him. "Enchanted Rahime, and may I say that you are every bit as lovely as your mother."

"Thank you sir." Rahime curtsied and looked up at the man through coquettish eyes, are you my daddy?"

Sema laughed, "She knows only that her father was an Englishman—long departed, yet still she hopes he will return."

Hawkspurr blushed as he replied. "Regrettably I'm not your father, but that doesn't mean that we can't go on a picnic together one day."

"Do you promise?"

"Cross my heart and hope to die!"

"Come along Rahime you must go back to bed, and if you are good you shall see Nyles Pasha tomorrow."

Hawkspurr grinned. "Does that mean that if I'm good I'll still be here in the morning?"

"We shall see. Now I really must bathe."

Sema kissed him quickly and with her laughter ringing in his ears, she took Rahime out of the room.

The next voice he heard made him start with surprise—he had no idea anyone else was in the apartment.

"Would you care to join Madame Sema now Nyles Pasha?" It was a young woman in the plain white robe of a Muslim maid.

Hawkspurr was if anything, a man of action. He rapidly slipped off his shoes and followed the maid along a corridor running the length of the wing. One door was ajar, and as the girl ushered him through he could hear the sound of running water.

Hawkspurr entered a bathroom, and through clouds of steam spied the figure of Sema silhouetted on the smoked glass of a shower stall; engraved in the glass a Satyr chased Nymphs across a wooded glen.

The maid departed silently and Hawkspurr wasted no time divesting himself of his clothes, and sliding back the glass panel.

Sema caught Hawkspurr ardently within the circle of her arms, and pulled him to her. Her long black hair was plastered down the length of her back, and water cascaded from the exotic waterfall of her breasts as she pressed proud nipples upon Hawkspurr's chest and kissed him passionately. Perfect teeth bit gently into his lips, and she caressed the male body that was rising to her demands and needed no more encouragement.

Hawkspurr lowered his head to anoint the woman's form with kisses—his mouth moved from full breasts to her belly, down to the soft mound of tight black curls, and back to her hungry lips.

He braced himself, as the sinuous woman wrapped her arms securely around his neck and raised slender legs to clamp her thighs onto his hips, then with a sigh of pleasure she lowered her loins to join with the man.

Sema's pelvis worked with the accomplishment of an experienced dancer, and Hawkspurr aided her—raising her firm bottom in his hands as with lips and bodies locked together they attained a perfect climax.

After a few moments of tender embracement, Sema murmured an endearment in Turkish, and released herself from Hawkspurr's clasp to kneel and complete his toilet.

Stepping from the confines of the shower, Sema draped herself and Hawkspurr in huge fluffy towels.

"Please follow me Nyles." She led the way into an annex, and indicated a wide massage couch. "Lay down and relax." She ordered.

Hawkspurr obeyed as Sema clapped her hands, and through an arch the slim maid entered carrying a tray of oils and unctions, and two long stemmed glasses filled with an Eastern nectar.

Hawkspurr accepted a glass and sipped appreciatively.

"Delicious—an aphrodisiac I trust?"

He finished his drink, and rolled over face down on the couch with a sigh of contentment as the masseuse poured perfumed oil onto her hands, and commenced to manipulate the tight muscles of his upper back and shoulders.

He turned his head in order to look at Sema. "Is the girl resident?"

"Certainly. One of the little pleasures of life, as well a nursemaid for Rahime."

Hawkspurr studied the woman's prominent cheek bones and the delicate planes of her beautiful face, which brought to mind a temple carving he had once admired, depicting courtesans in the royal court of an ancient civilization.

They both fell silent, allowing the masseuse to continue her skilled kneading and rubbing, revitalizing suppleness and circulation to weary muscles. The woman giggled and chattered rapidly in Turkish, when Hawkspurr—in the process of having his abdomen massaged showed unmistakable signs of returning vigor.

"Time to leave Elisha." Sema issued her instructions, and the girl left the annex twittering to herself like a bird in an Arabian garden.

"The bedroom is this way Nyles."

Sema guided Hawkspurr to an opulent room, filled with the melody of soft Oriental music and containing a canopied bed with an antique mirrored ceiling.

"Luxury and decadence—I like it!" Remarked Hawkspurr appreciatively as he lifted Sema and carried her to the bed and laid her gently upon silken sheets.

The woman reached for him. "Come Nyles Pasha. Make love with me."

Hawkspurr submerged himself in the beauty and desire of the Turkish woman, and later in the night they stood naked in front of the windows, their arms wrapped around each other for comfort as they watched the frightening power of a storm and as it passed over; the violence of nature was reflected in the tempestuous love making that followed.

# Finale

A week passed quickly. Seven busy days, during which Talon Troop listened and watched, waiting for a chance to compromise or capture Gunter Von Harzburg and seize the illegal arms shipment. Hawkspurr had established his cover as the eccentric Dr. Michael Johnson, scholar of antiquity, and as such was guided on his expeditions by Madame Sema and her daughter Rahime.

The doctor was to be seen poking around the coastal area at all hours searching for caves, and as yet undiscovered statues or ancient artifacts both ashore and below the surface of these mysterious waters. It was rumored that he spent nights of passion in the bed of the beautiful Turkish woman; lucky fellow the menfolk sighed, but then all the world loves a lover.

Nazim Avidar was in his element as skipper of the boat, and his crew had attained a piratical image that was the envy of their shore-based comrades. Craig Peters with his long hair, and already wild undisciplined streak looked as though he might very well have descended from English buccaneers. Peter Nelson the explosives expert bore the marks of his trade in the shape of a scar that traversed his scalp and crossed the cheek to a broken nose—a disfigurement he proudly displayed by keeping his head shaven. Jimmy McKenzie epitomized the wild highland clansman, but even out of uniform retained the bearing of a soldier.

Day eight just before dawn and the men in the villa were having breakfast with Hawkspurr, who had just arrived back from the town.

Clarke was maintaining a listening watch on the radio when a crackle of static alerted the group to an incoming message.

Clarke looked excited, "Boss, the harbor watchers have spotted Von Harzburg heading out to sea aboard a fishing vessel!"

Although Nazim had been shadowing any of the local fishing fleet that ventured near the 'Hermes', this was the first time that the German had personally sailed with them, and for Hawkspurr this could mean only one thing—the arms were coming ashore soon.

"Good! Then I'm off for a cruise too. Nobby, signal Nazim to sent a dinghy to the beach and pick me up. Billy, the rest of you stay alert and be ready to consolidate as soon as I send you a map reference, I want the whole troop in position, fully armed and in uniform when the arms are landed. Grivas is sure to send as many men as he has in this area to protect the shipment, so when I've sailed notify Jack O'Connor that he should organize a cordon of troops and police in case we fail to contain the terrorists."

Hawkspurr hurried down to the bay below the villa in the garb of a fisherman, but carried his uniform and carbine in a waterproof bag. Dawn was breaking in a clear sky as he scrambled into the little wooden dinghy, and Peters rowed him out to the fishing boat where Nazim and his crew met him with enthusiasm.

"Right lads, I have a feeling that before this day ends all our hard work will payoff. Peter," he addressed the explosives expert, "do you have enough demolition satchel charges made up?"

"Yes boss plenty, and a box of hand grenades."

"That's good, but please remember that we don't want to sink any boats or kill any unarmed fishermen. I believe from what I've heard that they're all working under duress, and our aim is to capture the arms only. Clear?"

The crew nodded their understanding.

"Avast skipper, up anchor and follow that boat!"

Keeping a safe distance from the vessel they knew Von Harzburg was on, Nazim steered a course for the last known position of the yacht 'Hermes'. The sea offered a gentle swell, but King Neptune appeared to be smiling on the amateur seamen and the boat ducked happily into the low waves without undue stress.

Hawkspurr was both disappointed and puzzled when still at a reasonable distance from the fishing fleet, he could see no sign of the Greek yacht through his binoculars. Was this activity by Von Harzburg simply a ruse to keep the security forces off balance, while the yacht made landfall on some other part of the island? He and his men had been extremely cautious, and Hawkspurr could not bring himself to believe that he had wasted their time on this operation.

Nazim was also carefully scanning the movements of the Greek fishing boats. "Hawk! Look at the last boat to the east, watch his net coming up."

Hawkspurr switched his observation to the far boat, and studied it intensely as he braced himself against the swell. The stern of the vessel was certainly well down in the water, indicating a very heavy catch of fish, but even as he looked he saw the unmistakable contours of a crate being hauled deliberately aboard the boat.

"Nazim," he called, "show me the charts of this area please."

Nazim hurried to Hawkspurr and spread a chart on the deck hatch. He ran his finger over the map until he found the right spot. "There, precisely over the Makiti shoal the most shallow sandbank in this sector."

"Clever! Bloody diabolical, and I'll bet the credit goes to Von Harzburg. The fishermen only have to dredge up the boxes, and deliver them at will to some prearranged rendezvous on the coast. Even if the navy had caught them red handed, they could deny any involvement and say they were going to report the find as soon as they returned to harbor."

"Ok Hawk, but what do we do now, we can't arrest seven boats and their crews—as soon as we approach one they'll all scatter."

"You're right Nazim, tack away—or whatever the correct nautical term is. I want to know where to intercept them on shore, otherwise I would have asked for naval support—not that there are any ships available they're still engaged at Port Said and Suez, so let's get as far from them as possible without losing contact."

Nazim changed course as if seeking a less crowded fishing ground, and whilst Hawkspurr watched from the stern, Peters and Nelson went through the motions of trawling the nets.

The day passed slowly for Hawkspurr and his crew, but the Greek boats in the distance kept busy and remained together until late evening. Was Von Harzburg going to attempt a night landing on the coast?

Hawkspurr pondered the question, and the pros and cons, which he conjectured were passing through his adversary's mind. No, a landing in the dark on a secluded beach with fishermen accustomed only to handling fish from boat to wharf would be dangerous and foolhardy. Dawn had to be the obvious choice.

Hawkspurr conveyed his thoughts to the Special Branch policeman, and conferred with Peters and Nelson as to their best plan of action. All agreed that a dawn landing made more sense.

"I think that the goods will be hidden somewhere, so that EOKA groups can collect them at their own convenience, and in small parties which won't attract attention. They can hardly expect to march undetected with a caravan of donkeys through our army patrols."

"So we're looking for a ruin, or caves close to the coast?" Nazim was smiling as if he already had the answer.

"Precisely, so where do you suggest we look?"

Nazim produced his maps again. "Here, about twenty-five miles east of Kyrenia where the road ends. There are plenty of unexplored caves on a very rough stretch of coast, and enough superstitious tales of gods and demons to keep the curious peasants away."

Hawkspurr studied the chart. "That makes sense to me, I suggest we head there now and hide in one of these little coves. I'll alert the lads ashore to be in place—this time they can use the Rovers with the machine guns and give EOKA a real fight."

It was after midnight when Hawkspurr went ashore in an unnamed cove, to meet Sergeant McDonald and the others of Talon Troop.

The villa had been left unattended, and Fab Faulconer and Tubby Wilson had set up a camp kitchen and first aid post in a sheltered spot that wouldn't be spotted from the sea. The soldiers ate a good meal, and sentries were posted on the cliff tops whilst those not on duty tried to get some sleep.

Hawkspurr was woken up by Billy McDonald offering a mug of hot tea before first light, and warned that the sentries could see navigation lights from several fishing boats approaching the coast.

"Great. At least I made the right decision. Rouse the rest of the lads, and make sure they have a solid breakfast it could be a hard day ahead. I'm going back to the boat now, but you know what to do, just keep the troop well spread out until we can pinpoint the exact location of the drop site. If we lose radio contact use your initiative and take any action you see fit, I know you wont let me down."

"No sweat boss—see youse later." Evil Billy went about his duties.

Hawkspurr sent for Kevin Richards, his underwater diving instructor. "Are the air tanks full Kevin?"

"Yes boss, all the SCUBA equipment is checked and ready for use."

"Fine. You and Jimmy get suited up, we're going for a swim."

Hawkspurr returned to the boat, and advised Nazim to keep the vessel out of sight until required.

"Jimmy and Kevin are coming with me, and I intend to stay underwater close to the shore until we discover the rendezvous. The lads on land have instructions to let the fishermen off-load their cargo and return to harbor unmolested—what happens to them later is a matter for the police."

"Right Hawk," Nazim agreed reluctantly, as he helped Hawkspurr into the rubber diving suit and air tank, "but I'll be monitoring the situation closely, and if you look like getting into trouble I'm coming out."

Richards and McKenzie were already in the water of the cove, floating so that only the black shiny heads showed, with their eyes looking up like a pair of tame seals.

Hawkspurr sat on the rail to pull on his fins, and then tipped over backwards to plunge into the still green depths. He stabilized himself, to twist around for orientation as the other divers joined him, circled thumb and forefinger 'Ok', and then pointed to the mouth of the cove and the northern Mediterranean beyond.

Each man was armed with a knife and two satchels of underwater demolition charges, as in a triangle of flight like wild geese they glided over sand dappled with growing light, until the sea floor started to drop away into a harder blue of deeper water.

As they descended Hawkspurr stopped for a moment, to tread water as the pressure equalized in his ears. He pointed west and kicked off strongly again, swimming parallel to the coast with underwater cliffs and towers eroded by time and earthquakes looming over them.

Ahead he saw a barnacle encrusted monolith, too perfect to be the careless work of nature, the stones it was constructed of were almost invisible under a blanket of russet brown sub aqueous flowers and weeds. To one side the sand layered up in great wrinkles to rest against a once mighty pillar, and beyond the bed fell into great squares which must surely outline the chambers of a town that was older than the Roman Empire.

Bright fingers of color darted away in panic, to seek refuge beneath clam shells that reminded Hawkspurr of elephants' ears silvered in moonlight on the African veldt.

A sudden burst of light exploded in oblique wavering shafts, as the sun popped above the unseen horizon at their backs, and Hawkspurr was so engrossed with the beauty of his surroundings, he might well have swum on unheeding, until he reached the shores of Crete.

It was a tap on his shoulder from McKenzie that brought Hawkspurr back to reality, and he paddled forward to come upright and stare around.

Hovering weightlessly and effortlessly he followed McKenzie's extended arm; two hundred yards away the black shape of a boat hull was rising and falling with the waves, and as the three watched silently and unseen, a box tumbled from the bulwarks and dropped in a trail of silver bubbles to come to rest on the sand.

Five more crates followed, before the throb of a motor increased to a muffled roar and its spinning propeller churned the sea in a spiral of power. As the boat disappeared into the distance, another arrived to take its place and more boxes fell to gather on the seabed.

Hawkspurr signed to Richards and McKenzie to follow him as he headed for the nearest point of the shore. Coming up against the corrugated walls of a cliff, he surfaced slowly to shelter behind a massive buttress that effectively hid their presence from the Greek fishermen.

Hawkspurr lifted the facemask and gratefully filled his lungs with fresh cool air, and as he steadied his body against a ledge he saw that they were close to a tiny beach nestled within arms of rock, and concealed from all human sight—surely gods and demons might just frequent such a place!

The divers crawled ashore on all fours and sat in the shingle.

"We've got them now lads—well done. Kevin, you swim back to Nazim and tell him exactly where we are, but repeat that I still want him to remain out of view unless he hears firing from the fishing boats. Get on the radio and give Sergeant McDonald our position, I want him to search for a cave entrance or path down the cliffs which could lead to a landing place."

He looked up, "There's certainly no way anyone could negotiate here with a load—not even a goat. Leave your satchel with us, Jimmy and I will maintain a watch from the surface until the boats have gone, then periodically check below, as someone has to collect the boxes. Better bring back an extra air tank and a flask of coffee, we'll make this beach our base, but if Jimmy and I are not here when you return you are not to come looking for us. Clear?"

"Got you boss."

"Off you go then." Hawkspurr watched as Richards replaced his mask, and crawled out into the water to dive in a wake of bubbles.

He turned to smile at his most trusted soldier and old friend. "At least we're not in hot water this time Jimmy!"

"No sir in fact it's a wee bit on the cold side, but then I always wanted a holiday on a Mediterranean island."

"Yes, and under different circumstances I could be quite happy living permanently on Cyprus." Hawkspurr sat quietly in thought until McKenzie spoke again.

"Are you serious about the Turkish lady sir?" The Scot asked a little reticently.

No other person—with perhaps the exception of Fab Faulconer would have dared to put the question.

Hawkspurr grinned. "You know me better than anyone Jimmy—I'm always in love—at least until we move on. Still, I have to admit that Madam Sema is a great deal more exciting than some of the women I've known."

With a brusque movement Hawkspurr reached for his mask and fins. "Come on you old agony aunt, let's get back to work!"

From the cover of a jutting rock, Hawkspurr and McKenzie scrutinized the last fishing boat to dump its cargo of weapons. The remainder of the fleet were hightailing it back to port as if Poseidon himself was holding his trident against their sterns.

McKenzie spat salt water from his mouth. "Sir!"

"I see them—down we go." Hawkspurr adjusted his mask, and let the weighted belt drag his body below the surface. Two figures were preparing to dive from the Greek boat, and he knew without a shadow of doubt that once again he was going out to confront Gunter Von Harzburg.

There was no point in swimming out to intercept the enemy. Hawkspurr first needed to know where they were headed, and to that end he kept close to the underwater cliff base, and kicked slowly along in its shadow. Occasionally small rocks fell from above and plunged down to add to the collection on the seabed.

Was this a natural occurrence, or were Talon Troop dislodging them as they searched the tops?

With a grunt of satisfaction Hawkspurr back-paddled and excitedly indicated a dark opening in the rock face—about five feet high and possibly twelve feet wide, with furrows leading in, not yet smoothed out by the tide and wave motion. He looked at McKenzie and the Scot nodded vigorously, this had to be the passage ashore and probably not the first time in history that smugglers had used this natural ingress.

Then Hawkspurr grabbed at McKenzie's arm urgently and pointed to the right. Two black-clad divers were also floating motionless above the seabed in a mirror image of themselves. For what seemed an eternity, Hawkspurr and Von Harzburg stared at each other across the intervening water—this time there could be no retreat and no quarter given.

Hawkspurr dropped the explosive charges from him and drew his knife from the leg sheath.

Simultaneously the four men scissored finned legs, and launched themselves to close the distance between them.

Instinctively Hawkspurr and Von Harzburg headed for each other and ignored their fellows; with arms extended like the knightly lances of combat they thrust deadly steel blades towards their adversary.

Hawkspurr's cold brown eyes glared across the decreasing gap into Von Harzburg's steely gray orbs and neither wavered or flinched, for both acknowledged the courage and determination of the other man.

They met in a crash and flurry of legs and arms, as each grappled to gain an advantage and slash at his opponent's body. Twisting and kicking in the alien environment, they clung together frantically lest one should free a hand and inflict a fatal wound that would terminate the encounter.

As they tumbled, the German's weight dragged his body below the Englishman, but his greater physical strength was overwhelming and he wrenched his hand free to slash at Hawkspurr's neck.

In a desperate maneuver Hawkspurr spun around, but underestimated Von Harzburg's agility, and in a powerful sweep the German's blade sliced through his air hose.

Choking as he was deprived of oxygen Hawkspurr, spat out the useless mouthpiece and attempted a last wild stab of his knife, then kicked headlong for the surface before he drowned.

For some inexplicable reason Von Harzburg did not attempt to pursue him, but as he broke surface gasping and spluttering, a second head bobbed up alongside and McKenzie reached out to assist him.

Hawkspurr coughed. "Are you Ok Jimmy?"

McKenzie lifted his mask. "Aye, what about you sir?"

"I'm fine now. What's happening below?"

"I topped the other diver sir, but Von Harzburg got away to the cave."

"Well he won't get far, give me your tank, then go back to the beach and collect Richards."

McKenzie knew better than to protest, and with a struggle managed to secure his harness on Hawkspurr.

As they floundered in the water, they heard a burst of gunfire from the cliff tops and an answering volley. Talon Troop was in action again.

"Go, go Jimmy!" Hawkspurr cleared his mask and propelled himself deep in a last anxious attempt to restrain Von Harzburg.

Skimming over the bottom he stopped only to retrieve the satchel charges from where he had jettisoned them, and headed for the cave.

As the entrance loomed closer he could clearly see marks in the shingle left by Von Harzburg and close by, McKenzie's adversary sprawled dead under the weight of his belt and tanks with a cloud of blood slowly dissipated above the corpse. Hawkspurr looked hastily around for sharks, but nothing moved as far as the eye could see, even the tiny damsel fish had fled in alarm.

Hawkspurr hesitated at the black opening under the cliff wanting to follow Von Harzburg and kill him with his bare hands, but commonsense and the natural instinct of survival stifled his desire. The cave could be the entrance to a grotto with a dry exit to the surface, and an armed terrorist waiting for any foolhardy intruder. Besides, Billy McDonald and his men were even now engaging the enemy above.

Hawkspurr was left with only one drastic course of action—and reaching into the demolition satchel he triggered the time switches and placed them against the inner wall at the base of the cave.

'Sorry Gunter, I would rather have killed you with a clean bullet.' Hawkspurr put all of his remaining strength into a rapid retirement, he had five minutes—plenty of time to escape the blast but still he kicked with all of his might. It would be a strange justice if the explosion engulfed him too.

As Richards pulled him from the water a panicky thought entered his mind—what if McDonald's men had entered the cave? No, the hammering of a .30 caliber Browning machine gun assured him that Talon Troop were still fighting outside.

The final detonation came with a muted roar, and a huge upsurge of water and shingle as the forward cliff face collapsed into the sea. A tremor reached the beach and the three men glanced anxiously up at the sheltering buttress.

"Come on you two, time to PUFO." (Pack up and fuck off). Hawkspurr dived into the sea, and started to swim swiftly back to the cove and Nazim's boat.

Royal Navy divers would later recover the illegal arms from the sea, and Gunter Von Harzburg had surely paid the price of his avarice and treachery.

Yet…some small challenge had gone out of his life.

His lips formed a cynical smile and he wondered; just where would his next assignment take him?

## THE END

# Other Books by the Author

## KOREAN RAIDER
ISBN 0-595-26351-8

After graduating from military school, Hawkspurr serves in the Household Cavalry, and at the age of nineteen he applies for active service, with armored unit fighting in Korea.

In his first action, MiG fighters wipe out his patrol. He finds his way to a beleaguered Commonwealth Company, and fights throughout the night in the trenches against masses of Chinese regular infantry. This description of the battle is authentic and typical of the bloody fighting engaged in by men of the United Nations Force.

His qualities are recognized, and he is recruited for service with a Wolf Pack group, operating from native Junks behind enemy lines on the west coast of Korea. On his first raid he captures the man destined to become his antagonist over the years ahead, Gunter Von Harzburg a German Communist officer.

The climatic raid is carried out from a submarine, utilizing rubber rafts. The operation is successful, but Hawkspurr is wounded as they escape pursuing communist troops. He is evacuated to a military hospital in Japan where a voluptuous American Sister nurses him.

During his treatment in Tokyo, Hawkspurr spots Von Harzburg who has escaped from U.S. Intelligence, and is being aided by Chinese agents.

Hawkspurr follows Von Harzburg to Hong Kong, where he is seconded to Special Branch. Hawkspurr locates Von Harzburg and continues his pursuit, but the German eludes him on the waterfront.

Hawkspurr is ordered back to his regiment in England but he is convinced that Von Harzburg will want to visit his home, in the Harz Mountains of Germany. Hawkspurr tracks down Von Harzburg, and chases him on skis to the German's village where he is captured, but treated as a brother officer.

Hawkspurr is released, but pursued by border guards, and after a fire fight escapes safely to England.

# THE GOLDEN KRIS
ISBN 0-595-26926-5

Follows the adventures of Nyles St.John Hawkspurr, as he serves with the elite Special Air Service. He is proud to be a member of the Household Cavalry, but during the celebrations for the Coronation of the new Queen, he enjoys the parties, and sexual favors offered by titled ladies, and actresses alike.

Hawkspurr learns that an old adversary from the Korean War, the German Agent Gunter Von Harzburg, is now advising the communist terrorists in Malaya. He volunteers for the SAS Malayan Scouts, who are actively engaged in the jungle war. Action against a ruthless enemy initiates Hawkspurr into the dreadful reality of jungle warfare but here he meets the extraordinary troop of men he will lead against the enemy.

On leave in Kuala Lumpur, Hawkspurr comes face to face with Von Harzburg and his deadly partner Ursula Kafka. There is a violent confrontation with Chinese communist sympathizers in a dance hall.

During specialized parachute training in Singapore Hawkspurr meets the Chinese Woman Detective Jennie Koo, and manages to find romance again. He is then assigned to protect a future leader of the country, on the island of Penang.

After a parachute descent into the jungle swamps, Hawkspurr again picks up the trail of Von Harzburg, and a treacherous Chinese agent.

A grueling and dangerous operation leads him to Von Harzburg and deadly confrontation.

Once more the author captures the authenticity of the land, its peoples, their food, and the lifestyles of primitive aborigines as well as the city dwellers.

Descriptions of parachuting techniques, and SAS operational methods are thrilling in their reality, and the jungle with its creatures graphically comes to life for the reader. Spiced as always with humor, and non-stop action.

# BLOOD ON THE PANGA

Major Nyles Hawkspurr and his former SAS soldiers are hired to lead an elite unit of native commandos against brutal rebels hiding deep in the jungles of the Congo.

Not a story for the faint hearted, but an authentic portrayal of guerrilla war and high action adventure in central Africa.

Murder, political intrigue, betrayal—and a little romance! Narrated graphically in the distinctive style of this popular military author. As always, the author draws upon his own experiences as a professional soldier, for the exciting action and locations, which are authentic, and colorfully descriptive.

## NURSE IN CONFLICT
ISBN 1-4033-5412-X

Emily McKerrow is a senior army nurse, serving in Saudi Arabia at the start of the Gulf War, 1991. Beautiful, intelligent and dedicated, Emily is introduced in London to the charming Captain Hugh Buckfast, an officer of the Grenadier Guards with whom she falls in love.

Emily's ambulance becomes lost in the desert during a storm and is found by an SAS patrol, commanded to her surprise by Hugh Buckfast. Hugh is furious at having his operation compromised and treats Emily with disdain.

Emily meets an intimate friend from university days currently employed by the Saudi Arabian government and the two renew their relationship. In the meantime, Hugh Buckfast has been seriously wounded, and captured by the Iraqis. Emily is summoned by Allied Commanders and asked to join a mission and render medical assistance. Guided by Bedouin tribesmen in company with the mysterious Colonel Nyles Hawkspurr, they cross into Jordan and operate on Hugh after an SAS team rescues him.

Many adventures befall the team as they journey south through historical Jordan disguised as Bedouin, and pursued by Iraqi agents.

# WAKE OF THE RAINBOW WARRIOR
ISBN 0-595-25856-5

Colonel Nyles St.John Hawkspurr former Special Air Service officer now retired, is living in New Zealand. In July 1989 he learns that Major Alain Mafart, convicted for his part in the bombing of the RAINBOW WARRIOR, is serving in the French Military Academy and has been promoted. In his anger Hawkspurr decides to kidnap Mafart and return him to justice in New Zealand.

To gather his old companions, Hawkspurr travels to Hong Kong, but French agents have now learnt of his intentions, and he and his friend are attacked. Hawkspurr renews his acquaintance with beautiful Chinese twins!

He journeys on to Borneo, where an old and trusted friend is running a medical clinic for the indigenous Iban tribe, and he spends a hilarious evening in the tribal Longhouse.

In Kenya Agents have again trailed Hawkspurr, but he and his former sergeant together with an old Mau Mau fighter, ambush and capture the agents.

Cyprus is the home of Hawkspurr's oldest friends who operate a converted attack vessel. Hawkspurr engages in an underwater fight and kills an assassin in a submerged cavern. He moves through Italy to France, where he is ferried to Jersey by an ex-Legionnaire turned smuggler, and by now he has discovered that the real leader of the bombing is an old antagonist the terrorist Gunter Von Harzburg.

The island of Jersey is base for the final operation into France, and Hawkspurr fights an exciting duel to the death with yet another French agent.

After a successful kidnap from Paris, the team and their prisoner escape by glider to the cruiser, which transports them to Egypt after a sneak attack by sea borne commandos.

The dramatic finale of the operation takes place in the Sudanese desert. An exciting, fast moving story of action, adventure, romance, fun, and colorful authentic descriptions of the locations and customs of indigenous people.

0-595-27341-6

Printed in Great Britain
by Amazon

12967343R00137